MW01156057

Wizard's Bane

Book one of the Sojurn Chronicles

By

Crystalwizard

1663 Liberty Drive, Suite 200
Bloomington, Indiana 47403
(800) 839-8640
www.authorhouse.com

This book is a work of fiction. Places, events, and situations in this story are purely fictional and any resemblance to actual persons, living or dead, is coincidental.

© 2004 Crystalwizard.
All Rights Reserved.

No part of this book may be reproduced, stored in a retrieval system, or transmitted by any means without the written permission of the author.

First published by AuthorHouse 09/02/04

ISBN: 1-4184-2311-4 (e)
ISBN: 1-4184-2312-2 (sc)

Library of Congress Control Number: 2004092960

Printed in the United States of America
Bloomington, Indiana

This book is printed on acid-free paper.

What others have said about Wizard's Bane

How does it feel to materialize onto a dump of garbage and not know where you are? Ask Dale and discover that this world is not as it seems and that he has a path of self discovery and personal development of epic proportions.

Rarely have I read a story that brings the elements of adventure, fantasy and science fiction into a fast-paced adventure and a very enjoyable story. After reading the first four paragraphs of Wizard's Bane, I could not put the book down. Crystalwizard has built a world where believing that nothing is impossible will change your present universe. Not since George Lucas' Star Wars has there been a story that mixes many genres into a glorious tale. The story flows so easily that you will be impatient for the next book in the Sojourn Chronicles.

Sit and read YOUR next big adventure!
Raymond Wilson - AIX Technical Specialist

Crystalwizard weaves a tangible, rich tapestry of magic and life lessons within her spellbinding Sojourn Chronicles. From the first few pages of Wizard's Bane, you are effortlessly drawn into an enchanted tale keeping you engrossed with every twist and turn of each character's journey. The characters are well rounded with just the right humanity and character flaws to entice the reader to truly care about them. Be prepared to burn the midnight oil as this riveting story keeps you thoroughly engrossed while wanting more!

Arianna -Producer/Production Manager

Oh wow Kelly... I am really impressed! I like this and I am SOOO intrigued! One of the things that makes me want to read a book is if it grabs me from the start. If it doesn't get my attention real quick I form an opinion and a lot of times put it down. This grabbed me right from the start... I would LOVE to read more... this is great!

Gail - Artist and Vendor, 3dcommune.com

Dedication

Life is full of many odd twists and turns. Strange, unexpected happenings, that change every plan you have and send you off in un-looked for directions. This book is the result of one of them. Last summer a friend of mine asked a casual question. That question got me writing again after a fifteen year absence from the notebook. Her encouragement, and enjoyment of what I was writing, kept me going. I would like to take this opportunity to thank her because with out her assistance, this book would never have been started, much less finished. Thanks Mel :)

I would also like to thank all the many people that proof read this book as it was being written, made comments, pointed out mistakes and told me that it was good enough to try and get published. Most especially I would like to thank four special people. Jeff, Raymond, Rayvin, Arianna...your assistance and feedback means more than you will ever know. Thank you.

It's been my experience that books should be dedicated to someone...or something...and with that in mind, this book is dedicated to Melanie, Laura and Morgan...my best friends in high school...and beyond...who stayed up many nights with me, fleshing out the universe that this story is set in, molding various characters and just plain having fun.

And it is dedicated to one of the most interesting and amazing people I've ever met...Norman Banduch. The world needs more dreamers that read. Norman...may you never run out of books :)

Kelly
March 2004

Table of Contents

Table of Illustrations

For more illustrations please see
http://igp-iupf.omnitech.net/~hub/sojourn

Chapter One

Darkness covered the city, flowing down the streets and collecting in the alleys. Silence sat heavily on the sleeping town, it's buildings swathed in a thick fog, light pooling in liquid puddles under the occasional street lamp. The town drunk stumbled down the street, his head spinning from the pots of ale he'd just finished off in the pub. Reaching the nearest alley, he leaned heavily against the wall then slid down to sit on the ground. Reclining against the building wall, he threw his head back and began singing loudly, and badly off-key. A brief flash of light a few feet further down the alley startled him and he peered into the darkness.
"Who's der?" he slurred, trying to make out anything in the inky blackness. No answer was forthcoming however, so after a few seconds he shrugged and went back to singing.

The reason for the flash stood silently several feet away, his eyes adjusting to the sudden darkness. The putrid smell of rotting garbage caused him to wrinkle his nose in disgust.
"Wonderful," he thought sourly to himself. "A backwater planet in the middle of nowhere. And where do I materialize? In the middle of their garbage dump!"
He closed his eyes for a second, then took a deep breath, settling his nerves.
"Well, it could be worse I guess. I wonder just how primitive these people are."

He picked his way slowly through the darkened alley, trying to avoid the larger concentrations of refuse. By the time he reached the street, the town drunk was happily snoring, the words to his song long forgotten in the stupor produced by the ale.
"At least" he thought to himself as he inspected the drunk, "I look like they do physically."
He squatted down beside the drunk and carefully pulled his tattered cloak aside then frowned.

"Clothing...that's another matter," he mused, dropping the cloak back down over the snoring man. He glanced down at his seamless, black jump suit and shook his head.
"I'll never fit in dressed like this," he thought, studying the drunk's ratty attire, then stood and glanced cautiously around the street. The fog drifted past, swirling slightly in the faint breezes as he watched, but no other signs of life were evident on the street. Satisfied things were relatively safe, he cautiously stepped out of the alley and turned left then made his way up the deserted street, hugging the rough brick wall of the building and trying to stay well out of the light as he made his way past silent store fronts.

The buildings ended fairly quickly and the street turned into a lane running out into the open land. The man stopped, then sighed and turned around.
"Better and better," he thought, shaking his head. "Backwater planet, primitive culture, local inhabitants who appear to have all the civility of poorly bred pigs and now this." He stared back up the street at the few buildings visible through the fog. "Maybe it's bigger if I go the other way. I need clothes."

He studied the buildings for a few seconds longer then shook his head again.
"No," he thought, correcting himself, "I need a farm. With a clothesline. And a sympathetic farmer."
He frowned, remembering the drunks singing and made a face.
"A farmer whose language I probably don't speak," he muttered then looked up at the invisible stars. "Why me!?"
He glanced over his shoulder into the blackness that shrouded the lonely countryside then turned back to the town again. If there was a farm out there it certainly didn't show up in the middle of the night.
"When I get my hands," he thought vehemently, "on the idiot that opened that warp..."

Light spilled suddenly out of a doorway a few feet ahead of him as the door opened, and he flattened against the wall. A couple strolled out, waving behind them at a fairly crowded, smoke filled room, then wandered off down the street arm in arm. He waited until they were lost in the fog before breathing a silent sigh of relief.

"Clothes now," he reminded himself. "And food. And sleep. Retribution later. After my powers come back."

He glanced around, then continued on up the street toward the alley he'd materialized in.

As it came in sight he could see a dark figure bent over the drunk who had been happily snoring away in it's entrance. He froze, watching as the figure drew a knife out of a sheath and silently cut the drunk's pouch from his belt. The man narrowed his eyes and glanced around. The street was still empty and the alley was only a few feet away. Trained reflexes took over and he advanced silently, little more than a shadow, as the figure opened the pouch and began rummaging through it. He paused for a moment, waiting until the thief was completely absorbed in the contents of the pouch, then stepped forward, one hand going to the thief's throat, the other grasping it's knife hand. In a single fluid motion he bent the thief backwards, lifted it off the ground to it's toes by the hand on it's throat and forced the knife hand open. The knife hit the ground with a dull thud and he shoved the arm up behind his prisoner's back. The other struggled slightly, stopping as his hand tightened around it's throat.

"You know, for a thief, you're not very observant," he growled, his voice low.

His captive grunted and he applied a bit more pressure to the arm behind it's back.

"Ow!" came the unhappy protest.

"Not only that, but your choice of targets is lousy," he continued, then waited for a reply.

"Let me go!" the other managed, then gasped as a bit more pressure was applied to his arm.
"Well," the man thought, "language will evidently not be a problem. That's one positive aspect to this."
"Let you go?" he asked in a low, dangerous voice. "Let you go? And then what? Wait while you pick up your knife and try to kill me? I think not." He squeezed slightly on the other's throat again.
"NO!" his captive cried out, sudden fear filling his voice. "Just let me go and I swear I won't.."
"No, you're right," he interrupted. "You won't...because you really won't like what I'll do if you try."
He twisted the other's wrist slightly, provoking another cry.
"I'll let go," he continued, his voice dark and threatening, "but you move and you die. Understand?"
"Yes," came the reply through tightly clinched teeth.

He let go and the thief stumbled forward, whirled around, then stood uncertainly in front of him, rubbing his wrist and watching him warily. The fog drifted slowly past behind him, diffusing what light the nearby street lamp shed and giving him an unearthly backdrop. The thief looked up into a pair of brown eyes that appeared faintly to glow and gulped, his blood running cold.

"Your name?" the man asked, looking down at the thief and crossing his arms.
"Why?" the other asked hesitantly.
"Because I asked," he stated bluntly.
"Kheri," came the response after a moment.
He nodded, then bent over and picked the knife up off the ground.
Kheri's eyes darted to the street but prudence kept him from moving.

"You can call me Dale," the man said, straightening up and handing the knife back to it's owner. Kheri looked at the knife suspiciously, then carefully reached out and took it, sheathing it quickly.

"So now what?" Kheri asked nervously, looking back up at the man who towered a full twelve inches over his slight, five and a half feet.
"First, give him back his pouch," Dale replied, indicating the drunk. "Second, you just became my guide to this place. To start with, I need other clothing. You're going to help me find some."
Kheri opened his mouth to protest, caught the look on Dale's face, nodded once, then dropped the pouch next to the drunk.

"What kind of clothes do you want," he asked, his gaze wandering over Dale's strange attire.
"Normal stuff," Dale told him. "What any average, working man would wear."
Kheri stared at the jump-suit for a couple more seconds then nodded.
"Alright," he replied apprehensively, "I know where you can get something but we'll have to leave town. The only stuff around here is either on someone's back or in a store. And they're locked."
"And stuff outside town isn't?" Dale asked.
"Well..." Kheri fidgeted and tried not to feel frightened. "My aunt's got a farm. It's several miles out. I can try to get you some of my uncle's old things unless you object to a walk?"
Dale caught his eyes and held his gaze for a moment until Kheri shivered and looked down.
"Alright," he replied, satisfied that Kheri was telling the truth, "we'll go visit your aunt. Which way?"
"Uh.." Kheri stammered, his heart pounding, "T...this way."
He moved cautiously past the larger man then stepped out of the alley and started up the street toward the center of town. Dale turned and followed silently behind him.

Kheri's thoughts raced as he walked past the silent wooden buildings that lined the street. The desire to dash off into the fog filled him and he fought it down, certain that he would fail in the attempt. His arm still ached from the pressure Dale had exerted on it back in the alley and he had no desire to find out just how strong he really was. He rubbed his throat, still feeling the ghostly impressions which Dale's fingers had left in it and shivered.
"Clothes..." he thought, trying to control his overly active imagination. "I gotta tell her something..."
He pictured the ancient steamer trunk locked away in his aunt's attic, full of his uncle's rotting clothing and frowned.
"Maybe I can just offer to clean up," he thought then shook his head. "She'll have it locked though. I gotta get her to give'm to me."
His arm twinged slightly and he rubbed at the shoulder, remembering the sudden, iron grip which had grasped his wrist, the ease with which Dale had lifted him from the ground, then held him on the tips of his toes, and shivered. The brief events in the alley sprang back to the front of his thoughts and overpowered his shaky attempt at planning. He swallowed hard and took a deep breath, then forced himself to consider what his Aunt might respond to. He was distracted, still deep in thought, when the last few buildings came in sight. Dale dropped a hand firmly on his shoulder, shattering his concentration and he jumped.

"Stop," came the soft command behind him. He froze instantly and glanced quickly around. A few seconds later a movement in the shadows a short way up the street caught his attention and he flattened against the wall next to Dale, holding his breath, watching. A figure detached itself from the shadows a moment later and crossed the street, visible now as one of the town guards. The two of them stood motionless, waiting as the guard glanced around, then made his way on down the street.
"Alright, let's go," Dale said quietly after the guard had vanished into the fog and his footsteps were no longer to be heard. Kheri

nodded silently, then looked curiously at Dale as they started walking again. Dale returned his gaze and lifted an eyebrow in question.

"Yes?" he asked.
"How'd you know he was there?", Kheri asked.
"I heard him," came Dale's quiet reply.
Kheri blinked.
"You heard him?" he repeated dubiously.
"Yes." Dale answered without explanation.
A shiver ran up Kheri's spine and he stopped, turned to face Dale and took a deep breath.
"Who...I meant what..." he stammered, unable to turn thoughts into words.
Dale sighed inwardly, then crossed his arms and looked down into Kheri's eyes.
"Are you sure you want the answer to that question?" he asked.
Kheri nodded, his eyes locked on Dale's face.

"At the moment," Dale told him, "I'm just a stranger who would prefer not to be noticed. You get on my bad side, I might turn out to be your worst nightmare."
Kheri swallowed nervously, unable to look away.
"You do as I ask, and behave, and I may turn out to be a valuable friend," Dale continued, still holding Kheri's gaze with his own. "You want more explanation than that, earn it. How far is it to your aunt's farm from here?"
"Uh..", Kheri stammered and shook his thoughts free from the somewhat frightening flight of fantasy they'd taken.
"About three...four miles...not far. A hour or so walk." he replied.
"She get up early?" Dale asked.
"Usually yes," Kheri agreed, "and this is market day. There'll be traffic coming into town in a while too."
Dale regarded him silently for a moment longer, watching the younger man fidget nervously.

"In that case," he suggested softly, a flinty edge to his voice, "I suggest you turn around and we get going."
Kheri broke into a sudden sweat and turned quickly around, leading the way out of town.

Chapter Two

The night had stretched thin and day was beginning to break around the clouds as they left the town. The fresh scent of newly mown hay drifted on the breeze and birds soared through the sky overhead, filling the air with a variety of calls as they greeted the new day. A smile tugged at one side of Dale's mouth as he looked around the open countryside.

"This might not be too bad," he thought, gazing at a colorful field of wild flowers which were turning their petals to the first rays of the morning. "I could almost feel at home here, if it weren't quite so primitive. Still, it's pretty...I could be stranded somewhere a lot worse."

He glanced up at the sky and silently watched the clouds shade from delicate pink to rich gold, then brought his gaze back down to the road and studied his captive for a moment. Kheri was slim, almost a foot shorter than Dale, with straight blond hair a bit past his collar and icy blue eyes. His pale skin was dusted with freckles, and he walked with the practiced ease of someone who traveled exclusively on their feet.

"Early twenty's," Dale thought, "and very inexperienced but not impossible to work with. Might even have decent potential, given enough time. We'll see."

"What do most people use for transportation around here," he asked, breaking the silence.

"Horses mostly. Mules sometimes. Carts or wagons for hauling," Kheri replied glancing at him. "Why?"

"Because I asked," Dale replied.

Kheri nodded uneasily, then returned to working out an excuse to get his uncle's mothballed clothing away from his aunt. Five minutes later he sighed, shook his head and stopped walking. Turning around to face his captor, he glanced up at him hesitantly then looked down at his own hands.

"Look," he tried, struggling to keep the tension he was feeling out of his voice, "I'm not really sure this is actually a good idea."
"Oh?" Dale kept his voice strictly neutral, waiting for Kheri to finish.
Kheri shivered slightly and picked nervously at a fingernail.
"Yeah, my aunt..." he explained, still looking at his hands, "well she's pretty sharp...and she's going to want to know why I want my uncle's clothes, you know?" He looked back up and met Dale's eyes apprehensively, "and well I can't..," he stopped as Dale crossed his arms again.
"Uh..." his knees threatened suddenly to give way and he swallowed then tried to finish, frightened now. "I...uh...I can't think of...of..."
He trailed off and dropped his eyes again then stood trembling, staring down at his hands, and Dale's feet. Dale sighed to himself, used to dealing with much more hardened individuals.

"Kheri," he said calmly, fighting his impatience and frustration with the current situation, forcing himself to treat his captive gently. "Let's just get to your aunt's farm. We can deal with what to tell her when we get there."
Kheri fidgeted a moment longer, then sighed. His shoulders slumped slightly and he nodded in resignation.
"Alright," he replied unhappily as he turned back to the road, "but don't say I didn't try to warn you."

The sun burst over the mountains a few minutes later, filling the air with golden shafts of light and painting the landscape with all the colors of elation. Clouds drifted lazily overhead, and the birds broke into a riotous chorus of welcome as it's first rays began to warm their nests. Dale found himself smiling and shook his head slightly.
"I might actually enjoy this," he thought. "If I can get past the hurdles of no clothes, no money, no food and no idea when my powers will return, if ever."

The thought was sobering and dulled the promise of the new day to a degree.

They walked along in silence, each wrapped in their own thoughts, for the better part of an hour. Dale kept a sharp eye out for any approaching traffic but the road remained deserted and finally the farm they were making for came into sight. It was a fairly small place, with a tidy yellow farm house not too far back from the road and a chicken yard nestled against the back fence. Tall rows of corn stood neatly to one side, golden tassels waving atop fat ears. A large swatch of tilled earth ran right up to the fence next to the road and the tiny tips of plants could be seen poking up out of it in places. A low mooing sound drifted towards them accompanied by the jangle of cowbells and the scent of manure. Dale grinned at the sound and looked around for the barn.

"She's probably milking the cow," Kheri commented. "It's about that time of day."
"And your uncle?" Dale asked.
"Dead," Kheri stated flatly.
"Oh," Dale replied, taken by surprise.
Kheri shrugged.
"Been dead for nearly thirty years," he explained. "Got drunk one night, thought he could fly, climbed a tree to try it. Didn't survive the fall. No loss."
Dale lifted an eyebrow at Kheri's back.
"My aunt says life got three hundred percent easier after he died, dunno though, I didn't know him." Kheri continued, rambling slightly. "He was already gone when I came out here to live after my parents died when I was six."
"Right," Dale thought and glanced around the farm again. "So your aunt lives here all alone then?" he asked as they neared the front gate.
"Yeah," Kheri replied. "Just her and the animals." He put his hand on the gate and paused, then looked up at his captor.

"Dale," he pleaded, "don't do anything to her, ok? Please?"
He stood motionless, his eyes locked on Dale's face. Dale looked down at him for a moment.
"Is there a reason I should?" he asked quietly.
"I hope not," Kheri muttered, then shook his head and opened the gate.

They made their way up to the house and walked around to the back. Kheri's aunt stepped out of the barn just then, a heavy metal pail in one hand and a basket in the other. She stopped at the sight of her nephew walking toward her across the yard then set the pail down and put her hands on her hips.
"Well now, I suppose there's something you want," she remarked. "Well it can wait. I've got eggs to fetch and breakfast to cook and chores to do."
"We just want," Kheri began and Dale interrupted him.
"It can wait till later," he said. "And we'd be happy to help you with your chores."
The aunt looked Dale over silently.
"You sure are dressed outlandishly," She commented after a few seconds. "where're you from boy?"
"A fairly long way off ma'am," he replied.
"Must be. You ever collected eggs before?" she asked.
Dale blinked and looked at her blankly.
"Uh..." he replied, "no, I haven't."
"Didn't rightly think so," she stated, then held out the basket. "Kheri, take this basket and go get the eggs. Take your friend with you. I'll be in the house."

Kheri bit his lip to keep from laughing at Dale's reaction and walked over to take the basket.
"Come on," he said, jerking his head to the side, "the hen house's this way."
His aunt watched them for a minute, shook her head and picked the pail of milk back up.

"City folk," she muttered. "Ain't never done a useful lick o' work in his life most likely. Well the hens'll give 'em some exercise." She lugged the milk into the house, the screen door slamming behind her.

The hen house and it's chicken yard were completely enclosed in a short wire fence. Kheri walked up to it, then paused before he opened the gate.
"Chickens are kind of funny," he explained, looking over at Dale. "They can't fly but they'll try to run out the gate. Don't let them or we'll be chasing them all day. Also, the hen's don't like it when we take their eggs, so they get kind of nasty and watch out for the rooster."
Dale glanced at the chickens milling around inside the chicken yard.
"Alright," he agreed then frowned slightly. "what's a rooster?"

Kheri looked at him incredulously.
"You don't know..", he began, stopped himself and pointed to a rather large, imposing chicken. "That's the rooster. He's the only male in there and he thinks it all belongs to him. He'll think we're invading his property once we go in there. He likes to pick fights and that beak's sharp. So are those spurs on the back of his feet. He'll cut you wide open if you're not careful, so watch out for him."
"Great," Dale thought to himself, studying the rooster as it strutted around the yard. "One more thing to add to the list...no clothes, no money, no food, no access to my powers and now I'm about to be a sparring partner for a bird with a bad attitude. I can't wait to see what else is lurking in the wings!"
He looked over at Kheri and nodded.
"Alright," he agreed unenthusiastically, "let's get this over with."
Kheri nodded, opened the gate and slipped inside, shutting it quickly behind him. Dale frowned slightly in the rooster's direction then followed suit.

The chickens scattered, squawking, as Kheri walked toward them, swinging the basket and the rooster gave a loud angry crow. Flapping his wings, he drew himself up to his full height, stretched out his neck and charged. Kheri fended him off with the basket and sprinted for the hen house, then disappeared inside, the rooster in hot pursuit. Dale stood there speechless, watching. A few seconds later Kheri came running out of the hen house with the basket over his head and the rooster close behind him. He vaulted over the fence, caught his foot on it and landed in a heap on the ground. The rooster, satisfied now that the intruder was gone, strutted off to take up his sentry duty among the hens.

"I see what you mean," Dale commented, trying not to laugh as he looking over the fence at the pile on the ground. "Did you get any eggs?"

A muffled sound came out from under the basket and Kheri pushed himself up on one arm.

"No I didn't get any eggs! Here!" He tore the basket off his head and flung it in Dale's general direction. "Let's see you do any better," he growled, his temper frayed beyond controlling for the moment.

Dale caught the basket with one hand and shrugged. He glanced over at the rooster who was eyeing him suspiciously and then looked at the hens who had scattered once more as Kheri came flying back from the hen house. Moving slowly, he made his way across the chicken yard, trying to avoid scaring them as Kheri had then paused at the hen house door. The rooster was still watching him but seemed content not to do anything since his hens still appeared unruffled. Dale opened the door quietly and slipped inside, shutting it behind him.

The hen house was small, and rather dark with the door shut. The smell of chicken hung heavily in the air, mixing with the scents of dust and old straw. He blinked a couple times then waited for his eyes to adjust, wondering just where the eggs were.

Boards with nests on them ran around the hen house wall and several chickens were nestled contentedly down on top of them. Peering curiously into one without a hen, he spotted several round, white objects.
"Ah, alright," he thought out loud and carefully retrieved the eggs from the nest, setting them gently into the basket. Working quickly, he removed the rest of the eggs from the other empty nests, then stood back considering the dozing chickens. There were only four settled on the nests and the basket was nearly full. The possibility of raising a squawk, then having to dodge flying rooster, out weighed the desire to see if there were eggs in the other nests. Dale opened the door quietly and looked around for the rooster.

The rooster was busily worrying a bug in the grass on the far side of the chicken yard and didn't appear to notice him. Dale stepped quietly outside the hen house, shut the door softly behind himself and made his way out of the chicken yard with as much stealth as he had used a couple hours before to sneak up on Kheri. He'd half expected to find the thief had fled while he was occupied with the eggs, and was pleasantly surprised to see him waiting patiently at the gate. He opened the gate, stepped through it and handed Kheri the egg basket with a slight grin.
"What was so hard about that?" he asked innocently. Kheri frowned at the eggs, glared at the rooster and stalked off toward the house carrying the basket, carefully avoiding Dale's question.

The smell of something cooking drifted from the house and Dale's stomach growled unexpectedly. He winced in pain, trying to forget the fact that he hadn't eaten in over two days, then followed Kheri into the kitchen after a moment.
"Here's your eggs," Kheri said, handing the basket to his aunt.

"Put 'em on the counter," she said over her shoulder from the sink. "You and your friend go wash up and then fill the water barrel. Bucket's by the pump. Get a move on or breakfast'll be cold 'for you're done."

"Yes ma'am," Kheri replied as he set the basket on the counter and headed back outside, running solidly into Dale who had just stepped through the door.

"OOOF!" Kheri grunted, and hit the floor, landing on his backside on the tiles. His aunt glanced over her shoulder, shook her head and went back to peeling potatoes.

"Clumsy," she grumbled. "How many times I got to tell you to open your eyes and look where you going?"

Dale winced from the impact as Kheri ran into him then reached down, grabbed Kheri's arm and hauled him to his feet then stepped back outside. Kheri followed, rubbing the back of his neck.

"You know," Dale commented as they walked over to the pump, "walking through solid objects is a skill I don't think you've had much practice with."

Kheri frowned at him silently then grabbed the pump's handle and pushed it down sharply.

"Yeah well..." he griped, as he picked up the bucket and set it under the pump to catch the water, "If you weren't so slow coming into the house," he pushed the handle down again, and water gushed out, missing the bucket completely, "you wouldn't have been in the door." He glared at the bucket and adjusted it's position, then shoved the handle down again.

"No," Dale agreed as he picked the bucket up and held it steady under the stream of water Kheri was forcing from the pump, "but if you were more observant it wouldn't have mattered where I was."

Kheri glowered at the pump and shoved the handle down again.

"Lay off already ok?" he growled angrily, "I've never been very good at this farm stuff."

"Which is why you're trying to make a living in town stealing from drunks?" Dale asked, setting the now full bucket back down on the slab.

Kheri jerked his head up, a furious retort ready and froze, staring at the house. Dale whirled then ran for the back door. Black smoke was billowing out of the kitchen window and he could hear the crackling of flames from inside. He jerked the door open then leaped aside as smoke flowed out, filling the air. Kheri still hadn't moved, his gaze fixed on the house. Dale slapped a control on his belt and sighed with relief as his force field shimmered into place.

"Small favors gratefully accepted," he said to no one in particular as he adjusted the controls then stepped into the kitchen.

The iron cook stove had flames shooting out it's top, the curtains over the sink were on fire and part of the countertop had started to burn. Kheri's aunt was crumpled on the floor next to one of the round, metal stove lids, unconscious. A nasty bruise had purpled one side of her face and for a moment Dale was unable to detect any breathing. He knelt swiftly and lifted her in his arms, then carefully carried her back outside.

"Kheri," he commanded sharply, laying the unconscious woman on the ground. "Water! Now!"

Kheri blinked, then hefted the pail and lugged it as rapidly as possible over to where Dale was kneeling beside his aunt, spilling about half of it in the process. He set the bucket down then stood there looking lost and confused. Dale stood up, grabbed Kheri by the shoulders and caught his eyes.

"Get your aunt away from the house," he directed. "How close is the nearest neighbor?"

Kheri blinked and looked up at him then suddenly realized Dale had asked him a question.

"Next farm, about half-mile," he replied.

"Carry her out of the way, " Dale commanded, "then go get help."
He picked up the bucket and plunged back into the kitchen.

Chapter Three

Dale ran to the stove and dumped what water remained in the bucket through one of the holes on it's top, drowning the wood inside, then headed back out to the pump. Kheri's aunt was still laying on the ground, unconscious but breathing, right where Dale had left her, with Kheri no where to be found.

Dale dropped the bucket, lifted her up and carried her to the barn. Laying her down gently on the ground, he paused long enough to make sure she was still breathing, then ran back to where he had dropped the bucket. Thick smoke filled the air in the backyard now, pouring like water through the open door. Dale grabbed the bucket, then ran to the pump and shoved the handle down as he'd watched Kheri do not long before. The pump creaked in protest but nothing happened. He frowned slightly, grasped the pump handle firmly and tried again. It took him several seconds to get it working once more, but finally a stream of water gushed out of it into the bucket.

"These people need to discover electricity," he thought as he grabbed the now full bucket from the slab and dashed back inside.

The fire was no longer shooting out of the stove top, but the counter was burning in several places. The curtains were gone, the rod they had dangled from was ablaze and the wall behind the stove was crackling. Dale tossed the water at the flames on the wall then spun and ran back outside.

"What I wouldn't give for a hose right now," he thought as he worked the pump handle once more, fighting to get water flowing again. "Come ON! Work!"

He put all other concerns aside, focusing only on the job of filling bucket after bucket of water then carrying them into the house as rapidly as possible. The fire danced around the kitchen, dodging his efforts as if it were a living thing, scorching the walls and ceiling as it did so. He fought back, slinging the water in wide arcs, attempting to hit as many of the infuriating blazes with each bucket as possible. He was so absorbed in the task that he dumped two extra buckets of water into the kitchen before realizing that the fire was actually out.

Gasping for breath, Dale stood in the middle of the drenched and blackened kitchen, looking around tiredly. Black water covered the floor a quarter of an inch deep, the walls and ceiling were dripping, the counter top was covered with scorch marks and missing chunks in it's surface. He stood motionless for several seconds, unable to move now that the emergency was over. His arms ached, his legs felt like rubber and as the adrenaline stopped flowing, he started to shake. He turned and stumbled back out of the kitchen, flopped down on the top step and dropping the bucket on the ground. Reaching for his belt, he barely managed the strength necessary to deactivate the force field, then closed his eyes and fought the waves of dizziness crashing over him.

The sound of hoof beats reached him a few minutes later and he looked up to see Kheri ride through the gate, followed closely by two strange men on plow horses. Kheri swung down off his aunt's horse, looked about wildly then ran to the barn and knelt next to her. The two men reined their horses in and dismounted, then one walked over to Kheri while the other ambled inside the house. Dale rubbed his eyes tiredly and leaned back against the door frame. A short time later, the second man exited from the house and stood nonchalantly on the top step.

"Fire's out," he observed around a piece of straw he was chewing on.
Dale nodded silently without opening his eyes.
"Kitchen's a mess," the man stated, taking the straw out of his mouth. He peered at it, then flipped it away into the grass and stuck his thumbs under his suspenders.
Dale looked up at him and nodded again, wondering if he was capable of noticing anything that wasn't blatantly obvious.

"Jerad," came the call from the barn, "come over here and help me."
"Comin'," he drawled, and descended the stairs then moseyed over to the others. The two men picked up the unconscious woman and carried her into the house. Kheri watched helplessly, then walked over to where Dale was and sat down on the ground, dejected.

"Who are they?" Dale asked, watching the men as they disappeared into the house.
"The neighbors," Kheri responded, pulling blades of grass out of the ground. "Old man Tucker and his son Jerad." He looked up and glanced through the kitchen door. "I hope she's going to be alright," he mumbled.
"She should be." Dale responded, tiredness coloring his voice. "She'll have a bruise for a while from that stove lid, but I don't think anything's seriously wrong."
"Yeah, well," Kheri trailed off still looking through the door. "She'd be dead if you hadn't been here." He looked away, his cheeks burning in embarrassment.

Dale raised an eyebrow at his odd behavior, but said nothing. Jerad walked back out of the kitchen door, looked down at Kheri and jerked his head inside.
"Pa wants you," he drawled, then turned and wandered back into the house.
Kheri glanced at Dale then levered himself up off the ground, and followed him in. Dale sighed and leaned heavily against the door frame. Exhaustion was beginning to set in. He fought to stay awake, unwilling to fall asleep in what was essentially enemy territory, but his energy was gone, drained by two non-stop days of struggling to close the warp which he had eventually fallen through. The spurt of energy that had sustained him while fighting the fire had taken what few reserves he'd had left and sleep overpowered him as easily as he had Kheri just a few hours

before. His eyes closed of their own accord and he passed out sitting on the back steps.

Kheri walked hesitantly into the bedroom behind Jerad, afraid of what he might see. The sight of his aunt awake and sitting partially up in bed sent a thrill of relief through him and the knot in his stomach loosened. She smiled weakly at him and patted the covers.

"Well son," she remarked, "guess it's a good thing you came to visit this morning, ain't it."

He walked over to the bed and perched on the edge of it, tears glistening in his eyes.

"Oh now stop that," she chided him gently. "Take more than that to do me in. Paw Tucker tells me the kitchen's a downright mess. I need to sleep a while but then I'll get up, wash up and make you boys lunch in a couple hours."

Kheri shook his head.

"It's gonna need more than a washing," he said. "It's pretty burnt."

"I'll round up the others and we'll get 'er fixed," Paw Tucker said from behind him.

"Yep," Jerad put in. "be good as new."

"I can't thank you enough Paw," Kheri's aunt said, then shooed them away with one hand. "Go on now, I need to sleep. Oh, and Kheri," she looked at her nephew. "Whatever that young man that's with you wanted, long as it's not my cow, he can have. Go on now, shoo."

She closed her eyes and slid down under the covers, pulling them up over her shoulder. Kheri bent over and gave her a hug, then stood up and followed the others out of the room, shutting the door softly behind him.

"Welp," Paw Tucker said, "Guess we better get started. We'll be back shortly."

"Yep," Jerad nodded. "Back later."
They strode through the kitchen and rode off on the plow horses without even a glance at the man sleeping on the steps.

Kheri walked over to the back door, his thoughts spinning around in circles. So much had happened in such a few short hours. He glanced down at Dale and his hand strayed to his knife handle.
"He's sound asleep," Kheri thought. "I could slit his throat and dump the body somewhere. He's not from around here, no one'd know he was gone." His fingers tightened around the hilt for a second then he forced his hand away.
"I can't do it," he thought. "My aunt'd be dead and her house gone if it wasn't for what he did."
He stood silently, struggling with himself for several minutes, then reached down and shook Dale slightly. The result was not quite what he expected. Dale's reflexes, trained for centuries, reacted and within the blink of an eye Kheri found himself pinned flat on the ground on his stomach, with Dale kneeling over him.
"Hey!" he managed to holler around a mouthful of grass.
Dale blinked, shook himself awake, then rolled Kheri over onto his back and stepped away.
"Did I mention that it's a bad idea to touch me if I'm asleep?" he asked.
"No, but I'll keep it in mind," Kheri replied with a groan, then sat up stiffly.
"Sorry," Dale said as he reached down and helped the younger man back to his feet. "What did you want?"

"I was just going to tell you that my aunt's ok and suggest you go sleep on the couch instead of the back porch," Kheri replied, fidgeting.
Dale regarded him for a moment.
"Before or after you tried to slip that knife into me?" he asked quietly.

"Uh..." Kheri flinched slightly and paled under Dale's gaze. Dale nodded then crossed his arms, looking down at him.
"How hard was it to talk yourself out of that?" he asked.
Kheri shrugged, looked away for a second then met Dale's gaze defiantly.
"Pretty hard," he admitted.

"You're honest at least," Dale replied. "A word of warning, don't try it. I react much differently to a weapon when I'm asleep." He held Kheri's gaze for a second longer. "And currently," he warned, "while I could easily rip you into several pieces before I had time to wake up, I do not have the ability to put you back together again," he paused for a moment to let his words sink in. "Understand?"
Kheri turned ashen, then nodded, unable to speak. His heart was suddenly pounding so hard it felt like it was about to leap out of his chest and his mouth became drier than old dust. He swallowed, tried to speak, and finally managed a whisper.
"Understood."
"Good," Dale rubbed his eyes. "Where's that couch?"
"In...inside. I'll show you," Kheri replied weakly, no longer defiant, and turned toward the house.

Kheri lead the way back inside, through the burnt kitchen, to the living room then watched Dale collapse onto the couch. He stood silently for several long minutes, staring at his unconscious nemesis and thinking. The unpleasant possibility of Dale suddenly exploding into action and ripping him to pieces ran through his mind in graphic detail. His imagination got away from him and he slowly backed into the kitchen, away from the terror that had taken over his life in the dark hours of the morning.

He bumped into the table and started, then blinked and stood looking around at the results of the fire. The curtains were gone, the rod they had hung on a scorched bit of wood that dangled from the wall over the sink. The window was blackened from the smoke but un-cracked. The counter was ruined, burnt completely through in places, the walls were covered with soot and the ceiling directly above the stove was charred. Paint had bubbled and burnt away on the wall behind the stove, the floor was still covered with sooty water and the entire room stank.

Kheri turned slowly around, staring at the damage then glanced back into the living room at the couch. The memory of Dale carrying his aunt out of the house to safety, the knowledge that he had spent himself trying to save her home, collided with the horrible fantasy that Kheri's imagination was building. He dropped his head into his hands and tried to think.

"Either he's evil, or he's not. He can't be both," he mumbled to himself, trying to calm his nerves. He looked around at the destroyed kitchen again and shook his head.

"He can't be evil," he muttered, confused. "Evil would have let her die, let the house burn. But," he turned and glanced at Dale's unconscious form stretched out on the couch once more. "He's not human, that's for sure. And he terrifies me."

His imagination took flight again, conjuring up all sorts of strange possibilities. Fear gripped his stomach and turned it into knots. "He knows what I'm thinking, I know that much," he mused, thinking back to several times when Dale had reacted to thoughts he hadn't voiced yet. "My aunt said he could have what he wanted. Well he wanted clothes. Maybe he'll take 'em when he wakes up and leave," he mumbled to himself, still staring at the couch and the unconscious form on it. The faint sound of the rooster crowing in the chicken yard drifted in through the open back door and Kheri shook himself back to reality.

"I can't just stand here," he thought, "I need something to do, get my mind off things." The idea of leaving while Dale was asleep flashed through his mind but he shook his head firmly.

"I'm not leaving till I know she's gonna be ok," he argued, "and I'm not leavin' her here alone with him, no tellin' what he'd do to her if he woke up and found I was gone."
He thought back to the alley and shook his head.
"Besides," he mumbled looking back into the living room, "He'd probably find me anyway if I did."
"...You get on my bad side, I might turn out to be your worst nightmare..." echoed through his mind and he shuddered involuntarily. "..do as I ask, and behave, and I may turn out to be a valuable friend.." he shivered then nodded slightly to himself and took a deep breath.
"Might as well get as much of this soot out of the kitchen as I can," he decided and went looking for the water bucket.

Quite some time, and all of his aunt's clean rags later, he stopped, stood up tiredly and looked around. The kitchen was still going to need work but the damage didn't appear quite as bad any more. The window was clean again, and the sunlight sparkled on the glass. The counter top was useless, but the walls were no longer black and he'd discovered it was only the area very near the stove that would actually need painting. The ceiling had survived with only a slight charring, once he'd gotten the soot off, and the smell was no longer over powering.
"She's gonna need a new curtain rod," Kheri thought, looking up at the now bare wall over the sink, "and a new counter." He squatted down in front of the stove and set about the unpleasant task of cleaning the soggy ashes out of it.
"At least the stove's not cracked," he thought as his eyes drifted over it's metal sides. He made a face, then carefully began scooping the mess that was left inside it into the bucket. He stepped outside with the last of the wood from the stove just in time to see Paw Tucker, and most of the neighboring farmers, along with their wives, coming in the gate. He dumped it on the ground beside the steps, then stood in the kitchen door, watching the crowd which was arriving noisily.

Paw Tucker pulled his wagon up next to the back steps and glanced at Kheri, then hopped down. Turning, he extended his hand up and helped an elderly man dressed in a long black coat out of the wagon.

"Watch the step Doc," he cautioned as the man climbed down.

"Thank you, now where's my bag," the man replied, feeling around under the wooden seat.

"Here," Paw answered, pulling a black bag out from behind the seat.

"Thank you" Doc repeated, taking the bag. He turned around and started for the back door then stopped.

"Ah, Kheri, back for a visit eh? Or did you get tired of life as a street rat?" Doc inquired with a glint in his eye. Kheri's face tightened noticeably.

"I'm not a ..", he began but the doctor cut him off.

"Where's your aunt?" he asked brusquely.

"In her room," Kheri responded, bristling noticeably, "this way." He turned and lead the doctor to his aunt's room, opened the door then stood aside.

"I'll be in the living room," he said as the door closed firmly in his face. His hands tightened into fists and he glared angrily at the door for several seconds, then spun around and stalked back down the hall toward the living room.

Chapter Four

The house was now buzzing with activity. The women were taking over the living room, getting ready to make new curtains and other homey touches for the kitchen while the men were busy with the task of ripping out the burned parts and putting in new wood. Dale opened his eyes slightly and lay there listening. He was still tired but no longer totally exhausted. He stretched slightly, then sat up and rubbed his eyes just as Kheri walked back into the living room. Kheri froze as Dale sat up, all his real and imagined fears flooding back through his mind. Dale opened one eye, looked at him quizzically then stood. The hen party in the living room ignored both of them, and noisily continued on with the business at hand.

"Excuse me," Dale said quietly, making his way with some difficulty through the maze of chairs, to the front door. He might as well have been invisible and silent for all the attention the ladies paid to him. He regarded them curiously for a moment, then shrugged and went outside, gently closing the screen door behind himself.

Kheri stood uncertainly in the hall and looked around.
"One of these days," he muttered, glancing back over his shoulder at his aunt's bedroom door, "I'm going to punch that Doctor right where it counts!"
He had a momentary, fairly satisfying vision, of pushing the doctor off the Goldwine bridge then slumped against the wall and stared into the living room. The women were already deeply in gossip, chattering about the lives of various neighbors and Kheri wrinkled his nose in disgust.
"Wonder how long it'll be before they start talking about me?" he thought, scowling slightly. The sound of sawing drifted to him from the kitchen accompanied by a burst of laughter. He glanced over and took a step in the direction of the men then stopped.

"I'll just get in the way," he thought, visualizing the crowded conditions of the small room. "Besides, I'm not good with a hammer anyway." He slumped against the wall again for a few minutes, listening to the chattering from the living room.
"...that nephew of hers...", one of the women said, the rest of her sentence drowned by a sudden clatter from the kitchen. Kheri frowned unhappily, then stood away from the wall and walked deliberately into the living room. The women pointedly ignored his presence, chattering gaily about the new addition to the Tucker family. Kheri waited for several seconds, then gave up and made his way to the front door. He glanced back at the kitchen, looked around the living room one more time then walked outside, slamming the screen door behind him with more force than necessary.

As he stepped out onto the porch, a bit of breeze blew the deep green scent of the nearby fields to him and he took a deep breath, then looked around. Dale had moved over to sit on the grass under the massive oak tree which dominated his aunt's front yard and was watching him. He stood silently on the porch, looking back over the last eighteen or so hours, digesting what all had happened, then stepped off the porch and walked over to the tree.

"It's hotter out here," Dale commented, "But a lot less noisy."
"Yeah, they get like that," Kheri answered, sitting down on the ground. "They'll be here till dark. They won't leave till everything's fixed."
Dale nodded slightly, then winced and wrapped his arms across his stomach and bent over, pain flashing across his face. Kheri frowned in confusion.
"What's wrong?" he asked, his mental fantasy's of what Dale might be colliding once again with the reality in front of him. Dale sighed in relief as the hunger pangs faded and relaxed.
"I haven't eaten for nearly three days now," he explained, leaning back against the tree. Kheri stared.

"Three days??" Amazement crossed his face.
Dale nodded.
"It's not by choice," he replied softly.
Kheri stared at him for several seconds, then got to his feet without another word and went back into the house.
"Do demons eat?" he muttered to himself as he walked back inside. The mental image he had built up of Dale collided once again with reality. In his imagination, Dale had become a supernatural creature, complete with fangs, horns and the ability to breath fire... but the pain that had crossed his face a few minutes before was a very human reaction to hunger. Kheri rubbed his eyes, trying to get ahold of himself, looked around the room, then walked deliberately up to Maw Tucker.

"You brought food right?" he asked bluntly.
"Sure did," she smiled up at Kheri, her hands still stitching on her part of the curtains.
"Where is it?" he asked.
"Oh, some's out in the wagon, some's in the kitchen. Why? You hungry child?" she replied.
"A little bit, but..." he glanced back out into the front yard, "Dale hasn't eaten in a couple days," he explained.
"Land sakes!" she exclaimed. "Why in the world didn't someone say something? Why no wonder he was sound asleep in the middle of the day!" She clapped her hands sharply. "Ladies, we can do this later," she stated loudly, rising to her feet. "We need to feed these menfolk right now!"

The hen party rose as one body and scurried into the kitchen. A great deal of shooing and "you can do that later", drifted into the living room for a few minutes then Maw Tucker stuck her head back out into the living room.
"Go call your friend and the two of you come eat," she instructed Kheri. He grinned as the smell of hot food drifted past his nose, then nodded and went back out onto the porch.

Dale was still leaning against the tree trunk, his eyes were closed and seemingly asleep once more. Kheri took a deep breath, walked lightly down the stairs then cautiously approached the tree. Dale opened one eye as he got close and looked up at him.
"I wasn't asleep," he commented.
"How'd you know..", Kheri began.
"Well..." Dale explained, sitting up away from the tree, "you know I'm still tired. I'm sitting here with my eyes closed and if I'd just recently had the shocking experience when I tried to wake someone up that you did, I'd be walking like I was afraid to get too close too."
"Oh," Kheri answered, thinking about this for a moment then shrugged. "There's food in the kitchen," he said, changing the subject, "they said to come eat."

Dale nodded and stood up stiffly, then stretched. Kheri watched in amazement as he seemed to grow almost two feet taller for a moment, then blinked.
"Dale..", he asked almost hesitantly, as if he really didn't want the answer he was sure he'd get.
"What?" Dale replied, looking at him.
"Where are you from anyway? I mean, you told my aunt it was fairly far away but..." Kheri's voice trailed off and he looked up at Dale in uncomfortable silence.
"I'll tell you later," Dale told him. "After I get some food in my stomach and all this commotion is over."
"Alright," Kheri replied, unsure if he was relieved to be put off or not. "My aunt said you could have whatever it was you wanted," he remarked, changing the subject again as they started back toward the front porch, "as long as it wasn't her cow."
Dale grinned.
"I don't have much need for a cow," he replied.
"Yeah, I know," Kheri answered.
"Where are the clothes?" Dale asked.

"Up in the attic, in an old trunk,"Kheri explained as they climbed the stairs up to the front porch. "I'm not sure how good they are though, they've been locked away up there for so long."
Dale nodded silently then went back into the house. Kheri punched the wall next to the door in frustration, then followed him inside.

The ladies had spread what looked like a veritable feast both in the kitchen and on several tables in the living room. The doctor had emerged finally and was happily stowing away a large sandwich when Dale walked back in. He glanced at Dale curiously, looked his jump suit over, then raised an eyebrow. Dale nodded slightly in his direction and disappeared into the kitchen.
"Now just where do you suppose," the doctor asked of Maw Tucker, "he blew in from. Mighty strange clothes he's wearing."
"Don't rightly know," Maw Tucker replied then looked at the doctor with piercing eyes. "And it ain't rightly none of my business either, less he brings it up."
The doctor flushed slightly. "Madam I beg your pardon, I certainly didn't mean anything by the question!" He bowed stiffly, then excused himself and found a less chilly place to sit.
Kheri snickered, watching the exchange. Maw Tucker had managed to deliver a very effective punch and it was extremely satisfying to watch the doctor crumple. He kept silent however and merely mumbled "excuse me" as he followed Dale into the kitchen.

Dale filled two plates with food and took them out into the back yard. He walked over next to the pump and sat down on the grass, then rapidly began devouring their contents. Paw Tucker wandered over and planted himself on the ground nearby then let out a satisfied belch. Dale looked up at him curiously.
"Good food," Paw commented, and stretched contentedly. Dale nodded and silently went on eating, trying to force himself to chew rather than simply swallow. He was fast losing the fight however

and Paw watched in amazement while both the plates emptied of their contents in the space of a few minutes.

"Something tells me you were a might hungry boy," he said as Dale finished the last bit of food. Dale nodded.
"I hadn't eaten in nearly three days," he replied, wiping his face.
"Now that's a record I've no desire to beat," Paw commented.
"Yes, well, it's a record I wasn't trying to set," Dale answered dryly.
Paw chuckled.
"Why'd you go so long without food then?" he asked.
Dale looked at him for a moment.
"I'm somewhat stranded here," he explained, "and I'm stranded without anything. No food, no money, and no way I can think of to get home, at least not any time soon,"
Paw turned this answer over in his mind for a few seconds then nodded.
"Yep that might cause a few problems. So who stranded you?" he asked
"Not who," Dale responded as Kheri sat down next to them with his plate.
"What."
"Ok," Paw replied, "I'll bite. What stranded you?"
Dale felt Kheri stiffen and shrugged. "Just circumstances beyond my control," he explained.

Paw nodded then gestured toward Dale's jump suit.
"Pretty strange clothes, you must come from a long ways off, " he remarked.
Dale nodded.
"I do," he replied. "Which is one of the reasons I was out here this morning."
"Oh?" Paw questioned, looking at him curiously.
Kheri stared at his food, forcing himself not to look interested. Dale glanced at him then nodded.

"Kheri said his aunt might have some old clothes she'd be willing to get rid of. I thought I'd ask her, but events didn't exactly give me that chance." he replied.

Kheri was visibly uncomfortable now, but he said nothing, just sat silently, shoving the food around on his plate. Paw Tucker regarded him for a moment. "You know your aunt'll never give those clothes away boy," he said at last.
"What were you thinking?"
Kheri shrugged.
"He's been dead thirty years," he said, looking up defiantly. "She needs to let go and move on. Besides, they're probably so old they're falling apart anyway!" He met Paw's eyes and glared at him for a moment.
Paw shrugged, then turned back to Dale.
"She won't part with 'em, that's all she's got left of that fool of a husband she had. But I tell you what son, you did something most men wouldn't have this morning and I'm obliged since she's my neighbor and friend. I've got some clothes that should fit you fine which I ain't gonna be wearing again. You're welcome to 'em if you want 'em."
Dale returned his gaze and smiled.
"Thank you, I'd be more than happy to take them off your hands," he replied.
"Well then, I'll send my wife and Jerad up to the house in a bit to fetch 'em for you," Paw told him. "I'm curious though," he went on, looking sideways at Dale. "Since you're stranded and all, where're you planning on living?"

Dale frowned slightly.
"I haven't figured that one out yet," he admitted. "I suppose I'll look around town and see if anyone's in need of help then go from there."
Paw nodded.

"Might be a couple, the inn's always looking for people. Take a piece of advice though, stay away from the crazy wizard to the east," he said.
Dale raised an eyebrow.
"The crazy what?" he asked.
"Wizard," Paw replied. "Least that's what he calls himself. Don't rightly know what he is. He's always coming to town with strange brews in bottles claiming they'll fix everything from warts to hangnails. They don't never fix anything," he went on, "and he's always looking for people to come help with some crazy experiments. No one's stupid enough to try that though." He nodded sagely to himself.
The side of Dale's mouth crooked slightly as a smile tugged at it.
"I'll keep that in mind," he responded. "Thank you for the warning."
"You're welcome," Paw replied. "Welp, think we better get back to work 'fore the sun goes down," he stood, brushed himself off and tromped back into the kitchen.

Kheri watched him go then turned and looked up at Dale.
"So..." he asked hesitantly, "Now what?"
"Explain?" Dale requested, looking at him.
"Well, you've got what you wanted," Kheri explained, "You've got clothes. So now what?"
Dale studied him silently until Kheri flinched then dropped his eyes and sat looking at the ground uncomfortably.
"Now I figure out where I am," Dale replied, "find some way to survive here until I can get home, then try to get home."
"What about..," Kheri tried again, looking back up at him.
"You?" Dale asked.
"Yeah, me." Kheri agreed.
"I told you this morning, you're my guide to this place. Remember?" Dale reminded him. Kheri nodded silently, picking at the grass. "So," Dale continued, "until I don't need a guide any more, nothing changes."

"But..." Kheri protested, a look of anger starting across his face. He fought with several rising emotions, his hands clenching into fists. Anger flooded through him, the fears he'd imagined swam up and did battle, and in the midst of chaos Dale put a very gentle hand on his shoulder.

"Settle down," he said quietly, his words cutting through Kheri's emotions like cold water. "We'll talk about it later, when all of these people have left. "

Kheri looked up into the face of someone he couldn't figure out then took a deep breath and nodded.

"Alright," he agreed reluctantly."

Dale nodded, picked up his plates and took them back into the house.

Kheri stared after him for a moment then finished his food and stood up. He wandered over to the chicken yard and stood there, watching the rooster. It eyed him suspiciously then flapped it's wings and crowed in his direction.

"Shut up you stupid bird," Kheri grumbled. "I'm not in your yard."

The rooster flapped it's wings again then strutted past a couple hens, showing off. Kheri glowered in it's direction then leaned dejectedly on a fence post.

"I can't win," he muttered, dropping his chin on his hands. "Everything hates me. What did I do to deserve this?"

He watched the rooster strutting around the yard for a few more minutes then jumped as Paw Tucker suddenly appeared out of nowhere next to him.

"He's a fine looking rooster, that one," the older man commented.

"Yeah, and he hates me." Kheri stated flatly.

"He just thinks you want his hens is all," Paw replied. "Just trying to protect what's his from being stolen."

"That's disgusting!" Kheri exclaimed, making a face. "The only thing I want his hens for is dinner."

"Yes, but he doesn't know that boy," came Paw's reply.
Kheri shrugged, dropping his chin back down on his hands on top of the fence post.

Paw stood silently for a few more seconds, watching him.
"You want to talk about it son?" he asked finally.
"What's to talk about?" Kheri shot back unhappily.
"Oh, I don't know, but something's eating at you mighty bad," Paw replied.
Kheri shrugged again.
"I doubt you'd understand," he muttered.
"Try me," Paw said, gazing at the chickens.
"My life sucks," Kheri responded. "Ok?"
"Things not working out in town?" Paw asked.
"Not really no," Kheri admitted angrily. "The rooster tried to kill me this morning, my aunt's house nearly burned down, she almost died, and one of these days I'm gonna punch that doctor right where it counts!" he complained, his voice rising to a shout as he finished.

"Well, the doc's gone now," Paw replied calmly, "Jerad took him off about an hour ago. The house's fine, and we're nearly done, your aunts ok, just needs a bit more rest and the rooster's on the other side of that fence."
Kheri shrugged.
"You could come back out here, help your aunt out. You don't need to be sleeping in alleys in town son." Paw remarked, still studying the chickens.
"I'm not sleeping in alleys," Kheri shot back defiantly.
Paw shrugged.
"Ok, have it your way," he put a friendly hand on Kheri's shoulder. "Just trying to help."

Kheri shrugged again, pulling away from the hand and Paw removed it, then stood up away from the fence. "Welp, we've got

some painting to do then we'll be out of here. I'll come back in a bit with those clothes for that friend of yours."
Kheri nodded silently. Paw waited for a few seconds longer then shrugged and went back toward the house.
"He's not my friend," Kheri muttered once Paw was out of earshot. "I'm not sure what he is."
Kheri glanced back at the house, half expecting to see Dale standing on the back porch watching him, but the doorway was empty. He stared at the house for a few more seconds then shrugged and walked back inside.

The kitchen was completely finished now and Paw stood in the middle of it, looking around with a smile on his face, satisfied at a job well done.
"Looks good boys, I'll go say goodbye to Matilda and we'll all meet back over at my place for some cards this evening." he said.
"Can't," one of the men remarked, "Cow's fixing to calf and I need to get home."
Paw nodded.
"Well get on with you then, and let us know how she does," he replied, clapping the man on the shoulder.
"Sure thing, you take care," the man responded.

The bedroom door opened and Kheri's aunt came out wearing an old, beat-up bathrobe. She spotted the men still in the kitchen and wandered over, looking around with a happy smile on her face.
"I declare, you boys did a wonderful job in here!" She exclaimed. "Why it looks brand new."
"You're welcome Matilda, can't see a neighbor without a kitchen." Paw smiled.
"Well thank you all," she replied, still looking around. "I'm much obliged. And tell Bessie that those curtains are just wonderful."
"I'll let her know," Paw agreed. "Careful with that wood now," he cautioned, motioning to the back yard. "I took a look at it what you

was burnin'. Mighty full of sap in spots. Probably what caused all this mess."
Matilda nodded.
"Probably," she agreed. "I'll chuck it round back of the barn and let it sit a while longer. Got some older wood from two years ago I still ain't burned."
"Right," Paw nodded. "I'll send Jerad over next week with another load. I just finished clearing a couple trees and it's ready to be split now."
"Why thank you," she told him. "That'd be right nice of you."

Paw glanced at Kheri as he walked in the back door then turned back to Matilda.
"Well you take care now," he finished. "Get some more sleep, Doc said you should rest till tomorrow."
"Oh what's he know," she replied, waving her hand to dismiss the comment. "I'm just fine cept for this bruise on my face."
"Still," Paw admonished.
"Bah, I'll be fine," she replied and turned to smile at her nephew. "Didn't they do a wonderful job?" she asked happily.
"Yeah, it's great," he muttered, then brushed past them and walked into the living room.
She sighed and shook her head.
"Sour all the time, that one. " she commented watching him as he deposited himself unhappily on the couch.
Paw nodded.
"Needs a woman," he commented. "Just to set him straight."
Matilda grinned then glanced out the backdoor as the sound of wagon wheels were heard.
"That'll be Jerad, back to get me and drop off those clothes." Paw explained. "Where's that friend of Kheri's?"
"Don't rightly know, might be out front," came the reply. Paw nodded and went outside.

Kheri glowered at his aunt as she walked into the living room.

"Now what's eating you," she asked, walking over to sit down by him on the couch.
He shrugged.
"Nothing," he grumbled.
"Mighty sour for nothing," she said.
"Just don't like it when people start lecturing me," he replied, glancing back into the kitchen.
She followed his gaze then nodded.
"Paw means well," she told him. "You know that."
"Yeah, but I'm tired of people trying to run my life!" he snarled, scowling.
She shrugged.
"Someone gives you advice, they're not trying to run your life boy," she explained. "Just trying to help you over the ditches."
Kheri shrugged.
"I can get over the ditches on my own," he muttered.

"Sure you can," his aunt agreed as she put her hand on his arm, "but everything's easier if you're not all alone."
Kheri sighed.
"I'm no good out here on this farm," he told her. "The chickens try to kill me, the cow hates me, I can't grow anything but weeds. I'm just not a farmer." His aunt didn't say anything and he shrugged. "So that doesn't give me many options. It's either try to live here or try to live in town. And town," he said without much conviction, "is working out just fine."

His aunt regarded him silently for a moment then nodded
"No one's trying to force you not to live there are they?" she asked.
Kheri nodded.
"Everyone I talk to. They call me a street rat, or tell me that my place is here, or," he stopped as his aunt patted him on the head.
"Calm yourself child," she said. "they're just trying to help. "
He shrugged, then stood up.

"I'm going outside. Maybe a tree'll fall on me or something and end the day proper," he growled and stalked out the front door. She watched him go, shaking her head, then got up and went back into the kitchen.

Dale had been sitting under the tree again, watching the world turn grey in the falling twilight, when Jerad drove the wagon back through the gate. He got up, stretched then walked around back, arriving just as Paw walked out of the kitchen door.
"Ah, there you are," Paw said as Dale walked up to him. "Wondered where you got off to. Here's the clothes." He reached into the wagon and produced a bundle, handing it to Dale.
"Thanks, I do appreciate it," Dale told him.
"No trouble," Paw replied. "A word of advice though," he cautioned, glancing back into the house. Dale lifted an eyebrow slightly in question. "Don't stick around Kheri too much. He's trouble. Always been," Paw warned, his voice low. "Always will be. He's living in town now, and if that boy's making an honest living, then I'm a horse."
Dale looked at him silently for a moment then nodded.
"Ok, I'll keep that in mind. Thanks," he replied.

"Might consider finding somewhere else to sleep tonight too... being as all the folk are gone now," Paw went on. "Hate to find out you died in your sleep or something."
Dale blinked and stared at him.
"Excuse me?" he asked, confusion written on his face.
"Like I said," Paw replied sagely, "trouble." He swung up onto the wagon then looked back down at Dale. "He's just never been caught at it."
He snapped the reins and the horses started to move.

Dale nodded and stepped out of the way, watching him turn the wagon then drive off.

"Now that," he remarked quietly to himself, "is a very observant man."
He watched the wagon leave then looked down at the bundle he was holding.
"I wonder if these fit," he thought then smiled slightly.
"Kheri," he addressed the darkness behind him, "If you're going to eavesdrop you'll need to learn to be a lot quieter on the approach."
Kheri shrugged, then stepped around the corner of the house.
"What'd you hear?" Dale asked.
"Nothing much," Kheri commented. "That I'm trouble." He shrugged. "Same thing they always say behind my back."
Dale nodded, looking at him silently.

Kheri fidgeted for a second, then met Dale's eyes again.
"So," he asked. "They're gone and my aunt's out of the way...can you answer my question now?"
Dale regarded him, a slow smile spreading over his face.
"You sure you want the answer to that question?" he asked.
"You asked me that this morning," Kheri replied. "Yeah, I want the answer to that question."
Dale nodded.
"Let it get fully dark first," he said.
Kheri stiffened.
"Why?" he asked, a trace of nervousness in his voice.
"Because I said," Dale stated bluntly. Kheri looked back at him for a moment, then nodded and looked away.
"Why can't I stand up to you?!" he muttered to himself.
Dale regarded him silently for a moment.
"You have a number of times," he replied.
Kheri shrugged and crossed his arms, glowering at the ground.
"Where can I change?" Dale asked, changing the subject.
"The barn I guess," Kheri told him, looking back up. "Just watch out for the cow."

Dale grinned, thinking back to the rooster, then nodded and headed for the barn.

Kheri watched him go, fighting with feelings of confusion, fear, and a faint feeling that he refused to put the name friendship on. "Demons don't eat and sleep," he asked himself. "Do they?"

The shot went wide as Dale's feet connected with it's abdomen and it lost its balance, stumbling backwards, the blaster flying from its grasp.

Chapter Five

Dale pulled the barn door open and stepped inside. The scent was overpowering and he covered his mouth, trying not to gag.
"Whew," he thought. "I don't know how many cows live in here but what do they feed them?!?" He flipped his force field back on and took a deep breath as the life support filters went to work, removing the stench.
"Man, I had no idea one cow could be so rank." he looked around in the dim light, trying to get an idea of the layout. Something squished underfoot and he looked down then sighed.
"Figures," he said to no one in particular. "Wonder just how long it's been since this place was cleaned." He made a face then pushed the door open and left the barn.

"I am not getting dressed in there," he muttered as he walked back outside. Kheri was no where to be seen and the yard was empty. He glanced around, then walked around behind the barn. The small space behind it was covered with weeds and high grass, thickly forested with tall thistles wound about with the vines of stinging nettles. A rogue squash plant was in the process of choking everything else out, it's vines covered with large, yellow flowers.

Dale sought a fairly open area, away from the nettles, and turned his force field off. He touched a recessed control on his belt then took it off and dressed rapidly, pulling the other clothes on over top of his jump suit. They fit and he grinned then threaded the belt through the loops on the pants. The jump suit's sensors detected the extra clothing and hummed for a moment. Various electronics came to life, re-patterned it's surface and it faded from sight, turning completely invisible.
"It would be nice," Dale thought as he waited for the suit to finish restructuring, "not to have to wear this thing all the time."

He thumbed a control on his belt and it too shifted slightly, becoming just another, slightly beat up, ordinary belt. The shoes that Paw Tucker had provided were too big and Dale looked at them for a moment then discarded them.

"My boots will just have to do," he thought. "Not much of them shows under these pants anyway. They could look more like leather though." He sighed inwardly and shrugged to himself. "No help for that, they'll just have to do," he thought, looking down their shiny black surface sticking out from under the legs of the work pants he was now wearing. Satisfied, he stuck his hands in the pockets, then brought out a handful of paper and looked at it curiously.
"I wonder," he thought, examining it, "if this is their currency or something else."
He studied it for a moment then stuck it back into his pocket and walked back around to the front of the barn.

Something detached itself silently from the darkness behind him as he started across the yard and slammed into his back. He hit the ground and rolled with the impact, rising to his feet in one fluid motion. His hand slapped now invisible controls on his belt, activating both the force field and infrared enhancements, and he spun around. Instantly three large humanoid figures sprang into view, their heat signatures blazing like the sun at noon day. A smaller figure could be seen huddled on the grass behind them, and Dale ignored it. "Lights," he ordered mentaly and his suit sprang to life. The scene changed dramatically as the daylight effects function activated and the lights were suddenly turned on.

Before him stood three Gorgs. Large, ugly creatures, almost eight feet tall, with massive muscles that rippled under leathery skin. Foul tempered and armed with blasters, they snarled at him, slowly advancing. Behind them he could see Kheri huddled on

the ground, his face a mask of terror. The largest Gorg stepped forward, snarling viciously.
"Why is it," Dale thought, dropping into ready stance, "that I always seem to wind up in a fight when I'm exhausted?"

"You come with us," the Gorg snarled in Galactic Standard, pointing his blaster at Dale's midsection. "Not likely," he thought, but said nothing, standing his ground and waiting. The Gorg roared in frustration at Dale's defiance, leveled it's blaster at his head and pulled the trigger. The shot went wide as Dale's feet connected with it's abdomen and it lost it's balance, stumbling backwards, the blaster flying from it's grasp. Dale rolled to a stand as he hit the ground, scooped the blaster up, ducked the shot from the second one and brought the butt of the blaster down hard on the first Gorg's head. The Gorg blinked as stars shot off through it's vision and let out a roar of pain. Dale swung around, brought the blaster to sight on the third Gorg, then thumbed the trigger.

A flash of incandescence lit the night as the Gorg vaporized. The other two took a step back, then vanished in flashes of brilliant light.
"Blast!!" the exclamation exploded out of Dale as they disappeared and he spun around, looking for other targets. The night was still once more and he took a deep breath, calming his nerves, then hit the safety on the blaster, and walked over to Kheri.

The younger man was huddled on the ground with his arms wrapped tightly around his knees. He looked fearfully up at Dale as he approached and shook his head rapidly.
"Are you alright," Dale asked gently as he knelt down beside him and put a hand on his shoulder. Kheri nodded wordlessly, then swallowed and looked into Dale's eyes.
"What...," he whispered, then tried again "What was... were...."
"Those," Dale explained, "were Gorg's. Nasty, evil, foul tempered creatures who only live to do one thing."

"What?" Kheri asked, his voice trembling.
"Kill for fun and profit," Dale replied. "In the most unpleasant ways they can."
He stood up, then reached down to help Kheri to his feet.
"And they are evidently after me for some reason," he continued as Kheri stood. "Which means we do not stay here. We're putting your aunt in danger."
Kheri nodded slightly.
"Where did they come from?" he asked in a shaky voice, his eyes still locked on Dale's face.

Dale studied the expression on Kheri's face for a moment, then nodded to himself.
"Backwater planet, lots of superstitions, should have seen this one coming," he thought.
"Kheri," Dale said, pointing up at the stars. "Tell me what those are."
Kheri glanced up at the sky, confused.
"The stars?" he asked, and Dale nodded.
"I dunno. Lights?" he looked back at Dale helplessly.
"No," Dale replied, shaking his head. "Those are suns. Like the sun that rises and sets every morning only they are so far away, they look like little dots. Millions and millions of them."

Kheri blinked and looked back up into the sky. He'd never thought much about the stars before. They were pretty, it was nice to have them in the sky when it was night but that was the extent of his scientific curiosity.
"Suns.." he repeated, looking up. "But why's it black then?"
"Because," Dale explained. "There's no air out there. There's nothing out there. It's not black really, it just looks that way because there's no light in the emptiness between the suns."
Kheri stared up at the sky for a long moment then shivered.
"Why..." he began, looking back at Dale again.

"And that," Dale interrupted him, "is where the Gorg come from. Out there. From another world. A really unpleasant place."

"They're not demons?" Kheri asked, an unvoiced fear finally breaking out of him.
"Guess that depends on your definition of demon," Dale replied. "They're flesh and blood, but that's about it. Their actions would fit most of the stories about demons I've ever heard."
"But you killed them," Kheri protested.
"I killed one. The other two fled," Dale corrected him. "They'll be back though and I'd prefer not to be anywhere near your aunt when they return. Things could get very ugly if they bring reinforcements."

Kheri shuddered.
"Are you..." he faltered and looked at Dale then glanced back up at the sky.
"One of the Gorg?" Dale asked.
Kheri nodded then shook his head rapidly.
"Yes, well no. Not one of them but...," he stumbled over his words.
"Yes," Dale replied quietly. "And I'm currently stranded here."
"How..." Kheri's face held a confused expression once again.
"It's a very long story, and you might not understand most of it. You sure you want to hear this?" Dale asked.
Kheri shrugged, looked back over at where the Gorg had been then took a deep breath and nodded.
"Yes," he replied. "I'd kind of like to know what else might show up in the middle of the night."
Dale grinned slightly.
"I thought you'd be begging to stay here with your aunt," he commented.
"You made it real clear earlier that I'm not free to do that," Kheri replied, "and," he looked back over to where the fight had taken

place, "I would really prefer not to get on your bad side...," his voice trailed off and he looked back up at Dale. "Ok?"
There was a certain attempt at bravado in Kheri's voice and stance but beneath it Dale could see the fear hadn't actually subsided. He nodded.
"Alright," he replied, then walked over to sit on the stump Kheri's aunt used when splitting firewood. Kheri followed, skirting the area where the Gorg had been with wary caution.

Dale looked up into the night sky for several minutes, searching for star patterns that might be even slightly familiar, then shook his head.
"I have absolutely no idea where I am," he remarked, more to himself than Kheri.
"So," he explained in a more normal tone, "I can't point out the exact location of anything. But I'll try to explain. Stop me if you get confused."
"Ok," came Kheri's subdued answer.
Dale looked up at the sky again.
"All the dots up there are suns, like I said. Some are the same size as the one you see every day. Some are smaller, some are much larger," Dale began, and launched into a short beginner's astronomy lesson. Kheri said nothing as he talked, listening and looking up at the sky once in a while. Dale paused after a few minutes.
"With me so far?" he asked.
Kheri nodded.
"Yes, kind of hard to believe though. So every one of those dots has a world? With people?" he asked, pointing up at the sky.

"No," Dale answered. "Most of them don't have anything, but enough of them do. Most of the worlds have decent people on them, but a few..." he glanced over at the bare patch of ground, "have creatures like the Gorg living on them."

Kheri shivered and looked around, half expecting to see more Gorg suddenly materialize nearby.
"Now the Gorg wouldn't be a problem," Dale continued. "They're too stupid to invent the stuff they need to get off their world, but there are some people out there who are greedy. And they use the Gorg to do their dirty work."
He looked at Kheri, trying to judge his comprehension level. Kheri was staring back up at the sky.
"So why doesn't someone stop them then?" he asked after a moment.
"We try," Dale explained. "Sometimes we win, sometimes they do."
"You're a guard?" Kheri asked suddenly, his mind conjuring up images of the town guards flying around space doing battle with the Gorgs.

Dale grinned.
"Something like that," he replied. "That's not quite the same as what I usually do, but it's close enough."
"So is that why are the Gorg after you then?" Kheri wondered, turning his gaze from the sky back to Dale.
Dale shrugged.
"Could be a lot of reasons. Maybe someone has a grudge against me, maybe I walked into the wrong bar in the past. Maybe they thought I was someone else. Who knows." He stood up off the stump. "Personally, I don't feel like sticking around to ask them."
Kheri shivered and nodded his head.
"Yeah, me either." he agreed.

"They won't be back tonight," Dale stated as they started back for the house. "Not their style. They didn't expect to lose and they'll have to go back, get new orders, probably get replaced with others...their employer's don't usually like failure." He made a face in the darkness then continued. "By the time they get back,

I intend to be very far away," he finished, watching Kheri for his reaction. Kheri stopped walking as Dale's last comment sunk in.
"Like..." he turned back to face him. "How far is far?"
"Well, far enough that they can't easily find me," Dale replied. "They'll search at least fifty miles around where they saw me last. So farther than that."
Kheri groaned.
"That'll take us completely out of the Barony," he grumbled. "and into the wilds."
"So?" Dale asked.
"So...do you have any idea what's out there?" Kheri questioned, his voice rising slightly.
"No," Dale answered flatly. "Do you?"

"Yeah, ogres and trolls, and dragons and Bilbeasts and bandits an...," Kheri responded, rattling off a long list of possible horrors. Dale stood silently waiting for him to wind down.
"And you've seen all these things?" he asked when Kheri finally finished.
"Well, no," the younger man admitted. "Not really...but I've heard about them!"
"You've seen the Gorg," Dale pointed out. "Do you honestly want to be where they'll be looking when they come back?"
"Uh," Kheri paused. "Not especially, no. But they're just coming back for you...aren't they?"

Dale said nothing, looking at him for a long, silent moment.
"Maybe," he replied when Kheri started to fidget. "But you were out here too. Exactly why were you sitting out here anyway?"
"I was waiting for you," he responded.
"Did they see you?" Dale asked.
Kheri shook his head then paused.
"I...don't know...I don't think so," he replied hesitantly.

"Then they might not come looking for you. But are you sure you want to take that chance?" Dale asked him, his voice cutting through the night air with a chill like an icy lake in winter.
Kheri shuddered.
"No," he responded quickly, shaking his head.
Dale nodded.
"My sentiments exactly," he agreed.
"Not that I have any choice," Kheri groused.
"There is that," Dale acknowledged. "But you could be in a lot worse shape."
"Yeah, I could be sleeping in an alley," Kheri grumbled sarcastically.
"You could be laying dead in the street at the end of one of the town guards blades," Dale stated bluntly.

Kheri bristled, then remembered how easily Dale had spotted the guard that morning, the one he'd never seen.
"Yeah, I guess," he agreed reluctantly. "But this would be a whole lot easier if you'd ask instead of ordering," he grumbled defiantly.
Dale said nothing, watching him in the darkness. Kheri set his jaw and met Dale's eyes for a few seconds, then wilted and looked down at his hands. "Well, it would," he muttered.
"You want that, earn it," Dale told him. "If you don't give me a reason to have to give orders, I'm much more likely to make requests."
Kheri shrugged, still staring down at the ground, then nodded. Most of the fight had left him, and he felt drained. The day had been one long shock after the other and his emotions were frazzled. Right up until he watched Dale take on the three Gorgs he'd still toyed with the idea of beating him in a fight but now he stood, looking down at his feet, and realized just how out matched he was. He resigned himself to being under Dale's control for a while, took a deep breath then looked back up.
"When do we leave," he asked, his manner subdued.

"As soon as it's light," Dale replied.

Kheri's aunt was quite happy to have them spend the night and made up the guest bed and the couch for them. She retired earlier than normal, still weakened after the events of the morning and Kheri followed suit soon after. Dale, tired as he was, found sleep elusive, and his thoughts kept returning to the Gorg. He'd only glossed over them when explaining things earlier, but now he turned them over in his mind, remembering everything he'd ever known about them.
"Too much of a coincidence," he mused. "That warp was no accident either, someone opened it on purpose. I should have been able to close it too." He thought back to his struggle with the wild energies that had comprised it. "It wasn't that big. Someone was fighting me to keep it open and I'm sure they're the same one that sent the Gorg. I wish I knew what this was all about."

He sat up on the couch and leaned back, looking at the ceiling.
"They'll be back," he thought, "and they'll be back soon. We'll have to leave no later than first light and get out of range as rapidly as possible."
Memories drifted through his mind, details he'd forgotten surfaced and he shook his head.
"Fifty miles won't be nearly enough," he thought, thinking about the Gorg. "Five hundred might be, but we can't possibly walk that fast. We'll have to ride...something...but these people aren't likely to just give their horses away...or anything else for that matter."
He reluctantly considered the possibility of stealing an unwatched horse but shook his head.
"No," he said to himself, "that'd cause more trouble than it would mend. And," he glanced toward the bedroom where Kheri was sawing logs, "He doesn't need to see me stealing anyway."

He got back up off the couch and went out onto the front porch, then sat down on the steps. The moon had risen, and it's light painted the landscape with a silvery sheen. He smiled, and sat there listening to the night noises. A chorus of crickets called to each other and in the distance he could hear the occasional whinny of a horse. Wings whirred softly through the air as an owl swooped down, then sailed away, a rabbit dangling from it's grasp.

"Why is it," he wondered out loud, "that I never get a break? This could actually be a nice place to stay for a while and what happens?" He shook his head at the thought, "I get chased by Gorg. If this were an inhospitable desert, I can guarantee nothing would even THINK of bothering me!"

He sat on the porch for a bit longer, listening to the night, then got up and went back inside.

Chapter Six

The sensors in Dale's suit went off as the first bits of light filtered through the window blinds and he awoke, then lay there listening to the sounds around him. All was still quite in the house, but the birds were starting their morning ruckus ritual. The clock chose that moment to chime five am and Dale sat up reluctantly. His suit hummed briefly, it's cleaning cycle automatically activated and he twitched. The cleaning cycle made it possible to wear the suit at all times, as it took care of disposing of sweat, dead skin and other problems, but the sensation was fairly close to being suddenly immersed in a bath of crackling, low voltage electricity. He'd long ago become accustomed to it, and usually never noticed it, but once in a while it hit the nerves just wrong. He reached up and scratched his neck, then sighed.

"It would be nice," he thought sourly, "to just once in a while, reach a state where I'm actually safe enough to take this thing off!"

He sighed and put the thought out of his mind for the thousandth time. The last time he'd taken the suit off, he'd been ambushed by a tribe of three foot high, spear wielding creatures that looked like a cross between a porcupine and a chimp. He'd barely had enough time to grab his suit and swing up into a tree, spears whizzing all around him, as he did so. That taught him a valuable lesson however.

"No matter how innocent a place looks, something is usually waiting to make you part of the food chain," he muttered, shook the memory away and stretched, then stood up and walked over to open the guest room door.

Kheri was sleeping across the middle of the bed, the blankets bunched up underneath him, and his feet dangling off the side. Dale blinked, shook his head, then knocked lightly on the door. Kheri didn't budge but his snoring turned up a notch. Dale tried again, knocking a bit louder, with less effect than his first attempt.

Kheri's aunt opened her door and came out, tying her belt around her bathrobe as she came.
"He won't wake up like that, sleeps way too sound. This'll get him though," she said, a twinkle in her eye.

Walking into the guest room, she picked up a pitcher of water from the table next to the bed and up-ended it over his head. Kheri jumped up, spluttering and looking around wildly.
"Get up," his aunt said in her no-nonsense tone of voice, then turned and walked out of the room. Dale collapsed against the door frame, shaking with silent laughter and Kheri glowered at him.
"Laugh it up," he growled unhappily. "I'll bet you'd look funny too if someone dumped a bucket of water on you when you were asleep."

"Probably," Dale agreed, catching his breath. "You must admit, it was effective."
"Yeah," Kheri agreed sourly. "It's also the main reason I moved out."
Dale nodded.
"Well come on, it's time we were on the road." he said, turning from the guest room toward the kitchen.
Kheri's aunt was busily pulling food out of the pantry, and wrapping it into a large square of cloth.
"I figure you boys might like some lunch later," she said. "Walking's hungry work."
Dale nodded, wondering just how much she knew or had guessed. She finished the bundle and handed it to him, then looked at him seriously.
"Take care out there on the roads," she said softly, her accent suddenly gone. "There are far worse things that lurk in the wild than the three that ambushed you in my yard last night."

Dale blinked.

"You saw that?" He asked.
She nodded.
"Of course I saw, and you did well against them, but," she shook her head. "There are far worse things in the wilds than those. So be very careful."
"I intend to," he responded, wondering how she had managed to guess where he was going.
"Well," she replied, looking him squarely in the eye. "As to that, I don't have to guess. You're broadcasting loud enough for a dead man to hear." Dale stared at her in shock and reflexively clamped down on his thoughts. "Don't worry though," she continued. "No one else around here can hear you. Just me."
Dale nodded wordlessly and she smiled at him then reached into her bathrobe pocket and pulled something out, then pressed it into his hand.

"You'll need horses, and they're not cheap. Take that. Should be enough there for two," she said, sticking her hand back into the pocket. "Talk to Paw Tucker, he raises 'em. Tell him I said to."
Dale looked down at the wad of paper in his hand, then back at her, an unasked question on his face.
"Take care of Kheri," she requested quietly. "He's got a good heart but he's been out of control all his life. Needs someone to straighten him up." She glanced at the guest room door which was now shut again with a faint smile on her lips.

Dale smiled slightly.
"Just how much have you overheard?" he asked.
"Enough," she told him. "And I'd already guessed most of it."
A bit of a grin crept over her face then she turned serious again.
"You're not the first we've had stranded around here, and probably won't be the last. This place seems to attract 'em for some reason," she explained. "My mother, dead these many years, she could tell when there was a stranger anywhere in the Barony. The sight

doesn't run that strong in me but it's enough." She smiled then shooed him gently out into the living room.
"You boys better get going," she said in a normal voice. "Sun's gonna get hot today."
Dale nodded, then studied her for a second.
"Does Kheri.." he began.
"Know what I can do?" she interrupted softly.
He nodded and she shook her head.
"No." she caught Dale's eyes for a second. "And I would like it to stay that way." she said pointedly.
Dale nodded.

She smiled again, patted him on the arm and walked over to the guest room door.
"Get a move on in there," she called, rapping loudly on the door. "I've got a load of wood that needs chop'n."

Kheri opened the door, tucking his shirt in and brushing the hair back out of his eyes.
"We can't..", he began and his aunt cut him off.
"I know, your friend told me," she said. "Got a walk to take this morning. Well get going then. Sun's hot early these days." She placed a small meat pie into his hands. "Might get hungry before lunch. Now scat, so's I can clean up that room you turned upside down."
Kheri sighed and moved out of her way. She bustled past him into the guest room and started making tisking noises as she set about straightening up the bed.
"Let's go," Dale told him, and headed out the front door. Kheri started to follow then impulsively ran back to his aunt, kissed her on the cheek then hurried of the house. His aunt watched him go, a fond smile creasing her face.

Dale was standing on the porch outside, waiting, as Kheri came out.

"Tell me what this is," he requested, opening his hand to display the bits of paper he'd found in the pants the night before. Kheri's eyes widened.
"Wow!" he exclaimed, staring at what Dale was holding out.
"I assume by your reaction that it's something either very good or very bad," Dale said dryly. "Which is it?
"Uh, good. Definitely good. Where did you get that?" Kheri asked.
"I found it in these pants," Dale explained. "What is it?"
"You don't know what money is?" Kheri asked rather incredulously.
"I know what money is," Dale replied. "But this hardly looks like anything I'm used to."
"Oh," came the response. "Well, that's probably enough to buy my aunt's whole farm twice over!"

Kheri reached over and picked one of the pieces up.
"This is a one doran note," he explained. "They're worth five-hundred gills. A gill," he looked at what Dale had, then shook his head. "You don't have any there, though. Those are worth two-hundred minigills."
"And a minigill?" Dale questioned. "How much would it buy?"
"A pint of ale maybe, or a night in the inn's cheap room."
Dale looked at the pieces of paper in his hand again then stuffed them back into his pocket.
"Alright," he said looking out at the country lane. "Which way to the Tucker farm?"
"What? Why?", Kheri asked, confused.
"Because I need to give them back this money before we do anything else," Dale explained, slight irritation creeping into his voice.
"Oh," Kheri replied, light dawning. He bit back a protest and pointed down the road. "That way, first farm we'll come to."
"Alright, let's go," Dale said, and stepped down off the porch, striding toward the gate.

Kheri shook his head, gave a glance around at his aunt's farm, then followed quickly afterward. As he stepped out onto the road, a curious feeling crept over him and he suddenly felt that he would never see his aunt again. He paused and stared back at the house, fighting with a wave of homesickness. After a few moments, he turned back to the road and found Dale standing silently, watching him and shrugged.

"Just saying goodbye," he muttered, then set off down the road in the direction of the Tucker farm.

Chapter Seven

They walked in silence for the better part of fifteen minutes, past open land covered with wild flowers of all shades. Kheri waited till they were out of sight of his aunt's house, then tossed the meat pie she'd given him into the grass.

"Not fond of her food?" Dale asked.

"Not her meat pies. She always burns 'em." Kheri replied, shaking his head. "Besides, Maw Tucker always gives me more food than I can finish every time I stop at her farm."

Dale grinned slightly to himself, remembering the woman from the day before, then grew serious again, troubled with thoughts of the Gorg. He glanced at Kheri, considering, then spoke.

"Kheri..." he began, speaking slowly. "Something you need to be aware of."

"What?" Kheri asked, turning to look at him.

"The Gorg are usually pretty single minded," Dale explained, "but there's always the possibility, albeit slight, that if they can't find me... they might pick other targets."

Kheri stopped walking and stared at him.

"Other targets...," he repeated. "Like my aunt??!!"

"Or anyone else," Dale clarified. "It's a very slight possibility, but it does exist."

"But..." Kheri protested and Dale cut him off.

"It's a very slight possibility," he repeated then crossed his arms and caught Kheri's gaze. "It's a guaranteed event if we stick around however."

Kheri looked back at him, his fists clinched.

"You could have said this last night," he responded tightly, fighting the urge to turn and run back to his aunt's farm.

"I spent most of last night remembering everything I knew about them," Dale replied.

"I only remember one incident ever being recorded where the Gorg were known to kidnap random people... and that might have been a set up."
Kheri stood there, his eyes flashing, and fought down the fury that threatened to consume his self-control.
"Alright," he said at last. "But if anything happens to my aunt, I'm holding you responsible for it!"

Dale looked at him for a moment, then nodded in acceptance.
"If anything happens to your aunt, I'll fix it if I at all can," he agreed.
Kheri stood for a moment longer, then forced himself to unclench his fists.
"Why couldn't you have been stranded some where else?" he complained bitterly, his emotions still overriding his common sense.
Dale shrugged.
"I have no idea," he replied. "I had all I could do to keep from being torn apart by the forces I was trying to control. Figuring out what planet to land on was the last thing on my mind. Besides," Dale pointed out. "I'm not the one who was robbing drunks, and breaking the law, in the dark."
He held Kheri's gaze silently. The younger man glared back for a few seconds, then dropped his eyes.
"Sorry," he mumbled, his emotions finally back under control.
Dale nodded. "Can we continue now?" he asked and Kheri nodded, then set off once more toward the Tucker farm.

The farm came into sight a few minutes later. It was quite a bit larger than Kheri's aunts, and several horses trotted up to the fence to greet them as they approached. The gate was a full five minutes walk further down the road and Dale had begun to wonder if one even existed when they finally reached it. Kheri pushed it open and was immediately engulfed with bounding dogs. He laughed, scratching one of the dogs behind the ear then pushed his way through them. Dale stepped inside the gate and closed it behind him, one eye warily on the dogs. They ignored him however, and bounced around Kheri's feet as he attempted to wade through them to the farmhouse.

Paw Tucker was sitting on the porch as they approached, whittling on a piece of wood. He nodded slightly to himself, a bit of a smile playing on his face at Kheri's obvious discomfort then whistled. The dogs dashed up onto the porch and flopped down, panting happily. He put his whittling aside, wiped his pocketknife and stood up, shoving it in a pocket.
"Well, you boys is out early this morning," he remarked as they stepped up onto the porch with him. "How's your aunt feeling?"
"She's fine," Kheri replied. "Up making the beds and kicking us out to get fresh air."
Paw smiled at the thought.
"So what you boys need?" he asked.
"I found this," Dale explained, pulling the money out of his pocket, "in the pants you gave me and I thought you might like it back."

He handed it to Paw and the others face lit up with a smile.
"Well now, don't that beat all," he mused. "Who'd a thought I'd left anything like that in those pants."
He looked it over, then handed one of the doran's back to Dale.
"I'm much obliged," he told him, pocketing the rest. "Why don't you boys come in and have breakfast. Maw should be setting it on the table right about now."
Kheri grinned, then glanced at Dale who nodded.
"We'd be glad to," he replied.
Paw reached over and opened the screen and the dogs, sensing a chance to invade, dashed into the house ahead of them, followed closely by Kheri. Dale didn't move.
"There is something else," he said. "If you've the time."
"Certainly," Paw agreed affably, "What is it?"

"Kheri's aunt suggested you might have a couple horses you'd be willing to sell," Dale explained.
"I might at that," Paw nodded thoughtfully. "Let's go eat breakfast first, before there's none left, then we'll go take a look."

The table was loaded with food and already crowded with members of the Tucker household. Paw ambled over and took his place at the head of the table.
"Now you young'ns watch your manners this morning," he cautioned as Dale sat down in the only empty spot. "We've got guests." He reached over, picked up a platter of biscuits and took one. The table erupted in activity at his signal. Silence, broken only by requests to pass this or that reigned for several minutes as everyone concentrated on the rapidly vanishing food. At last Paw pushed his plate back, and gave out a loud belch of satisfaction.
"Good breakfast Maw," he remarked, patting his stomach. "That'll hold till lunch."
She smiled and stood, then began clearing the dishes.
"Well now," Paw said, standing. "Shall we go look at the horses?"
Dale was taken by surprise, but stood at once, leaving part of his food unfinished.
"Lead the way," he replied. Kheri glanced up at him, then shrugged and returned to eating.

Paw led the way out of the house and over to one of the far pastures. Several horses trotted over to the fence at their approach and Paw reached up to scratch one on the muzzle.
"Take your pick," he suggested. "How many you need?"
"Just two," Dale replied.
"You got a cart?" Paw asked, looking at him curiously.
"No," he admitted, shaking his head. "We're riding them."
"You got tack?" Paw asked.
"Well...no," Dale responded. "I still have to buy that."

Paw nodded.
"Tell you what," he said after a moment. "Since you were so honest and all, brought back all that money you found, I'll give you the horses."
Dale looked at him silently.
"But tack, I don't have," Paw continued. "I can give you a couple halters, but you'll have to go visit Jhopar to buy tack."
"Jhopar?" Dale asked curiously.
"Yep. He's the blacksmith in these parts," Paw explained. "Nice fellow, but a little pricey. Still, his stuff's well made."
"How do I find him?" Dale asked, looking back at the horses.
"Just go back to town and ask around for him," Paw replied. "Kheri should know where his shop is." He paused, and looked at Dale for a moment.
"You ever ridden a horse boy?" he asked suddenly.
"Not recently," Dale answered, studying the horses.
Paw nodded, then climbed over the pasture fence.
"Well let's see about getting you acquainted with a couple."
He hopped down on the other side and stood waiting.

Dale fought back a momentary panic, then climbed the fence and jumped down beside Paw. The horses eyed him for a moment, and one bent it's head down, sniffing at his pockets.
"She's looking for sugar," Paw explained, taking a small cube out of his pocket. "Here, give her this."
Dale took the cube and looked at it curiously, then tried to offer it to the horse.
"Not like that son," Paw chided him. "Put it on your palm, open your hand up."
Dale opened his fingers as Paw instructed then cautiously held out the cube in front of him. The horse snorted, then happily took the offered cube and munched on it.
"Learn something new every day," Dale commented, wiping horse slobber off his hand onto his pants.

Paw grinned slowly.
"You seem a might nervous," he observed and Dale nodded.
"A bit," he agreed.
"Haven't ever ridden at all...have you?" Paw asked.
Dale shook his head.
"No," he admitted sheepishly, "but I don't have much choice."
Paw nodded.
"Figured as much." Paw said. "These guys, they'll get you where you need to go but your backside'll be sore for a few days." He grinned. "Kheri can teach you how I reckon," he continued. "He's not bad on a horse."
The horse, having finished the sugar, suddenly chose that moment to nip at Dale's hair.
"Hey!" he exclaimed, jerking his head away and Paw grinned.
"She wants more sugar," he explained. "Here."
He handed Dale several more cubes.
"Here," Dale said, giving the horse another cube. "Leave the hair alone."
The horse accepted the cube and munched on it happily.
"Looks like you've made a friend," Paw said. "Think that one'll be yours. Now," he looked around. "Where is that boy?" Kheri still hadn't joined them and Paw shook his head.
"You sure you know what you're doing son?" he asked Dale seriously. "I warned you, he's trouble."
Dale nodded. "I know what I'm doing."
"Alright, suit yourself." Paw commented. "But if you want to get going anytime today, you better go roust him out o' the house. The morning's not getting any earlier."
Dale nodded, then climbed the fence again.
"I'll be back in a minute," he said, jumping down on the other side, and starting for the house.

Kheri had just finished off his second plate when Dale walked back inside.

"You planning on eating all morning?" he asked and Kheri looked up, startled.
"No," he replied, standing a bit too quickly. His chair went over backwards and hit the floor with a crash. He winced, then bent down and picked it up.
"Well then come on, the day's not getting any younger," Dale commanded, plainly irritated. Kheri's face fell and he nodded.
"Coming," he muttered, and followed Dale back out to the pasture.
Paw stood, watching them walk toward him over the grass and shook his head.
"That's trouble brewing and no mistake," he said to himself. A dark cloud had settled on Kheri's face and Paw didn't miss the angry glare he gave Dale's back. He thought about that, wondering, but kept his thoughts to himself.

Dale climbed up on the fence once more and jumped down into the paddock again. Kheri followed reluctantly, eyeing the horses and avoiding Paw's gaze.
Paw glanced at Dale, then shrugged.
"See if you can make friends with one 'o these," he directed Kheri, and leaned against the fence. Kheri looked them over warily. The horses regarded him just as cautiously, tails swishing back and forth. One of the males snorted, then turned and trotted away. Dale said nothing, and turned his attention back to the horse he'd fed the sugar to. She nuzzled his pocket again, then happily accepted the last cube he had left. Kheri shrugged then reached up and gently stroked the nose of the nearest horse. It snorted and he pulled his hand back slightly, then tried again.

Paw continued leaning against the fence, watching the scene silently. His mind was busy though, running over the events of the previous day. He thought about the brief interactions he'd witnessed between Kheri and Dale that morning as well and finally nodded as he came to a conclusion.

"Finally picked a fight with the wrong person," he mused silently. "Got himself into hotter water than he knows how to get out of by the looks of it."
He watched as Kheri led the horse he'd been making friends with over to the fence, then swung himself on it's bare back.
"Well, who knows. Might be good for him." Paw thought. "Got to be a durn sight better than thieving in the town, whatever happens."
He didn't have any proof Kheri actually had been thieving but most folks who knew him assumed that was how he spent his time. He wasn't well liked by most in the community.

"Boy's fortunate the guards haven't run him through by now," Paw continued his musings. "Or tossed him in the Baron's dungeons."
He watched Kheri as he turned the horse and rode bareback across the pasture then nodded.
"Looks like he's found a match," he commented to Dale. "Don't suggest you try riding without a saddle though. Might uncomfortable less you're used to it."
Dale nodded.
"Wasn't planning on it," he replied. "You said something about halters?"
"Yep," Paw agreed, and stood away from the fence. "Let me fetch 'em." He climbed back over the fence and walked off toward the barn.

Dale watched him go, then turned back to the horse. She'd tried for more sugar, and was now attempting to chew on his shirt.
"Stop that," he said, pulling the collar out of her mouth. "There's no more sugar and that's not edible." She tossed her head slightly, then bumped him in the chest with her nose.
"Demanding aren't you," he said, reaching up to stroke her nose as he'd watched Paw do earlier. "There's still no more sugar."
Kheri rode back up at that moment and swung down. He met Dale's eyes, then shrugged.

"He'll let me ride him," he said, then looked down at the ground. "Uh, Dale..." he fidgeted.
"Yes?" Dale looked at him, wondering what was upsetting him now.
"Sorry I lost my temper," Kheri mumbled, more to the ground than to Dale personally.

Dale nodded.
"Apology accepted," he replied. "I'm sorry I got irritated. I'm just worried about the Gorg and any delay is hard to deal with right now." Kheri looked back up, taken completely by surprise at Dale's reaction, then nodded.
Paw came back out of the barn with two halters a moment later and ambled over to the pasture.
"Here we are," he remarked, climbing back over the fence. "You ever used one of these?" he asked Dale, handing him a halter.
"No," Dale answered, shaking his head.

"Here," Paw said, handing Kheri the other halter. "He don't know nothing about horses, you're gonna have to teach 'em." Kheri glanced at Paw, took the halter then looked over at Dale.
"That true?" he asked.
"Pretty much," Dale responded.
Kheri stared at him for a second, then nodded. He turned the halter around in his hands.
"Look," he explained, turning the halter around in his hands, "this part goes over the horses nose, and this under his chin...watch." He slipped the halter onto the horse and buckled it into place then turned to Dale. "See? Like that."

Dale looked at the halter in his own hands for a moment then nodded.
"Playback the last sixty seconds," Dale thought, activating the event log in his suit. "Half speed." The air in front of his eyes sparkled and a slow motion replay of Kheri's instructions

presented itself. He turned the halter around, then slipped it on the horse, buckled it into place then stood back.
Paw nodded.
"Nicely done," he observed, pleased. "You're a fast learner."
Dale shrugged and said nothing.
"Be a little different when you try riding her though," Paw grinned, "bit different than riding on a wagon."
"I'd imagine," Dale responded, then forced himself to relax.

"Thank you," he said, extending his hand. "I really appreciate this."
"Think nothing of it," Paw replied, grasping Dale's hand firmly. "Always glad to help out a neighbor."
He shook Dale's hand then suddenly turned to Kheri.
"How long you going to be gone?" he asked.
"I don't..", Kheri started to answer then stopped and glanced at Dale. Paw nodded.
"Thought as much," he remarked and Kheri tensed. "Let me give you a piece of advice boy, whether you like it or not," he continued, looking at Kheri pointedly. "I don't know what you've gotten yourself into this time, but don't follow your usual tricks and get yourself in worse," Paw told him, all jesting gone from his voice. "You've been just a hair away from landing in the Baron's dungeons for some time now. Everyone knows it. You know it." He frowned at Kheri and continued. "And don't look at me like that. Won't do you any good to argue, facts is facts. You behave yourself, you hear? Don't go giving Dale here any trouble and you just might live to see thirty."

Dale said nothing, but regarded Paw with a new sense of respect. Kheri reddened, and he bit his lip then nodded sharply.
"Don't take no lip from him," Paw said to Dale, "'Bout time someone took him in hand and made him straighten up. Come on, the gate's over here." He led the way to the gate and let them out of the pasture onto the road.

"Thank you again," Dale told him and Paw nodded.
"You're mighty welcome," he replied. "Go visit Jhopar and get that tack."
Dale nodded. "That'll be our next stop," he replied.
Paw smiled then turned to Kheri.
"I'll keep an eye on your aunt," he promised, "so don't you worry none."
Kheri nodded silently, holding the halter's lead tighter than necessary. Paw shut the gate behind them, waved once then ambled off toward the barn. Dale watched him go then glanced over at Kheri.
"Don't let it eat at you," he admonished quietly.
"I'm trying not to," Kheri replied through clinched teeth. "But it's none of his business!"
"Regardless," Dale responded. "Let's just go find Jhopar and then see if I can actually stay on a horse."
Kheri grinned at the image of Dale falling off the horse and relaxed.
"We have to go back to town," he replied and started off down the road.

Chapter Eight

The day had turned hot and the road dusty. The sun was nearly at noon when they finally re-entered the town. It was bustling with activity and noise, the streets full of horses, carts and various traffic. Kheri threaded his way expertly through the street, avoiding as much of the confusion as possible, then turned down a small side road. From not too far ahead the ringing sounds of a hammer hitting an anvil could be heard. They made their way up the side road and finally paused in front of a large wooden building.
"This is Jhopar's shop," Kheri explained, then wrapped the lead of his halter around a rail. Dale looked at the lead he was holding and attempted to secure it to the rail. Kheri shook his head.
"Your horse won't be there when you come back if you tie it like that," he explained, taking the lead out of Dale's hands, "Look, like this." He wrapped it around the rail and secured it, the stepped back. "See?" he asked and Dale nodded.

They stepped around the horses, entering the blacksmith's shop and Kheri made his way to the back door.
"Jhopar!!" he called, his voice lost in the ringing of the hammer. He stepped out into the yard and walked over to the burly man.
"Jhopar!" he shouted again, and the blacksmith stopped pounding, then turned to look at him.
"Get lost kid," he growled, a look of irritation on his face. "I got nothing to say to the likes of you."
"I brought you a customer," Kheri told him defiantly. "One with money this time."
"Likely story," Jhopar grunted, but he put the hammer down and wiped his hands on a towel. "I find out you're tryin' ta scam me runt.." he warned and Kheri took a step back.
"I'm not," he protested, raising his hands slightly and backing away, "he's inside."

The blacksmith glared at him, then strode toward his shop.

Dale glanced over at them as they entered.
"You must be Jhopar," he said and the blacksmith grunted.
"Yeah, that's me," he replied. "And you are?"
"Dale," came the reply. "Paw Tucker said you might have some tack to sell."
A smile wrinkled the blacksmith's face.
"Ah, Paw sent you in, well that's alright then," he replied. "Paw's a good man. I've got some tack," he continued, "Saddles and stuff. Not here though. What all did you need?"
"I guess everything," Dale responded. "I've got two horses but Paw didn't have the tack for them so all they have is a halter each."
The blacksmith nodded.
"We'll have to take a walk over next door," he explained. "All the leather stuff's over there."

He turned and glared at Kheri.
"You can take off now runt, I ain't paying you for this," he snapped.
"He's with me," Dale interrupted before Kheri could speak.
The blacksmith narrowed his eyes and scowled at Kheri for a moment then nodded.
"Alright, but if he causes me any trouble.." he warned and Dale shook his head.
"He won't." he promised.
"We'll see," the blacksmith glowered threateningly in Kheri's direction. Kheri stepped back out of his way and pointedly avoided his gaze.
"This way," the blacksmith said, motioning toward the door.

They followed him over to a small building on the other side of the forge. Inside there were several saddles piled in a corner and

various other leather objects hung on the walls. He walked over to a saddle and hefted it, then looked at Dale.
"Where're the horses?" he asked.
"We left them out in front of your shop," came the reply. The blacksmith nodded, then handed him the saddle. "Here, take this." He picked up another one then looked at Kheri and jerked his head. "Get some reins runt, and the blankets," he commanded, "and make it fast."

Kheri shot him an angry glare but moved to obey, gathering up several blankets from a dusty corner. A mouse who'd made her home in the pile squeaked in fright and dashed for safety. Kheri jumped, startled, and fell backward against the wall. The impact jarred the wall, knocking a number of the reins and halters loose and they cascaded down on top of him. The clattering crash stopped Dale in his tracks and he turned to see Kheri standing, his hands over his head, in the center of the shed, draped with leather straps. He bit his lip to keep from laughing.
"You ok?" he called.
Kheri nodded, trying to untangle himself from the straps. "I'll be right there," he managed, rubbing his head where the metal bit of a bridle had smacked him.
"Alright," Dale replied, then went to join the blacksmith.

The tack was all used but still in fairly good condition and after a short while both horses were outfitted properly. The blacksmith even had a set of saddlebags someone had left him as surety and never reclaimed. He looked the lot over then grunted.
"Horses need shoeing," he commented. "give me sixty minigills and I'll throw that in."
"How long will that take?" Dale asked, considering the time.
The blacksmith looked the two horses over.
"Bout an hour," he said. "Not long. Save you a lot of trouble down the road."

"Alright," Dale agreed reluctantly. The blacksmith nodded, took both horses by the reins and led them around to the back of his shop.

Dale pulled the money Kheri's aunt had given him out of his pocket and looked at it. None of the markings matched any of the bits he'd returned to Paw earlier and he doubted that the blacksmith would be able to change the one doran note he'd been given as a reward for honesty. He frowned slightly.
"Your aunt gave me this," he said, holding the bills out where Kheri could see them.
"How much is this one worth?"
Kheri glanced at the bills, then picked one up.
"This is a minigill. That one," he explained, pointing to one of the others, "is a moll, it's worth ten minigills. That one's worth five, it's called a doll." He dropped the minigill back into Dale's hand and glanced at the street. "Put it away," he said quietly, "we've got company."

Dale stuck the money back into his pocket and followed Kheri's gaze. A pair of shifty characters were walking toward them down the street. As they got closer he felt Kheri stiffen, his hands clinching.
"Someone you know?" Dale asked softly.
"Yeah," came Kheri's tense reply. "You could say that."
Dale thumbed the force field control on his belt, turning it on to the lowest power, then stepped out into the street, and faced them.

The men looked at each other in slight surprise, then one tipped his hat.
"Afternoon," he said pleasantly.
"Yes," said the other, "Afternoon. Doing a little business with the blacksmith today?"
"Perhaps," Dale replied, watching them. Behind him, he could feel Kheri's tension. "If that's any of your business."

"No need to get testy," the first one remarked, "just being polite and all."

"Yes," the second one agreed, his eyes going behind Dale to where Kheri stood on the walk outside the blacksmith's shop. "We just have a bit of business to conduct here ourselves."

"Do you now," Dale asked, his voice neutral. "Well then, don't let me stop you."

"You know," the first one decided suddenly, glancing at his companion, "perhaps we'll just come back later."

"Yes," the second one agreed, bobbing his head. "Perhaps later. Have a good afternoon will you?"

Dale said nothing, watching as they turned and began to walk off.

"Duck," Kheri hissed behind him and time slowed to a crawl, the light seeping to shades of red, as his suits protective functions kicked in. As the two men took another step, they turned back in tandem and flung daggers aimed at his heart. He watched them sail slowly towards him, then knocked them both out of the air with one motion. The daggers clattered to the ground at his feet and Dale glanced down at them as time returned to normal, then looked back at the two would-be thieves. They stared back at him, then suddenly broke and ran. He watched them go, then bent down and picked up the daggers.

Kheri broke out laughing, watching them flee.

"Now that's a beautiful sight," he remarked, chuckling."

Dale smiled slightly, and handed the daggers to Kheri.

"Here, you have more use for those than I do," he said.

"Thanks," Kheri replied as he accepted the daggers and stowed them away. "Teach me how to do that?"

"Do what?" Dale asked innocently. Kheri made a face at him in response.

"Move like that," he clarified.

"We'll see," Dale replied and grinned at him.

Kheri grinned back, suddenly happy for some reason.

"Now," Dale told him, "We still need to find food and supplies. And something to hunt with."
Kheri nodded, the sobering thought of the wilds Dale was determined to take them into returning to his mind.

They walked back to the main street and Kheri led the way to the general store.
The place was bursting with activity when they entered and Dale looked around, confused, trying to make sense of it.

The store was lined with shelves up to the ceiling, barrels standing around in corners, large display cases and a general assortment of partly opened crates. A woman carrying a bag full of flour passed him, jostling him out of the way. The shopkeeper was busy and catching his eye proved nearly impossible but at last Dale succeeded in the endeavor.

"What can I get you," the harried man asked him, barely pausing for breath.
"Some basic supplies for a long trip," Dale responded, and the shopkeeper nodded.
"Hard tack then," he said. "Beans too. You got pans?"
Dale shook his head.
"Got a couple in not too bad shape," the shopkeeper explained, leading the way to another part of the store. "Bit beat up but no holes in 'em." He scurried around the shop, pulling things off shelves and out of crates, then piled it all on the counter. "Got bags?" he asked.

"Uh," Dale shook his head. "Not big enough for all of that."
"Need blankets too most like," the shopkeeper said and set off again.
"There, that should do it," he said as he returned and set the rest of the items on the counter. "Got blankets, rope, food that'll keep, some sacks, a couple tinderboxes and extra flint. Ponchos for rain

and a tarp case you need to make a tent." he nodded, satisfied. "Think that's everything. Knives, hatchet, stuff like that you'll have to get elsewhere."
"Alright, how much I owe you?" Dale asked, fishing in his pocket.
"Two dolls and three minigills," the shopkeeper replied, holding out a hand.
Dale pulled out the money and paid him, then started putting stuff in the sacks. They stepped back out onto the street fairly well loaded down and Kheri sighed.
"Now I know what a pack mule feels like," he complained.
"You'll live," Dale commented and started back toward the blacksmith's shop.

The smith was done with the horses by the time they returned and Dale paid him for services rendered then paused.
"Do you happen to have a hatchet?" he asked, remembering the shopkeepers comment.
"Might," the blacksmith replied. "You fixing to travel for a spell?"
Dale nodded. "Fairly long trip?" The blacksmith asked.
"Maybe," Dale said and the blacksmith nodded.
"Got a couple that might do you," he said, walking back into his shop. Dale put his load down by his horse then followed him inside.

Kheri watched them go then turned his attention to loading the horses, finishing just as Dale walked back outside. Dale walked over to the horses then handed Kheri a hatchet.
"Here," he said, "he had two. He also," Dale continued and handed Kheri a hunting knife twice as heavy as his dagger, "had a couple of those."
He looked at the bedroll Kheri had made and attached to the back of the saddle, then at the bulging saddlebags on the back of each horse.
"Everything fit?" he asked and Kheri nodded.

"I'm amazed," Dale remarked, trying to figure out how he was going to get up on the back of the thing.
"So was I," came Kheri's dry comment. "Anything else we need here?"
"Probably," Dale replied, "but I can't think of anything."
"Then can we please leave?" Kheri requested.

Tension colored Kheri's voice and Dale glanced over at him. The younger man was standing beside his horse, waiting.
"Yes," Dale responded, "Provided I can figure out how to get on this horse."
Kheri grinned, boredom momentarily forgotten.
"Here," he explained. "I'll show you. First, always mount from the horse's left side." He stuck a foot in the stirrup and swung up onto the horses back. "Like that, see?"
Dale glanced at the horse, looked at the stirrup, the nodded.
"Somehow I think it's not long enough," he said, looking at how short the stirrup was.
"Probably not," Kheri replied, swinging down. "They're adjustable though. Here, watch."

He walked over to Dale's horse and showed him how to let the stirrups down, then waited. Dale managed to clumsily scramble up onto the back of the horse and shook his head.
"They're still too short," he said.
"I'll let 'em out the rest of the way then," Kheri offered. "But you don't want them too long, your foot'll slip out and you'll fall off."
"Which you are just waiting to see me do, aren't you?" Dale asked dryly.

Kheri grinned.
"Who, me?" he said innocently, concentrating on lowering the stirrups the rest of the way down. "There, how's that?"
Dale sat for a minute, then nodded.

"That feels ok," he agreed at last.
"Good," Kheri replied. "Because that's as far as they go. Any more and you'll have to wait a year while someone makes you a special saddle." He gathered the reins together and handed them up to Dale. "You use these to tell the horse what to do," he explained as Dale took them from him. "It's not that hard, but your horse probably knows you don't have any experience. It might not do what you want. Watch me and you should get the hang of it pretty quickly." Dale nodded and tried to adjust his body to the uncomfortable saddle.

Kheri swung up onto his horse then looked back over at Dale. "The horse will go where it's head is pointed," he lectured. "That's basically all there is to it. You put his head where you want him to go and he goes." He pulled gently on the reins and his horse obediently turned to the right. "Like that. Pull back if you want him to stop."
Dale watched him, then tried pulling slightly on the reins himself. The horse ignored him, and flicked a fly off it's flank with it's tail.
"Kick her in the ribs," Kheri suggested, nudging his horse with his heel. "You have to teach her who's boss or she'll never do what you say."
Dale frowned slightly in thought then tried a sharp, experimental kick. The horse snorted, but turned and took a couple steps in the direction he was trying to get her to go.
"Yeah," Kheri nodded in approval. "Like that. Ok, so where do you want to go?"
Dale thought for a second.
"We just need to get away from your aunt's house so about any direction will do but," he considered. "We probably should get away from this town too and the Tucker farm."

Kheri nodded.

"We'll go south then," he said then grew serious. "The roads aren't safe though, and once we're out of the Barony, no where's safe." He shook his head and looked over at Dale, thinking.
"We really," he said after a moment, "should at least have swords."
"Do you know how to use one?" Dale asked.
"Well, no," came the reply. "But I can learn."

Dale thought for a moment. It hadn't been all that long since he'd had to use a sword extensively, but he wasn't too comfortable with the idea that Kheri might be swinging one anywhere near him. Still, if the wilds were as bad as Kheri and his aunt seemed to feel, swords might be a good idea. As would crossbows. Or maybe even a fully rigged battlemech. He grinned at the idea.
"Yeah, you're probably right," he said. "Any idea where to get them?"
Kheri glanced back at the blacksmith's shop.
"I don't suppose he had any?" he asked hopefully but Dale shook his head.
"No," he replied, "the knives were the biggest things he had."
Kheri shrugged.
"Then we go to a city," he stated. "That's the only place I can think of that might have them."
"Alright," Dale agreed, "which way to the nearest city?"

"There's Marshbow," Kheri said, thinking out loud. "it's about three weeks ride to the south." He frowned then brightened. "We could always go east to Villenspell."
"What," Dale asked, "is Villenspell?"
"It's sort of a city, well mostly. It's where the wizard's college is. There's a city that kind of grew up there, around the college." Kheri answered. "It's said you can find everything there."
Dale looked at him considering.
"How far is it," he asked at last.

"I'm not sure," Kheri answered, "but I don't think it's much farther than Marshbow."

Dale watched the expression of excitement flicker over Kheri's face and thought it over.

"Probably not nearly as interesting as he seems to think," Dale thought. "But it might have some useful items. And when the Gorg come back, there could be worse places to be than in a city full of wizards." "Alright," he agreed aloud, "We'll head that way."

Kheri grinned, then turned his horse and headed away from the blacksmith's shop. Dale kicked his horse in the ribs again and tried to follow.

Chapter Nine

"There are a number of things they never tell you," Dale thought several hours later when they finally stopped for the night. "One is just how badly it hurts to sit in a saddle!"
He sat on the ground, rubbing the soreness out of his legs. Kheri glanced up from where he was busily laying a fire and grinned.
"Something wrong?" he asked innocently.
Dale made a face in his direction.
"Not a thing," he grimaced. "Except that I think my legs are permanently bent."

"You'll get used to it," Kheri grinned. "At least your horse stopped arguing."
"Yes," Dale agreed dryly, "finally." He thought back over the few hours ride.
Everything that could have gone wrong, did, in his opinion. His horse refused to obey him, insisting on sauntering along at the slowest walk possible and stopping to munch on every interesting plant they passed. His saddle had come loose and slipped to the side, dumping him into the road, then just after he'd gotten that fixed and remounted, his horse had spooked into a mad dash through a stand of trees. He rubbed at the scratches on his face where the branches had cut him as they dashed past and shook his head ruefully.
"I seriously hope nothing worse than a mosquito happens along tonight," he remarked, trying to stretch the kinks out of his knees. "I really do."

Kheri shrugged.
"Yeah, me too," he muttered and concentrated on getting the fire to burn.
Dale stood up and stretched, then set about trying to take the saddles off the horses. The buckles where tight but not impossible and after some effort he finally got them undone. They spread the

blankets out on the ground near the fire and Dale sat back down on one of them.
"You know," Kheri observed after a couple minutes of rummaging through the saddlebags, "We don't have any water."
Dale stared at him silently for several seconds, then sighed in resignation.
"You're right," he agreed tiredly, "we don't."
They had passed a stream several minutes before but there was no water anywhere near where they were now.
"We also," Kheri remarked less than helpfully, "don't have anything to carry it in."

Dale closed his eyes, then lay down on his blanket and stared up into space.
"That," he muttered after a few seconds, "wasn't something I needed to hear."
Kheri shrugged.
"Sorry," he replied. "thought you better know."
"Thanks," came Dale's irritated reply.
"We can always go back and buy a couple water bottles," Kheri suggested.
Dale didn't respond and Kheri quietly put their stuff back into the saddlebags. He stood after a few moments, stretching his legs and went to check on the horses. They were tethered to a tree by the halters that Paw had given them and stood happily grazing on the grass growing nearby. Kheri brushed his hand over his horses's flank, then stood silently, looking back at where Dale was still laying on the blanket, staring up at the sky.
"It isn't my fault," he muttered darkly, nervous knots beginning again in his stomach, but somehow he didn't quite believe himself. Dale had been so clumsy on the horse that he'd forgotten his fears for a while but the irritation in Dale's voice had triggered them again. He stood looking back at the fire for a bit longer then turned and quietly walked off into the night.

Dale looked up at the stars, thinking. It would take them several hours to get back to the town if they were to go return and buy water bottles. He hated to do that, but unless there was an inn or something on the road ahead, they didn't have much choice. He wished briefly for a crash kit, but his suit didn't come equipped with such a thing. He wondered if it wouldn't be a good idea to move back down the road to the stream at least for the night then rubbed his eyes tiredly. The sky was clear with no moon as yet and the stars glittered at him like sparks against a velvet background. He sat up finally, and looked around. Kheri was no where to be found and he frowned. Closing his eyes, he concentrated, listening to the night noises. Nothing. The bugs and birds which frequented the darkness called out undisturbed. He stilled his breathing and listened harder. Still nothing. He took a deep breath and tried to force his powers to unblock. A horrible resistance arose in him as he fought against the residual effects of the warp and he broke out into a sweat. At long last, just as his head felt ready to explode, something gave way. He blinked in surprise. He hadn't regained much, but it was far better than nothing. He closed his eyes against the night and tried to reach out mentally. His scanning range was severely limited, barely fifty yards in all directions, but his spirits rose dramatically.
"It will take me time," he thought. "but I'm not stuck here forever." He sighed with relief, then set about trying to find where Kheri had gone.

Kheri had walked off aimlessly across country into the darkness, with no planned direction in mind. He wasn't intending to leave, just walk for a while and get his emotions back under control. However the countryside was unfamiliar, it was pitch black and in short order, he was totally lost. It would be quite some time before the moon rose and the darkness made it impossible to see what might be underfoot. He stopped after a few minutes, then looked around. The land was rolling and hilly, with stands of trees and thickets covering it. No distinct features stood out and he realized with a sinking feeling he had no idea which way the road lay.

"He's gonna kill me when he finds out I'm gone," Kheri thought, imagining Dale's fury. Everything he'd gone through for the last twenty-four hours overwhelmed him and he sank down to the ground, then dropped his head in his hands.
"Why me?!" he muttered after a minute, and stared up at the night sky. "Why me? What did I ever do to deserve this? What?!"

He snatched up a rock and tossed it with as much force as he could manage. There was a loud thunk as the rock hit a tree then a low growl sounded.
"Oh crud!" Kheri thought, and slowly stood, then begin backing away from the growl. The growl came again, a bit closer and Kheri fought down rising panic. His foot slipped as he stepped backwards and he fell, then tumbled down the steep slope of the hill he'd unknowingly been standing on top of. He covered his head with his arms as best he could and tried to stop rolling, coming to a stop at last at the foot of the hill against a tree. He groaned then tried to sit up. Everything protested but nothing appeared to be broken.
"I'll probably be black and blue tomorrow," he thought, looking around. The hill he'd tumbled down blocked out most of the landscape and he suddenly felt very lost, alone and frightened.
"Dale," he thought helplessly, "I don't care if you beat me within an inch of my life, just come find me!"
He looked up at the sky through the branches of the tree, hugged his arms across his chest, and fought down the desire to cry.

Dale stood up and keyed the sensors in his belt, turning on the infrared then looked around the camp. The ground was covered with fading footprints, their heat dissipating rapidly. He keyed his location into his suit, and detached part of it, setting up a beacon he would be able to find from several miles away. Looking around, he noticed a single set of footprints that went away from the camp and out into the empty landscape. He flipped his force field on, activated the suits sound dampers and followed them as quietly as a wisp of cloud. They were already fading rapidly and Dale forced himself to a run, counting on the suit's sound dampers to keep anything from hearing him as he moved. After a bit they led up a hill and Dale topped it just in time to hear Kheri smack into the tree at the bottom on the other side. A low growl sounded from his left and he turned. A large shape, low to the ground, stood there. He switched to the suits daylight effect sensors and the lights came on, showing him a rather shaggy wolf not too far away.

"Get lost dog," he muttered, then slowly removed the blaster he'd liberated from the Gorg from his belt and set it on stun. The wolf growled again then readied to spring. Dale brought the blaster up and thumbed the activation switch. The energy beam caught the wolf as it leaped and it fell, unconscious but unhurt, a few feet away from him. He set the safety, put the blaster away, then switched off the suits daylight effects. Looking around he could see a large swath of heat signature where Kheri had rolled down the hill and at the bottom of it, a much brighter mass. He switched back to the suit's daylight effect sensors then sighed in relief.

Kheri sat next to the tree he'd smacked into and rubbed his neck. He hadn't hit the tree with anything major but the impact had jarred him and everything hurt. The thought of trying to climb the hill he'd rolled down crossed his mind and he shoved it away.
"Maybe tomorrow," he thought, "after it's light and whatever's up there's gone."
"Kheri," came a familiar voice out of the darkness and he jumped, startled, then looked around as Dale appeared to materialize out of the night. He gulped then stood up, crestfallen.

"I'm sorry," he managed, looking down at his hands then flinched. His imagination had gotten the better of him again and he stood,

trembling, afraid of what might be coming. Dale placed his hand gently on Kheri's shoulder.
"That was foolish," he said. "Are you all right?"
Kheri nodded and looked up, confused.
"You're not mad?" he asked, trying to see Dale's face in the darkness.
"No. Just worried. If you can walk we'd best get back to the horses." Dale replied.
"That wolf will be waking up shortly."
"I can walk," came the subdued answer, "nothing broken, just bruised."
"Alright then let's get out of here," Dale responded and set about climbing back up the hillside, with Kheri following slowly behind.

The footprints Dale had followed were completely gone by the time they reached the hilltop but the wolf was still unconscious. He turned around slowly, letting his suit detect the homing beacon, then nodded as it came into sight.
"This way," he stated, then set off down the hill.
Kheri tried to keep up but Dale moved at a much faster pace than he was capable of and after a few minutes he stopped and stood looking around, confused.
"Dale!" he called, fighting down the panic that tried to well up again, not caring if the wolf heard him or not. Dale stopped, shook his head and backtracked.
"Sorry," he apologized as Kheri came back into view. "I forgot you can't see in the dark."
"And you can??" Kheri asked incredulously.
"Yes," Dale replied without explanation.
Kheri shook his head in disbelief.
"Is there anything you can't do?" he wondered aloud and Dale smiled faintly.
"Yes," he admitted. "Lots. Now, can we get back to the horses please?"

They made their way at a slower pace back to the camp and at last, after several very tense minutes, the fire came back into view. Kheri relaxed and sighed in relief.
"Thank you," he said. "That was really stupid."
"It wasn't overly bright," Dale agreed. "What possessed you to walk off like that?"
Kheri shrugged and went over to sit on his blanket.
"I got upset," he explained. "I wasn't going to go far, just wanted to walk it off."

"Might I suggest that next time you stick to the road?" Dale commented and Kheri shook his head.
"Not going to be a next time," he promised. "That was enough."
Dale nodded, picked up the part of his suit that had been the beacon, and reattached it. Kheri looked at him curiously.
"What was that?" he asked.
"Part of my jump-suit," Dale responded as he reconnected it and tested it's function.
"Huh?" Kheri replied, looking blankly at him.
Dale grinned.
"My jump-suit," he said. "Remember what I was originally wearing?"
He keyed the suits sound damper back off and set down on his own blanket. Kheri nodded, still confused.
"Alright, watch," Dale instructed him, then took his shirt off.
The jump suit's sensors detected the change and it flickered back into visibility. Kheri raised an eyebrow in question.
"I'm still wearing it," Dale explained, "it's just invisible when I've got other clothes on."
"Why're you still wearing it?" Kheri asked.
"Well," Dale told him, as he slipped the shirt back on and the suit vanished again. "It's kind of like armor. I wouldn't die without it but it sure makes surviving easier."
"Got a spare?" Kheri asked seriously.

Dale shook his head.
"I wish I did," he replied. "You could use it, especially if those Gorg come back any time soon. But they're made specifically for the wearer and keyed to their signature. That prevents theft but it also makes it very hard to replace them."
Kheri looked at him, then nodded.
"Now," Dale said, getting back to his feet. "I think we better move camp back down to that stream for tonight."
Kheri started to protest, but thought better of it and silently went to re-saddle the horses.

The rest of the night passed uneventfully. They moved the camp back to the banks of the stream, and made a very boring supper out of some hardtack and cold water. Kheri made a face as he worked at a corner, trying unsuccessful to break part of it off.
"I swear," he complained, "this is made out of iron!"
"Probably," Dale agreed, also struggling with a piece. "Or grave dust. At least that's what it tastes like."
"That," Kheri growled, dropping his piece, "was not appreciated."
He picked the hardtack up and shoved it back into the bag then lay down. Dale sat silently in the dark, still worrying bits off his piece and thinking.

"Dale," Kheri asked quietly after several minutes, "Why'd you come after me?"
"Because," Dale responded.
"Because why?" Kheri tried when no further explanation was forthcoming. He sat up and looked over where Dale still sat, half-hidden in the shadows of the dying fire.
"Would you have preferred I hadn't?" Dale asked him.
Kheri shook his head emphatically.
"No, I'm glad you did," he said. "Just wondered why."

"Well," Dale explained, "I need your help for one thing. Second, I told your aunt I'd keep an eye on you and third," he finished, giving up on the hardtack and shoving it back into the bag. "I'm starting to like you. Ok?"

Kheri digested the answer, turning it around in his mind.

"But," Dale went on, breaking into his thoughts, "that doesn't mean I'm going to pull you out of every stupid situation you get yourself into."

Kheri nodded, a bit of a grin breaking over his face.

"It also doesn't mean I don't have limits on how far you can push me," Dale warned, from the other side of the firelight.

"Didn't think it did," Kheri acknowledged, the grin widening, "wasn't planning on finding out neither."

He laid back down on his blanket and looked up at the night sky, a sense of relief mingled with an unfamiliar happiness spreading through him. The stars twinkled back at him and he stared at them for a bit then shook his head. "Hard to believe they're suns," he mumbled to himself. "They sure don't look like it."

"Go to sleep Kheri," Dale commanded gently as the firelight died to embers. "Tomorrow's going to be a long day."

Chapter Ten

Morning came far earlier than Dale wanted it to. He was awakened by his horse nuzzling his pocket for sugar as the sun peeked over the tops of the hills. He groaned and sat up, shoving her nose away, then remembered why he hated sleeping on the ground

"Don't remember any boulders under this blanket," he grumbled, standing up stiffly. His horse snorted and bumped him playful in the chest, sending him sprawling onto the ground.

"Oof!", he grunted then struggled to sit back up. "You know," he remarked to the horse as she stuck her nose down into his face, "you should work at breaking that addiction. I don't have any sugar for you."

Kheri snickered and Dale looked at him sideways.

"What's so funny," he demanded, pushing the horse away again.

"You," Kheri replied with a grin, then set about rolling up his blankets. Dale grunted an unintelligible reply then stood up, shook his blankets out and followed suit.

"We going back to buy water bottles?" Kheri asked as he finished.

"Do we have much choice?" Dale answered without looking up.

Kheri shrugged.

"There should be an inn or something on down the road," he replied. "There usually are. I'm actually surprised we didn't find one before dark yesterday."

"And if there aren't?" Dale asked, walking over to where they'd piled the saddles. "Then what?"

"Well," Kheri responded, "I can't imagine there not being one, but I guess it would be faster to go back now, instead of this afternoon."

Dale said nothing. He really didn't want to go back at all. The possible return of the Gorg loomed over him like a black shadow and he regretted having to even delay long enough to sleep during the night. He walked over to his horse, grabbed the halter's lead

and tethered her to the tree again, then tried to remember how to saddle her without relying on his suit's instant replay.
"Not like that," Kheri said from behind him as he struggled with the unfamiliar activity. "Here, let me. You watch."

Kheri took the saddle away from him, put it on the horse then slowly went through the steps, taking time to point out where all the straps went and how to tighten them.
"Think you got it this time?" he asked when finished. Dale nodded.
"Yeah," he replied. "Now let's see if I can remember it."
Kheri grinned, then went back to securing his saddle bags to his own horse. Dale managed to be slightly less clumsy when mounting than he had the day before, then groaned. Leg muscles, unused to riding, complained bitterly and he shifted around in the saddle, unable to find a comfortable position. Kheri snickered then looked away quickly, trying not to laugh.
"It's not funny," Dale grumbled.
"Yes it is," Kheri replied, "but you'll get used to it. Just take a few days riding."
Dale shot him a glare then turned and studied the road, thinking.
"About the inns you mentioned," he asked over his shoulder. "How far from the towns are they usually?"
"A days walk, maybe a little farther," came the reply. "At least that's what I've been told."
Dale turned and looked at him.
"How far could you walk in one day then?" he asked. "Farther than we rode yesterday?"
Kheri thought for a moment then nodded.
"Yeah, we went pretty slow for most of it and you took that detour," he grinned at the image of Dale's horse as it spooked off the road the day before, then turned serious again. "we probably could've gotten a lot farther on foot."
Dale nodded, ignoring the reminder of the previous days misadventures and looked back at the road.

"Alright, here's what we'll do," he decided, glancing up at the sun which had climbed slightly up above the horizon. "We'll ride for another hour. Baring mishaps," he went on, and shot Kheri a look. "If we don't find an inn by then, we'll turn around and go back to town."
"Sure," Kheri replied innocently. "Lead the way."
Dale reached into his saddlebags, pulled out the piece of hardtack he'd been worrying the night before, then convinced his horse to step out on to the road.

The sun sprinkled gold across the landscape as they rode and Dale found suddenly to his amazement that he had relaxed. The Gorg's return was still looming, they still had no water and hadn't found an inn and he was still stranded, but a feeling of hope had come back to him and refused to be ignored. He smiled to himself and tried another mental scan. His range had not increased beyond fifty yards but it hadn't vanished again either. He rode in silence, watching as trees, rocks and animals not yet visible to the eye, sprang into mental view around him. He reined suddenly as something large across the road up ahead came into the edge of his mental vision and motioned to Kheri. The younger man stopped his horse, and looked at Dale curiously. Dale sat motionless for several minutes, his eyes closed. Scanning cautiously, he searched the countryside around them for anything more menacing than a rabbit, then shook his head and opened his eyes.

"Is there a reason," he asked Kheri, turning to face him, "for the road to be blocked up ahead?"
Kheri lifted his eyebrows at the question, glanced at the road then frowned.
"Bandits maybe. But," he looked harder at the road, "I don't see anything blocking it."
"It's on the other side of that curve up ahead," Dale explained. "You can't see it from here."
Kheri looked at him silently, thinking, then nodded.

"Well, unless a tree fell in the last storm, it's probably an ambush." he decided, glancing around.
"When was the last storm?" Dale asked.
"Couple weeks back," Kheri replied.
"Long enough for someone to have come along, and moved the tree?" Dale asked, closing his eyes and mentally probing the barricade ahead.
"Might be," came the answer and he nodded then struggled to increase his scan range again.

The residual effects of the warp fought back with fury and he broke out into a sweat then sighed, giving up for the moment. He opened his eyes and sat there, rubbing them, and trying to think. After a few moments he turned and looked at Kheri who was watching him, a look of confused concern on his face.
"You ok?" he asked as Dale turned to face him.
"Yeah, just frustrated," he replied.
"You always glow like that when you're frustrated?" Kheri asked.
"What?" Dale asked, and blinked. "Glow like what?"
"You started glowing," Kheri explained. "Kind of a blue color. It's gone now."
Dale sat still for several seconds thinking, then shook his head.
"I have no idea," he said at last. "Unless it's got something to do with what stranded me here." He shrugged, then turned his attention back to the road. "How likely is it, do you think, that we're about to ride into a roadblock?" he asked at last.
"Well..." Kheri responded slowly after a few seconds silence, "We're still in the middle of the Barony, and banditing isn't legal. Still..." he continued, thinking out loud, "the Baron's patrols never come out this far and the Baron...who knows. Spends most of his time collecting taxes and getting fat from what I've heard."
"So," Dale said, looking over at him, "we assume that we're about to be ambushed just in case."
Kheri nodded.

"Yeah," he agreed. "Seems odd they'd set up an ambush here though. Not a lot of traffic on this road."

Dale shrugged then looked around the countryside. The ground ran up a hill to their right, and a thicket of trees crowned it's top. To the left was the fairly thick beginnings of a forest that the road curved into about thirty yards ahead. He sat there considering, then turned his horse and started up the hill toward the thicket on the top. Kheri glanced around, then followed quickly behind.

They reached the thicket without incident and rode under it's trees. The sun had already started to turn hot but the shade was cool and the horses seemed to welcome the change. Dale dismounted then led his horse through the thicket on foot. After a few seconds he stopped and stood looking back down at the road.
"There," he said, pointing to the road down below. Kheri dismounted as well and came to stand beside him.

The curve in the road was visible from their high vantage point and a clear barricade of logs could be seen placed across it. Kheri studied it for a moment and frowned.
"Yeah," he said, "Definitely an ambush, but I don't see anybody."
Dale nodded.
"I can't either, but we're too far away up here." he said, "I'd have to be a lot closer."
He looked around at the hills then back down at the road.
"Well," he said after a moment, "We've got three choices. We can try to ride over the hills and not get spotted. We can try to cut through that thicket down there or we can stick to the road and hope it's not too large a group waiting for us on the other side of that barricade."

Kheri stared silently at the barricade, thinking.

"Let's cut through the woods," he said after a few minutes. "The hills are too open, and I really don't like the idea of walking up to a trap in broad daylight." Dale nodded, then remounted his horse. They retraced their route back down the hillside to the road, then Dale dismounted again and lead his horse into the woods to the left. Kheri followed closely behind, nerves on edge.

"Something else they fail to mention," Dale thought as he stopped his horse, "in all the various books, is that horses can not walk through underbrush without making noise. And you can't," his thought continued as he looked around the forest, "just park them out of sight like you can a speeder."
"Kheri," he said softly, "we need to leave these horses behind till we find out what's going on."
Kheri nodded, then looked around for a moment.
"They should be fine right here," he decided. "Plenty for them to munch on till we get back."
They tethered their horses to a couple trees out of sight. Dale keyed the sound dampers in his suit, then pulled the hunting knife out of his saddle bags and strapped it to his belt.

They made their way slowly through the trees and finally reached the road on the other side of the barricade. Dale stopped before they stepped back out onto the road and stood quietly scanning. Kheri touched him on the arm after a couple seconds and he opened his eyes, glanced at Kheri, and then looked where the younger man was pointing. A thin wisp of smoke drifted up into the air from somewhere on the other side of the road behind the hill. He nodded and then stepped back into the woods. They made their way back to where they'd left the horses, then rode them back through the woods to the other side of the barricade. The rising smoke was thicker now and Dale sat still watching it for a moment, thinking.

"You want to get rid of them?" Kheri asked, as they sat there.

"I'm considering it, yes," Dale responded. "If we have to come back this way they'll still be a problem."

"Plus they might have water bottles," Kheri put in practically.

"They might, but that wasn't my main concern," Dale said, glancing around. He turned and looked silently at Kheri for a moment.

"How many do you think there are?" he asked and Kheri shrugged.

"Not very many or they'd have someone on this fence all the time," he said, motioning to the barricade. "Probably just two or three." Dale glanced back at the hill and thought for a moment, then turned his horse and headed up the road, away from the barricade.

Chapter Eleven

The cut Dale was looking for occurred several yards up the road on the other side of a sharp bend and he dismounted, glanced around then led his horse into the woods.
"This," he thought as he secured the halter lead to a small tree, "is going to get real old, real fast."
Kheri tethered his horse beside Dale's, loosened the hunting knife in it's sheath, checked his daggers, then squared his shoulders and followed Dale across the road and into the cut behind the hill. They moved cautiously up the cut, making their way to where the smoke could still be seen. Dale stopped after a bit and tried another scan then glanced at Kheri.
"Three." he said, his voice barely above a whisper. "That's all I find." Kheri nodded, glancing around then fell back a pace. They moved forward quietly, then slipped into a small stand of trees at the end of the cut, and stood out of sight looking down at a hollow behind the hill.

A fire was burning merrily and three men sat around it, talking. A large pile of stuff lay on the ground to the side and Kheri started then touched Dale's arm. Dale glanced at him, followed his gaze then shrugged.
"What am I looking at?" he whispered.
"That's the Baron's insignia," Kheri breathed, pointing at the pile of stuff. "Only members of the Baronial House can wear it."
Dale shot the three men a look then raised an eyebrow.
"Don't look very much like nobility," he observed.
"Not only that," Kheri continued, "I think that's the personal insignia of the Baron's family."

Dale turned and looked at him silently.
"The Baron's family?" he asked and Kheri nodded.
"Yeah," he replied. "I'm pretty sure that belongs to him."

"Then either they've killed someone they shouldn't have," Dale observed, turning back to study the tableau below them, "or someone's living a double life."
Kheri raised an eyebrow.
"What makes you say that," he asked and Dale pointed to the youngest member of the three.
"Because he's wearing the same insignia," he said. "Watch when he moves." Kheri frowned then watched the young man Dale had pointed out for a moment and nodded.
"Yeah, I see it," he agreed, nodding. "On his jacket."
Dale thought for a moment longer.
"I'm not so sure," he decided finally, "that I really want to deal with this, whatever it is." He glanced at Kheri. "It could either get messy or difficult fairly quickly."
Kheri looked at him silently. Dale caught the look flickering through Kheri's eyes then sighed.
"Alright, come on," he said, giving in. "Let's get this over with. But," he caught Kheri's gaze and held it, "I don't want to hear you complain if you don't like the results later."
Kheri nodded in reply and made ready to follow Dale out of the trees.

Dale activated the force shield on his belt, turned off the sound dampers and stepped out of the trees into plain sight of the three in the hollow below.
"Good morning gentlemen," he said, crossing his arms as he regarded them. "Would that road block down there belong to any of you?"
Two of them jumped, startled, but the largest of the three looked him over then laughed.

"Pretty good job, sneaking up on us like that," he said, fitting a bolt into the crossbow he was holding. "Not sure how you managed it but you shoulda kept going."
Dale shook his head.

"I really wouldn't do that if I were you," he warned and started walking slowly forward.
"You take one more step," the man growled, "and it will be your last."
Dale adjusted his force field to block solid projectiles and continued walking forward.

A loud twang sounded as the man loosed the crossbow bolt and Dale's time slowed to a crawl as his suits protection sensors detected danger on a direct course for his head. He reached out as the bolt neared him and caught it out of the air, snapping it in two, mentaly ordering his suit to release. Time returned to normal and he dropped the bolt on the ground, then took another step forward toward the bandits. The man with the crossbow was staring at him, his mouth hanging wide open.
"I said," Dale growled, his voice low and dark, "not to try that."
The man stared in disbelief, threw the crossbow aside and drew his sword.
"Get away from me!" he commanded, holding the sword in front of him with both hands. Dale shook his head and kept walking slowly forward, his eyes steely and fixed on the other man's face.
"I can't think of any reason three law-abiding citizens should set up a road block," he said conversationally, watching the largest of the men. "Care to explain why it's there?"
The man gripped his sword tighter and narrowed his eyes.

"None of your business," he snarled then charged.
Dale ducked under his swing and caught him with a punch in the midsection. He doubled partly over from the blow and Dale landed an uppercut on his unprotected chin. The man's head snapped back and he toppled over, then lay still. Dale watched him for a second to make sure he wouldn't be getting back up then glanced around at the other two. Kheri had just pinned the youngest on the ground, the knife point pressing firmly on his neck. The second man froze,

dropped his sword with a clatter on the ground, and slowly raised his hands in the air.

"Smart," Dale told him. "Now, since your partner can no longer answer my question, perhaps you'd like to try?"
He took a step toward the second man.
"It was his idea!" the man blurted out, pointing at the young man on the ground under Kheri's knife. "Ask him!"
"I'm asking you," Dale replied and took another step forward.
"He wanted to see what it felt like to be a bandit," the man said hurriedly. "We weren't really going to hurt anyone. Honest."
Dale lifted an eyebrow at him and said nothing.
"We weren't!" He protested, backing away. "We would have taken the roadblock down soon as someone came along."
He backed away again and started to shake as Dale took another step toward him.
"Someone came along," Dale pointed out. "And they didn't find the joke funny."
He glared at the man who paled visibly.
"What were you going to do?" he growled, his voice still dark. "Rob some poor farmer, scare him to death then laugh at him as you rode away?"
The man shook his head, backing up slowly.
"Or maybe you were going to kidnap some poor farmer's wife," Dale continued, watching the others reaction, "then hold her for ransom in the hills and rape her every day?"
The man swallowed with difficulty, then shook his head again.
"N...no," he stammered, his eyes wide with fear. "Nothing like that! Nothing! We'd have taken the barricade down and let them through."
Dale motioned to the unconscious man on the ground and shook his head.
"Somehow," he commented, "his actions leave me doubting that."

The second man took another step back, tripped over a rock and sprawled on the ground.
"Now," Dale said, closing the gap between them with lighting speed, and hauling him back up to his feet. "How about you tell me exactly who you people are." The man gasped then fainted. Dale looked at him for a second then dropped him in a heap and looked around.

Kheri still knelt over the youngest of the three, a look of fury on his face. Dale walked over to him and put a hand on his shoulder.
"Easy," he said. "Let him up."
Kheri relaxed slightly, then stood up and stepped back.
"Get up," he commanded, "and do it slowly."
The young man stirred, then pushed himself up to stand. He brushed his hands off, threw his head back and crossed his arms, then stood looking at them with an air of disdain.
"You'll pay for this," he declared haughtily.
Dale lifted an eyebrow and looked at him.
"Oh?" he asked, "let me guess. You're the Baron's son eh?"
"That's right," the other replied, giving him a withering look. "And you, peasant, will be dog food when my father gets finished with you."
"Really?" Dale replied, completely unimpressed. "What makes you think your father will ever even know we have you?"

The Baron's son blinked, his composure shaken slightly, then tossed his head again.
"He'll find you when you send the ransom note," he asserted imperiously.
Dale glanced over at Kheri who shrugged.
"Ransom note?" he asked, studying the Baron's son. "What ransom note?"
"The one I'm sure you'll be sending," he responded. "Won't do you any good though, my Father will just find you then string you up."

"I see," Dale said, then tossed Kheri a rope. "tie him up."
Kheri grinned, and caught the rope. A look of anger flashed over the young man's countenance.
"You can't tie me up you idiot!" he snapped arrogantly, and slapped Kheri in the face.
Kheri blinked then narrowed his eyes and punched him hard in the stomach. The Baron's son gasped for air, doubled over, then lay on the ground moaning. Kheri knelt over him quickly, and tied his arms tightly behind his back.
"I hate people like you," he snarled. "Be glad you're not dead!"
"Ow!" came the response as he jerked the ropes taught.
"Stupid little..," he snarled and stood up then pulled his foot back and aimed a kick at the young man's unprotected backside. It landed with a thud, provoking another cry.
"That's enough," Dale said, restraining him. "We'll deal with him in a bit. Go get the horses."
Kheri glared at the Baron's son for a second, then looked up at Dale, his eyes still flashing.
"Now Kheri," Dale said firmly, "the horses".
Kheri took a deep breath, nodded once and complied.

Dale turned and walked back over to the man who had fainted, then shook him awake and dragged him to his feet.
"How many of you are there?" he asked as the man regained consciousness.
"Uh," he blinked, trying to think. "Just the three of us," he replied, his words slurring, then seemed to realize what he said. "but there are more on the way," he added hurriedly. "A lot more. Like twenty more."
Dale caught his eyes and held his gaze silently for a moment.
"Don't," he warned, his voice low, "lie to me."
The other man paled, then fainted again.
"Worthless," Dale muttered and dropped him on the ground again.

He glanced over at the Baron's son who was struggling ineffectually with the ropes.
"You know," he commented thoughtfully, studying him, "I'll bet your father doesn't even know where you are. Wonder if he cares," he added, watching for a reaction. The young man stiffened and tried to look up at him, a look of anger on his face. "Thought so," Dale remarked, and turned away.
"He does so care!" came the angry reply. "You wait, you'll see! You'll be swinging from a noose before dark."
Dale shook his head and walked over to look at the man he'd sucker punched. Bending down, he touched the body then keyed the sensors in his suit. The heads-up display scrolled in the air before his eyes and he studied it for a moment, then nodded.
"Well, you'll have quite a headache when you wake up, but you'll live," he told the unconscious form as he turned the display off. "And just maybe you won't be quite so quick to threaten a stranger in the future."

He looked up as Kheri walked back into sight leading the horses.
"Thank you," he said, standing. Kheri nodded, and shot an angry glance over at the Baron's son.
"Get a handle on it," Dale admonished him. "We've got a mess here to clean up."
"What do you want to do with them?" Kheri asked, looking at the other two.
"Leave them," Dale replied. "Strip them first, and leave them. Maybe they'll learn a lesson out of this."
"And him?" Kheri asked, pointing at the Baron's son.
"He," Dale replied loudly enough for their prisoner to hear, "really deserves to die, but we'll let him live." The Baron's son stiffened slightly then pretended he hadn't heard. "He comes with us however," Dale continued. "He might be useful."
"You're not taking that nonsense about a ransom seriously," Kheri asked him surprised.

"No," Dale explained. "Money's the last thing on my mind." He shot a glance back over at their captive and raised his voice slightly. "We might need something to feed that dragon you mentioned."
Kheri bit his lower lip to keep from bursting out laughing as the Baron's son paused in obvious shock then frantically resumed his efforts to untie the ropes. "Now," Dale continued, turning back to the task at hand, "help me strip these two. Pile their stuff over there. Put the food, water and anything useful that's unmarked over here."
He bent down over the unconscious form on the ground and began pulling the clothing off of him.

They worked silently for several minutes and in short order had two piles, one considerably larger than the other. Dale stepped back and looked around. They'd stripped the two erstwhile bandits down to their underwear, then tied them together against a tree. All of the clothing was marked with insignias, as were the trappings for the horses which Kheri had found hobbled not too far away, and various other things such as blankets and backpacks. The horses themselves bore the brand of the Baron and Dale shook his head.
"No," he said in answer to Kheri's question. "nothing with the Baron's markings. That's trouble waiting to happen."
They un-hobbled the horses, removed their halters, and let them go, watching as they trotted away into the hills.
"That will slow them down," Dale commented, glancing at the two men tied to the tree, "and give them something to think about."
He looked around the camp one last time then turned his attention to the pile of marked items. Drawing the blaster, he adjusted the controls, then fired several short bursts. The pile grew indistinct then vaporized, leaving a slight ozone stench in the air. Kheri glanced from where the pile had been to the weapon Dale held.
"I want one of those," he said.
"So beat a Gorg and take one," Dale commented.
"No thanks," Kheri responded shaking his head. "I'll pass."

They stowed the food in their saddle bags, and Dale looked the swords over, searching for markings.
"Interesting that these don't bear any insignia's," he said, looking at the scabbards.
"That's cause they ain't the Baron's," came a growled comment.
Dale looked around at the two men tied up to one of the trees and lifted an eyebrow.
"Oh really," he asked. "And why's that?"
"Cause the squirt there," the larger man said, jerking his head toward the Baron's son, "wanted to play bandit," he replied, spitting on the ground, "so he had to look the part. Swords are better'n what you'd get from the Baronial armory anyhow."
"So you're carrying unmarked swords and wearing marked clothing?" Dale asked, and the man grinned.
"Wasn't my idea," he replied, "like I said."
"Exactly how long have you been playing bandit?" Dale asked, turning back towards him.
"Long enough," the other said, eyeing him. "Me at least." A nasty grin spread over his face.
"Yeah," Dale said, "I thought as much."
The other shrugged and met his eyes defiantly.
"You've got quite a punch on you," he commented. "Ain't met many men that could lay me out like that."
"There's always a first time," Dale responded, drawing the sword and checking it's balance. The other chuckled.
"Yeah," he agreed. "win some, lose some."
"Yep," Dale replied, turning the sword over and sighting down its edge, "and this time you lost."
The man shrugged.
"I'm still alive," he remarked.
"True," Dale agreed, "You are that."
He turned his back on the man for a second then spun back around and touched the sword's point to his throat.

"But you won't be for long if you succeed in untying those ropes while I'm still here," he warned and the other relaxed.
"No problem," the man responded quietly, eyeing the sword. "I got no desire to fight you again. And no reason either," he went on, glancing over at the Baron's son. "I ain't got no special fondness for the kid."
He relaxed back against the tree and prepared to wait until Dale was well out of sight before continuing to work on the ropes.

There wasn't much else they could use, as almost everything had been marked. The swords were in decent shape however and there were several unmarked water bags. Dale looked them over and hung them on the horses, strapped one of the swords on his belt and handed the other one to Kheri.
"Do not," he cautioned as he handed it to him, "draw that and swing it anywhere near me until I have a chance to teach you how to use it."
Kheri nodded, a grin spreading over his face, and strapped the sword on happily. Dale walked over to the Baron's son and stood, looking down at him. The young man's arms and wrists were red, nearly raw in places, where he'd struggled against the ropes without effect. He twisted his head around as Dale's feet came into view and tried to look up at him.
"You'll pay for this," he spat the words out angrily. "How DARE you lay a hand on me??!!"
Dale reached down and dragged him to his feet, then backhanded him sharply. His head snapped to the side and a trickle of blood appeared at the corner of his mouth.

"That is a warning," Dale told him, his voice low and menacing. The Baron's son jerked his head back around and Dale caught his eyes, holding them with his gaze. "You are NOT in your father's courtyards with guards around you, to back up your threats and scare those who might object. You are in the middle of nowhere. Alone." He narrowed his eyes slightly and continued. "Perhaps you thought it would be a lark to scare the local folk, play at stealing their money and their goods, but I doubt they found it fun. Regardless," he continued before his captive had a chance to respond, "this is no longer a game. You are now my prisoner and if you wish to live, you'll watch your step. I'm not sure who you thought you were dealing with, but you guessed very, very wrong."

The Baron's son looked back into his eyes and for the first time in his life began to realize just how little power he might really possess. He set his jaw, determined not to let Dale see the uncertainty that was beginning to pick at him. Dale returned his gaze silently for a few more seconds until young man's resolve wavered enough for him to look away. Dale nodded, satisfied, then reached over and ripped the insignia off his jacket. The Baron's son jerked his head back around to glare at him again but said nothing.

"You'll be coming with us," Dale told him, searching the rest of his clothing for markings. "As of right now, you're nobody. You behave yourself and maybe I won't feed you to the first wolf I see."

He glared at Dale silently, and struggled slightly with the ropes.

"Kheri," Dale called, "come over here and untie him."

Kheri made a face but walked over to them and reached for the ropes. The Baron's son waited till they were loose, then suddenly shoved Kheri out of the way and dashed off toward the road. Kheri drew his dagger, cocked his arm back and let it fly. It hit the fleeing figure in the upper left arm, spinning him around and he let out a scream then fell to the ground and lay there screaming, kicking his feet and clutching at his arm.

"Good shot," Dale commented as they watched his hysterics.

"I missed," Kheri remarked, "I was aiming for his head."

"You were not," Dale replied, looking sideways at him and Kheri grinned back.

"Naw, not really," he agreed, "but I sure wanted to."
They watched him for a few more seconds in silence, then Kheri shook his head.
"He's a dunce Dale," Kheri grumbled. "Why do you want him?"
Dale shrugged.
"He might be useful," he replied, then walked down to where the Baron's son still lay on the ground, sobbing now and clutching his arm. "Besides," he explained, glancing over at Kheri, "someone needs to teach this kid a lesson."

Dale strode over to the boy then bent down and hauled him up to his feet.
"Get up," he commanded, "you're not damaged."
"My arm!" he wailed, clutching at the dagger which was still stuck in the flesh. "My arm!"
"Keep screaming," Dale warned him, "and I'll let him stick a few more daggers in you."
The young man's face went white and he struggled to become silent. Kheri reached over and pulled his dagger out of the arm causing blood to ooze out of the wound. Dale sighed, wished momentarily for a first aid kit, then grasped the arm tightly to stop the flow.
"OWOWOWOWOW!" came the response and the boy tried to twist away.
"Keep it up," Dale growled in warning and his captive stopped struggling.
"It hurts!" he whined as Dale turned him around.
"You'll live," Dale replied shortly, "now move."
He shoved him slightly and the three of them walked back up toward the horses.

"I need a couple strips of cloth," Dale said in Kheri's general direction when they reached the horses. He turned the Baron's son around to face him. "Take your jacket off," he commanded, loosing his hold on the young man's arm.

The other tried briefly to obey but the wound in his upper left arm made it impossible. Dale reached over and pulled the jacket off of him a bit rougher than necessary.
"I warned you," he asked as another muffled cry escaped his captive. "Did I not?"
He tossed the jacket over to Kheri.
"Here, cut some strips out of that."

Kheri caught it one handed, nodded and began ripping the seams apart. Dale turned the young man back around to face him. His demeanor had changed drastically. He still clutched his arm, but instead of a haughty ruler, his face reminded Dale far more of a trapped rabbit in a cage.
"One little prick with a dagger," Dale thought to himself, "and he folds this badly. I hope we don't run into anything serious for a while."
"Take your shirt off," he commanded and waited while the Baron's son struggled to get it over his head without using his left arm.
"Turn around and let me see your arm," he instructed, taking the shirt away from him. He looked the wound over and nodded then tossed the shirt to Kheri. "Burn it," he directed, as it landed on the ground near where Kheri was sitting. "you got any strips yet?"
Kheri nodded and handed him several narrow strips of cloth from the jacket.
"That'll do," Dale told him, taking them and binding the wound on his captive's arm. "Burn what's left of the jacket too."
Kheri lifted an eyebrow but stuffed the clothes into the fire and poked at them with a stick.
"Any reason why?" he asked after a minute.
"Because," Dale explained as he tied off the last strip of cloth. "They have his blood on them."

He turned the Baron's son around to face him again. The young man stood sullenly in front of him, anger flickering through his eyes.

"I warned you to watch your step," Dale chided him. "I told you this wasn't a game. Behave or feel the consequences." His captive clinched his teeth but kept silent, waiting.
"What's your name?" Dale asked after a moment.
"None of your..." he began then flinched as Dale lifted his hand to strike him again.
"No!" he exclaimed, flinging his right arm up to shield himself. Dale grasped his wrist and forced the arm down.
"Answer me," he commanded, his voice low and unfriendly.
"Faran," came then unhappy reply.
"He's lying," Kheri commented as he poked what was left of the clothes deeper into the fire. "None of the Baron's sons are called that."

Dale narrowed his eyes slightly and the young man shook his head.
"I'm not lying," he protested. "It's a nickname."
"Then what is your real name," Dale asked, irritation creeping into his voice.
"Alain Herauso Feliks the fifth of House Eleriem", the Baron's son shot back. "Satisfied?
Dale glanced at Kheri who nodded.
"Yeah, that could be him," he acknowledged, poking at the clothes. "Thought he was a little older than five though."
The boy's eyes glittered and he rounded on Kheri.
"I'm sixteen," he snapped, then winced as Dale twisted the wrist he still grasped.
"Ow," he protested and looked back at his captor.
"That will be enough," Dale commanded, his tone icy. "We'll call you Faran. One more outburst like that and I let him use you for target practice. Understand?"
Faran glanced sideways at Kheri, then nodded crossly.
"Good," Dale replied, then let go of his wrist.
"Leave those," he said to Kheri, "they'll finish burning on their own. Let's get going."

Kheri nodded and stood up then snickered as he caught sight of Faran.
"You're gonna make him ride like that?" he asked, looking the boy over. Faran started to glare back, then caught the expression on Dale's face and prudently looked somewhere else.
Dale shrugged.
"You got another shirt to give him?" he asked and Kheri shook his head.
"Then I guess he goes without for now," Dale replied, and swung up onto his horse.
He reached a hand down for Faran, who hesitated, then reluctantly mounted behind him.

They rode down the cut, then Dale turned back up toward the barricade. Kheri looked at him questioningly but said nothing. The barricade had been made from several thick logs positioned across the road in such a way that a cart or wagon would be unable to pass. Dale reined his horse to a stop in front of it then turned to his passenger.
"Get down and move those logs out of the road," he instructed.
"Me?!" Faran responded incredulously, then shrank away slightly as Dale turned deliberately around to look at him.
"Yes," he replied, "you. Now."
Faran bit his lip but slid down off the horse and walked over to the logs then grabbed one with his right hand. He struggled briefly to pull it aside but it was far too heavy for his strength and didn't budge. He stopped after a second and stood panting beside it. Kheri sighed and started to dismount, then stopped at a glance from Dale. He lifted an eyebrow in question, then shrugged and settled back on his horse, content to watch. Faran tried again, then turned around.
"This is impossible!" he complained, stamping his foot. "It's too heavy! I shouldn't have to move these anyway, I didn't put them here and it's demeaning!"
Dale said nothing, watching him.

Faran drew himself up, his eyes flashing imperiously and faced Dale down recklessly. Dale waited for a few moments then dismounted. Faran's bravado vanished suddenly but he held his ground, albeit nervously. Dale walked over to him and he suddenly wished he'd kept his mouth shut. He took a step back, shaking his head. Dale stopped in front of him, crossed his arms and looked down into his eyes.
"Would you care to repeat that?" he asked, his voice quietly intense.
Faran swallowed and shook his head, looking up at him.
"If the logs are beyond your strength," Dale continued, "then ask for help. But do NOT," he commanded sharply and Faran flinched, "EVER," Faran flinched again, "speak to me in that tone of voice again. Understand?"
Faran looked up into Dale's eyes and nodded quickly.
"Yes," he managed, stepping back again and running into the log he'd been trying to move.

Kheri sat silently on his horse watching, trying very hard not to laugh. He was well acquainted with just how intimidating Dale could be when he wished and he felt a bit of sympathy for Faran. "Poor kid," he thought, biting his lip to keep from chuckling out loud. "He's really out of his element. All this time he thought he was something special, somebody important," he shook his head. "At least I knew I didn't matter much. He's got a lot of pride to swallow." He watched as Faran regained his balance and quickly turned back to the log again.

Dale stepped back and waited, watching as Faran struggled with the log, trying to get it to move. After a few more minutes the boy gave up again and turned around to face him.
"I can't.." he began and looked at Dale helplessly.
"Do you want help with it?" Dale asked and Faran nodded.
"Then ask for it," Dale said and stood waiting.

Asking for anything was not something Faran was familiar with. He was used to giving orders, demanding, threatening. He stood now in the road, dripping with sweat, totally at a loss for how to phrase such a request. He fidgeted for a moment then mumbled something under his breath.
"Say it louder," Dale told him. "I can't understand you."
He took a deep breath and looked up at Dale uncertainly.
"Can you move this log?" he tried.

Dale looked at him silently then beckoned to Kheri. Kheri slid down off his horse and walked over to the barricade.
"Kheri," Dale asked, glancing at him. "If you needed my help, is that how you'd ask?"
Kheri shook his head.
"No," he replied. "Not if I actually wanted your assistance." He looked at Faran who shifted uncomfortably. "But I'm not a spoiled rotten brat who's lived in a castle all my life and never been taught manners either," he declared pointedly, then shrugged.
Faran looked back at him, anger flashing across his face. Dale nodded silently, then grasped the end of one of the logs.
"Grab that end and help me get this out of the road please," he said to Kheri, ignoring Faran completely now.

Faran watched as they dragged the logs back out of the way then walked past him back to the horses. He felt small for the first time in his life and wondered what was going to happen to him. Dale looked back at him after they had re-mounted then pointed to Kheri. Faran shivered slightly, then walked over to Kheri and looked up at him.
"Get up," Kheri told him, then reached a hand down and helped him mount.
Dale waited till Faran was settled, then turned his horse and headed them up the road into the unknown.

Chapter Twelve

The sun continued it's climb through the sky as they rode and the day became hot fairly quickly. The air was dry and dusty now and the hills slowly flattened out to become an endlessly rolling plain. Kheri wiped the sweat off his face, then took a short pull from the water bag. He sighed and kicked himself for suggesting they go east. He'd forgotten the Ramsiern plains lay between them and the wizards city. There were a few scraggly stands of trees in sight now that they'd left the hills behind but nothing near the road and the sun was beginning to bake down as it reached the noon zenith. He nudged his horse in the ribs and rode up even with Dale.

Dale's suit compensated for the heat as they rode, keeping the temperature comfortable but one look at Kheri's reddened face was enough to warn him that the others were in danger of heatstroke. He reined his horse up and looked around then pointed at the closest stand of trees.
"There," he said, and turned his horse toward it. Kheri nodded, relieved, and followed willingly. The shade was quite a bit cooler and Kheri shivered as they rode under the trees, then sighed in relief.
"I was beginning to feel like one of my aunt's meat pies," he remarked, as he reined his horse to a stop. Dale grinned at him then swung down.
"Burned to a crisp eh," he said, stretching. Kheri nodded then turned around to look at Faran.
"Dismount," he ordered, and Faran blinked then looked around confused. He wiped the sweat away, blinked again, then slid clumsily off the horse and stood looking around at the trees.
Kheri climbed down, took one look at Faran's bare back and shook his head. The sun had blistered the skin and turned it crimson. Faran looked at him then suddenly passed out, crumpling to the ground.

"Dale," Kheri called, somewhat alarmed. Dale turned toward him then walked over.

"What happened?" he asked.
"I'm not sure," Kheri replied, squatting down beside the body. "He was standing there then just fainted."
Dale knelt down beside Faran and let the suits sensors do their job. He studied the heads up display for a moment, then flicked it off and nodded.
"Too much sun," he said. "My fault. I wasn't thinking. We'll stay under the trees till evening. Get some water into him," he directed, handing Kheri the water bag. "I'll see if I can find something to fix that sunburn."
He turned the suits auto detect on, then keyed in a request for plants with healing properties.

Pictures began flickering through the air in front of him and he narrowed the request down to sunburn. Several pictures flickered faintly on the display and he turned slowly then began walking. The pictures remained ghostly for several minutes then suddenly one brightened and a small patch of leaves on the ground began to glow. He knelt down beside it and careful dug around, unearthing the plant that matched the display after a few seconds. He flicked the display off and studied the plant, then keyed the suits flora guide. A description of the plant flickered into life in the air, along with instructions for it's use. He read it over then nodded and keyed the display back off. He searched around for several more minutes, uncovering a few more specimens of the plant, then made his way back to where he'd left the horses.

Faran was awake and sitting on a stump when he returned, while Kheri knelt beside a small fire he was coaxing to life. Dale ignored both of them, and went to the horses to extract one of the pans from the saddlebags. Walking back to the fire, he stripped the leaves from the plants and crushed them into the pan, then poured a small amount of water over them and set the pan carefully on the burning wood.

"You get him to drink?" he asked, watching the water as it began to heat up.

"Yes," Kheri answered. "Some. He's not disoriented any more at least but he's in quite a bit of pain."

"This'll help with that," Dale said, swishing the leaves around in the water and watching it change color slightly.

"I'm gonna go get some more wood," Kheri stated, standing and Dale nodded.

"Kindly don't get yourself lost, ok?" he requested and Kheri made a face at him.

"It's not the middle of the night," he replied, then turned and walked off.

Dale waited till the liquid in the pan had become a dark green then took it off the fire and set it aside to cool. The smell rising from it was not too much different from rotten eggs and he made a face then double checked his guide. It confirmed that the plants were indeed a correct solution for sunburn but said nothing about the smell. He added a rather terse note to the entry, then turned off the display. The woods were quiet except for the occasional buzzing of an insect. The air was hot and stuffy, no wind stirred the leaves and Dale sat there, staring at the fire and considering the possibility of several days ride across the plains. They evidently weren't going to be able to cross them in the heat, which left riding at night, something he really was loath to do. He glanced over at Faran who was sitting on the stump, bent over in pain and shook his head.

"Day is definitely out," he thought, "At least till we find him another shirt."

He glanced up as Kheri deposited an armload of wood nearby.

"Kheri," he asked, "What kind of creatures roam the plains at night around here?"

Kheri paused in thought, then shook his head.

"I really don't know," he answered. "I guess probably wolves. Maybe nighthawks. why?"

"Well," Dale replied, swishing the liquid around in the pan to hasten it's cooling, "We can't very well ride while it's hot. That leaves early morning, late afternoon, evening and night. We can't afford to risk any more sunburns like Faran just got."

Kheri glanced over at the boy, then nodded.

"Yeah, it's pretty bad," he agreed.

Dale handed him the pan with the now tepid liquid in it.

"Here," he instructed. "Go pour that gently over his back. It's cool enough now. Make sure you get all the blisters."

Kheri looked at him for moment then nodded.

"You're sure this putrid stuff isn't going to poison him?" he asked, sniffing at the pan and making a face.

Dale nodded.

"I'm sure," he replied, "just don't drink it."

Kheri walked over to where Faran was moaning in pain and rolled his eyes.

"You act like you're dying," he said, slightly disgusted.

"I am," came the plaintively whined response.

"Not likely," Kheri remarked, dribbling the pans contents over Faran's blistered back. He was rewarded with a yelp of pure agony.

"Oh sit still and shut up," he growled. "And grow up, this isn't hurting you."

Faran clinched his teeth and tried to hold still as Kheri finished pouring the foul smelling liquid over his back. The effect was almost instantaneous. As the liquid cascaded over the sunburn, the blisters shrank then vanished and the red turned to a light brown. Faran sighed in relief as the pain vanished completely and sat up.

"There," Kheri said, emptying the last few drops on his back, then turned and walked off in search of a stream he'd crossed while gathering wood. He located it after a few minutes, knelt down and rinsed the pan out. "I wonder," he mused, picking up one of the

boiled leaves that still clung to the side of the pan and looking at it closely, "how he knew?"
He turned the leaf over, examining it, then tossed it away and finished washing out the pan.

When Kheri got back to camp, Dale had a small pot of beans boiling on the fire and was no where to be seen. He looked around, spotted Faran sitting in a dejected heap not too far away and stopped, thinking. His thoughts went back to the log barricade and the fact that Dale had almost consigned the boy to nonexistence after his lousy attempt to ask for help. He sighed, wondered what Faran had tried now and walked over to the horses to put the pan away. Faran glanced up at him then looked back at the stick he was meticulously snapping pieces off of. Kheri buckled the saddlebag, then walked over and squatted down beside him. Faran glanced up, shrugged, and looked back at his stick.
"What happened now," Kheri asked and Faran shook his head, then wiped tears from his face.
"Nothing!" he snapped, breaking the twig in half.
Kheri looked at him for a moment longer, then shrugged and stood back up.
"Suit yourself," he said and walked over to tend the fire.

Dale returned a few minutes later with several handfuls of leaves and squatted down beside the fire.
"Found some herbs," he explained to Kheri's unanswered question. "No salt though, and we didn't buy any."
Kheri shook his head resignedly.
"Sorry," he replied. "I knew I was probably forgetting stuff."
"It's fine," Dale responded, breaking off bits of the leaves and adding them to the beans. "Would you refill the water bags please?"
"Sure," Kheri responded, stood up, collected the water bags from the horses and walked off to the stream.

The woods were hot and stuffy, without even the faintest breeze to stir the leaves on the trees. Kheri dropped the water bags down on the bank of the stream, then stripped and wadded in. The water was cool and he sat in it for several minutes, then climbed out and stood on the bank dripping. A sound in the water behind him caught his attention and he turned just in time to see a large fish leap from the water. It snapped at a fly then fell back into the water and he grinned. Pulling his clothes on quickly, he gathered up the water bags and nearly ran back to camp.

Dale looked up from stirring the beans as he reappeared.
"You're wet," he remarked. "Fall in the creek?"
"No," Kheri answered him. "Got in on purpose."
He hung the water bags on the saddles then turned around, eyes shining.
"You should see the size of the fish down there!" he exclaimed. "He's huge!"
"I saw," Dale replied. "Earlier, when I was getting the herbs."
"We could catch him and make several meals out of him," Kheri said hopeful.
"With what?" Dale asked, looking up at him. "You experienced at fishing by hand?"
Kheri shrugged.
"Wouldn't hurt to try," he responded.
Dale regarded him for a second then grinned slightly.
"You want to try to catch that fish," he stated finally, "be my guest. I'll stay here and stir the beans."
Kheri grinned, and glanced over at Faran then looked at Dale who nodded slightly.
"Come on," he said, walking over Faran and nudging him with his boot, "let's go catch a fish."
Faran looked up, glanced over at Dale who ignored him, then stood and followed Kheri down to the stream without comment.

The fish was still leaping after flies when they reached the bank and Kheri stood looking at it for a moment, then sat down and pulled his boots off. Faran didn't move, just stood looking at the water. Kheri looked up at him and shook his head, then pulled his other boot off.
"What's the problem now," he asked, a hint of sarcasm tingeing his voice. "Afraid of the water?"
Faran surprised him completely by nodding his head.
"Yes," he whispered, his eyes still glued to the stream. "I nearly drowned once..."
Kheri turned and squinted at the stream then looked back at Faran.
"It's not deep enough to drown in," he said bluntly, "Now come on before I push you in."

Faran glanced at him quickly but Kheri was busy pulling his pants off and his expression was unreadable. He looked back at the stream and shivered, then stripped down and stood nervously on the bank. Kheri waded out into the water searching for the fish, then suddenly slipped on a rock and landed on his rump with a very surprised look on his face. Faran grinned slightly, and cautiously put a toe into the water. It was cold and he jerked it back out quickly. Kheri stood up, shaking the water out of his eyes and looked around. Faran was still standing on the bank and he motioned.
"Come on," he called. "He's over here."
Faran shook his head.
"No," he refused. "It's too cold!"

Kheri looked at him for a second, then waded out of the water.
"Yeah it's cold," he agreed, tossing his dripping hair back out of his eyes. "So?"
"So I choose not to get into it," Faran replied, a hint of the imperiousness from the morning creeping back into his voice.

"Oh really?" Kheri asked as he walked back over to where Faran stood. He looked at him silently for a moment, then grabbed his uninjured arm and pulled quickly.
Faran was caught off guard and stumbled forward then went sailing into the water face first. He scrambled up, spluttering and glared at Kheri, his hair dripping into his eyes. Kheri burst out laughing, then waded back in.
"Now," Kheri asked, as he approached, "was that really so bad?"
"I guess not," Faran replied, then suddenly shoved Kheri over backwards into the water.
"Hey!" Kheri exclaimed as he went under momentarily. He came up spluttering and shook the water out of his eyes, then glanced at Faran who was standing several feet away grinning.

"Yeah, you'll think it's funny when I'm done with you," he warned in mock anger and tossed a double handful of water in his direction.
Faran dodged and slipped on a rock, sitting down in a mildly deep pool. He jumped up, startled and looked down into the water.
"Hey, look!" he exclaimed, staring at something below the surface.
Kheri walked over cautiously, expecting another dunking.
"What?" he asked and Faran pointed into the pool.
"What are those?" he asked, his eyes on the water.
Kheri glanced into the pool then smiled slightly.
"Those are frogs," he replied. "haven't you ever seen frogs before?"
Faran looked up shaking his head.
"No," he responded. "We don't have any in the castle gardens."

Kheri looked at him for a couple moments in silence then shook his head.
"You're kidding," he said. "No frogs?"

Faran shook his head again, watching the frogs as they skittered across the stream bed. "No, just some fish in the ponds and roses. Lots of roses..." he replied softly.
Kheri looked at him in disbelief, then reached down into the pool and gently captured a frog.
"Here," he said, holding the frog out to Faran, "cup your hands."
Faran obeyed and watched the frog curiously as Kheri poured it into his hands. It swam around for a moment as the water drained away, then hopped up onto a thumb and jumped back down into the pool. He grinned, his face a mask of wonder for a moment.
"Frogs," he whispered, as if some new and amazing thing had just been added to the world, then lost his balance and sat back down in the water.

They spent quite a while in the stream, attempting to catch the fish but discovered that the reason most people used fishing line was because it's very hard to hang onto a fish when he's wet. The afternoon was well along when they finally called it quits and wadded back out to stand dripping on the banks. Faran shook the water out of his hair, then glanced over at Kheri. Kheri was halfway through pulling his boots on when Faran spoke.
"Kheri," he asked, his tone slightly subdued.
"Yes?" Kheri replied, standing up and stamping his foot down.
"Do you .." Faran began, then shook his head. "Never mind."
"What?" Kheri asked again, looking at him curiously.
Faran crossed his arms over his chest and hugged himself, looking away.
"Nothing, just a stupid question," he muttered.
"Obviously it ain't nothing," Kheri replied, mimicking his aunt, then walked over to stand in front of him. Faran looked away, refusing to meet his eyes.
"Hey," Kheri said, putting a hand on his shoulder, "talk to me."
Faran said nothing for a few moments then turned and looked at him.
"Do you guys hate me?" he asked in a small voice.

Kheri raised an eyebrow at the question.
"Now where did that come from?" he asked.
Faran shrugged and Kheri nodded.
"Yeah, well I don't hate you," he replied. "At least I don't any more. I did. But you're a pretty decent guy when you want to be. Just need to learn the whole world doesn't belong to you is all."

Faran looked at him silently then glanced back toward the camp.
"Dale, well I don't know. You haven't exactly given him much reason to like you, have you?" Kheri responded. "You were cruel to the people guys like you and your father are supposed to take care of. How many innocent people did you hurt while you were playing bandit? " He asked then continued without waiting for a response. "You were obnoxious, nasty and demanding, then rude and disrespectful to Dale when you needed help moving the logs. And you acted like both of us should fall at your feet and worship the ground you were standing on."

Faran started to protest but fell silent at the look on Kheri's face.
"Granted I guess you don't know any better," he went on. "Or maybe you do now but you didn't. But if you're still confused on that," he finished, crossing his arms in imitation of Dale, "I suggest you get the idea through your head right quick that you don't own nothing out here, not even your own skin. Not unless Dale says you do."
A cloud passed briefly over Faran's face.
"I got the message," he replied, no longer meeting Kheri's eyes. "I'm not stupid."
"Well then maybe you should try apologizing to him," Kheri suggested bluntly. Faran looked at him in surprise.
"Apologize? Why?" he asked, honestly confused.
"Because," Kheri explained, "you acted like an ass. Get something clear Faran," he said. "You might be the Baron's son, but until Dale lets you go, IF he lets you go, you're nobody. So you might as well stop acting like nobility and start acting like normal folk.

Unless you want to spend the next few weeks on his bad side. And trust me," he said seriously, "you really don't want that."
Faran glanced down at the finger Kheri was poking him in the chest with, then looked back up at him.
"But," he protested innocently. "I don't know how."

Kheri sighed and dropped his head into his hands in mock frustration, then looked up at the sky.
"Why me?" he asked the trees in general, then turned his attention back to Faran. "You don't know how what?" He asked. "To act like normal folk or to stop acting like nobility?"
Faran nodded.
"Both," he said. "I guess."
"Oy," Kheri muttered and took a deep breath. "Ok, kid, pay attention. For starters keep in mind that the only things you've got the right to order around any more are your own feet, and maybe a horse if Dale lets you have one. You try pulling rank on me, I'll ignore you, unless I'm in a bad mood, in which case I'll punch you. You try it on Dale and there's no telling what might happen, but whatever it is, trust me, you don't want it. You ask for things, not demand them, you apologize when you do something stupid and you don't sit on your fanny when there's work to be done, you get up and help. And," Kheri said, thinking back to that morning, "I don't suggest you ever try slapping anyone again."

Faran's eyes flickered as he also thought back to the morning then he nodded.
"I guess that wasn't real smart," he admitted.
"Not really, no," Kheri replied. "Pretty dumb to throw your weight around like that unless you can back it up. But then," Kheri added with a shrug, "guess you never had anyone put you in your place before did you?"
Faran shook his head.
"No," he admitted, looking away uncomfortably.
Kheri nodded.

"Thought not," he stated. "Well I suggest you learn some manners fast, unless you feel like not eating for a few days."
Faran glanced up at him in shock, but Kheri was through talking. He pulled his shirt over his head and walked off back toward camp. Faran watched him go then looked around. It was cooling off as the evening fell and he looked back out at the water. It suddenly seemed like the morning's events had happened to someone else a long time before and he shook his head.
"I want to go home," he thought then sat down on the bank. "Except I'm not sure why."

He thought back to the castle full of continuous activity, an ever changing horde of Nannys bustling around. Brief glimpses of the man who was his father once in a while and no clue who his mother was. A large number of brothers and sisters, all a year or so older than him, who acted like he didn't exist. People gave him attention when he spoke there, and they did what he demanded, but it never chased the loneliness away. They cowered, and begged and pleaded with him when he threw fits, which he did frequently, or fawned on him when they wanted something, then talked about how much they detested him when they thought he couldn't hear. He looked out at the stream, thinking about the afternoon spent trying to catch the fish and realized that for the first time in his life, he'd actually spent more than a few minutes not being bored, angry and miserable.
"I can't remember ever laughing that much before," he thought out loud. He glanced back toward the camp and then suddenly decided that he didn't want to be hated.
"...try apologizing to him..." Kheri's words flitted through his mind again.
"I'm not sure it'll work," he said out loud, "but I'll try."
He pulled his pants back on and stamped his feet down into his boots then walked back to camp, trying to remember all the things the people at his father's castle did when he was angry.

Dale had already eaten and was sitting a distance from the fire, leaning against a tree, when he got back and Kheri was just finishing his food. He noticed there wasn't any set aside for him and gulped slightly, remembering Kheri's threat, then summoned up his courage and walked over to where Dale was sitting. He stood there silently for a moment until Dale noticed his presence and glanced up, then knelt down clumsily on the ground in front of him.
"Can.." he started then corrected himself, "May I speak with you," he asked. "Please?" he added with difficulty.

His voice was strained and Dale could feel the tension in him. He regarded him silently for a moment then nodded.
"Yes," he said, "what about?"
Faran looked down at the ground for a moment, nervous, then met Dale's eyes. "I...", he took a deep breath, "want to apologize for my behavior this morning. I was way out of line."
Dale said nothing, watching him silently as he struggled with the unfamiliar act of trying to humble himself. Faran dropped his eyes, his heart sinking at Dale's apparent lack of response.
"I'm sorry," he said almost in a whisper. "it won't happen again."
"Sit," Dale told him, "and look at me."
Faran sat down on the ground, then looked back up and met Dale's gaze.
"Which actions are you apologizing for?" Dale asked.
"All of them," Faran answered, spreading his hands in a gesture of totality.
"Oh?" Dale responded. "And what brought this on?"
Faran struggled for words to explain.

"I," he shook his head after a moment. "I don't know," he replied, "everything I guess. No one's ever even raised their voice to me before," he went on, "much less slapped me. That was the worst thing I think that's ever happened to me. That scared me...badly. I hated you and I couldn't do anything to stop you." he bit his lip but continued. “I’m still scared but,” he glanced over at Kheri who was pointedly ignoring the both of them, “this afternoon was different too. No one’s ever acted like I actually mattered.” He frowned slightly, trying to put feelings he hadn’t completely sorted out into words. “I just....I’m sorry,” he finished lamely and looked down at his hands. “Please don’t hate me.” he pleaded, staring at the ground then looked back up and met Dale’s gaze again. “I’m not stupid, honest. I can learn, change, whatever, just give me the chance,” he paused then added, “please?”

“Alright,” Dale agreed, his face softening slightly. “You have your chance. There’s some beans in the pan over there, go eat and then help Kheri get the horses ready to ride.”
Faran nodded, and started to rise then stopped, confused.
“What now?” Dale asked.
“I’m not sure what I’m supposed to call you,” he replied.
“Dale,” came the answer. “Just use my name.”
He nodded again then stood up and walked over to the fire.
Kheri looked up at his approach.
“Everything worked out?” he asked as Faran picked up the pan then looked around for a bowl.
“Sorta,” he responded. “He’s talking to me at least. I’m still in trouble though, I think.”
“You’ll have to eat out of the pan,” Kheri told him, and finished his beans. “We only have two bowls. Which means you’ll wind up eating last too until we can get another one.” He stood, then handed Faran the spoon he’d been using. “Clean it off when you’re done with it, and make it quick, the lights fading.”
Faran looked at the spoon for a second, then noticed Dale watching him. He turned his attention to the beans without another word, and ate, determined not to give Dale any further reason to be angry at him, at least for that day. They were a far cry from the food on the fancy tables at his father’s castle. They didn’t even match up with the food he’d gotten used to while camping out playing bandit,

but they satisfied the hunger that had been gnawing at him and he finished quickly.
"Take the pan, the bowls and the spoons down to the stream and wash them out, " Kheri instructed as he finished. "and don't leave any food in them to spoil."
Faran nodded silently, collected the utensils and headed back for the stream.

Chapter Thirteen

As the shades of evening deepened into twilight, they re-mounted the horses and set out on the road again, Faran riding behind Dale once more. The wind had picked up and it sighed over the plains, carrying with it the wild smells of summer and a faint promise of the coming autumn. Kheri had no idea how long they'd have to ride to reach the other side of the plains and Dale had resigned himself to a schedule of riding in the evening, sleeping in the dead of night, riding in the morning and sleeping in the heat of the day. The miles rolled beneath their horses as they pushed them to a gallop and the world seemed to fade into a soft grey nothing around them. As darkness grew complete, they rounded a stand of trees and saw lights twinkling on the road ahead. Dale reined his horse to a walk, studying them. Kheri slowed to a trot then moved up beside him.

"An inn, do you think?" Dale asked.

"Might be," Kheri answered. "Don't know of any settlements out here."

"Faran," Dale turned slightly in the saddle. "Do you know what that might be?"

Faran looked at it for a moment then shook his head.

"No," he responded. "I don't."

"You didn't ride down this road before?" Dale asked.

Faran shook his head.

"No," he answered, "we never came this way. My fathers castle is to the south."

"We are, however," Kheri muttered, "still in the Barony," and he glanced over at Faran. Dale caught his eyes and nodded but said nothing in response.

As they drew closer to the lights it became quiet evident they were approaching a small cluster of buildings. The largest had several horses and two small wagons parked in front of it, while the rest nestled around it. An ancient oak tree spread it's branches over the road and a sign with the picture of a green pig on it swung from one of the branches, creaking in the breeze. Dale reined his horse in front of the building and motioned for Faran to dismount then swung down himself. Kheri pulled up next to him and dismounted then looked around cautiously.

"I guess it's an inn," he remarked after a moment.
"What makes you think that," Dale asked innocently, tethering his horse to the hitching post. Kheri looked at him sideways.
"The smell of ale floating out the door might have something to do with it," he responded. Dale grinned then looked at Faran. The boy was staring up at the oak tree, watching the sign swing back and forth.
"I've never seen a tree like this," he said.
"It's an oak," Kheri commented, coming over to where they stood. "They get bigger even than this up in the northern forests."
"It's big enough," Dale responded then turned his attention back to Faran. "We're going inside," he said. "You watch yourself."
Faran looked at him quickly and nodded.
"I'll stay out of trouble," he promised.
"You too," Dale warned, catching Kheri's eye.
"Me?" Kheri asked innocently, then ducked his head grinning. "I'll keep my mouth shut," he replied and straightened his sword belt.

A grassy lawn stood in front of the inn, dotted with benches and a few tables. Light from several oil lamps which were mounted on top of poles spilled over the grass, giving it a warm, welcoming feeling. Several people were scattered about on the lawn, and they glanced up as the trio approached but no one bothered them. The inn door opened as they reached it and a man, with two buxom girls on his arms, walked out. The girls giggled and one pinched Kheri on the cheek as they passed by. Kheri stared at her bouncing chest, and watched them as they walked off, his mouth agape, then realized that he was being watched. Faran was grinning broadly at

him and Dale was leaning on the wall of the inn, his arms crossed, studying him quietly. He reddened and cleared his throat.
"Finished?" Dale asked and he nodded, embarrassed.
Dale grinned at his discomfort, then stood away from the wall and opened the door, leading the way inside.

The inn was busy and quite loud, the sounds of singing mixed with talking and loud bursts of laughter. It took several minutes to find someone who wasn't incredibly busy but finally a large man came over, wiping his hands on his apron.
"Welcome," he remarked, looking them over. "What can I be doing for you this evening?"
"How much is a room?" Dale asked, trying not to shout and still make himself heard above the din.
"For the three of ya," the man replied, "five minigill. You got horses?"
Dale nodded.
"Yes," he responded, "two of them. Out front."
"Stabling is another three minigill, so eight," he declared.
"Is there anywhere nearby we can also buy some supplies?" Dale asked and the innkeeper motioned around with his hand.
"This is it," he stated, "but we have a good stock of most things. What would you be needing?"
"Staples mostly," Dale responded. "Salt and stuff like that."
"I'll see what I can do to fix you up," the innkeeper nodded. "Let me get you that room first."

He walked behind a large counter and scribbled in a book then handed Dale a key.
"Here you go," he said as Dale handed him the money. "It's at the top o' the stairs, third door to the right. I'll send someone up to see to the fire in a bit."
"Thank you," Dale replied, looking at the key, then glanced around for the stairs.

"Supper's in the common room," the innkeeper continued, "unless you'll be wanting it private?"
"Private would probably be best," Dale agreed, "if there's no extra charge?"
The innkeeper shook his head.
"No extra charge," he replied. "I'll send Malita up to see to it. Take your horses round back to the stables and tell that lazy cuss Thorat I said to put 'em up."
Dale nodded, then led the way up the stairs to the room they'd been given.

"I thought," Kheri remarked as they reached the landing on the top, "that my aunt's hen parties were loud!"
"Never been in an inn before?" Dale asked, unlocking the door.
Kheri shook his head.
"No, just the pub in town," he replied stepping into the dark room.
"One thing that's universal," Dale commented, looking around for something to light, "on just about every world," he continued, as he picked up the oil lamp, "is that inns are loud, full of smoke and over-priced." He took the chimney off the oil lamp then frowned. "No wick," he grumbled. "and no oil in it either."
He set it back down and flipped his suit's daylight effect sensors on, then walked over to the window and threw the shutters open. Light from the lawn outside filtered in the window through the branches of the oak tree, filling the room with weird dancing shadows. Kheri looked around then shrugged and sat down in a chair.

Faran stood in the doorway, looking at the room and not saying much. A knock sounded on the wall directly behind him and he jumped, then spun around. A boy of about his age stood there holding a burning oil lamp.
"'Scuse me," he said, "but the girls is all busy so I brung you yer lamp."

Faran moved back out of the way, and the boy stepped into the room, replacing the empty lamp with the lit one he was carrying, then scurried back out the door. He was back directly and made for the hearth.
"Will you be wanting a fire?" he asked, looking around and Dale shook his head.
"No," he responded. "that's not needed."
"Ok then," the boy replied. "Yer dinner'll be up sometime, though you might get it faster if you go downstairs."
He bobbed his head, then headed back out the door and was gone.
"Whew!" Kheri commented, looking after him. "I could use some of that energy."
"Come on," Dale said, standing back up. "Looks like we're stuck with the common room if we actually want food tonight." He stopped at the door and looked at Faran.
"Have you ever been in an inn before?" he asked and Faran nodded. "Several," he answered.
"And I suppose they fell all over themselves getting you what you wanted?" Dale replied.
"Well..." Faran began, then nodded. "Yes, they pretty much did."
"Don't expect that tonight," Dale cautioned. "Remember what I told you this morning."
Faran met his gaze and nodded quickly. "I'll behave," he replied.

They went back downstairs to the common room and Dale found a table that wasn't too dirty. He sat down gingerly in a rickety looking chair and was mildly surprised to find that it actually held his weight then closed his eyes and leaned back, scanning the room and listening around him. Kheri stretched his legs out under the table and drummed his fingers on it, wondering how long food would be. Faran made a face at the state of the table then sat down, trying not to touch it's surface.

The inn was full and Dale had plenty to capture his attention. A group of farmers at one table were discussing the summer's current weather conditions, at another table two men were plotting out an expedition to retrieve some sort of treasure and one of the barmaids was busily trying to secure a companion for the night. As he shifted his attention from group to group around the room he slowly became aware that a hooded and cloaked figure in the corner was watching them with growing interest and frowned slightly. He opened his eyes and sat up but was distracted by the arrival of food as large steaming trays were deposited on the table in front of them.

"Here you go ducks," a bouncing barmaid said, smearing the table once around with a dirty rag. "Ale's at the bar."
She flounced off to tend to another customer and Dale glanced at the food then looked around for the figure he'd spotted. The corner seat was empty now, however, and he frowned, then searched the room. No sign of the man, or woman, and he gave up after a few minutes, turning his attention to the food. Kheri and Faran were already hard at work on the meat piled on one of the trays. Dale picked up a chunk of bread, then suddenly became aware that a short, fat man, dressed in bright colors was making his way purposefully toward their table. He put the bread down and watched him come.
"Greetings fellow travellers," the man said as he reached their table, doffing his cap and putting on a smile. "You strike me as some gentlemen that know the value of a coin."

Kheri ignored him, his concentration absorbed by his food. Faran looked up, gave him the once over and decided he wasn't worth bothering with, but Dale silently regarded him, waiting to see what he wanted.
"Yes, well," he said to Dale as the others made it clear they had no interest,

"My name is Cerot," he said. "Cerot the well-traveled. And I have a wagon just bursting with goods waiting for some discriminating parties to look them over. Now you strike me as a man who'd be interested in a bargain," he continued, warming up.
"You're a trader?" Dale cut him off and he nodded in agreement.
"That I am," he replied. "And a good one at that. Would you be interested in a few bargains this evening?"
"I might," Dale stated, "later."

The man shook his head.
"Might not be here later," he explained. "I've got to get this load on down the road to the next town. I just stopped here for a quick bite,"
"And discovered you couldn't pay your tab perhaps?" Dale interjected.
"Why now sir," the man responded, feigning hurt. "You cut me to the quick. Cerot always pays for what he gets." He glanced around the inn then bent down conspiratorially. "Of course, sometimes I forget that little, out of the way places like this, can't always handle large sums of money."
Dale nodded, then put his chin in his hand and leaned his elbow on the table, looking the man over.
"So," he asked, as if considering the possibilities, "exactly how long will you be sticking around tonight?"
"Oh, I might be here for another quarter hour," Cerot declared, glancing around, "or less. Depends on how fast I can make a few sales."
"I see," Dale replied. "And just what all do you have to sell?"
"Oh all manner of things," Cerot responded, launching into his sale's pitch. "Cloth from distant lands, made of silk and woven with strands of shinning gold. Exotic scents for the ladies and pans made of the purest beaten copper. Magical and Mystical toys to delight the most sophisticated tastes." His spiel was interrupted by Faran who suddenly choked and started coughing violently.
"Here now," the trader complained, looking down at his clothes.

Some of Faran's food had found it's way across the table and now decorated his jacket.
"Sorry about that," Dale apologized, picking the food off. "He tends to eat too fast."
The trader looked a bit put out, then nodded.

"So where's your wagon?" Dale asked him, brushing the last bits of food from the man's jacket.
"It's right out front, my good sir," the trader told him. "Right out front and easy to spot."
"Alright," Dale replied. "Give us a few minutes then we'll come see what you have."
"Take your time," the trader smiled. "I'll be waiting right outside."
He placed his cap back on his head, tipped it then made his way back out of the inn. Dale watched him swagger across the floor, stopping at several other tables on the way and shook his head, then turned to Faran.
"You ok?" he asked and Faran nodded, wiping streaming eyes.

"He's a liar," Faran declared, when he could talk again. "What a scam!"
"Oh?" Dale asked, then glanced back over at the trader who's brightly colored cloak was just disappearing out the door behind him.
"Yes," Faran replied and coughed again. "He came to the castle last year. Supposed to be selling the same stuff even. My father's currently looking for his head."
"His stuff isn't quite what he makes it out to be?" Dale asked and Faran shook his head.
"Not hardly. He sold some ... exotic something...I'm not sure what it was but all the ladies were after it, and right after he left, the castle started stinking like rotten meat. Took a week to get the smell out. Plus all those magical and mystical toy's ", he intoned, imitating the traders words badly, "don't work long. The ones he sold Count Lyalat's daughter all exploded a couple days after he

left. Made a mess of the rose garden and killed one of the guards. She didn't get hurt though, unfortunately."

Dale lifted an eyebrow at him.
"Don't like her much?" he asked and Faran shook his head. "No," he replied, wrinkling his nose. "She's ugly and her breath stinks. And she's always trying to kiss me."
Kheri snickered then clapped a hand over his mouth as Faran glared at him.
"Sorry kid," he said sympathetically. "No one said romance was ever easy."
Faran started to respond but Dale interrupted him again.
"So what about the other stuff he sells?" Dale asked. "Does he carry anything more mundane?"
Faran shrugged.
"I wouldn't know," he answered. "If he does, he didn't try to sell it to us."
"Alright," Dale replied, making a decision. "Let's finish up here then check out what he has real fast. If he's got a couple decent pans, I'd like to get them. As well as another bowl and maybe see if he's got any clothes that might fit any of us."

They finished relatively rapidly, and made their way outside. The trader was standing by his wagon, displaying a piece of gaudy looking cloth to two women, gesturing grandly as he talked. The wagon was hung about with all sorts of things, which Dale thought made it look more like a rolling junk shop than anything, but the women were entranced with the trader and a small crowd had gathered around the wagon. He finished up with a flourish and collected the money that the women handed him then bowed.
"Thank you ladies," he told them. "You'll be delighted with whatever you make out of that I'm sure." They smiled, thanked him and went their way, chatting gaily and examining the cloth.

He stood up, put his cap back on then noticed Dale standing a couple feet away. "Ah, excellent," he exclaimed. "You've come just in time. I was about to close up shop."

"You mentioned something about pans?" Dale said as he walked over.
"Yes good sir, that I did," the trader replied, flinging open a flap on his wagon. Behind it was a wall hung with several shining copper pans. Dale keyed his suit's sensors then walked over to the wagon and let the metal content register. The heads- up display told him that most of them were nearly paper thin, and full of micro- cracks but one of them, a rather dingy looking item, registered as being in good condition. He pointed at it.
"How much for that one?" he asked. The trader glanced at it then shook his head.

"You don't want that one sir," he explained. "Why it's old...used... battered. You want one of these new wonders of modern science," he continued, taking the most expensive of his copper pans off the wall. "Guaranteed never to change the flavor of the most delicate dishes cooked within it's dazzling embrace."
"How much," Dale repeated firmly, "for that one?"
The trader sighed and hung the pan back on the wall.
"Sir," he stated, "I do so hate to part with an old friend, but", he added quickly as he sensed he was about to lose a sale, "I'd be willing to sell it to you for five minigills."

"Five minigills!?" Kheri burst out, "That's.."
"We'll take it," Dale interrupted and pulled the money out of his pocket. "Now, do you happen to have any clothing in that wagon?"
The trader bobbed his head and pulled out a large trunk from under the wagon's skirting. Flipping the lid on the trunk he pulled out a hideous shirt of flaming reds and greens.
"This fine work," he began and Dale cut him off.

"Obviously you mistake us for someone else," Dale explained. "We're not interested in flashy, expensive, magical, or otherwise wonderful items to be displayed at a party among noble guests. We're interested in normal, mundane, useful things that will stand the wear and tear of a long journey through inhospitable territory." The trader blinked and his spiel died on his lips. "Now," Dale asked calmly, "do you have anything like that to sell?"

"Well, sir," the trader replied with some difficulty, and sighed as he put the shirt back into the trunk. "I might have a few things of that sort, but you realize of course, I'll be forced to sell them to you for a bit more than they may be worth. I can't make much of a living on such trappings you know."
"How much I'm willing to spend," Dale told him, "will depend on just how good the items in question are. Can we see them please?"
The trader shut the trunk's lid and shoved it back under the wagon, then pulled a smaller, battered trunk out and opened it.
"This is what I have," he explained. "Not much, some old things from several trading runs ago, but you're welcome to look through them." Dale nodded and began going through the trunk.

It turned out to contain three shirts and two pairs of pants that would fit Faran, a pair of pants, a pair of boots and two shirt's in Kheri's size and one shirt in his. There were also several blankets of tight weave in good condition as well as a couple wooden bowls and spoons, a leather backpack and two small leather pouches. He looked them over then turned to the trader.
"Alright," he asked. "How much for this?"
The trader studied the items, glanced at Dale sizing up how much he might be able to squeeze out of him then smiled.
"I can let you have all this for the paltry sum of only thirty-five minigills, kind sir," he responded. Kheri winced but Dale nodded his head and silently gave the trader the money.

"Thank you," Cerot said as he accepted it, stowing it quickly away. "It's been a pleasure doing business with you, I must say. A pleasure."

"You're welcome," Dale replied, gathering up the items and handing part of them to Kheri. They started to walk off then Dale suddenly turned as if he'd forgotten something.

"Oh, and," he remarked, stopping the trader in the act of climbing back onto his wagon. "I wouldn't be visiting the Baron again any time soon if I were you. Rumor has it, he's a tad upset with something you sold him last visit." He waved and turned back toward the inn. Behind him the trader stood frozen, staring at the three of them as they vanished into the inn. His face darkened for a moment, then he climbed onto the wagon and drove off into the night.

As soon as they were back in their room, Faran burst out laughing, unable to contain it any longer.

"Did you see his face!" he chuckled. "I thought he was going to explode when you insisted on buying that pan."

Dale grinned.

"Yeah," Kheri agreed, "and boy did you let the air out of his bubble when you told him you weren't interested in his junk."

"Well," Dale said, sorting the clothes out into three piles. "What I told him was true."

"Yeah," Faran agreed, "but I don't think even Count Ellingath could have done a better job of insulting him. That was classic!"

Dale smiled slightly.

"He had it coming," he responded, "I simply let him know I was on to his scam. His desire to make money just wouldn't let the sale pass. I'm not sure where he got these," he went on, looking the clothes over, "But I'll bet that pan is the one he normally cooked in. The others wouldn't have lasted three meals."

He pulled the backpack open, examined the inside of it then tossed it to Faran.

"That's yours. So are these," he explained, handing him the clothes that had fit him, one of the bowls and a spoon. "Put them away and make sure you take care of them."
Faran nodded then started to shove the clothes into the backpack. He paused as Dale crossed his arms, and looked up, his hand still in the pack. "What'd I do now?" he asked, confused.
"Fold them, don't just shove them in there," Dale instructed. "Kheri, show him how."
He opened the door and went out into the hall.
"I'll be back in a few minutes, I need to talk to the innkeeper and take the horses to the stables." He shut the door behind him and they heard footsteps fading away down the hall.

Kheri sighed and walked over to Faran.
"Not used to doing much for yourself, eh?" he asked, taking the clothes away from him.
Faran shrugged.
"No," he replied, "didn't have to."
"Watch and learn," Kheri responded and showed him how to fold the shirt up into a small, neat, bundle. "Like that," he admonished, when he was finished. "They take up less room in your pack that way. They don't get wrinkled either and are less likely to get holes in them."
Faran nodded and tried unsuccessfully to fold the next one.
"Keep trying," Kheri advised, "you'll get the hang of it eventually."
Faran shook the shirt back out, looked at it distastefully, then tried folding it up again.

Chapter Fourteen

Dale made his way down to the common room again then looked around for the innkeeper. The activity had partly ceased and he found the man busily clearing platters.
"Would you have a moment?" he asked over the din. The innkeeper nodded his head.
"Half a minute, if you don't mind," he replied. "Just let me get this lot to the kitchen and I'll be right with you." Dale nodded and went to wait by the front desk. A few minutes later, the innkeeper came back out of the common room, wiping his hands on a towel.
"What can I be doing for you sir," he asked.
"I'd prefer to speak to you in a more private place, if possible," Dale requested, glancing around. The innkeeper raised an eyebrow, but nodded and led the way to a room at the back.

"What do you need?" he asked when the door was shut. Dale fished the one doran note that Paw Tucker had given him out of a pocket and handed it to him.
"Is there any way you can break this for me?" he asked simply.
The innkeeper looked at it, then thought for a moment.
"I might be able to," he decided. "We've had a fair run of business lately. I can't promise though. I'll have to check."
"If you can, I'd really appreciate it," Dale replied. "It's all I have left and I have yet to find anyone that can change it."
"Let me check and I'll tell you in the morning." the innkeeper told him. "Was there anything else?"
Dale thought for a moment then nodded.
"Yes, I'm rather in need of another horse. I don't suppose you might have one for sale perhaps?" He asked hopefully.
"Now that I can help you with," he declared, smiling broadly. "I've got several I'd be willing to part with. They're all sturdy lots. Not the kind you find in the Baron's stables spoiling for battle mind, but good horses who ride well and should be just what you're looking for."

"They sound perfect," Dale agreed, smiling back. "Any possibility we could look at them right quick?"
"Certainly," the innkeeper chuckled, "if you don't mind picking out a horse in the dark. I might suggest waiting till the morrow though. When the sun's up."
Dale grinned.
"Yeah," he replied, "I guess that might work a little better."
The innkeeper nodded.

"Anything else for tonight then?" he asked.
"Yes," Dale said, "we're headed to Villenspell. Would you happen to have any maps or possibly current information about the roads between here and there?" The innkeeper shook his head.
"No," he admitted, "I'm afraid I don't. 'Bout all I can tell you is that once you leave the plains you're likely to meet up with all sorts of trouble. Those mountains are full of the worst sorts of critters, and rumored to be crawling with outlaws of every kind imaginable."
"Alright," Dale replied and stuck the doran back into a pocket. "Thank you, I'll check with you in the morning."
A loud commotion broke out in the common room as they stepped out of the office. The innkeeper grabbed a broom that was sitting in the corner and dashed off to keep the peace without another glance at Dale. Several loud crashes could be heard then the innkeeper reappeared, escorting two men by their collars. One of the barmaids opened the door and he tossed them forcefully outside then shut the door. Dale watched nonplused, then made his way back up stairs, the exertions of the day beginning to tell on him.

The room was dark when he entered and he looked around then frowned. Kheri and Faran were both gone, the lamp was out and the shutters had been drawn over the window. He hit the controls on his belt reflexively, flipping the force shield on to maximum then froze, listening. The only sounds that reached him were the faint noises from the common room downstairs. He keyed the suit's daylight effect sensors and looked around.

Nothing appeared out of order in the room, but something seemed wrong. He didn't move, but stood, years of experience having taught him to pay strict attention to his intuition, and very carefully began to scan in an ever widening circle around himself. Nothing untoward presented itself and he frowned. He glanced at the closed shutters then realized what was nagging at him. He had opened them to let in the light before they were brought a lamp and left them that way. He could understand Kheri turning the lamp down, or possibly even turning it off, but it made no sense that he'd also close the shutters if he was leaving, and then have to walk back into a dark room.

He concentrated on the shutters then, turning off the daylight effects and keying other sensors on his suit. Nothing. He took a step forward, watching the area around the window. On his third cautious step a very faint, blue line appeared across the floor about a foot in front of the wall. He nodded then stopped and slowly turned around, studying the room. More blue lines appeared snaking across the walls and over the floor as he moved his head. He kicked the gain up on the display and a glowing blue net covering the insides of the room sprang into view. The heads up display scrolled as his suit tried to categorize the energy creating it then spit out a reading he didn't like at all.

The energy registered as ninety percent arcane, something he hated to deal with. Wizards were usually unpredictable, and more often than not, unpleasant to boot. He looked down at the floor and realized he was standing on some of the arcane netting. "What the?" he thought, and looked closer. The netting appeared unable to detect his presence for some reason and he smiled slightly. "Alright, perhaps not too powerful a wizard," he thought, "or maybe one that just hasn't had much experience." He turned and looked back at the door which was still partly open. The netting ran across the inside, but until the door was shut, it appeared impotent. He studied the rest of the room, satisfying himself that there was no one in it with him, then keyed on his suits locate function. The display scrolled as the sensors went to work, tracing the energy that the netting was composed of back to it's source. A map of the inn sprang into view and several small dots flashed in an area behind it.

He shrank the display, moving it to the side and out of the way of his vision, then made his way carefully out of the room, shutting the door softly behind him. There was a faint smell of ozone from inside the room as the door shut, triggering the trap and he crooked one side of his mouth up, imagining the wizards confusion when his trap failed to deliver a victim.

"Now," he thought, "let's see if we can find you."
The hall was lined with doors, with a window at one end. A second set of stairs exited to the back of the inn through a sturdy wooden door next to the window, however anyone outside would be sure to see the blaze of light from the hall lamps and easily target someone attempting to descend them. Dale didn't even give them a second thought. He returned to the common room, then took the innkeeper aside and quietly asked him if there was an exit to the back that might be less visible.

"Through the kitchen," the man replied and looked at him curiously. "Why?"
"A long story," Dale responded. "Let's just say I need to retrieve a young man who's not supposed to be out in the dark, without being seen while doing so."

The innkeeper looked at him then nodded.
"Boys will be boys," he said, knowingly.
"That they will," Dale agreed.

"The kitchen will be the best for that," the innkeeper decided, "follow me."
He led Dale through the busy kitchen to the garden entrance on the side and let him out.
"Now this door's locked from the outside," he cautioned as Dale stepped out into the darkness. "So you'll have to come back in through the front."
"That'll be fine," he replied. "Thank you."

The innkeeper nodded, then shut the door. There was an audible click as it swung to. Dale stood silent for a moment then checked the location display. The blinking lights hadn't moved and the map indicated they were a ways off, directly behind the inn. He keyed the daylight effects, toned the light down so that the display was still visible, and flipped on the sound dampers.
"Let's see just how good your magic is," he thought, adjusting the energy signature of his force field. He activated his suit's molecular-computer and watched the display change, stopping when the force field no longer registered.
"Dangerous," he thought, "but I won't be leaving it like that very long. I'll have to recharge it for a couple days before I use it again though."
He took a deep breath, stilled his nerves, then looked around the garden he was standing in for a rock.

There were several fist sized rocks scattered around the garden and he collected three then silently made his way to the back of the inn. He moved through a wide arc, designed to carry him around behind the flashing dots and hopefully allow him to spring an ambush of his own. He had dimmed the suit's daylight effect down almost to twilight so that he could still see the map display and it made the going a bit slow but at last he found himself behind the wizard he was hunting.

About ten yards in front of him was an interesting sight. A man, wearing long robes and a tall pointed hat, stood facing the inn, his head bent and his attention fixed on something he was holding in front of him. Another man, dressed in weather-worn clothes squatted nearby cleaning a dagger. Kheri and Faran were both tied up not too far from the second man, and Dale could see that Kheri already had one hand free, though it was out of sight of his guard. Faran was sitting, his hands tied behind his back, and a look of absolute fury on his face. He had been gagged and he looked about ready to explode.
"Probably shot his mouth off," Dale thought, imagining Faran's probable outburst at being kidnapped. Dale took careful aim with one of the rocks just as the guard reached up and poked Faran with his dagger point.
"Papa's gonna pay a pretty penny for you," he chuckled nastily. "I think I'll send you back to him one little piece at a time."

Faran struggled against the ropes and muffled sounds escaped him. The guard laughed and poked him again. Kheri slipped his other hand free at that moment and extracted a dagger from his sleeve then threw it. It hit their guard in the throat and his eyes went wide. He gurgled slightly then toppled over onto Faran and lay there bleeding to death.
"Silence!" the wizard commanded, not looking up. "You're breaking my concentration!"
Dale cocked his arm back and threw. The rock sailed soundlessly through the air and hit the wizard on the head. He dropped something shiny and stumbled forward, then fell to the ground and lay still. Kheri rid himself of the rest of the ropes as fast as possible and dragged the dead man off of Faran then pulled his gag loose.
"Take it easy," he said as Faran lost control of his stomach and bent over, retching on the grass. He patted Faran on the shoulder then set about untying him.

Dale flipped the map off, kicked the daylight effects to normal, and ordered his suit to reset his force-fields signature, then walked over to the wizard and looked down at him. The wizard rolled over suddenly, pointed a wand in his general direction and snapped out one word. Fire shot out of the wand, splattering on his shield and throwing Dale backwards ten feet through the air. He hit the ground and rolled over his shoulder as he landed, ending on his feet, then raised another rock. The wizard had another wand out now, and it was pointed at Kheri. A beam of blue light enveloped him, freezing him in place. Dale pulled his arm back and the wizard shook his head.

"Don't be a fool," he warned, "unless you want to see him die horribly."
"You can't hold all three of us off forever," Dale replied, dropping his arm and letting the remaining rocks fall to the ground. "So now what?"
"Obviously we're at an impasse," the wizard stated. "We both want the same thing, and one of us is going to have to die, I'm afraid, in order to get it."
"That doesn't leave much room for negotiation," Dale remarked, keeping his hands loose at his sides.
"No," the wizard agreed, "I'm afraid you're probably right."
"What exactly is it you want?" Dale asked, his mind racing as he tried to think of a way to force the wizard to drop the wand pointed at Kheri.
"Why, money of course," the wizard explained. "What else would I want."
"Money?" Dale asked, "and just how do you think killing anyone is going to get you that?"
"It won't," the wizard admitted, "but your little friend there is worth at least two-hundred gill to me."

He smiled slowly as Dale glanced at Faran then looked back at him.

"Just what makes you think this?" he asked.
"Don't play the fool with me," the wizard warned. "Everyone knows what the Baron and his sons look like. This brat will bring me a fine ransom."
Dale paused for a moment and the wizards smile grew.
"Alright look," Dale said, "you're wrong, but if you're after money I'll make a deal with you. You release both of them and leave, and I'll pay you the ransom you think you'd get elsewhere."
The wizard thought about this for a moment then shook his head.

"You hardly look rich enough to pay my price," he decided.
Dale shrugged and reached into a pocket, flipping the controls on his belt at the same time. The force shield overloaded suddenly and the night was lit with a blinding flash. His suit reacted, shutting out all light and he pulled the blaster free then fired, guided only by his suit's heads-up display. The blast hit the wizard in the center of his chest and Dale flipped the sensors off briefly, continuing to fire as the night returned to normal brightness. The wizard was wreathed in blue flames, one hand stretched out in front of him with a ball of blue energy building before it, the other holding the wand steady on Kheri. Dale kicked the blaster up to a higher setting and the flames around the wizard increased. Suddenly, the wizard let out a groan, and crumpled to the ground. The wand deactivated instantly as it left his grasp and Kheri whipped out another dagger then threw. The dagger buried itself in the wizard's temple, black blood gushing out of the wound. The wizard convulsed suddenly then let out an unearthly shriek, and his body crumbled to dust. Dale flipped off the blaster, then ran over to the others.

Kheri turned as he ran up then drew a deep, shaky, breath.
"That is the last time," he declared, sitting down heavily on the ground, "that I want to have to fight a wizard."
Dale nodded, then knelt down beside Faran and put his hand on his shoulder. Faran looked up at him, his face pale, and shuddered.

"You ok?" he asked, as he untied the ropes binding his arms. Faran nodded and rubbed the wound on his left arm.
"Yes," he said, shivering, "just kinda cold."
Dale nodded, and stood then helped both of them back up to their feet.
"Look around on the ground and see if he dropped anything," he instructed, then caught Faran as the boy suddenly passed out and fell.
"Bit too much excitement," Kheri commented, his own voice still shaking slightly. Dale laid Faran down on the grass then stood and looked the area over.

Kheri retrieved his daggers, including the one in the dead man's throat, then went through the thief's pockets.
"Why is it," he asked, as he stood up at last, "that the ones I have to kill never have anything worthwhile on them?"
"Because," Dale explained, standing up and dropping the wizard's robe back on the ground. "You pick the wrong targets." He was holding five wands and a couple small vials of glowing liquid.
"Here," he directed, handing them to Kheri. "Take these but do NOT point them at anything."
Kheri took them gingerly, turning them around to look at the writing carved on their lengths.
"And don't try saying anything written on them either," Dale added.
Kheri bit his lip and tore his eyes away from the wands.

Dale reached down and picked up a round, dark globe. It glowed slightly as he handled it and he nodded.
"Thought as much," he said, turning it around. "This is what he used to spring the trap."
He glanced over at Faran still passed out on the ground.
"I wonder who else recognized him in there?"
"Probably not many," Kheri replied, "there really aren't a lot of people that know what the Baron looks like. He never comes

around here so about the only ones that would recognize him or anyone related to him are people that have been to the castle."
"I hope you're right," Dale replied, handing him the globe. "I don't exactly relish the idea of any more kidnapping attempts."
Dale bent down, and shook Faran awake gently, then helped him to his feet. "Come on," he said as he steadied the boy, "let's get back inside."

No one had noticed the fight behind the inn and they made their way back to the front, then went inside, trying to avoid attracting any undue attention from the few people still sitting under the oak. The night was getting on and most of the customers had left due to the lateness of the hour however the innkeeper was still busily at work, cleaning up the common room when they came back inside. He tipped his head to Dale, a knowing look on his face, then went back to sweeping. They made their way up the stairs and Dale paused outside their room for a moment then opened the door. Faran froze and shook his head.

"There are monsters in there," he whispered, staring into the room.
Dale blinked and glanced at him. Kheri nodded.
"Yeah, there's something in there," he agreed. "Or at least there was earlier."
Dale frowned, thinking about the arcane netting that had covered the insides of the room.
"Probably just an illusion that the wizard cast," he replied. "It's likely gone now that he's dead. However to be on the safe side, I'll be right back." He left the two of them standing in the hall and went back downstairs to find the innkeeper.

The innkeeper was just finishing when Dale walked back into the room.

"I hate to be trouble," Dale said, his voice strained and tired, "but would it be possible to get a different room for the rest of the night?"
"I suppose," the innkeeper agreed, looking at him curiously. "Mind if I ask why?"
"I'll show you," Dale replied, and turned toward the kitchen.
The innkeeper followed him, a look of interest on his face, as they exited the kitchen door and stood outside in the darkness.
"It's around back," Dale explained, and set off for the rear of the inn.
He led the way to the place where the dead man lay and pointed.

The innkeeper's eyebrows shot up as he regarded the dead body, now lit fairly well by the light of the rising moon. Dale walked over, picked the wizards robe off the ground, and handed it to him without a word. The innkeeper looked it over, a puzzled look flickering across his face, then shook his head.
"Might a known those two were gonna be trouble," he grumbled and dropped the robe with disgust.
"They tried at least," Dale agreed. "But they did something to the room and I can't get either Faran or Kheri to go back in there. They claim there are monsters inside."
"Monsters?" the innkeeper thought for a moment. "Don't see how there's monsters in my inn."

"There aren't," Dale replied, "but they refuse to sleep in the room anyway. It's probably an illusion," he added, kicking the robes. "But I don't have any way of getting rid of it."
"Well now, that just might be useful," the innkeeper mused out loud.
"Yep, might just find a use for that," he repeated, nodding to himself, then looked at Dale.
"I've got another room y'all can have," he said, still nodding. "Not as nice, but it should do fine."
"Thank you," Dale replied, rubbing the back of his neck tiredly.

"No problem," the innkeeper smiled, and started back to the front of the inn.
"We'll dispose of the body tomorrow," he added, "after it's light."
Dale nodded in agreement then stopped.
"The horses," he muttered, "I completely forgot them."
"Don't worry your head about it," the innkeeper told him. "I'll see they get stabled."
"Thank you," Dale responded, fighting back the urge to yawn. "I appreciate it."

The innkeeper gave him a different key then accompanied him upstairs to look at the room. He peeked inside then shrugged.
"Doesn't see any monsters," he commented, shutting the door, "but I'll deal with it later. You boys have a good night now."
He walked off down the hall and disappeared down the stairs. The new room was smaller, and had only a small couch and a single bed. Dale retrieved their belongings from the other room, then sat down on the bed and pulled off his belt. He looked at it carefully then turned it over and began tinkering with something on the back. Kheri looked around, then cleared his throat.

"Uh, Dale," he observed, "there's three of us."
'Yes." Dale answered, not looking up. "And?"
"Well there's only two places to sleep," Kheri pointed out.
"Yes," Dale replied, still not looking up. "And?"
"Well there are three of us," Kheri tried again.
"So someone sleeps on the floor," Dale replied, carefully adjusting one of the controls on the back of his belt. It hummed for a second and he nodded in satisfaction, then threaded it back through the loops on his pants. Kheri looked at him uncomfortably, then glanced at Faran.
"Who's sleeping on the floor?" Kheri asked, turning back to Dale.

Dale regarded the two of them silently for a moment. Faran met his eyes, then swallowed and looked away. Kheri chewed on his lip for a moment, then shrugged.

"I'll take the floor," he sighed, a note of resignation in his voice.

"No," Dale told him, "though it's nice of you to volunteer. Faran come here."

Faran looked up, then walked over to stand in front of him.

"Any idea how that wizard knew who you were?" Dale asked. Faran shook his head.

"You're sure?" Dale asked again.

"I'm sure," came the answer. "I never even saw him before."

"Tell me what happened then," Dale requested, watching his face.

"You left," Faran explained, "and someone knocked on the door. Kheri opened it and suddenly the room went dark. Something grabbed me, there were all these things growling and I think I screamed. Then we were suddenly sitting on the grass and I was tied up. That's all."

"That's about the size of it," Kheri agreed, "except that he started yelling about how they were going to hang and what his father was going to do to them."

"I did not!" Faran declared hotly, rounding on Kheri.

"You did too!" Kheri yelled back angrily. "I heard you!"

"Enough!" Dale commanded sharply, stopping both of them. He looked back over at Faran who met his gaze and shook his head emphatically.

"I didn't," he insisted. "I swear."

Dale looked into his eyes for a moment then nodded.

"Alright," he said, "the wizard probably had some kind of spell on you. However Kheri wouldn't lie about this, so accept the fact that you did tell them, even if you don't clearly remember."

"But," Faran protested and Dale interrupted him.

"I'm not saying you had any control over it, or that it's your fault, but you DID tell them."

Faran shut up, anger written on his face, then glared suddenly at Kheri. Dale glanced around just in time to see Kheri wipe a smirk off his face.
"Alright," he declared, fed up with the bickering, "you can BOTH sleep on the floor!"
"What!" Kheri exclaimed.
"No!" Faran yelled, then stood glowering at the floor. Dale crossed his arms and locked gazes with Kheri. The younger man gulped, and quickly dropped his eyes.
"I'm sorry," he mumbled, staring at the floor.
Dale looked at him for a few seconds in silence then turned his attention to Faran who was staring at Kheri in disbelief. He swallowed, met Dale's eyes for a moment then looked down.
"I'm sorry," he whispered, suddenly remembering how thin the ice he was on might be.
"Now," Dale stated, "it's late. I'm exhausted and I'm not in any mood for this. Morning comes very early and we've a long day ahead of us tomorrow. I don't much care who sleeps where but no more arguing! The two of you work out where each one sleeps and then do so. Now!" He reached over and blew out the lamp, then lay down on the bed.
Faran stood for a moment in partial shock, then carefully made his way through the darkened room to where Kheri was sitting. He felt very confused at the moment, and very much alone. Kheri looked up, then stood and motioned to the couch.
"Lay down," he said, a bit rougher than necessary. "I'm used to the ground, you'll never get to sleep."
"Thanks," Faran replied, his tone subdued. "I'm sorry I yelled at you."
"Forget it," Kheri responded, "we're all tired. Let's just go to sleep."

Kheri lay on the floor by the hearth and tried to force himself to sleep. The floor was cold, the blanket scratchy and he couldn't find any position that was comfortable. He gave up after several minutes and sat up. He thought back over the wizard's attack, and how stupid he'd behaved. Everything he'd done wrong, every opportunity he'd missed, replayed itself in his mind. He growled and pulled on his boots, tucked in his shirt and quietly left the room.

The inn was dark now, and moonlight poured in through the window at the end of the hall. Kheri walked softly down the hall and stood looking out of it, then turned the door handle and went down the stairs to the grass outside. The wizard's robe still lay where they'd dropped it, but the other body was gone, the grass was flattened as if it had been dragged away. He frowned, a knot growing in his stomach, then ignored the clear sense of danger and carefully followed the track it had left, trying to stay out of the light as much as possible.

The body had been dragged away from the inn and into a small stand of trees that flanked it. He stood in the shadows at the edge of the stand, listening. Everything was silent. Even the bugs had stopped singing, and he felt the hair rising on the back of his neck. Suddenly, following the track in the middle of the night seemed like a very, very bad idea. He wished desperately that he had never left the inn, but to go back to it now meant crossing a large swatch of moonlit ground unprotected. Just as he summoned up the courage to move, a crackling sounded through the underbrush and he stood frozen, listening as something heavy was dragged further away. He waited, unable to move, until the sounds faded into the distance, then slowly backed away from the stand. Nothing seemed disturbed by his movement and he retraced his steps to the inn as rapidly as possible, then climbed the back stairs and let himself back into the hall.

He closed the door softly, then turned around and bumped solidly into Dale. He looked up into the taller man's eyes, and swallowed nervously.
"What is it with you," Dale asked, looking down at him, "and walking straight into danger in the middle of the night?"
"Uh..." Kheri responded, then shook his head.
"I couldn't sleep," he explained. "I was going to go outside and unwind, then noticed that the body was gone. So.."
"So you followed it and nearly got yourself eaten," Dale finished for him. "I know, I watched."
Kheri chewed on his lower lip, then nodded silently.
"Kheri," Dale said after a moment, "would you like to know what took the body?"
Kheri fidgeted, then nodded.
"It was large," Dale replied, "About four feet high. With long hair and short black wings. Four footed. And there were five of them."
Kheri turned pale and glanced back out the window.
"They're gone," Dale stated, "They didn't like the stun ray."
Kheri turned back around to face him.
"Which," Dale continued, "I almost didn't have the power for. I used most of the charge up on that wizard. The blaster's useless now for the next twenty-four hours."
Kheri swallowed again, not daring to interrupt.
"As is most of my equipment," Dale went on, "which means the next time you get yourself into trouble, I might not even be able to find you in time, much less rescue you."
Kheri nodded, crestfallen.
"And regardless of how fast you might think I can move," Dale finished, driving the point home and watching Kheri squirm, "I would NEVER be able to cover the distance between the inn, and where you were just standing, in the length of time it would take for one of those creatures to kill you." He looked at Kheri silently for a moment, then added, "much less five of them."
Kheri nodded again, chewing on his lower lip.

"I'm sorry," he replied, when it was evident that Dale had finished. "I honestly didn't mean.."
"I know," Dale interrupted him, "but from now on, while it's dark, you don't go more than ten feet away from me without my permission. Understand?"
Kheri nodded, the image of the beast Dale had just described burning in his mind.
"Understood," he replied and shuddered at the thought of what had almost happened.

The rest of the night passed uneventfully. Kheri was shaken enough by his misadventure, that his blanket now looked inviting instead of uncomfortable. He lay down, covered up and was sound asleep in less than a minute. Dale sighed to himself, then pulled his boots back off and wondered if it would be safe enough to do without his suit for the night.
"Probably not," he decided, "especially with my belt out of commission till sometime tomorrow. He watched the others as they lay sleeping for a few more minutes, then lay back down and joined them.

Chapter Fifteen

The sun poured through the window a few hours later, and streamed across the room, bringing with it the promise of an uncomfortably hot day. Dale woke and set up groggily, kicking himself for not turning the suit's alarm clock off, then reluctantly pulled his boots on and stood up. The others didn't move, and he yawned then checked the time.

"Five am," he grumbled to himself. "Why does the sun come up so early in the day here?"

The tree's branches moved in a faint breeze outside, scattering bits of golden light across the floor. He went over and opened the blinds completely, letting the sun shine directly on Kheri's face, then shook Faran awake. Faran mumbled something, jerked his arm away and turned over with his back to Dale. He looked at the boy for a moment then stripped the blanket off him and left him shivering on the couch. Kheri was sitting up, blinking, wiping the sunlight out of his eyes as Dale turned around.

"It's too early to be morning," he complained, rubbing his eyes.

"That's the price for not going to sleep," Dale told him, shaking Faran again.

"Lemealone," Faran grumbled, and curled into a ball on the couch.

Dale swatted him sharply on the rump and Faran jumped.

"HEY!" he yelled as he came fully awake, then blinked and remembered where he was.

"That hurt," he pouted, sitting up and looking around for his clothes.

"Not nearly as much as it could have," Dale replied, then walked over to the door. "I smell food," he observed, opening the door. "I'll be downstairs. You two want anything to eat before we leave, I suggest you get a move on."

He walked out and closed the door behind him. Faran made a face and picked up his pants, then looked at them in disgust.
"Something wrong?" Kheri asked, yawning.
"Yeah," Faran grumbled. "These are filthy."
"So wear a different pair," Kheri suggested, "and wash those the next time we find a stream."
"A stream?" came the incredulous response.
"Or somewhere else with water," Kheri replied, pulling his clothes on.
"Me?" Faran asked in disbelief, still not sure he'd heard Kheri correctly.
"Yeah," Kheri said, then glanced at him. "You. Who did you think was gonna wash 'em?"
Faran set his jaw and wadded up the pants unhappily, stuffing them into his pack, then pulled a clean pair out and started getting dressed.

"You better not let Dale see those wadded up like that," Kheri pointed out as he buckled his belt. Faran opened his mouth to respond and Kheri cut him off. "And you better watch that attitude," he warned, "or you're gonna land in trouble before we even get back on the road. Is that how you want to start the day?"
Faran glared at the pants, then shook them out and folded them without comment.
"Well?" Kheri asked when he didn't reply.
"No," Faran grumbled. "Not particularly."
"Then straighten up and stop pouting," Kheri suggested. "All that's gonna get you is the backside of Dale's hand again."
He walked over to the door and opened it.
"I'll be downstairs," he said as he walked out of the room, leaving Faran to himself.

Faran rubbed his cheek which was still slightly sore from the backhanding Dale had given him the day before and tried to swallow his ire. Mornings never agreed with him and he was used to being coaxed out of bed by terrified servants pleading with him to please get up. He'd even sent several to the dungeons for daring to wake him before eleven am in the past and his habits weren't ready to accept the abrupt change in his routine. But he also had no desire to feel Dale's hand across his face again. He finished folding the pants, stuffed them into his pack and stood up.

The thought crossed his mind to tell the innkeeper who he was and he pushed it away.

"What could he do?" he asked to the air, "even if he did believe me, dressed like this. Besides," he continued out loud, sitting down on the floor, "my father doesn't even know I exist. So who cares."

He picked up a boot and looked at it critically. "At least Dale cares enough to yell at me," he finished defiantly, then pulled on his boots, brushed the hair out of his eyes and followed Kheri downstairs.

The inn was mostly empty as yet, but a few people were up and had wandered into the common room. Dale looked around and spotted the innkeeper then walked over to him. The innkeeper looked up then smiled, lines crinkling in his weathered face.

"Ah," he said pleasantly. "Good morning to you. And how did your group sleep last night?"

"Just fine," Dale replied, hiding a sudden yawn. "Once we got to sleep."

The innkeeper nodded sagely in his direction.

"Boys that age'll give any father grey-hair," he observed conversationally and Dale grunted in response. The innkeeper grinned and wiped his hands on a towel attached to his apron.

"So would you care to look at the horses this morning?" he asked and Dale nodded.

"Yes," he replied. "If you have the time."

"Right this way," the innkeeper said, and led the way to the stables.

The innkeeper had several horses he was willing to part with, left over from past patrons that had tried to leave without paying for services rendered. A chestnut filly caught Dale's eye and tossed her head as he walked up to her, then looked at him sideways as if to say "Just you try and ride me." He grinned, then studied the horse for a moment. She was in very good shape and didn't look to be much more than five years or so.
"What's the story on this one?" He asked the innkeeper, indicating the filly. The innkeeper reached up and stroked her nose, smiling. "Ah she's a fine lady, this one," he declared. "Full of sass. She came in with a pair of rogues one night and after they failed in their attempt to rob me, she stayed behind." The horse tossed her head again, and nickered, then stamped her foot. Dale chuckled, watching her.

"Think she'd be willing to accept a new rider?" He asked, reaching up to stroke her neck. The innkeeper shrugged.
"Can naught but try," he replied. "Who'd you have in mind to rider her?"
"Faran," Dale answered, watching the light gleam on her coat as he stroked it. "He lost his."
"She might," the innkeeper agreed amiably. "If not, I've got a nice, placid old timer who will."
Dale grinned again, imagining what condition such a horse might be in.
"Where's the lad?" the innkeeper asked.
"He'd better be downstairs by now," Dale replied, "unless he doesn't want breakfast."

Faran clattered down the stairs, jumped from the second to the last and hit the floor with a loud 'THUD', then grinned to himself as everyone glanced up to see what had happened. His mood shifted slightly at the look of annoyance on several faces and he snickered, then imperiously tossed his head and strode into the common room.

"Great," Kheri thought to himself, watching Faran's entrance, "here comes trouble."

Faran swaggered over to the table and plopped down onto an empty chair. Kheri put his elbows on the table, leaned his chin on his hands and looked at Faran silently.
"What?" Faran asked. "Can't I have any fun?"
"Yeah," Kheri replied, "can you be any noisier?"
"Sure," Faran said, rising, "watch me."
He turned around and spotted Dale walking back into the common room accompanied by the innkeeper.
"Maybe later," he muttered and sat back down quickly.
Kheri bit back a chuckle and sat there, waiting while Dale walked over to their table.
"What's funny?" Dale asked, as he sat down.
"Nothing," Kheri responded, watching as Faran tried to play innocent. "Just waiting on food."
Dale raised his eyebrows slightly, glanced at both of them, then shrugged as he sat down.
"The innkeeper's got a horse he's willing to sell," he remarked after a moment then looked at Faran. "How well do you ride?"

Faran looked around after a moment.
"Me?" he asked, suddenly aware that Dale was looking at him.
"Yes," Dale replied. "How well do you ride?"
"I'm the best rider in the Barony!" Faran bragged, sticking out his chest.
"Really?" Dale asked, "Alright then we'll see how the horse likes you after we eat."
Kheri rolled his eyes at Faran's blustering and shook his head slightly. Faran ignored him and stuck his feet out straight under the table, then put his hands behind his head and settled back.
"I once out-rode Duke Relet," he bragged, "and no one beats me at the jumps."
"Jumps?" Dale asked, his tone carefully neutral.

"Yup," Faran replied, warming up. "The jumps are a contest." His voice took on a condescending tone. "You have to jump your horse over fences and hedges and a creek and sometimes even people. I NEVER loose." he gloated, a look of conceit on his face.

"I see," Dale replied, trying to ignore Kheri as he rolled his eyes again then pretended to suddenly be gagging. "Well good," he continued calmly, "I'm sure we'll get a chance to see you in action." Faran leaned back slightly, a smug, self-satisfied expression playing across his face then suddenly fell over backwards.
"Hey!!" He exclaimed as he hit the floor, arms flailing. Dale shot Kheri a glance but
Kheri's attention was solidly fixed on one of the barmaids on the other side of the common room.
"You ok?" he asked Faran who was still laying on the floor, grimacing.
"I'll survive," Faran groaned, as he untangled himself and got back to his feet, then righted the chair. He looked at it suspiciously, glanced sideways at Kheri, then sat back down carefully. A sudden frown crossed his face, he clinched his teeth and stamped. Kheri let out a yell and jerked his foot back under his chair. Faran glared at him for a second then sat up looking victorious.
"Kheri," Dale said, and Kheri froze, then looked at him guiltily. "Kindly do not kick Faran's chair over again." Dale continued, turning slowly to look at him as he finished. Kheri muttered something under his breath but was spared the embarrassment of having to explain what he said as breakfast suddenly arrived at their table.

The food was good, solid fare, much like what Maw Tucker might have had on her table and they were given far more than they could finish. It was getting close to eight am when they were finally done and Dale sent Kheri upstairs to retrieve their belongings while he took Faran out to the stable to meet the horse. She snorted and tossed her head as they walked in, then stepped over to the stall gate. Faran glanced at her and a look of wonder crossed his face, then he walked over to the stall and stood, stroking her nose gently. "She's magnificent!" He whispered breathlessly, not taking his eyes off the filly. Dale watched him for a moment, then went back inside to find the innkeeper. Kheri reappeared at the top of the stairs, loaded down and looking unhappy, just as Dale walked back in the door. He shifted the bundles around and said nothing but something was very clearly wrong. Dale frowned slightly and Kheri shook his head, then glanced at the innkeeper. Dale nodded briefly, then turned to the task at hand, as Kheri took their possessions outside.

The innkeeper wanted two-hundred minigills for the horse and another twenty for the salt and other dry staples Dale had requested. They bartered for a few minutes then Dale handed him the doran. The innkeeper disappeared into a small room, returning a few minutes later with a handful of bills.
"Here you go," he said, handing Dale his change. "See cook on your way out. The tacks in the stable, just give this to Thorat and he'll see you're taken care of."
He handed Dale a bill of sale for the horse and it's tack then shook his hand. "Been a pleasure doing business with you," he said. "Be sure to stop in anytime you're out this way." "Thank you," Dale replied, extracting his hand from the big man's beefy grip. "I'll be sure to do that."

Thorat looked the bill of sale over when Dale handed it to him several minutes later, then scratched his head slowly and turned around.
"A-yup", he drawled, "tack's around here somewheres. Jest you wait a spell whiles I finds it." He moseyed off, scratching his rump and talking to himself. A few minutes later he returned, lugging a very beat up saddle and near worn-out bridle with him. "This here's the tack," he drawled, dropping it on the ground in a heap. "Got a might dusty, it did."

Dale squatted down and looked it over, then stood up and crossed his arms, his face unreadable. He looked silently at Thorat for a moment.

"Somehow," he said quietly, "I'm having a hard time believing you found the right equipment." Thorat opened his mouth but Dale wasn't finished. "I'm pretty sure, that for the price I just paid, the innkeeper would have made mention of such worn out pieces." Thorat tried again and Dale stopped him once more. "In fact, I believe I'd better get a refund if this is truly the correct saddle and bridle for this horse." Thorat raised a finger, but Dale interrupted him yet again. "Faran, go get the innkeeper!" he commanded sharply. Faran jumped, took a quick look at the pile of useless stuff on the ground and ran full tilt out the door.

He was back and out of breath a few minutes later, the innkeeper right behind him, a look of worry on his face.

"Here now," the innkeeper said. "What's all the commotion about? Is someone hurt?"

"No," Dale replied. "Not yet at least," he motioned to the tack laying on the ground. "But that's likely to be the case very quickly if I try to put that on a horse and use it."

The innkeeper frowned, looking at the pile of equipment, then put his hands on his hips and addressed Thorat.

"What do you mean," he asked, irritation creeping into his voice, "by trying to pawn this off on our customers."

"But," Thorat tried. The innkeeper wagged his finger in his direction.

"Don't but me boy," he lectured, "just go put this back where you found it and retrieve the correct equipment."

Thorat sighed, clearly frustrated, picked up the saddle and bridle, then lugged it back out of sight.

"I'd better go make sure he doesn't get confused again," the innkeeper remarked, walking off after him.

"Yeah, sure," Kheri muttered, "you and my grandmother."

"Drop it," Dale told him, watching the innkeeper's vanishing back. Kheri narrowed his eyes in the innkeeper's direction but nodded and went back to saddling their other horses.

When the innkeeper and Thorat returned a short while later, they were carrying a slightly worn saddle and blanket, a fairly new bridle and a halter in good condition. The innkeeper handed Dale two extra saddle blankets as Thorat dropped the saddle on the ground.
"Here," he said, "I hope this will make up for the incompetence of my help. I also have a pair of saddle bags without an owner, if you'd like. They're nearly new though so I have to ask five minigill for them."
"Thank you," Dale said, looking the equipment over. "If they're not too small I'll take them off your hands." Thorat ambled off to fetch the saddle bags at a nod from the innkeeper, and Dale handed the halter to Faran.
"She's your horse," he said. "Let's see what you can do with her."

Faran took the halter with a grin, then opened the stall door and held it up for the horse to look at. He talked softly, letting her smell it then slipped it over her nose and buckled it in place. She looked at him sideways and he smiled slightly, then led her out of the stall.
"I hope you know how to ride," the innkeeper commented. "That gal's got the fire in her for sure."
"I can ride," Faran replied simply, tying the halter to a ring next to the stall gate. He tossed the saddle blanket expertly on her back, gathered up the saddle and settled it in place, then cinched it. "One...two...three!" he counted under his breath, then suddenly kneed the horse in the ribs. She gave a surprised snort, letting out the breath she'd been holding, and he pulled the cinch up the rest of the way. "Now," he told her, picking up the bridle, "let's have done with this game. You and me are going to be good friends,

I can just feel it." He looked the horse in the eye for a minute then slipped the bridle on and settled it in place. She gave him a wicked look then flattened her ears. He reached up and flicked one smartly, provoking another startled snort. "Don't even think it," he warned, then untied the halter and slipped it off of her nose. Gathering the reins, he vaulted into the saddle with the practiced ease born of many years experience and settled into place, testing the length of the stirrups. He frowned slightly, then slid down and lengthened them.

"Well," the innkeeper commented at length. "Perhaps you can ride after all lad."

"I said I could," Faran replied, then took the saddle bags Thorat was holding, stuffed the halter in one side, and tossed them onto the horse.

"I best be getting back to my customers," the innkeeper said. "You boys have a good journey." He tipped his head in Dale's direction then headed back to the inn.

They led the horses out of the stables to the front of the inn then mounted and walked them back to the road. Dale turned and looked at Kheri as soon as they were out of sight.

"What happened?" he asked and Kheri frowned.

"When?" he asked.

"Inside," Dale replied. "What were you so upset about as we were leaving?"

"Oh," Kheri said, "I found that kid, the one that brought us the lamp last night, in our room digging through our stuff. Scared the pants off of him and sent him packing."

"Did he take anything?" Dale asked and Kheri shook his head.

"No," he replied. "Tried to I think but everything was accounted for."

Dale nodded, then turned and looked at Faran. The boy met his gaze and waited silently, a hint of nervousness about him.

"Do I have to warn you about trying to run?" Dale asked after a moment and Faran shook his head quickly.

"No," he responded. "I'm not stupid. I didn't ask you for a chance to prove myself just to hear myself talk either. I'll do what you say."

Dale watched his expression for a moment longer then turned, satisfied that he was being told the truth, and headed them down the road, deeper into the plains.

Chapter Sixteen

The plains stretched endlessly into the distance and Dale forced them to a gallop, pushed by the need to cover as many miles as possible before the day got too hot. The sun beat down as they traveled, sending waves of heat rippling into the air from the road ahead. The temperature increased steadily and as the sun climbed to zenith, Dale turned his horse and headed them into a thick grove of trees not too far from the road. The shade closed over them like a welcoming plunge into water and Kheri sighed in relief. They stopped the horses in a clear area and dismounted gratefully. Dale looked around, stretched tiredly, then unsaddled his horse.
"I'll be back in a few minutes," he said when he was done. "I'm going to see if there's any water around." He keyed the sensors in his suit, then turned and walked off into the trees.

Kheri finished unsaddling his horse, then looked around at the small clearing. It was covered with short, wiry grasses and clumps of nettles. Flies buzzed and flitted about ceaselessly, filling the air with a hypnotic droning. Faran had wandered over to the other side of the clearing and was staring up at a large hornet's nest in one of the trees, his horse still saddled and untended.
"Hey!" Kheri called. "Get back over here and take care of your horse!"
Faran ignored him, engrossed in watching the hornets. Kheri frowned, then strode across the clearing and grabbed him by the arm. Faran jerked his arm away, then glared at Kheri.
"You can't tell me what to do!" he snapped. "You want my horse unsaddled so badly? Fine, you go do it!"
Kheri growled, grabbed Faran by the arm again and jerked, sending him stumbling toward the horses a few steps. Faran clinched his fists, fury written across his countenance, and swung. Kheri blocked the swing then threw a punch of his own. Faran dodged backwards and Kheri's fist whistled past his nose, striking only the air. Faran lowered his head and charged, ramming Kheri in the

stomach. Kheri grabbed him around the torso as he fell, dragging Faran down with him and they rolled over on the ground, each intent on the others destruction.

Dale walked back into the clearing just in time to see Kheri jerk Faran by the arm. He watched silently until they were both engaged in a grappling match in the dirt, then walked over to them. Grabbing both of them by an arm, he hauled them effortlessly to their feet, yanked them apart then dropped them unceremoniously back on the ground on either side of him. They both hit the ground in unison, then sat there, blinking in surprise. Kheri glared briefly at Faran, then looked up at Dale and tried not to seem worried. Faran returned the glare then realized Dale was watching him. He wiped the glare off his face rapidly and looked up to meet Dale's gaze apprehensively.

"Explain what I just witnessed," Dale requested, gazing down at Faran, his face expressionless.

"Uh," Faran looked up at him, chewed on his lip for a moment, then shook his head.

"We were just fighting," he explained. "That's all."

"Fighting." Dale repeated, his voice carefully neutral. "And why were you fighting?"

"Ummm," Faran thought furiously. "I dunno," he finished lamely, "we just were."

"Right." Dale commented, then turned to Kheri.

"You have a better explanation?" he asked, crossing his arms. Kheri glanced at Faran, then met Dale's eyes again.

"Yeah," he responded. "I told him to tend to his horse and he got mouthy."

"Oh?" Dale asked, glancing over at Faran for a moment. "And why were you telling him to tend to his horse?"

"Because he was over here playing with a hornet's nest instead of taking the horse's saddle off!" Kheri exclaimed.

Dale regarded the two of them silently for a moment then pulled his belt off.

"If the two of you wish to act like children," he stated, as he grabbed Kheri by the front of his shirt and dragged him up to his feet, "then I will treat you like children."

He released Kheri's shirt, then folded his belt in half. "Turn around," he commanded.

Kheri stared at him in shock and shook his head.

"Turn around," Dale warned, his voice hard, "or live to regret it."

Kheri winced and turned around, his fists clinched, waiting. Dale swung once and the belt cracked solidly across Kheri's backside, provoking a muffled cry. "That was for ordering Faran around without my permission in the first place," he said, then reached down and hauled Faran up off the ground onto his feet. Faran's eyes were wide and he shrank back slightly.

"Turn around," Dale commanded. Faran shook his head and stared aghast at the belt Dale still held in his hand.

"Now!" Dale ordered and Faran jumped, startled, then reluctantly turned his back and tried to look over his shoulder. Dale grasped his shoulder, put one foot in front of him and swung the belt at his unprotected backside. It connected with a loud

"THWACK!" and he let out a yelp then rapidly put both hands over his rear. "That was for lying to me," Dale told him gruffly, "when I asked you what the fight was about. Move your hands!"

Faran tensed, then slowly moved his hands, his eyes squinted shut. Dale swung the belt again, provoking another cry. "That was for not tending to your horse," Dale told him sternly, "before doing anything else." He threaded the belt back onto his pants and buckled it, then grasped them both by the shoulder and turned them back around to face him.

"Now," he warned, locking eyes with each of them in turn, "I have had ENOUGH of the bickering and fighting between the two of you." Kheri cringed and looked at the ground silently, his manner subdued. Faran wiped tears off his face and chewed on his bottom

lip, waiting nervously for what might happen next. "The next time the two of you decide to get into a brawl," Dale continued firmly, "expect me to end it with about ten times what you each just got."
Kheri looked up and shook his head quickly.
"No Dale," he whispered, pleading, "please."
"Then control your temper," Dale ordered, "or I will control it for you."
"Yes sir," Kheri managed, shivering.

Dale released them, turned and walked back across the clearing without another word, then sat down under a tree and began tinkering with his blaster. Faran sniffed, wiped his nose on his sleeve, then glanced at Kheri. Kheri looked over at him, glanced across the clearing at Dale, then took a deep breath.
"Truce?" Kheri asked and Faran nodded, still sniffling.
"Yeah," he agreed, blinking back more tears, his voice trembling slightly.
"We'd get along a lot better," Kheri commented, "if you'd quit forgetting you're not in charge around here."
Faran started to glare at him then glanced over at Dale and rubbed his behind.
"That's not real easy to do," he muttered, wincing instead.

"Yeah, well," Kheri replied, "I don't think he is real happy with either of us right now. And I, at least, have no desire to experience a repeat performance."
"I said truce," Faran responded. "I'm just not real good at this."
"Yeah," Kheri agreed. "I've noticed. I suggest you get better at it fast unless you don't want to be able to sit down for a while."
Faran looked at him for a moment, fighting off the glare that threatened to cross his face, then nodded.
"I'm trying," he muttered.
He walked back over to his horse and silently unsaddled her, then brushed her down and left her to graze. By the time he was done,

Kheri had vanished into the trees in search of firewood. He glanced around the clearing, and rubbed at his still smarting backside, then looked over where Dale was sitting, engrossed in tinkering with the blaster, and chewed on his bottom lip. He stood silently for several more minutes, working up his courage, then walked over to Dale and dropped down to his knees before him, looking down at the ground, in imitation of what he had personally demanded out of various servants in his father's castle whenever they had earned his dissatisfaction, then waited tensely.

Dale deliberately ignored him for another minute or so, then looked up from the blaster.
"Yes?" he asked, displeasure still evident in his voice.
Faran swallowed hard.
"I'm sorry," he responded, his voice trembling, not daring to look up.
"For?" Dale asked without emotion.
"Lying," Faran replied, still staring at the ground. "And fighting with Kheri. And not taking care of my horse. And," he bit his lower lip, took a deep breath, then added, "forgetting my place."
Dale said nothing for a moment and Faran forced himself to remain silent, waiting nervously.
"Is it going to happen again?" Dale asked finally and Faran shook his head.
"No," he whispered. "It won't."
"Look at me," Dale commanded and Faran lifted his head, trembling slightly. He said nothing, but met Dale's gaze silently.
"I thought we had this clear yesterday," Dale stated bluntly.
Faran looked miserable but nodded.
"I dislike having to repeat myself," Dale told him, "and I would prefer not to have to use force on you."
Faran nodded again.
"However," Dale continued, his voice quiet but firm, "I will if your actions require that. It's your choice really." He paused, then

studied Faran for a moment. "Do you honestly want me to be mean, harsh, or iron-fisted with you?"
Faran shook his head.
"No," he replied. "I've just never..." his voice trailed off and he fell silent, unable to voice his thoughts.
"Finish," Dale prompted after a moment.
Faran struggled with himself then tried again.

"I've always made the rules," he said at last. "Everyone's always done what I said, what I wanted. I've never had to do this before, and it's not easy."
Dale raised an eyebrow slightly and regarded him silently, studying his expression.
"You've never had to obey any rules at all?" he asked after a moment.
Faran shook his head. "No." he answered simply. "Never."
"And your father never got upset at you for ordering his staff around?" Dale asked.
A look of resignation mixed with anger crossed Faran's face for a second.
"My father?" he growled, bitterness coloring his voice. "Why would HE care? He doesn't even know I'm alive!"
Dale blinked.
Faran abruptly sat down cross legged on the ground then roughly pulled up a handful of grass and threw it to the side.
"You know how many brothers and sisters I have?" Faran asked, glancing up at Dale.
"Twenty-seven. There are twenty-seven other kids all older than me. All better than me. All more important than me. All with different mothers than me!" Faran wiped angry tears out of his eyes and continued. "Shoot, I don't even know who my mother IS! Some girl he had hanging around the castle for a while!"

Dale thought briefly about the picture Faran was painting as his frustration spilled out and shook his head.

"So who took care of you when you were younger?" Dale asked.
Faran shrugged. "Different Nannys, or other servants," he responded. "Whoever didn't get out of the way fast enough and got stuck with me."
Dale said nothing, letting him vent, but privately wondered what sort of man the Baron was to have been party to such a situation.
"I hear them all the time," Faran went on, his voice shaking with rage. "Talking about me when they think I'm not listening. The names they call me. How much they hate me. They deserve what I do to them! They deserve worse!"
Dale watched him silently, waiting for him to wind down as Faran ripped a couple more handfuls of grass out of the ground and threw them forcefully aside, then stopped and wiped his eyes again.

"Finished?" Dale asked after a moment and Faran nodded, his emotions drained from the outburst. "Feel better now?" Dale asked and Faran shrugged slightly then nodded.
"Yes," he replied, his voice quieter. "Some."
"Alright," Dale responded. "Then from now on, let the past stay in the past. You have rules now, and I expect them to be obeyed. You have boundaries that I don't suggest you cross. You do not have the right to order either myself, or Kheri, to do anything, but if you ask, politely, you'll likely get what you're after. Unless it's dangerous, stupid or something I don't approve of."
Faran nodded, listening silently, still picking at the grass.
"However," Dale continued, "if something is bothering you, come talk to me. As long as you're not disrespectful I'm more than willing to listen."
Faran nodded again, waiting for Dale to finish.
"Do I need to make the rules clearer or do you have a fairly good idea of what I expect of you?" he asked.
Faran shook his head.
"I know what you expect," he replied. "You already made that clear."

"Then explain to me," Dale requested, "why the fight between you and Kheri happened earlier."

Faran picked at the grass, thinking.
"Well," he explained after a moment, "Kheri's not you. And he didn't ask, he demanded. And I wasn't going to take that, not from him."
"Oh?" Dale asked and Faran held his hand up.
"I'm just telling you what went through my mind," he explained quickly. "I'll do what he says from now on unless you tell me different."
Dale nodded and Faran continued. "I guess I didn't really expect you to do anything either, well maybe yell some, but that's all."
"Then why didn't you tell me the truth about the reason for the fight?" Dale asked and Faran shifted uncomfortably.
"Habit," he muttered, looking down at the grass he was picking at.
"Habit?" Dale asked, a warning tone in his voice. "What else have you lied to me about?"
Faran looked up quickly and shook his head.
"Nothing! I swear!" He met Dale's gaze and swallowed then shook his head. "I haven't lied to you about anything else!"
Dale said nothing, watching him.
Faran bit his lip and shook his head again. "Honest. I haven't," he protested, frightened again.
"I suggest you make that the one and only time then," Dale admonished him after a moment and Faran nodded quickly.
"And as a word of advice," Dale warned, "I don't suggest you try telling me half-truths or twisting things. I WILL eventually find out and you WON'T like the results. You'll get in far less trouble if you tell me when you've done something wrong than if I hear it from someone else or find out about it some other way." He held Faran's gaze for a moment before continuing. "I also suggest," Dale finished, "that you keep this in mind. If you lie to me, you'll

get in trouble twice, once for lying and once for whatever it was you shouldn't have done."

Faran gulped slightly, then nodded. "What are you going to do with me?" he asked after a moment, changing the subject completely.
"That depends," Dale replied, picking the blaster up again, "on how hard you make it on yourself."
Faran waited silently, watching him. Dale flicked a switch on the blaster, nodded in satisfaction as it's gage swung to full charge, then placed it back on his belt.
"Are you ever going to let me go?" Faran asked uneasily when Dale said nothing else.
Dale regarded him seriously, and Faran tensed.
"That also depends," Dale replied, "on your actions and what you push me to do. At the very least," he continued, "not until you grow up and learn how to be a decent, respectful, human being, instead of an out-of-control, spoiled brat who thinks the universe revolves around his every whim."
He stood, then dropped a hand on Faran's shoulder.
"Since your father didn't care enough about you to do that job, I'll do it. After that, we'll see." He smiled slightly at a suddenly, very confused, young man, then walked over to the horses and began rummaging through the saddlebags.

They spent several hours in the grove, waiting until the sun was well on it's way toward evening. At last, as the shadows were deepening, they left the grove and headed back to the road. Dale paused as they left the shelter of the trees, and looked around, a feeling of unease suddenly overtaking him. There, under the eves of the grove, stood a hooded and cloaked figure, watching them. He reined his horse and turned to look at it but it stepped behind a tree and vanished from sight. Keying the sensors in his suit, he turned carefully around, looking at the trees. The heads-up display remained empty of everything except small birds and beasts. He shut his eyes and concentrated, scanning the area as far as possible.

Again, nothing, as if the figure had never existed. He frowned and opened his eyes, then shook his head. He was sure it was the same person as had been watching them in the inn, but what it's motives where he had no idea. He resolved to keep a sharper eye out, then headed for the road, and the next step of their ride.

Chapter Seventeen

They fell into an easy rhythm over the next few days. Taking to the road at first light every morning, they rode until the sun reached noon and the heat had become near unbearable. A grove, a thicket or some sort of cover was usually not too far away from the road and once the heat began, they took to the first available shade, resting and waiting for evening. As the afternoon settled toward night, and the heat began to dissipate, they took to the road again, riding until near midnight. In this way, they covered nearly thirty miles a day, and Dale had begun to breath easier. They passed a number of side roads that joined them from various places on the plains and several more inns but Dale avoided stopping at them, not wanting to run the risk of anyone else recognizing Faran.

The afternoons were much too hot to do anything strenuous but Faran had developed a keen interested in insects, and Dale spent quite a bit of time with him, using his suit's sensors to identify the new, amazing creatures Faran was discovering then watching them with him as they went about their lives. Kheri spent the afternoons throwing knives at twigs, and trying to learn to walk softly on dry grass and leaves. The nights were different as the temperature was cooler and the second night out from the inn, Dale began working on Kheri's swordsmanship. Kheri was completely unfamiliar with such a large, heavy object and after the first near mishap, Faran prudently stayed at the edge of camp, well out of his way.

As the days went past and the miles fell beneath them, Dale found himself still bothered by a nagging worry that they were being watched, but his scans produced nothing. At last, in the distance, they could see a faint darkness which resolved into distant mountains as they traveled. Days became weeks and at last, a little over a month out from the inn, they entered the foothills at about ten am one morning. There was far more cover now, and the ground became rolling, somewhat rocky and covered with thick, lush grass. The temperature dropped several degrees shortly after they began the trek through the foothills as the wind, cooled by the snows on the mountaintops near at hand, blew past them on the way to the sun drenched plains. They rode through the day instead of stopping, and at last as the shades of evening were falling, Dale turned from the road into a small hollow he'd spotted.

"I think that's far enough for today," he decided," dismounting tiredly. "We'll camp here for the night."
The others reined to a halt and dismounted, then set up camp. There had been no more arguing between the boys, although Kheri had to bite his tongue at times when Faran's ego got the best of him. At such times however it usually didn't take very many minutes before Faran's ego also earned him Dale's slight displeasure and he straightened back up quickly.

The wind was picking up as they finished preparations for the night. Clouds began to gather in the sky and Kheri looked around, his eyes shining. "Rain," he murmured and took a deep breath. He watched the clouds for a few more moments then dug out their tarp and began setting up a shelter.

Dinner was finished, and the fire was beginning to die down as night closed in. The crickets and other night creatures had begun their evening symphony and Kheri leaned back against a tree. He smiled to himself, watching the flames flickering on the bits of wood that had not yet become coals and thought back to what he'd been doing just a few weeks before. He shook his head, bemused, at the turns his life had taken in such a short time, wondering what would have occurred if he'd remained in the city. After a few minutes, he closed his eyes, and dozed off. Dale watched him for a moment, then picked up both sheathed swords.
"Here," he said, handing them to Faran. "These need polishing, see what you can do with them please."

Faran nodded, and took them, then went over to sit at the edge of the firelight with the swords in his lap. He drew one of them carefully and inspected the blade. Firelight flickered down it like molten gold and he grinned then sighted down the edge looking for nicks.

Dale was restless, bothered by a feeling of impending doom. He stood up and walked over to the other side of the camp, then detached the blaster and disengaged the safety. He activated the force field on his belt, setting it to maximum deflection and keyed the sensors in his suit. The heads up display flickered to life and he quickly ran a perimeter scan, searching for anything that might have triggered his nervousness. The scan turned up nothing, but the feeling increased and he flipped the display off, kicking on the daylight effect sensors. Three seconds later, there were five simultaneous flashes of light on the other side of the campfire and Dale found himself suddenly facing several Gorg, all armed with long, curved, blades and snarling viciously in his direction.
"Kheri!" he shouted, leveling the blaster at the closest one and thumbing the trigger. Energy shot out of it and splashed harmlessly on the Gorg's armor. Dale flipped the safety back on and tossed the blaster into the underbrush then drew his hunting knife and dropped into guard stance.

Time stood still as his suit reacted to his actions and the light turned into shades of red. He stepped forward and grabbed the blade hand of the closest Gorg, placed the point of his knife against it's throat then mentally ordered his suit to disengage the time stop. The Gorg crashed into him as it charged forward, carrying him backward several feet and burying his knife in it's throat. It toppled forward, spewing acidic blood in an arch as it did so. He jerked his knife free and jumped backward out of it's way. As his feet touched the ground, he tripped over a partially buried rock and landed flat on his back with a jarring thud. The impact stunned him for a moment and lights went off in his head. He blinked, looking up at three Gorg bearing down on him, and struggled to move. As he did so, one of the Gorg suddenly fell over, blood spewing out of a deep wound in its back.

Faran appeared behind it wielding both swords. As he jerked the sword in his left hand out of the Gorg's body, he swung the other sword in reverse and sliced the head off of the second Gorg's shoulders. Turning slightly, he shoved the sword in his left hand into the third Gorg's side. It bellowed, then grasped at it's side. It's eyes bulged, and Faran opened his right hand, dropping the sword he held, then grasping the one in the Gorg's side with both hands, he rammed it all the way in to the hilts. He let go of the sword as the Gorg fell, whirled and retrieved the other one from the ground and spun quickly back around.

Dale froze, and stared at the now still bodies of the Gorg laying around the camp, then looked at Faran in amazement. The young man was standing in the middle of the Gorg, his expression one of pure hatred, as he studied them to make sure they were dead. Kheri pulled his Garrote free of the Gorg he had strangled, wrapped it around his hand and carefully stowed it back in a hidden pocket in his shirt, then walked over to Dale and held out his hand. Dale grasped it and stood up, wincing slightly as he put weight on the foot that had been beneath him when he fell.
"Thank you," he said, still slightly stunned. "I am in debt to both of you."
"You're welcome," Kheri replied, glancing back over at the Gorg. "I thought we'd shaken them."
"So did I," Dale replied, wiping the Gorg's blood off of his hunting knife. "I was wrong."
He looked around for a moment, then walked over and picked the blaster up from where he'd tossed it, reattaching it to his belt. "Didn't expect them to be wearing energy- resistant armor either," he commented, then walked over to the fire, sank back down to the ground and closed his eyes, trying to steady his nerves.

Faran satisfied himself that the Gorg were not going to move again, then extracted the second sword from the corpse he'd left it in. Once it was free, he walked over to Dale and sat down next to him on the ground then carefully began cleaning the blades. Dale opened his eyes after a moment and watched him silently.
"That was amazing," Dale said after a couple minutes. "How did you learn to fight like that?"
"Well," Faran replied, examining the first blade for nicks along the edge. "One of the people that got stuck with me a lot was the captain of the guard. So," he looked around then picked up a rock, "I grew up playing warrior. I've been learning from him since I was two." He looked at the rock critically, then carefully drew it over the swords edge, sharpening it where it had been damaged slightly. "And," Faran continued, "I wasn't going to sit there and let you get killed." He glanced over at Dale and grinned. "Even if it would have spared me getting in trouble again."
Dale grinned back at him, then reached over and tousled his hair. Faran grinned back happily, and set to work on the swords in earnest.

Dale stood after a few minutes, and set about stripping the Gorg of any useful items, then turned the blaster on them. Bereft of their armor, the bodies vaporized instantly under it's disruptive power. Kheri wandered over to the pile of left overs and picked up a knife and looked it over, then shivered. The knife was a wicked creation, composed of a curved blade with a serrated edge on one side and backward pointing spikes on the other.
"That would rip a huge chunk out of you," he remarked, examining the spikes.
"That's exactly what it's designed to do," Dale responded, vaporizing the last of the corpses. "They have several standard weapons that they fight with," he continued. "A maul with explosive barbs, that knife, a blaster and a net. The explosive barbs on the maul are rigged to shoot into whatever they hit if the wielder so

wishes, the net has millions of glass shards embedded in it's ropes and that knife is designed so that after they drive it into a target they can literally pull it's organs back out of the wound. They've also been known to pick up whatever happens to be laying around and use that as a club. Stuff like branches, furniture, people, and whatever. But they only do that if they've been disarmed and are still standing."

He looked around the camp and shuddered suddenly.
"Three Gorg is usually enough to overpower anyone. Five is overkill."
He shook his head, then looked at the others with a serious expression on his face.
"Whoever sent them must want me pretty badly," he said, his voice tense.
"We're much farther away from where they first encountered me than I actually ever expected them to hunt."
Kheri looked around quickly as if he expected to see more Gorg either step out of the bushes or materialize out of thin air.
"And they found me much more rapidly than I thought possible," he continued. "They will be back. Not tonight, but they will be back and in greater numbers I'm afraid."

Faran looked up at him, worry written across his face. He and Kheri exchanged glances then Kheri spoke.
"How many do you think they'll send next time?" he asked, his own voice tense.
Dale shook his head.
"I don't know," he replied. He leaned his back against a tree and covered his eyes with his forearm for a moment, then looked up at the sky. Wiping his eyes quickly, he crossed his arms and shook his head.
"I don't know," he repeated, then stared down at the ground. "I don't know," he said for the third time, his voice almost a whisper, "And I'm afraid of the answer."

Kheri stared at him in shock for a moment. Dale had seemed unbeatable to him, a tower of unassailable strength and unimaginable power, and suddenly he was face to face with the fact that Dale was scared. Not just scared but very nearly terrified and trying not to show it.

He stood silent for a moment, then squared his shoulders.
"Well," he declared, his voice firm, "they're not here now and nothing's set in stone. We'll just have to make sure we're ready for them if they do come back."
Dale smiled slightly at Kheri's resolve.
"It's not that easy," he thought, visualizing the huge army they could easily send after him if they so desired, "but it's nice to know someone's willing to stand against them with me."
"Yeah," Faran agreed, as he sheathed the sword he'd been working on, "and they'll have to go through me first."
Dale smiled gently at both of them.
"Thank you," he told them, genuinely touched, "both of you. You don't know what it means to me to hear you say that. However," he continued seriously, "I'll feel a whole lot better once we get to Villenspell. I think we need better equipment and reinforcements, and I can't think of a better place to find either."

Chapter Eighteen

The hour was getting on toward midnight and the clouds had now covered the sky completely. Flashes of light could be seen crackling through them high above as the lighting began a magnificent show. The far off crashing of thunder could be heard now every few minutes and the air felt alive with anticipation. They double checked that everything was as protected from the rain as possible, then tried to go to sleep under the shelter that Kheri had rigged. The rain held off just long enough for sleep to descend upon them, then with a resounding explosion directly over head to herald it's arrival, it cascaded down in a flood of gigantic proportions. Hail came crashing down as well, smashing through the branches of the trees in chunks nearly two inches across. Dale came instantly awake as the thunder sounded and glanced out at the downpour, then ducked as a chunk of ice hit the tarp above him and bounced off his head.

Flipping his force field on, he grabbed the tarp with one hand and keyed the area control with the other. The field expanded, enclosing the area under the tarp bare instants ahead of the avalanche of falling ice. The others were awake by now and Faran huddled close to Dale, shivering and striving to turn himself into a ball. Kheri blinked, looked at the water pouring under the edges of the tarp and sighed. Conversation was impossible and they sat in a rapidly forming puddle of mud, protected from a drenching by Dale's shield, watching while the ice covered the ground three inches deep and listening to it bounce off the tarp. The cloudburst ended as rapidly as it had started, but the ground was soaked and water continued to pour under the tarp, running down the slope of the hills around the hollow to pool at the lowest point of ground.

Dale waited unmoving for several minutes after the downpour had finished, and the water had stopped flooding around the edges of his shield, to make sure it wouldn't start again, then let go of the tarp and flipped his force field off. He crawled back out from under the near-worthless shelter and stood, then looked around. Kheri shook Faran, got him out from under the tarp then set about trying to rescue their possessions from the flood.

The horses were gone, vanished into the woods in search of somewhere no ice pounded down from the skies, and Dale suddenly felt overwhelmed, unable to deal with any thing else that might go wrong. He glanced over at the others who were wringing the water out of their blankets and stood watching them for a few moments.

"What am I doing," he thought, "dragging them along with me, out into the middle of nowhere. Kheri at least," he thought watching the younger man kicking the ice out of the way, "has done what I needed. I should have let him go back at the first inn."

He looked over at Faran then shook his head. "No, I took that responsibility on and I have to see it through. He needs a chance that he will not get if I send him back to his father. I just hope I can keep the Gorg from killing him when they return." He fought with his emotions for several more minutes, then pushed his concerns away for the moment, and walked over to assist in cleaning up the mess.

The saddlebags had been waterproofed but nothing was tightly sealed and the rain had gotten into even the smallest cracks. Dale pulled out his blaster and melted the ice covering the ground around the campsite, then dried out the fire pit. The wood was soaked but it too dried under the blaster's ray then caught fire and blazed brightly against the blackness of the night. Working meticulously, he played the blasters beam across the ground, drying the mud as he did so, stopping when he got too close to the bushes and trees. Drying their blankets and other equipment proved to be a harder task, as the blaster would ignite them or even disintegrate them long before they would reach a usable state. They hung everything they could on the branches of the underbrush, then sat next to the fire trying to keep warm.

The air was quite chilly, and the storm raged on in the distance, but the clouds were breaking overhead and the wind had died to almost nothing. Dale sat and stared into the fire, thinking. The horses, if they weren't dead, would likely return by morning and if not, he would worry about tracking them then. But the prospect of being caught in another sudden downpour as they rode through the hills worried him and he tried to think of some way to improve their shelter. He looked up to find Kheri watching him, concern written on his face.

"Everything ok?" he asked and Dale nodded.

"Yes, just trying to think of some way to keep from getting wet the next time it rains," he replied.

"We should have bought a tent," Kheri responded with a grin.

Dale looked at him sideways.

"Oh now you tell me," he said with mock sternness. Kheri chuckled.

"Well," he replied, "at least we didn't get pounded to death."

"True," Dale agreed, "and hopefully it'll stay that way."

Faran said nothing, just scooted closer to the fire and huddled in front of it, shivering. Dale reached over and put a hand on his shoulder.

"You ok?" he asked.

"I'm c-cold," came the answer. His voice was tense and hinted at something more than just chill air. Dale just nodded and said nothing but made sure he stayed close to Faran for the rest of the night.

Morning found the three of them sleeping on the bare ground next to the now dead coals.. The sun spilled through the branches and turned the swirling motes in the air to bits of fairy dust. Dale yawned, and sat up stiffly. The air was still cool, and somewhere off in the trees, a dove began cooing. He looked up through the branches and was rewarded with the sight of a cloudless, deep blue sky. He smiled slightly, then got to his feet. His suit kept the chill off but it did nothing to ease the hardness of the ground and he ached all over. He stretched then looked around to see if the horses had come back.

The two that Paw Tucker had given them were standing close by, grazing on grass that hadn't been vaporized by the blaster as Dale had dried out the mud hours before but the one that he'd bought at the inn was no where to be found.
"Figures," he thought to himself. "Wonder if I can find her."
He keyed the sensors in his suit and punched in horse, then scanned Faran briefly to use as an energy signature. The heads up display in front of him scrolled as his suit tried to detect anything in the near vicinity that matched both settings. Slowly he widened the search out and at last, about three-hundred feet away, a blip appeared. He nodded then shook Kheri awake.

"Hunh?", Kheri mumbled, then groaned and sat up rubbing his eyes. "Oh man, who knew that dirt could be so hard!" he complained.
"Tends to get that way when baked with blaster fire," Dale remarked. "I'll be right back, Faran's horse is still missing. See if you can find any food that didn't get ruined by the rain."
Kheri nodded and stood, then bent backwards and let out a sigh as his back popped loudly.

Most of the food was soggy but not ruined and Kheri pulled it out to dry off in the air which was beginning to warm now that the sun was fully up. Faran woke while he was doing so and looked around confused, then got up and stumbled over to the bushes. Kheri looked up as the unmistakable sounds of retching drifted to his ears then Faran stumbled back out of the bushes and plopped down on the ground looking miserable.
"Not feeling too good?" he asked and Faran shook his head.

"No," he mumbled, dropping his head on his knees. "My head hurts."

Kheri looked at him sympathetically. His aunt would have known what to do, and he wished momentarily that she was there, then got up and set to work building a fire. Dale walked back into camp a few minutes later, Faran's horse in tow. He was tying it to a sapling when Kheri walked up to him.

"Dale," Kheri said, his voice low. Dale glanced around at him.

"Yes?" he asked, wondering what was up.

"There's something wrong with Faran," Kheri responded. "He's been throwing up and he's over there by the fire acting like he's freezing."

"Wonderful," Dale replied, "since there's not a dry blanket in our possession, and we're miles from any kind of help. Why am I not surprised?"

He walked over to Faran and squatted down beside him then put a hand on his shoulder.

"Faran?" he said, his voice gentle. Faran glanced up at him, squinting in the sun.

"What's wrong?" Dale asked, letting his hand remain on Faran's shoulder. He keyed the sensors in his suit as he did so, and scanned over the readout on the display.

"I don't feel very good," Faran responded, his voice hoarse. He dropped his head back on his knees and shivered. The sensors were reporting an elevated temperature, though not to dangerous levels. Nothing else seemed to be wrong, at least at the moment and Dale nodded to himself, then stood. He walked over to the blankets and checked them, but they were all still soaking wet. Turning back to the display again, he ran a check on Faran's chemistry, then ordered his suit to synthesize something to combat the fever. A complex formula scrolled across the display and Dale read it over, then requested a search for plant life that would most closely match it. The display scrolled again but remained blank then the words Not Available flashed briefly in the air in front of him. He sighed, keyed the sensors off, and walked over to Kheri.

Kheri had dug out one of the pans and was in the middle of boiling water over the campfire. He looked up, then stood as Dale approached.

"He's got a fever," Dale said, gesturing in Faran's direction, "and I can't seem to locate anything around here that will combat it."

"He'll just have to sweat it out then," Kheri replied practically, "that's what my aunt always did with me."

Dale glanced over at Faran, and nodded.

"We'll stay here till it breaks," he decided. "I hope those blankets don't take too long to dry."

They wound up camping in the hollow for several days while Faran fought with the illness. The fever reached a peak on the third day just as night was falling and by the morning of the fourth day he was back to normal, though still a bit weak.

Dale had spent the time while Faran was ill wrestling with himself.

"I have to let Kheri go home," he had told himself several times over the preceding days, but each time something had come up. Now, with Faran over his fever and the ride deeper into the mountains at hand, he forced himself to stop procrastinating. After breakfast was finished, he walked over to the edge of the camp, then looked back at Kheri. The younger man was methodically repacking what hadn't been totally ruined of their equipment, absorbed in the task at hand.

"Kheri," he called softly, his voice carrying on the still, morning air. Kheri looked up, then stood and walked over. Dale looked at him for a moment, then spoke. "You've done what I wanted," Dale told him "and you're free to leave, go back home, if you wish."

Kheri blinked, surprised.

"I.." he faltered, then his face clouded. He looked down at his hands for a moment, glanced around the camp, then looked back at Dale again.

"Can I have some time to think about this?" he asked. Dale nodded.

"Certainly, but we're about to head into the mountains and the way back will become increasingly more dangerous each mile we travel." He studied Kheri's face for a moment then continued. "I'd like you to decide this morning, before I leave this campsite."

Kheri nodded. "Give me half an hour," he requested, "I need to think."

Dale nodded, then left him standing alone with his thoughts.

Chapter Nineteen

Kheri stood silently for several minutes, then left the camp and climbed up the slope of the hill. Standing on the top, he looked out over the countryside, then turned and stared up at the mountains in the near distance. The sun glanced off the snow on their tops, and the air sparkled around him. He stood, thinking about the last few weeks, then turned back and looked out in the direction that he knew his aunt's home lay. Memories of his life there, the town, the people he knew, drifted through his mind.
"That didn't happen to me," he thought, "that was someone else, a very long time ago."

He came to a sudden realization that he had no desire to go back to that life. Back to hiding in dark alleys, stealing to exist and being spit on by those who took any notice of him at all. He thought for a moment of his aunt, alone on her farm, then recalled Paw Tucker promising to look after her.
"She's fine," he told himself. "I can't live with her anyway, not for more than a day or two once in a while."
"You're a fool boy," his aunt's words to him when he moved out coming back to his mind. "You're a dreamer, always got your head in the clouds and your mind full of fantasies. You don't get those feet on the ground, you're gonna be walking off a cliff and you won't see the bottom till you hit it!"
He smiled to himself at the memory.
"Well I've got my feet on the ground," he told it, "and there's nothing wrong with dreaming."
He thought a moment longer then turned and walked back down to the camp, certain of what he was about to do.

Dale had finished re-packing their equipment and was currently sitting with Faran, scratching numbers in the dirt and explaining basic math concepts. Kheri waited silently, watching, until Dale noticed he was there.

"Here," Dale said, as he handed the stick he'd been using to Faran and stood, "try to figure that problem out. I'll be back in a minute."
He brushed his pants off then walked over to where Kheri was waiting. Faran chewed on the stick and frowned down at the numbers in the dirt, trying not to be interested in what Kheri was saying to Dale.

"I made a decision," Kheri said, "but I'm not real sure how to say this."
Dale nodded but waited silently for him to continue. An image of Paw Tucker rose in Kheri's mind and wagged it's finger at him.
"Don't beat around the bush boy," the image admonished, a memory of some years past,
"Jest say what's on yer mind. Ain't no call to go being fancy about it."
"Alright," he thought back at it, then looked up at Dale. "I don't want to go back there," he explained simply. "I don't want to go back to living like that. There's nobody other than my aunt that I really want to see again and I made a promise to you the other night not to let you face the Gorg alone." He struggled with words for a moment, then continued. "I don't know how to say this right, but I think I'd be dead by now if you hadn't dragged me out of that town and I owe you." Dale smiled slightly, but Kheri wasn't finished. "There's a thing knights do," he continued, "when they tell a king they'll fight for him to the death if they need to. I don't know the words, but that's how I feel."
"It's called a fealty oath," Faran put in, obviously listening closer than he should have been.
Dale glanced at him for a second, then turned back to Kheri.
"Yeah," Kheri agreed, "that's what I heard someone say one time. And that's what I'd like to do."
Dale took a mental step back, touched deeply and astounded. He stood silently, studying him.

"Do you have any idea how an oath like that to me would bind you?" he asked quietly after a few moments. Kheri nodded. "Remember Kheri," he cautioned, "I'm not from this place. The rules that govern me, that I am required to live by, might be very hard for you to deal with but you will be required to live by them as well. An oath like that will be something you can not break, or ignore, if you decide you didn't want to live up to it any more."

"I understand that," Kheri replied, "but that's still how I feel."

"You also understand," Dale went on, looking down into Kheri's eyes, "that such an oath is for life, not just for a year or two? Or until I leave and go back home? You realize that even though I'm stranded here now, I won't be forever. If I leave, and you're under an oath like that to me, you'll have to leave too...and go wherever it is I go?"

Kheri thought for a second then nodded.

"And you still wish to do this?" Dale asked, studying Kheri's face for any sign of reluctance.

"Yes," he replied, meeting Dale's gaze and holding his own steady.

Dale studied him silently, thinking. Such an oath went both ways, and he would be in far more trouble than Kheri if he accepted it then failed to keep his end of it.

"Am I really up to that sort of responsibility?" he wondered, searching Kheri's face. "He's nervous and he hasn't really got any idea what he's asking. He's sincere, that much is evident, but I hope he doesn't come to regret this when he learns just how binding this will be on both of us." He turned things over in his mind for a few more moments. "I could tell him no, but I doubt that would change his mind..." he took a deep mental breath, stilling his emotions. Kheri said nothing, waiting and Dale nodded finally. "Alright," he agreed. "The words don't really matter, it's the intent behind them. Are you absolutely certain you want to do this?"

"Yes," Kheri responded without hesitation.

"Then swear to me," Dale instructed, tensing himself for what he knew would happen, "in your own words."
"I swear," Kheri promised, "my loyalty to you until such time as you decide you no longer want me in your service."
"Accepted," Dale said softly.

Kheri jumped as the air between them brightened suddenly. The brightness thickened rapidly into a glowing rope of light which spun in the air between them for an instant, then wrapped quickly around them, tendrils shooting out of it's length, and enclosing them in a glowing net of brilliance. Dale closed his eyes, feeling the net settle down around him, as various unearthly forces went to work, binding them unbreakably together. As it settled into place he became aware of the tenseness running through Kheri and the unvoiced fear that was building in his mind. He reached over and placed a hand on Kheri's shoulder, steadying him.

Kheri stood frozen as the rope wrapped around him, and time seemed to stand still, unsure what was going on. As the tendrils shot out and the net settled into place he became intensely aware of Dale's presence and fought down a rising panic that he would be destroyed by whatever was happening. He bit his lower lip and forced himself not to move, then relaxed suddenly as Dale dropped a hand on his shoulder and a feeling of safety filled him. The net continued to brighten for a few seconds then constricted suddenly, and vanished. Kheri blinked, and looked confused.
"I can still feel it?" he whispered, looking down at himself and Dale nodded.
"Those energies are part of what not only now binds us together," he explained, "but also will ensure that you keep that oath, like it or not. You'll know where I am, even if I'm not in sight and I'll know where you are. It will also make it impossible for you to hide anything from me, so keep that in mind."

Kheri looked back up at him, then nodded, the confusion gone and replaced with a solid determination Dale hadn't noticed in him before.

"We can now also," Dale thought at him, "talk without words."
Kheri blinked.
"How?" he thought and Dale chuckled.
"Just like that," he thought back. "Just pretend you're talking to me but think instead of opening your mouth or making sounds."
Kheri nodded, unsure if he liked this development or not, then grinned. He felt happier than he had in a long time, with a real sense of purpose. The deep black hole in his life, which had opened when his parents had died and left him with no one but his aunt, was suddenly gone. If an army of Gorg had materialized right then and charged Dale, he would have waded into them without hesitation.
"Dale was right," he thought privately, "That's one oath I don't think I'll ever succeed in breaking, but I wouldn't have given it if I hadn't meant it."
"Now," Dale declared, relaxing finally and looking around the camp, "the morning's getting late and we need to get on the road."
He walked back over to Faran to check the math he'd given him to figure out, leaving Kheri to saddle the horses.

"Then what would you rather be called?" Dale ask.
"Aerline," she replied, "If you don't mind."

Chapter Twenty

They took their time getting back on the road, and finally left the place about noon. White clouds floated over head and the air was filled with the scent of pines borne down from the mountains above. Dale kept them to a more gentle pace that they'd used in the plains as the road through the hills was winding and sometimes quite steep. Kheri glanced around nervously as they rode, constantly turning to look behind them and staring into the shadows under the trees they were passing. Dale ignored him for the better part of an hour, then reined his horse to a stop and turned around in the saddle to face him.

"What, exactly, is it that you are looking for?" he asked. Kheri shrugged.

"I don't know," he responded, "but I keep seeing something, only it's not there when I look right at it."

Dale frowned slightly, then closed his eyes and slowly searched the area around them as far as his scan would reach. The trees were thick now, covering the hills with a dense forest, and hundreds of animals lived among them. Birds filled their branches, squirrels darted through their tops, while rabbits, moles and other small burrowing critters made their homes around their feet. A bear stood out starkly in his mind, but she was busy teaching her cub to fish in a small stream and wasn't aware of their presence not far away. He sat silent, allowing himself to become passively aware of everything going on around him in a complete circle fifty yards wide, waiting. Kheri shifted slightly in his saddle, and wondered why he was suddenly watching a skunk sniffing in a hollow log. Faran yawned, the heat of the sun making him feel drowsy, and stretched.

The air became hot, and the wind died to nothing. Even the buzzing of the flies faded away to silence and still Dale sat, unmoving, waiting, his thoughts passive and little more than a ripple to any passing observer with such a talent. Just as he was about to give up a flicker close to the edge of his scan range caught his attention. A cloaked and hooded figure materialized beneath the trees. It stood silently, watching them, then carefully began slipping closer to the edge of the road, an aura of magic flowing around it and making it difficult for Dale to detect its presence.

"I am beginning to hate wizards," he thought in Kheri's direction. Kheri blinked, then froze, seeing the figure clearly as Dale mentally showed him what the scan was picking up. He very slowly removed a special dart from the lining on his belt and readied it. The figure came closer, almost to the edge of the trees, but still hidden from normal sight in the shadows, and stood watching them. Kheri turned suddenly and tossed the dart in a lightning fast motion. The figure looked up, then fell limply to the ground and lay there motionless. Kheri swung down from his horse and dashed into the trees, instants ahead of Dale who hadn't realized what he intended to do. They reached the figure at the same moment, and Kheri quickly knelt down beside it, then rolled it over and pulled the dart out of it's neck. The hood fell back reveling a finely chiseled face framed with raven-dark hair. Dale looked down at the unconscious woman for a moment, then keyed his suit's medical scanner.
"What did you do?" he asked Kheri after his sensors informed him that her heart was indeed still beating.
"Stuck her with a sleep dart," came the response. "She'll be out for at least an hour."
Dale nodded then also knelt down beside her.
"That, he remarked, as he examined the cloak she had been wrapped in, "was quite a shot."
Kheri grinned then put the dart away.

Dale pulled the cloak apart, took it off of her, then handed it to Kheri.
"Take this," he directed, "and go put it in one of the empty saddle bags."

Kheri stood, took the cloak, and walked back to the horses. Dale keyed the sensors in his suit again, and studied the unconscious person laying on the ground before him. Now that the cloak was gone, the aura of magic that had made it hard to detect her was also gone and the display scrolled information almost faster than he could read it. He flipped it off after a moment, then methodically set about de-fanging her.
"Kheri," he thought as he worked, "bring me back an empty sack please. A small one."
Kheri jumped, not yet used to suddenly hearing words in his head, then retrieved an empty sack and took it to Dale.

The woman was wearing a large number of magical artifacts and Dale stripped her of them one item at a time. Kheri watched fascinated as rings, bracelets, necklaces, earrings and other types of jewelry were dropped into the bag. Dale stopped finally, turned his sensors back on, then sighed and pulled her clothes off. Kheri gasped and turned brilliant red. Dale ignored him and set about removing various objects that had been attached to her skin in less than public places, dropping them into the bag as well, then checked the suit's sensors again. Nothing registered this time, either on her body or the clothing she had been wearing and Dale nodded in grim satisfaction, then flipped the sensors back off and re-dressed her clumsily.
"She's not going to be happy about leaves down her back," he remarked as he laid her back down on the ground, "but I have no desire to become the target of anything she had at her disposal."

A hum suddenly began to issue from the bag that Kheri was holding, growing rapidly louder and rising up the scale in pitch. He turned and threw the bag down the road with as much force as he could manage, then ducked. The bag hit the ground, and green flames suddenly spouted from it's mouth, increasing to a fountain fifteen feet high. Faran dismounted rapidly as the fountain began, grabbed the three horses by their reins and led them quickly into

the trees next to where Dale stood. With a loud chiming sound, the fountain exploded into a brilliant light and vanished. Standing where the bag had been was a tall, black, figure. It's eyes flamed red as it looked around, its arms crossed over its massive chest. It looked directly at Dale, then inclined it's head slightly.
"Oh great," Dale thought to himself, "that's trouble with a capital T."
"Stay here, both of you," he commanded, then strode out of the trees.

He walked over to the figure which towered almost seven feet above him and looked up.
"Fancy meeting you here," he remarked and the figure grinned, sharp teeth flashing in the sunlight. "Lose another bet?"
"No," came the thunderous reply, and Dale winced, "let my guard down."
"Tone it down will you," Dale requested, rubbing his right ear. The figure grinned broader, then looked around.
"What manner of place is this?" it asked, its voice still booming.
"Class one, blue coded planet," Dale responded, "in the Gamma quadrant."
"Class one..." the figure replied, as if the words were highly distasteful, "oh how terribly thrilling."
"Yeah well, the Gorg are making it interesting," Dale responded dryly, looking up and shading his eyes, "and I told you to tone it down."
"Fine!!", came the booming reply, then the figure snapped it's fingers and a dark cloud swirled around it. Blue and green lighting flashed out of the cloud which shrank, then dissipated, leaving a normal looking man of slightly less than Dale's six foot, six inch height, standing in the road before him. He was dressed in a jump suit nearly identical to the one Dale wore and he crooked the corner of his mouth up into a lopsided grin then ran a hand through his short, auburn hair.

"I was out of energy anyway," he commented, straightening his sleeve slightly, then flicking a bit of imaginary dust off his chest. "So now what?" He looked back up at Dale, mischief sparkling in his green eyes, and grinned.
"So start by telling me," Dale began, then changed his mind. "Belay that, you can tell me after we finish something. Come on."
He turned and walked back toward where Kheri and Faran stood, watching in fascination. The other man shrugged, then followed after.

The woman was still unconscious and the new arrival looked at her in disgust.
"You're letting her live?" he asked and Dale looked at him askance.
"Is there a reason I shouldn't?" he asked. The man shrugged.
"I wouldn't," he replied, "that's all."
"Is it her fault you got yourself enslaved here?" Dale asked.
"Who says I got enslaved?" The newcomer asked, looking at Dale sideways.
"The fact that you were stuck in that ring leads me to think that," Dale answered, crossing his arms as he regarded the stranger. "Also, the fact that I now apparently have total control over your actions if I want lends a fair amount of weight to that conclusion."
"Yes, well..." the other looked embarrassed and quickly changed the subject. "So, what are you going to do with her?" he asked.
"I haven't decided," Dale replied, "beyond neutralizing any attack she might have been planning on."
"She wasn't going to attack you," the other remarked, "she's just an apprentice wizard."
"Then why has she been following us?" Dale asked.
"Curiosity maybe," came the reply, "or maybe she thought you could help her."
"Great," Dale grumbled, "now I get to rescue damsels in distress."
The other man grinned at him.

"Something, as I recall, you do quiet well," he remarked and Dale glared at him.
"Quiet you," he commanded, trying to ignore the fascinated interest both Kheri and Faran were displaying, "make yourself useful and help get a fire going."
He was rewarded with another grin, then the man made an elaborate bow.
"At once oh high and mighty master," he responded, then ducked quickly out of Dale's reach and strode into the trees.
"Who," Kheri asked, watching him go, "is that?"
"I'll tell you later," Dale replied, "just go get firewood. We're going to be stuck here until your sleep dart wears off."
Kheri glanced down at the woman then walked off into the trees as well.

Faran looked after him, looked at the horses, thought for a moment, then shrugged and began unsaddling them.
"Well," he remarked out loud, "at least we're not being rained on."
Dale sighed, then knelt down on the ground and began clearing a place for the fire.
"No," he agreed as he worked, "we're not being rained on. But we're also not likely to get any farther today."
Faran nodded, feeling slightly left out of the events that had just transpired. He tethered the horses to a sturdy bush close by then sat down on the ground and started picking at the grass.
"What's wrong?" Dale asked, looking over at him.
"I dunno," Faran replied, "just feeling kinda lost I guess."
Dale looked at him for a moment, then stood up and walked over to where he was sitting.
"Here," he said, sitting down next to him and picking up a stick, "let's see if you can solve this problem."

Kheri was burning with curiosity about the stranger, who obviously was someone that Dale knew well. He picked up a few sticks, then

spotted him and walked over. The man had already collected quite a few larger pieces of wood, but he stopped when Kheri walked up, then cocked his head slightly and looked at him.
"You planning on starting a fire with that?" he asked, indicating the few small twigs
Kheri was holding. Kheri grinned and shook his head.
"No, just thought I'd offer to help carry what you've got," he replied.
"Thanks, but I'm fine," the stranger replied. He shifted his hold on the wood slightly, then grinned at Kheri, "and I'm not going to answer your questions right now, so you'll just have to wait a while longer."
Kheri made a face at him and he chuckled.
"It's written all over your face kid," he explained, "but you'll just have to wait. See you back at camp."
He walked past Kheri, and headed back toward the road. Kheri grumbled to himself, then concentrated on collecting wood.

The sleep dart finally wore off about three hours later, and the recipient of it sat up groggily, rubbing her head. She blinked, looked around, then realized that something had gone terribly wrong. Her cloak had vanished, and she felt nearly naked. It took her a few more seconds to realize that every magical object she had possessed was also gone, even those which had been attached to very private places. She looked around the area where she'd been sleeping, then wet her lips nervously.
"Well," Dale commented as she moved, "look who's decided to wake up and join us."

A fire was burning brightly not too far away, and she eyed it, wondering if she was close enough to grab one of the flaming branches to use as a weapon.
"Don't try it," Dale interrupted her thoughts, "you'd die before you got more than two inches."

She looked at him then glanced up and realized that Kheri was watching her casually with a dagger in his hand, poised to throw. She relaxed back down onto the ground then looked around.

"Well," she said after a moment, "I guess you have a few questions for me?"

"Perhaps," Dale agreed, watching her. "I am a tad curious why you've been following me. How about you start by explaining that."

She licked her lips again and Dale interrupted before she could reply.

"I must caution you," he warned, "that if you lie, I'll know. And if you lie, I'll revise my opinion about how long we should allow you to live."

She blinked again and stared at him.

"So I suggest," he finished calmly, "that you carefully consider your words before you speak them, and don't leave out any important details."

She looked at him incredulously for a long moment then nodded, "I'll keep that in mind," she replied. "Before I tell you though, I need to ask...", she glanced around again, "what happened to all my things?"

"Most of them were destroyed," Dale explained simply, "the cloak I have put away."

"And who," she asked, looking at him as she spoke, "was the thief?"

"If you mean, who was it that stripped you, and removed them," Dale clarified for her, looking back at her with an icy stare, "I did." His voice was still calm, but there was an edge to it now and the tone was decidedly less than friendly.

"I see," she replied, licking her lips again, "well then, I guess that settles that."

"Your explanation," Dale prompted, and she nodded, feeling like she had awoken in a den of wild cats.

"Yes," she agreed, "let's see...I noticed you in the inn several weeks back, and I wondered about him." She gestured in Faran's direction. "I was intrigued and wondered what reason the Baron's youngest son could have for being there, with no guards in sight. Being the curious type, I resolved to find out. I happened by chance to be outside the inn when you slipped out the kitchen door and when I watched you defeat Magnus and Boor, I quit being curious about the Baron's son and wanted to know more about who you were. You fascinated me, and I decided to find out where you were going. I also thought that if I were to observe you, perhaps I could learn some of your secrets."
"And have you?" Dale asked, interrupting her explanation.
"No," she replied, shaking her head, "I haven't the faintest idea how you do all the amazing things I've seen."
He nodded and gestured for her to continue.
"Well then," she went on, "I knew that if I were to follow you on horse, you'd know and I decided to watch from a distance. So I used magic to transport ahead of you on the road, then consulted a seeing stone. When you passed me and got too far ahead, I used magic to transport again. I must admit," she stated contritely, "I felt kind of sorry for you in that hailstorm, but you must understand I didn't want you to know I was watching, so there really was nothing I could do. You survived it anyway."
Dale frowned slightly.
"And if someone had been killed in that, what then?" he asked but she shook her head.
"No one was hurt." she pointed out, "but had things been different, perhaps the ice larger, I am not sure what I would have done. I probably would have tried to help at least a little bit."
Dale said nothing but the feeling of unfriendliness grew on her and she looked around like a cornered rabbit, then cleared her throat.
"Any way," she continued, "to go on, I realized that there had to be more to you than I was seeing, and I was working up my

courage to approach you. It seems however," she finished, "that there is no need to do that now."
Dale read over the results on the display then nodded.
"Alright," he said as he turned it off, "it appears you're telling the truth. Kheri, you'll have to practice on some other target."
Kheri grunted, but put the dagger away and sat down on the ground next to the fire.

"Thank you," she told him, relaxing slightly. "May I ask what you intend to do now?"
"I'm still making that decision," Dale replied, "I'm not through with the questions either."
"Oh," she said, and waited for him to continue.
"Why were you in the Inn to start with?" he asked.
"I had been traveling," she responded, "and had stopped there for the night."
"And just like that you changed all your travel plans," Dale asked, "and decided to follow me?"
"Well," she explained, "it's not like I had any plans to change. I was just wandering really."
"Oh?" Dale said, "alone?"
"Yes," she agreed, with a nod of her head, "alone."
"Yeah," the newest addition to the group interjected, "that's what happens when you're the worst wizard in the college. They kick you out and no one wants anything to do with you any more."
"I was NOT the worst wizard," she snapped, looking offended.
"That is the other question I have for you," Dale interrupted. "You had a ring. Gold, with a green stone in it. Rather large."
"Yes," she agreed, "it was very expensive too. It contained a demon, and they're not easy to capture. He was the most annoying thing, but he was useful so I kept it around."
"A demon?" Dale asked, raising both eyebrows.
"Yes," she replied, "the sorcerer that crafted it for me had a horrible fight after he summoned him. Nearly lost his life. His tower was a shambles."

"Really?" Dale asked.
"Yes," she responded, nodding her head emphatically. "He charged me double because of all the trouble it gave him. It really made a terrible mess of his tower, blew the roof right off of it and the door too."
"Shoulda offered him a drink," Dale commented sarcastically and she looked at him curiously.
"A drink? Demons don't drink", she stated.
"Oh? and how many have you known on a personal basis?" Dale asked.
She looked at him and shook her head.
"Well none of course," she replied. "You don't make friends with demons, you just summon them to do your bidding. That WAS my major in college you know...Demonology..I know quite a bit about them."
"Yeah and you flunked it," came a comment from someone behind Dale. She glanced up quickly and looked at the stranger.

"And just how would you know that?" she demanded.
He grinned, then stepped away from the tree, walked over to her and squatted down beside her. She pulled back slightly, a rather worried look on her face.
"Because," he explained, his face mere inches from hers, "I happen to be that Demon. Only you don't control me any more Weezee."
She blanched and looked about ready to faint.
"Jarl," Dale said quietly, "was that really necessary?"
"Probably not," Jarl replied, getting back to his feet, "but it sure felt good. She's right though," he grinned, stepping back slightly, "I did make rather a mess of that old geezers tower. I'd have gotten away too, but he zapped me with something and I couldn't think straight for a while."
"And what were you doing that got you into this mess in the first place?" Dale asked.
Jarl looked at him, and scratched the back of his neck.

"Ummm," he hedged, looking rather embarrassed, "random porting. Landed in the middle of his pentagram by mistake."
"Serves you right then," Dale declared, looking over at him. "I warned you before about random teleports and what could happen."
"I was bored!" he protested.
"And now you're stuck!" Dale pointed out. "And don't ask me to undo the enchantment because I have no idea how."

"Oh you can't undo it," the woman explained, watching the exchange between them with a bemused expression on her face. "Part of the extras I paid so much for was a special spell that guaranteed the enchantment couldn't be broken. You'll have to take the ring back to Sourbane and have him undo it."
"I'm afraid that's not possible," Dale stated and she glanced back over at him.
"It is a bit of a ride," she agreed, "but I'm sure he'd be willing to undo the spells, for the right price of course."
"That's not the problem," Dale explained, then looked back at Jarl who now appeared quite uncomfortable. "The ring was destroyed. Evidently there was a trigger on something you were wearing. It went off in a rather impressive display and everything that was in the bag with it, which was everything but your cloak, was removed from existence."
"Oh dear," she exclaimed, "that's terrible!"
"Yeah," Jarl groused, "tell me about it."
"Well," she replied, "at least you're free of the spell now."
"I'm not free of the spell," he complained, "that's the problem."
"When I pulled that ring off of you," Dale explained, "evidently ownership shifted from you to me. When the ring was destroyed, he was not and the spell is still very much in force."
"Well..." she said, then smiled slightly, "I'm not sure what to tell you. I don't know if Sourbane can undo it without the ring. But I must say," she commented to Jarl, "after all the annoying things

you've said to me, the way you've embarrassed me terribly a number of times, I'm rather enjoying this."

Jarl made a face in her direction, then leaned back against a tree, crossed his arms and looked up into it's branches, pretending to ignore her. Dale grinned, watching his reaction.
"Do you know," she remarked, looked back at Dale as she talked, "that he had the most annoying habit of suddenly blurting out horrible comments in the middle of class?" she frowned over at Jarl who was studying something above his head. "I don't think there's one professor on that campus who he hasn't insulted in some way."
"They deserved it," Jarl told the tree above him. "Bunch of idiots!"
"Jarl," Dale admonished him, "idiocy is it's own reward, there was no need for you to insult them."
"Yeah, I know," Jarl commented, looking back at Dale. "but you should have heard some of the things they were teaching!"
"Regardless," Dale replied, then turned his attention back to the woman. "Where's Sourbane at?" he asked.
"His tower, or what is left of it, is located just outside of Villenspell," she explained.
"Which is where we were headed anyway," Dale said. "Good." He looked back over at Jarl, then stood. "What condition are your powers in?" he asked and Jarl frowned.
"Oh, they're mostly all there, I just can't use them at will," he replied, "and my teleport's limited to a five mile range."
"See if you can find a couple wild horses then," Dale requested, "and bring them here."
Jarl nodded once, vanishing from sight, and Dale turned back to the woman.

"Back to you and following me," he went on and she nodded. "What I can do, you can not learn. It's not magical in nature. However I might be able to help you improve the skills you currently have.

You can come with us if you want and I'll see what I can do. However," he cautioned, looking at her seriously, "if you come, be aware that I am the target of a rather nasty group of creatures called the Gorg. You might have seen a few of them invade our camp the other night. When they show up, I can't guarantee you'll be protected."
"Yes," she replied, "I saw them. They didn't look very impressive."
"Looks are deceiving," he said. "They're far more impressive than you might guess."
"Well still," she responded, "when compared to several other things I've encountered, they didn't look all that powerful. But I'll stay out of their way if they show up again."
"Alright then you can come with us, providing Jarl finds those horses and we can tame them," Dale replied, "but if you do, you'll pull your own weight around the camp."
"I always do," she responded, "and I can tame the horses, if he finds any. The one thing I actually can do well is control animals. Just not very many at one time and not if they're much bigger than a horse."
"Very well," Dale agreed. "What was it that he called you?"
She wrinkled her nose in disgust.
"A name they called me at school," she responded. "Something I'd prefer to forget."
"Then what would you rather be called?" Dale asked.
"Aerline," she replied, "if you don't mind."
Dale nodded.
"Aerline it is," he agreed then stood and brushed his pants off.

"It's now mid-afternoon. By the time Jarl gets back here," he stated, looking around at the others, "it will probably be dark... knowing him. We'll just plan on camping here for tonight. Kheri, there's a stream not too far off that way," he gestured off into the forest. "Would you and Faran please go fill up all the water bags and pots."

Kheri nodded and stood.
"We're on it," he replied, dragging Faran to his feet. They collected the water bags, dug the pots out of the saddlebags, and headed off into the trees. Dale pulled the cloak back out of the saddlebag Kheri had stuck it in and handed it to Aerline.
"Here," he told her. "You can have this back."
"Thank you," she responded, as she took the cloak from him and put it around her shoulders.
"That wasn't," she commented as she fastened it, "a very gentlemanly thing to do, you know, stripping me while I was asleep."
"If you'd acted more like a lady," Dale responded, "instead of an enemy, I wouldn't have felt the need to do so."
She stood up, and then shook the leaves out of her shirt.
"Those things also cost me a considerable sum," she said as she finished. "I don't suppose you're going to pay me for them."
"It is hardly my fault that they were destroyed," Dale said, "but yes, I will attempt to pay you for their loss. As much as I can at least. I haven't exactly got any way of making money at the moment."
"Well," she replied, "that certainly wasn't what I expected you to say. Don't worry about it." She brushed the leaves out of her hair. "Most of them were priceless and couldn't be replaced if you did pay for them. I'll just have to do without. At least for now. Perhaps when we reach Villenspell I can pick up a few other things."

Dale picked up one of the saddlebags and began pulling out packets of dried food.
"Do you honestly need that much hardware?" he asked as he stacked the packets on the ground.
"If I'm alone?" she replied, "Yes. I really don't have much ability without them. It makes things easier and much safer."
"What all can you do?" Dale asked, sniffing at one of the packets. He made a face and opened it then poured its contents out onto the ground.

"Not much," she responded, sitting back down on the ground. "I can tame animals as I said, as long as they're not real big or there aren't too many of them all at once. I can talk to some kinds, and understand what they're saying. And I can usually get them to do what I want. It depends on the type of animal really, how well that works."

Dale glanced at her curiously but didn't interrupt.

"Dogs I never have a problem with," she explained, "but weasels? They're impossible. Annoying little things with minds that never pay attention to anything for more than thirty seconds. Well unless they're hungry of course. Horses too," she continued, "I usually don't have a problem with, except for the ones that already have an owner. Then, if they don't like their owner they'll do what I ask, but I can never order them like I can a dog. The wild ones are different, don't ask me why."

"What about large, black, hairy beasts that stand about four feet high, have short wings and leave tracks like cats," Dale asked, remembering the creatures that had almost killed Kheri back at the inn. She stared at him in horror.

"Those aren't animals!" she exclaimed. "They're minor demons. Where did you see them?"

"Back at the inn. Late at night after the fight with those two fools."

She shuddered and shook her head.

"Those must have belonged to Magnus", she said, "and after you killed him they were set loose. I hope they aren't following you seeking revenge."

"If they are," he responded, "they haven't shown up." he thought back to how easily they'd fallen to the stun ray and shook his head.

"Minor demons," he thought. "Everything not from this world is a demon to her. I wonder where they actually come from."

Kheri and Faran returned a few moments later, lugging the full containers. They handed the pots to Dale then set the bags by the saddles, out of the way. The sun was dropping down toward the horizon now, and the shadows were lengthening as night drew near. The wind had picked back up slightly and a comforting breeze blew through the trees. Dale had found several more packets of food that hadn't actually been watertight enough to survive the rainstorm a few days before and had discarded them, then started supper. They ate as the shadows deepened and night arrived to the many- voiced chorus of crickets and other creeping things. Jarl still hadn't reappeared and Dale was becoming concerned. He stood up and walked to the edge of the firelight, looking out into the forest, thinking.

"He's either lost," he thought, "unable to find any horses, or he found an inn and is taking a detour."

He closed his eyes, feeling for the spell that currently had Jarl under his power. It was easy to locate, standing out in his mind like a beacon of light. He reached for it, then yanked mentally. There was a loud 'BANG' and Jarl appeared. He looked startled then realized where he was.

"No horses to be found?" Dale queried.

"Not close," Jarl replied. "I've been all over these hills."

"So why didn't you come back and let me know?" Dale asked.

"Well," Jarl answered, looking frustrated. "You didn't say I could. You said, find a couple wild horses and bring them here."

"I said, see if you can find a couple wild horses and bring them here," Dale corrected him.

"And the spell interpreted that," Jarl argued, "as a requirement to keep looking till I found some. You have to be careful how you phrase things," he explained. "It does it's own interpretations and I can't fight it, I've tried."

"Wonderful," Dale remarked dryly. "This could be either very annoying or fairly funny."

"I don't find it the least bit funny," Jarl groused. "I doubt you'd find it funny either if our positions were reversed."
"Maybe I'll just leave you under that spell," Dale said calmly, watching him. "This might be just the lesson you've needed for a long time."
"You wouldn't!" Jarl protested.
"I just might," Dale warned, "you could use the discipline."
Jarl crossed his arms tightly, an angry expression playing across his face.

"It's not like you're back in the Altherian slave pens again," Dale pointed out. "Or the mines. Or stuck on a prison planet. Or.." Jarl looked at him unhappily. "I'm getting tired of rescuing you when you do something stupid," Dale continued, crossing his own arms. "Maybe this'll fix that little problem. And stop glaring at me," he continued as Jarl's expression darkened. "You have only yourself to blame for the mess you're in, as usual."
Jarl looked at Dale silently for a moment then the glare vanished from his face.

"Now," Dale told him, "come with me."
He turned and walked over to the road. Jarl uncrossed his arms and followed, ignoring the others who were sitting around the campfire watching them.
"We need two more horses," Dale explained as Jarl joined him in the middle of the road. "Unless you want to walk."
"Not particularly," he replied, "but do I have to do this tonight?"
"I'd appreciate it if you would," Dale responded. "I'd really like to be able to get going at first light. I wasn't kidding about the Gorg."
"Yeah, alright," Jarl agreed reluctantly. "Not like I have any choice anyway, but do me a favor would you?"
"Depends on what it is," Dale told him.
"Don't go overboard with the orders ok?" Jarl requested. "I'm really getting tired of this."

Dale regarded him silently for a moment.
"We'll see," Dale decided. "That'll depend on how irresponsible you act." Jarl said nothing, but nodded his head in reluctant acceptance. "And just to close any loopholes," Dale continued, looking at him firmly. "You know good and well what I don't consider acceptable behavior, correct?"
Jarl took a deep breath, then nodded.
"Yeah, I do," he replied, a note of resignation in his voice.
"Then if you know I wouldn't approve of something," Dale instructed, "from now until that spell is broken, don't do it."
Jarl winced briefly, then nodded.
"Understood," he responded, "but that sure takes the fun out of a lot of things."
"Yeah?" Dale asked sarcastically. "That fun, as you put it, is what gets you into trouble."
"I get out of it," Jarl countered, a hint of defiance in his voice.
"Oh?" Dale challenged, "And just who is it that usually has to get you out if it?"
"Ummm..." Jarl hedged, looking away uncomfortably.
"Answer me," Dale demanded, unwilling to let him off the hook.
"You," Jarl admitted without looking back at him.
"Yes," Dale agreed. "Me. Every single time."

Jarl turned back and looked at him, a slightly sour expression on his face.
"I'll stay out of trouble," he stated. "You can stop the lecture."
"I wasn't lecturing," Dale informed him. "I was pointing out facts. Right now," he continued, "I'm going to be responsible for whatever problems you cause, because that spell basically makes you my property. And I do not want to have to clean up after you yet again. I will if I have to but I'm going to be real unhappy with you if I'm forced to."
Jarl said nothing, a dour expression written on his face.
"In fact," Dale continued thoughtfully, "I seem to remember Sssversth warning you the last time, that if you got in trouble

again and I had to get you out of it, you might wind up under my control permanently anyway. Shall we see if he's available to pass judgment on this situation?"

Jarl winced and shook his head quickly.

"No," he replied. "I'd rather not."

"Then how about you straightening up," Dale suggested. "Or I WILL call him and let him decide your fate."

Jarl sighed, then nodded.

"Alright," he agreed, giving in. "I'll behave. What do you want me to do?"

Dale gestured down the road.

"Follow this road in that direction until the hills come to an end," Dale explained. "You'll find that it's crossing a very wide, grass covered plain at that point. There are a number of herds of wild horses which roam that plain, we passed several on our way here. Find the closest herd and choose two horses out of it that are about the same size as those," he continued, gesturing at their horses, "and bring them back here. Aerline can tame them, so don't waste time trying, just find them and get back."

Jarl nodded but Dale stopped him before he could vanish.

"Don't spend all night on this," he clarified, "the moon comes up around two am right now. If you haven't got them by moonrise, just come back without them."

"Thank you," Jarl replied gratefully. "Anything else?"

"Not currently," Dale decided. "Come back if you get into danger, if the moon rises and you haven't gotten two horses or the minute you do get both of them."

Jarl nodded again and was gone.

Chapter Twenty-One

The night was getting late and the moon had just begun to rise when Jarl rematerialized just outside of camp. With him were two horses who appeared to be frozen in the act of grazing. He looked around, then left the horses standing like statues in the middle of the road and walked over to where the campfire had burned down to coals. Sinking down onto the ground beside it, he wrapped his arms tiredly around his knees, dropped his head onto them and let out a sigh of relief. He sat there next to the fire, staring into what was left of it, trying to stay awake. He had been forced to use nearly all of his skills to find the herd and by that time he was running low on energy. Suspending the horses in time stop then returning with them had exhausted him. He shook his head, blinking sleep away, and glanced over at Dale, willing him to wake up.

Dale yawned slightly after a moment, then sat up rubbing sleep out of his eyes.
"You get them?" he asked when he saw Jarl on the other side of the fire.
Jarl nodded tiredly.
"Yes. They're in stasis," he, gestured toward the road. "Over there."
He blinked, forcing sleep away again. Dale nodded and stood.
"Get some sleep," he suggested, "morning'll be here soon."
"I can't," Jarl responded, his words barely audible. "If I do, the time stop will end and they'll take off."
"Give me a few minutes then," Dale requested, and bent down to shake Aerline awake.
She blinked, and looked up at Dale confused, then sat up groggily.
"It's not morning," she remarked, looking around.
"No," Dale replied, "but Jarl's back and I need you to tame the horses he brought."

"Oh." She wiped sleep from her eyes and got to her feet. "Where are they?"
Jarl climbed tiredly to his feet and motioned with his head. "Over here." He turned then stumbled back to the road.

The moon was shinning full on the two horses, turning their coats to silver and giving them the appearance of some finely crafted metalwork. Aerline walked up to them curiously, and touched one on the neck.
"What's wrong with them?" she asked, stepping back.
"He's got them frozen," Dale explained.
"Oh," she answered. "I've never seen a freeze spell do this before."
"It's not..", Jarl began but Dale motioned him to silence.
"Well," Aerline continued, ignoring Jarl's attempted explanation. "Unfreeze them so I can talk to them." Jarl nodded, then released the closest of the two.

It lifted it's head and snorted in surprise, then paused and looked at Aerline. She was mumbling softly, spreading her hands apart and focused entirely on the horse. It snorted again, and pawed the ground, then twitched an ear. She moved her hands slightly, and it twitched the other ear, then trotted over to the camp and stood, eyeing the other horses.
"He's willing to come along," she explained. "But he won't let anyone put a saddle on him. Or a bridle."
"That's going to make it real comfortable," Dale observed. "Think he'll at least allow a blanket?"
"I'll ask him, but can I talk to this other one please?" Aerline requested, turning her attention to the other horse. Jarl nodded and released it, then staggered sideways into Dale.
"Sorry," he whispered as Dale steadied him, "I am about to pass out."
"Not just yet," Dale replied, helping him stand back up. "Let's get back to the fire first."

Jarl struggled to remain on his feet as Dale helped him back to camp, then sank down onto the ground next to the fire.
"Go to sleep," Dale told him quietly and Jarl crumpled, asleep before his head touched the ground.
Aerline walked back into camp a few moments later followed by the second horse. She led it over to the others, and spent several minutes talking to all of them then nodded in satisfaction.
"Well," she declared happily, "they're all friends now, and he's agreed to allow a blanket. The second one said you could use a saddle if you wanted but no bridle either."
"Thank you," Dale replied with a smile. "That will make things much easier."

Morning burst through the trees in a glorious display of golden sparkles as the slanting sun turn specks of dust floating through the air into bits of light. Dale sat up stiffly as his suit woke him and yawned, then stretched and looked around the camp. Everyone else was sound asleep, each wrapped in their own land of dreaming. He sat there for a bit, thinking about what had happened in such a short time and running back over the entire journey in his mind. Kheri woke suddenly, and sat up as well.
"Morning Kheri," Dale thought softly. Kheri nodded, yawning as he did so.
"Morning," he thought back as he rubbed his eyes. "Man this camp is getting crowded."

Dale nodded slightly as he looked around at the number of bodies still stretched out on the ground.
"Yes," he agreed silently. "Hopefully we won't collect any more."
Kheri grinned then got to his feet and stepped out of sight to tend to more personal business.
Dale reached over and nudged Faran awake.

"Goway," Faran grumbled, curling up into a tight ball. Dale shook him harder and Faran kicked empty air then sat up furious. He blinked and looked around, then made a face.
"Why do we have to get up just cause the suns up?" he grumbled.
"Because otherwise we wind up only riding for an hour or two," Dale explained.
Faran climbed to his feet unhappily, and disappeared into the trees for his own private early morning ritual. It took nearly an hour to get everyone up, breakfast over and all the horses sorted out that morning. The two extra saddle blankets that the innkeeper had given Dale now came in handy and after a bit of difficulty they finally got back on the road.

Jarl sat on his horse silently, plodding along at the back of the group. His head was pounding worse than if he'd been on a three-week binge. Every inch of his body protested the fact he'd had to sleep on bare ground and he was grumpy. "This is so not fair!" he complained to himself and rubbed the back of his neck. "It wasn't my fault that stupid old geezer thought I was his demon. I shouldn't have to be stuck here like this!" His mood was the darkest shade of black and he raged silently against the entire universe for tricking him into his current situation.

Dale ignored him for nearly half an hour, then suddenly reined his horse to a stop as his temper got the better of him. The entire group came to a stand still and Jarl realized guiltily that Dale had turned around in his saddle and was looking straight at him. He sat up self-consciously and tried to look innocent. Dale dismounted after a moment, motioning for Jarl to do the same, and stalked into the trees on the other the side of the road. Jarl slid off the horse and handed its reins to Kheri then followed him into the forest. They walked out of earshot of the others then Dale stopped and spun around to face him.

"Exactly what is your problem this morning?" he demanded, irritation filling his voice.
"Just in a bad mood," Jarl responded, not meeting Dale's eyes.
"That mood going to last all day?" Dale asked darkly and Jarl looked up, narrowing his eyes.
"How should I know?" he shot back, glaring furiously at Dale. "My head hurts, my body aches, I feel like I'm hung over only I didn't have the fun of getting there first!"
"And blaming everything on me is going to fix this how?" Dale snapped, his own mood deteriorating rapidly.
"I'm not blaming everything on you!" Jarl fumed, clenching his fists.
"No, just most of it," Dale shot back angrily, his eyes flashing. "I've been listening to you feeling sorry for yourself for the last twenty minutes and I'm just about fed up!"

The two of them faced off and glared at each other fiercely, energy crackling through the space between them. The air hummed dangerously as their anger mounted and the ground began to vibrate beneath their feet. The smell of smoke arose around them as small fires ignited in the leaves on the ground and several branches cracked as they gave way to the mounting pressure. With a loud crash, an older and not well rooted tree fell over not far away, sending shock waves echoing through the forest. A high pitched whining started, centered slightly above their heads, and the air began to swirl dangerously as reality threatened to come apart.

The escalating battle ended suddenly as a blinding flash of brilliant white light occurred between them. They winced, flinging their arms up in unison to shield themselves. Dale rubbed his eyes, trying to force the after image to fade. Jarl blinked then tried squinting through one slightly opened eye. When they both could finally see again several long moments later, the image of a large creature dressed in billowing red robes was floating in the air,

regarding them both. Blue and green lighting crackled around it and it hissed slightly, its voice filling their minds.
"Enough!" it commanded, "This disturbance ceases now!"

Jarl paled and quickly stepped back, placing Dale between himself and the glowing image floating in the air. Dale took a deep breath and relaxed.
"Sssversth," he said, and bowed slightly. "My apologies for disturbing you."
"This was not to happen again!" the words floated through their minds as air around the image shimmered. "Too much of a problem you have become Jarl! I will stand no more!"
"No!" Jarl pleaded in terror as blue crackling lines of force shot out of the image and encased him. He screamed and struggled wildly against them as his form began to fade.
"Wait!" Dale exclaimed. "Please!"
The image turned and regarded him.
"He has passed the limits," it declared, "and has once again caused me problems not soon to be repaired. I will waste no more time on his existence!"
"Then let me have him and I'll keep him in line," Dale responded quickly. "Please."

Jarl was transparent now and still struggling frantically with the energies that surrounded him, terror written on his face. The image appeared to consider for a moment.
"This only will I allow," it decided. "Nonexistence he deserves and no more use have I for him, but your request I will grant. However," it warned, and Dale jumped slightly as he felt a link come into existence between Jarl and himself. "YOU will answer for his errors as of now! Keep him under control or pay the price!"
The crackling ceased suddenly and Jarl became fully solid again. He fell to his hands and knees on the ground, panting heavily. Dale glanced down at him then looked back up at the image.

"You!" it commanded sharply and Jarl jerked his head up to face it fearfully, shaking. "Your life is his. Give him no reasons further to be angry with you or you cease to exist!!"
Jarl shook his head quickly.
"I won't," he gasped. "I won't...ever."
The image vanished in the same brilliant flash that had announced it's arrival.
Dale took a deep breath then sighed in relief and looked down at Jarl, still on his hands and knees on the ground.
"Can you stand?" he asked reaching a hand down to him. Jarl shivered, then grasped his hand and stood shakily.
"I think so," he replied, his demeanor changed dramatically. He glanced back at where the image had hung in the air and shuddered.

"Thank you," he said, greatly subdued, turning back to Dale.
"You're welcome," Dale replied, mentally touching the link that had been forged between them. "However I suggest you remember his warning this time." Jarl flinched as Dale made him aware of the link, then nodded still shaking.
"I heard," he acknowledged, trying to calm down. "Very clearly." He shuddered again and closed his eyes. "I could feel myself being erased," he whispered after a minute, his voice trembling. "Slowly, bit by bit." He shook his head and swallowed hard, then took a deep breath and looked at Dale. "I don't ever want to feel that again."
"I don't blame you," Dale responded, "I wouldn't either."
Jarl shivered again then dropped his eyes.
"Thank you for interceding," he told the ground. "I owe you a debt I can't ever repay."
Dale smiled slightly.
"Just see if you can't curb some of that temper," Dale requested. "Alright?"
Jarl nodded, looking back up at him, his face serious.

"I'll do the best I can," he promised. "I'm sorry for this morning."
"Apology accepted," Dale told him. "Now, shall we try to see how much farther down the road we can get today?"

They put out the few small fires that were still burning in the leaves then walked back to the road in silence. The others were sitting unmoving on the horses, staring at the woods as they walked out. Faran swung down suddenly and ran to Dale, throwing his arms around him.
"What happened???!!" he demanded, obviously frightened. "It looked like the whole forest was going to explode!!" Dale stopped, hugged Faran tightly for a few seconds then pried him loose.
"I lost my temper," he explained. "And things got a bit intense."
"Lost your temper?" Faran asked incredulously, and shook his head. "Remind me not to ever make you that mad!"
Dale smiled at him and tousled his hair.
"You'd have to work really hard at it to make me that angry," he responded as they walked back to their horses and re-mounted. "That's a skill not many possess." He glanced back at Jarl who reddened and looked down, embarrassed.

Kheri said nothing. He had wound up with a front row seat due to the bond he shared with Dale and had watched the entire thing through Dale's eyes. His curiosity was eating at him and he was dying to ask questions, but he could feel the anger still simmering inside Dale and decided prudently that later would be a much better time to broach any subject more emotional than lunch. He kicked his horse into motion and tried to concentrate on the ride.

Chapter Twenty-Two

The hills were becoming much higher and the road snaked around their feet. Every now and then, a small stream ran across the road and occasionally they passed a game trail or other small track that lead away from the road and into the forest. Dale kept them moving until late afternoon, not even stopping for lunch. At last as it was beginning to look like evening was well on its way, he turned off the road into a small clearing and reined his horse to a stop. The others joined him and began dismounting.

The clearing was fairly large, though it had looked small from the road and Kheri became intrigued by sounds from behind a thick set of bushes. He forced his way through them, then stopped, staring at a small lake that they had hidden. As he watched, a fish leaped from the water, after a fly that had buzzed too closely to the surface. His face lit up and he returned quickly to camp.
"Dale!" he exclaimed as he burst back into the camp.
"Yes?" Dale asked, looking up from the campfire he was attempting to coax into life.
"I found a lake!" Kheri explained excitedly. "With fish in it!"
"We still don't have anything to catch fish with," Dale pointed out.
"I can try to make a net or something," Kheri suggested, refusing to be dissuaded.
"You're welcome to try," Dale replied, watching the tiny flames and slowly feeding more bits of dry twigs into the fire. "While you're at it, look around for turtles, crawfish or other, slightly slower, critters."

Kheri grinned and started digging through the saddle bags. Aerline watched him for a minute, then walked over.
"I can help you," she suggested and Kheri glanced up.
"You have a net?" he queried. She shook her head and smiled, dimples showing on both cheeks.

"No," she responded. "Something better. Come see."
He stood up, curious, and walked back to the edge of the lake with her. She paused on the bank, looking at the water for a moment, then knelt down and put her hands under the surface. Closing her eyes, she began whispering something, the words of which Kheri couldn't quite catch. A few moments later she lifted her hands out of the water and held up a wiggling fish. His mouth fell open and he stared.
"How did you do that?" he wondered aloud and she smiled.
"It's part of my animal talent," she explained. "Fish are very easy to control."
She looked around then turned back to Kheri.
"You didn't bring anything to put them in?" she asked and he started.
"Ooops," he replied, and disappeared back into the bushes, leaving her standing on the edge of the lake with the fish dangling from her fingers by its gills.

He was back a few moments later with the larger of the pots. She dropped the fish into the pot then in rapid succession pulled six more out of the lake. The last was much too big for the pot however and she could barely lift it with both hands. Kheri blinked.
"No," he decided. "We've got plenty. Put him back."
She released the grateful fish back into the water and watched it swim away.
"Couldn't eat something that's been around long as he has anyway," Kheri commented as the fish vanished into the murky depths. "Just wouldn't be fair."
She smiled, then washed her hands in the water.
"They're all yours," she told him happily, and went back to camp, leaving him with a pot full of fish to clean.

The smell of frying fish soon filled the air and Aerline found that she'd become quite popular all of a sudden.

"Imagine," she thought to herself. "My worthless talent turned out to be so useful after all."
She thought back to all the times in her life when she'd been told what a waste of time it was. Her mother had lectured her constantly about not spending her energies on such a useless thing.
"Concentrate on real magic," she'd been told over and over from the age of three.
"Don't you know that you'll never make a living with THAT?" her professors had lectured her each time she'd mentioned what her talent was in response to their questions. "You want to be something, you need to learn to conjure," one had admonished, "You need to be able to shoot fireballs," another had told her. "Who would EVER need a wizard who could talk to cats??!!" a third had scoffed.
"But it's so easy," she thought, "and everything else is so hard."

She sat down on the ground not too far from the campfire and for the first time in her life enjoyed knowing that other people appreciated what she could do. She looked up a few minutes later, her happy daydreaming shattered, to see Jarl re-enter the camp, his arms loaded with wood. He deposited the wood off to the side, then walked over to where she was sitting. She sighed to herself and tried to maintain a pleasant look on her face in spite of wishing he would suddenly cease to exist. He stopped next to her and sat down. She frowned in disgusted annoyance, then unobtrusively scooted away from him slightly. He nodded, aware of her action.

"I would like to talk to you if I might," he requested. She looked at him suspiciously.
"What about?" she asked, her voice guarded.
He picked up a stick and tossed it into the campfire.
"I'd like to apologize for being such a jerk," he responded, watching the stick catch in the flames.
"You were a bit more than just a jerk," she pointed out bluntly.
He nodded.

"You're right, I was," he agreed, looking down at his hands. "I was upset at being trapped and I took it out on you."
"Well, it's nice that you've finally realized just how rude and infuriating you were," she responded. "But don't expect me to suddenly want to be good friends or something."
He shook his head.
"I'm not expecting anything," he answered, glancing at her. "I just felt I owed you an apology. Is there anything I can do to set things right?"
"After getting me kicked out of college?!" she exclaimed incredulously. "I HARDLY think so!"
She stood up and brushed off her skirt with several sharp flicks of her hand.
"No," she finished angrily. "I can think of NOTHING you could POSSIBLY do which would mend that! Excuse me!"
She flounced away from the campfire and went down to sit at the edge of the lake.

Jarl flinched at her outburst then sighed and sat watching the flames eat away at the wood.
"I tried," he thought after a minute.
"That's all I asked you to do," Dale thought back.

The fish were done a few minutes later and dinner seemed like a veritable feast compared to what they had been eating for weeks. Darkness fell completely as they finished the last of the food and the soft, velvety night silently covered the dozing forest. Aerline was sitting under a tree, talking to an owl that had landed on her shoulder. Faran and Dale were standing off to the side, staring up at the stars, while Dale attempted to explain basic astronomy to him. Kheri walked back into the camp carrying the dishes he'd just finished washing and put them away then looked around. Jarl was off by himself in the darkness at the edge of the firelight and everyone else appeared engrossed in their own activities. Kheri wiped his hands on his pants, then walked over to Jarl.

"You busy?" he asked and Jarl glanced at him then shook his head.
"No," he responded. "Just listening to the night."
"Can I ask you a couple questions then?" Kheri requested.
Jarl crooked the corner of his mouth up at the eagerness in Kheri's voice.
"What about?" he replied.
"How'd you meet Dale?" Kheri asked, nearly tripping over his own words, so anxious was he to gain the answer.
"Now that," he replied, "is a loaded question."
Dale glanced over at him and grinned slightly, then nodded his head and returned his attention to Faran.

"Ok," Jarl said in response to Dale's approval, "this might take a while. Want to take a walk?"
"I can't," Kheri replied. "It's dark."
Jarl looked at him blankly.
"I kept getting in trouble after dark," Kheri explained, "So Dale's restricted me to not going more than ten feet away from him at night."
Jarl stared at him for a second.
"This I gotta hear," he declared. He walked over to the campfire and sat down, motioning for Kheri to join him. "So tell me," he asked conversationally as Kheri sat down on the ground beside him. "What happened?"

Kheri made a face, then explained about the walk he'd taken to calm his nerves ending with a roll down the hill.
"Not real bright," Jarl commented when he was finished, chuckling at the image of Kheri tumbling down the hill.
"Yeah," Kheri agreed, slightly embarrassed.
"Not to mention what happened that night at the inn," Dale put in from the other side of the fire where he was now sitting.
Kheri turned bright red and looked away.

"What happened?" Jarl asked curiously, glancing between the two of them.

Kheri mumbled something and Jarl lifted an eyebrow.

"I can't understand a word you're saying," he remarked innocently.

Kheri sighed then turned back to face him.

"I couldn't sleep," he explained. "So I went for a walk..." His thoughts went back to the darkness outside the inn, the moon drenched silence on it's back lawn and the creatures Dale had very nearly not been able to rescue him from. He shuddered and shook his head, the images flashing through his mind in graphic detail.

Jarl blinked as Dale allowed Kheri's thoughts to flow to him then nodded.

"Yeah," he agreed, "I can understand him being rather upset at you for that."

"So anyway," Kheri replied in an attempt to change the subject. "How'd you meet Dale?"

"I met him in a bar," Jarl stated without explanation.

"How long have you known him?" Kheri asked, interrupting.

Jarl thought silently for a few moments.

"A long time," he answered reflectively. "A very long time."

Kheri sat silently, waiting for him to continue. Jarl paused in thought for several more minutes then shook his head.

"A very long time," he repeated. "Didn't realize it had been as long as it has actually."

"So what happened?" Kheri prodded.

"Well," Jarl said, "I was young and foolish. Older than you though. I was about thirty-four at the time. Some of the guys back home had dared me to stow away on a ship. I wasn't going to but there was this girl...pretty little thing too..." He paused and shook his head, a crooked smile on his face. "She told me how big, and brave I would be in her eyes if I took the dare. Fluttered her eyelashes and gave me one of those looks that leave a guy helpless. So naturally I stowed away on the ship. And naturally the captain found me after we were too far out of port to turn back. He was less than happy but thankfully he let me work for passage until we got to the first port. Then he kicked me off." Jarl shook his head at the memory then continued. "So there I was, with very little money in my pocket, not nearly enough to buy a ticket home, no idea what I was going to do, or even if I spoke the language of the locals."

"So what'd you do?" Kheri asked, enthralled with the account.

"He got drunk," Dale interrupted and grinned at Jarl.

"I did not," Jarl argued, making a wry face at him. "I just got a little tipsy."

Kheri snickered and Jarl turned back to him.

"Where was I?" he mused. "Oh, right. No idea of what I was going to do. So I did what anybody would do in like circumstance. I found the nearest bar. I figured that maybe I could find a sympathetic ear or something in it. I did find some ears but they weren't very sympathetic and they belonged to a rather large individual who had a distinct hatred of humans...which meant he didn't like me at all."

"Humans?" Kheri asked, looking slightly confused. "Wasn't he a human too?"

"Ummm..." Jarl hesitated for a moment. "No, he wasn't. Not even slightly close."

"Oh," Kheri replied. "Sorry, didn't mean to interrupt."

"That's ok," Jarl grinned. "Now let's see...Oh right. Anyway, he decided he didn't like me and got insulting. I'd had a drink or two..."

"A drink or ten you mean," Dale interjected and Jarl made a face at him.

"Tell it right," Dale told him. "You'll have Kheri thinking you're the universe's prime example of virtue."

"But I am," Jarl protested innocently and ducked as Dale tossed a pine cone at him. He grinned then turned back to Kheri.

"So, ok, I'd had a few drinks", he admitted. "and I was feeling them somewhat. The guy got insulting and I had to prove he wasn't as big as he looked. Unfortunately, he actually was. He hit me and I broke a table by falling on it. That made me mad and I tossed him through a window. Which didn't do much for his temper. We'd just started warming up to each other..."
"Because the place had caught on fire," Dale added
"...when someone called the law." Jarl continued, ignoring Dale's comment. "They interrupted us just as I was about to finish the fight, and arrested everyone, even the barkeep. I woke up in a cold, smelly.." he said.
"It wasn't smelly," Dale interjected. "Until you threw up in it."
"..jail cell," Jarl went on, "The judge sentenced me to three weeks and told me I had to pay this huge fine."
"Yeah," Dale agreed. "To pay for the bar you wrecked."
"Wasn't wrecked that badly," Jarl argued and Dale grinned.

"Anyway," Jarl continued, turning his attention back to Kheri, "they let me out three weeks later and Dale was waiting for me. Asked me where I was going to go. Well I still didn't have the money for a ticket back home and they weren't going to let me out of that port till I'd paid that fine anyway. So I told him i didn't know. He pointed out that if I didn't have any where to stay, they'd toss me right back into jail for vagrancy, which I really didn't care to have happen. So I accepted when he offered to let me stay at his apartment."
"So how'd you meet him at the bar then?" Kheri asked.
"Oh, well..." Jarl paused, glancing at Dale who was listening to the account with a grin on his face. "He was the officer that arrested me."
Kheri grinned broadly.
"Go on," he prompted, fascinated, "what happened next?"
"Not much," Jarl explained. "I started sleeping on his couch and got a job so I could pay the fine off. By the time I had, we'd become pretty good friends."

"Not to mention I could drink you under the table," Dale commented, "and you were still trying to beat me at it."

"I still say you were cheating," Jarl insisted and Dale chuckled.
"You know better," he responded. "I don't have to, you just can't handle the alcohol."
"Anyway," Jarl said, turning back to Kheri. "I paid the fine off then decided to hang around the port anyway, because there wasn't much reason to go back home and I'd made several friends there."
"Yeah, since it took you nearly ten years to pay it off," Dale put in.
"That's cause it was so big," Jarl griped.
"That's because you stopped paying on it over and over again," Dale reminded him, "and the judge kept heaping extra fines on top of it." Jarl stuck his tongue out at Dale then ducked as another pine cone whizzed over his head.

"So how long have you known him?" Kheri asked and Jarl looked thoughtful then turned to Dale.
"How long's it been?" he asked.
"Close to three thousand years," Dale replied.
Kheri's mouth dropped open and he stared at Dale in shock.
"Wow!" he managed after a moment. "That's incredible."
"What's incredible," Dale responded before Jarl could speak, "is that he managed to get into so much trouble so often in that time."
"Yes, well..." Jarl coughed, then grinned at him. "I had to give you something to do."
"I had plenty to do," Dale retorted, "without having to rescue you every time I turned around."
Jarl grinned at him then turned back to Kheri.
"So that's how we met," he finished.
Kheri shook his head.

"That's amazing," he exclaimed. "I didn't know anyone lived that long. Not even wizards live that long."
"Here maybe," Jarl replied, then shrugged. "It's different in other places."

The night was getting late and Kheri found himself yawning uncontrollably. He blinked a few times and rubbed his eyes then gave in and curled up in his blanket. The others soon followed his example and silence fell over the campsite, broken only by the occasional snort of one of the horses. A mist drifted over the ground, thickening as the night wore on, covering everything in a film of wetness. When the sun rose, it looked down on a world shrouded beneath thick fog. It's rays struggled to penetrate the thick roiling mists, succeeding only in reaching the ground as a weak, watery beam. Dale was first awake as usual, and he sat up then looked around.

The fog was thick enough to obscure everything more than fifteen feet away. He rubbed the sleep from his eyes and stood, searching for the horses, then took a couple careful steps toward where the cold coals lay and was finally rewarded with the sight of the horses standing at the edge of their campsite, steam rising from their noses. He reached over and nudged Kheri awake with his foot.

"Up," he commanded gently, as Kheri stirred then sat up shivering in the clammy air. Kheri squinted one eye open and looked around at the fog, then made a face. He stood up yawning, stretched, then began sorting out the relatively dry wood in an attempt to make a fire. In a few minutes, there was a bit of a blaze crackling happily and Dale had roused the rest of the camp. Water was dripping steadily from the branches of the trees, their hair and everything else the fog could find to condense on. The company ate as rapidly as possible and got back onto the road, wrapped in somewhat damp blankets against the chill.

Chapter Twenty-Three

The road wound its way around the base of a hill and then up a bit of a rise. On the other side they discovered that the road forked into three legs, each running off through trees with no clear indication of which way led to Villenspell. Dale sat and thought for a moment, studying them, then turned to Jarl.

"Jarl," he thought, "I need you to port down each of these for a couple miles and let me know where they're going."

"I can't," came the reply. "Sssversth blocked my teleport yesterday. I'm stuck with feet and a horse, just like you."

"Great," Dale thought back. "What else did he block?"

"Nothing," Jarl responded, then paused. "At least not that I am aware of."

"Aerline," Dale said out loud, turning to the woman who was staring off into the forest. She blinked, then turned looked at him, a question in her eyes. "Any idea which road leads to Villenspell?" he asked but she shook her head.

"No," she replied. "I didn't travel this way when I left the college. I've never been through here before."

"Alright," Dale replied and studied the roads for a few more minutes. "We'll take this one," he decided, turning his horse to the leg on the far right, "and if it doesn't go where we want, we'll come back and take a different one."

The leg that Dale had chosen twisted back and forth across the hill as it descended through the trees and at last they found themselves back on level ground. The forest was dense here, and the fog covered the ground in a thick blanket. The air was clammy and the feeling of unfriendly eyes watching them began to grow on the entire company as they rode. Dale checked his suits sensor reading every few minutes but nothing dangerous appeared to be nearby. He keyed the force shield on his belt anyway, unsure of what type of attack might be coming, and tried to ignore the feeling.

The company rode on for a few more minutes then suddenly stopped as if some unspoken agreement had been reached. The air was heavy with anticipation and the feeling of danger was nearly overwhelming. They sat silently, looking around at the trees which were so close together that nothing could be seen in their shadows.
"I don't like this," Faran commented, glancing around with a slight frown on his face. "It feels evil."
"Yeah," Kheri agreed, looking quickly behind himself. "I don't like it either."
Dale nodded slightly then glanced over at Aerline. She was staring at something unseen ahead of them, her face pale and her lips moving slightly, whispering quietly. Dale frowned, then swung down off his horse.
"Alright," he decided, "dismount. Let's find out what's going on."

All except Aerline swung down and cautiously moved up to stand beside him. The fog billowed around the road a few feet away, as if something had moved and stirred it.
"No heat signature," Jarl commented, looking at the readout from his own sensors.
"Fan out," Dale instructed the company. "And watch the fog."
The four of them spread out across the road. Kheri drew his dagger then stepped into the shadows under a tree, vanishing from sight. Faran drew the sword Dale had given him, and turned sideways slightly, watching the fog as it billowed around on the road ahead. Jarl cracked his knuckles then looked at Dale and nodded.

As they stood watching, the billowing in the fog began to move, coming slowly closer to where they stood. Dale waited until it was about ten feet away then drew his blaster and fired a short burst into the road just ahead of it. It stopped moving suddenly.
"Now is that really necessary?" a raspy voice asked. "Very un-neighborly of you I must say."

"You're the one that's invisible," Dale replied. "You want to talk instead of fight, how about showing yourself."
"So jumpy, these youngsters," the voice mused. "Very well, but call your youngling back first, he's making me nervous."
"Kheri," Dale directed over his shoulder. "Step back out on the road."
Kheri moved back out of the trees cautiously, his eyes fixed on the spot where Dale had fired.

"Well now," the voice said again, "that's a little better."
There was a wavering in the air and slowly a long, snaky head became visible. The body followed a few moments afterward and they found themselves looking at what could only be a dragon. It stretched its wings then swung its head slowly around, regarding all of them one by one.
"Now what might you be doing out here all alone," it wondered aloud, and turned its attention back to Dale. "You don't look much like knights on errantry."
"We're not," Dale responded. "We're trying to find the road to Villenspell."
"Villenspell," it repeated thoughtfully. "You most certainly won't get there on this road. This road leads to the swamp."

"Do you know what road we need then?" Dale asked.
The dragon cocked its head to the side, studying him.
"You," it mused, ignoring his question, "just might be the reason for that dream I keep having."
"What dream?" Dale asked, curious in spite of himself.
"A dream," the dragon explained. "Or perhaps you would call it a vision. Falling stars is how it begins. A few, then more, then all, falling far away. And where they fall an army appears. Creatures I've not seen before. They swarm like ants and the land crumbles. A strange knight rides out of the darkness then, wielding a fire from heaven."
Dale felt like he'd just been hit with a tree.

"What," he asked, fearing the answer. "Do the creatures look like?"

"Big," the dragon explained. "large, like the hill giants or ogres. And powerful. Their faces are shrouded, but their weapons are not."

"Wait," Dale said, and walked over to his horse. He pulled one of the Gorg knives out of the bag where he'd placed it and walked back, unwrapping it as he did so, then showed it silently to the dragon. It looked at the knife then regarded him again.

"Yes," it acknowledged, its voice dropping like a stone into the pit of his stomach. "That is one of them."

Dale fought down the urge to flee and wrapped the knife back up.

"King Yaybar must not die." The dragon stated flatly. Dale looked at him and frowned slightly.

"Who is King Yaybar?" he asked.

"I have no idea," the dragon replied. "But in the vision I see two roads. If he dies all is lost and the army devours all life. If he does not, victory is certain and the army is vanquished back to the heavens from which it fell."

Dale took a deep breath and tried to steady his nerves.

"Can you tell us the way to Villenspell?" he asked at last. "I think it just became critical that we reach there as fast as possible."

The dragon swiveled its head around, looking them over again, then turned back to Dale.

"Go back the way you came," it explained. "For you surely will not reach there by entering the swamp. But I can not give you better instructions than this, for I do not know where it lies."

"Alright," Dale replied. "Thank you. We'll try one of the other roads."

"So you intend to fight this swarming army?" The dragon asked, looking intently at Dale as it did so.

"I can't fight an army that size, if your vision is accurate, alone," Dale replied. "But I don't think I have much choice. I'm afraid I'll have to try. I'm hoping to find reinforcements in Villenspell. Maybe I can find some wizards there who don't have any common sense and want an adventure."

The dragon chuckled.
"That would define most wizards I've ever had the displeasure to know," it remarked.
"And maybe they can tell me who this King Yaybar is," Dale went on, ignoring the dragon's comment. "Or where I can find him at least."
"Perhaps," the dragon agreed. "I wish you success in your quest, knight of heaven."
Dale looked at him and lifted an eyebrow.
"I wasn't aware I held such a title," he commented.
"You do now," the dragon responded dryly. "I just gave it to you."
Jarl snickered and Dale looked at him sideways.
"Besides," the dragon continued and looked at Dale strangely. "The vision names you such as well."
"I'm beginning to wish I'd gotten stuck in that warp," Dale grumbled.
"Fare well," the dragon told him, ignoring his reply. "I wish you good fortune...you'll need it."
It vanished back into invisibility and the fog billowed for a second then was still.

"Well," Kheri remarked, relaxing finally. "That was unexpected."
"Yeah," Faran agreed, sheathing the sword. "I thought dragons were huge, breathed fire and ate you."
"Only if you try to take their treasure," Kheri replied as he put his dagger away.
"I doubt that one has any treasure to speak of," Dale commented, still looking at the road where the dragon had stood. He shook

himself after a moment then turned to look at Jarl who had his arms crossed and was watching him.
"This is not my fault!" Jarl responded in mock protest.
Dale grinned faintly.
"I know it's not. I'm not sure whose fault it is but I'm beginning to piece things together and I don't like what I'm looking at."
"What?" Jarl asked but Dale shook his head.
"No," he replied, "I'm still working on it. I'll tell you when I've got all the parts."

They remounted and turned the horses, then rode back the way they had come. By the time they reached the fork in the road, the sun was nearly at zenith and the fog had lifted. White fluffy clouds floated through the sky and a light breeze blew past them, cooling the air and bringing with it the heady smell of pines from the mountains close at hand. Dale stopped once they reached the fork and studied the remaining two legs for several minutes.
"Fifty-fifty chance," Kheri commented unhelpfully.
Dale glanced at him, then nodded.
"Yes," he agreed. "So you pick."
"Me?" Kheri looked surprised.
Dale nodded again.
"Yes," he replied. "You."

Kheri looked at the remaining two legs for a moment then swung down off his horse and walked over to examine the ground. After a few minutes he stepped back then pointed at the middle leg.
"That one," he decided. "There's been a lot more traffic over it since the last rains than there has this other one."
"Very well," Dale agreed. "We'll go that way."
The forest was more open than it had been on the right handed leg and the sun streaked through the tree branches to light their path. Ferns grew thickly between the trees and patches of brightly colored wildflowers could be seen every now and then. The road began to climb after about an hour, switching back and forth as it

proceeded to the top. They rode out of the trees into a clearing about thirty minutes after beginning the climb and found themselves looking at a dark green sea of tree- tops. The mountains were very close now and a thin line where the road began its climb into them could be clearly seen.
"Lunch," Faran suggested and Kheri grinned at him.
"Well?" he asked, looking at Kheri defiantly. "I'm hungry."
"Lunch is probably a good idea at that," Dale agreed, swinging down off the horse. "But I don't want to be here more than an hour."

The day was pleasant and they ate sitting on the grass as the horses grazed nearby. They were nearly done when Aerline looked up and then pointed.
"Look!" she exclaimed, staring up into the air. They glanced up in time to see a brilliant light streak across the sky and disappear behind the mountains.
"I wonder what that was," Jarl said.
Aerline giggled.
"Villenspell lies that way," she explained. "That was most likely the professor of extemporaneous travel, missing his entry point again."
Dale stared at her.
"The professor of what?" he asked.
"Extemporaneous Travel," she clarified. "He teaches magical travel. He's a wonderful professor, just a bit absent minded. And every now and again he misses his entry point. I do hope he didn't break anything this time." She shook her head. "The last time he hit the roof over the auditorium and put a huge hole in it."
Jarl grinned.
"I remember that," he remarked.
"Yes, you would, wouldn't you." Aerline asked, smiling at him sweetly.
"Considering you forced me to fix it," he replied, catching her eyes. "Yes. I remember it pretty vividly."

"Well that's what you were for," she responded, her dimples showing as she smiled. "You did a pretty good job though. The Dean was quite pleased. He even forgave you for setting his pants on fire while he was wearing them that time."
"That," Jarl protested, "was a complete accident."
"Oh really?" Aerline asked, lifting an eyebrow at him.
"Yes," he responded innocently. "I was aiming for his shoes."
He grinned at her and she tossed a chunk of bread at him.
"You're impossible!" She exclaimed.
"Not completely," he replied, ducking out of the way of the bread. "I just wasn't happy about being trapped like that."

Faran had finished eating and was sitting next to Dale, watching the two of them banter, a look of complete fascination on his face.
"What's the school like?" he asked when they paused for a moment.
Aerline looked over at him and smiled slightly, shrugging.
"It's like most schools, I guess." she replied, "It's old, the buildings have stood for centuries and they're covered with ivy. It's always crowded, because anyone that wants to learn magic goes there. At least if they want to be good at it. It was fun to be there," she sighed wistfully, "but I guess I never should have gone. It wasn't my idea anyway."

"Whose idea was it?" Faran asked curiously.
"My parents," Aerline replied. "Pretty much from the day I was born I guess. I remember always being told that I was special and when I was old enough I was going to go there and learn to be a very important wizard." She rolled her eyes.
"You didn't want to be an important wizard?" Faran asked, looking at her curiously.
"Oh I wouldn't have minded," she responded. "It's just that I'm no good at magic. I never have been. And my animal talent wasn't what my mother, or the professors at the school for that matter,

considered important. But I tried. I didn't want to disappoint anyone. That's why I was wearing all that stuff. It worked too, until someone caught me."

"They got mad huh?" Faran asked.

"Yes," she replied. "They got very mad. They kicked me out of the school and told me not to come back."

"What'd you do?" Faran asked.

"Well I couldn't go home," she explained. "I mean, if I'd walked back into my parent's house and told them I'd been kicked out they'd have died of shame or something. So I decided it was a good time to go see the world. Travel and find out what other places looked like. That decided, I left the school and traveled for a couple years. Until you showed up at the inn. That was the most interesting mystery I'd run across in months and I just had to know what was going on."

Faran grinned, then paused suddenly, staring across the grass at the trees.

"Look!" he whispered in awe.

The others turned to look where he was staring and everyone froze. Under the trees at the edge of the clearing, a soft glow surrounding it, stood a unicorn. It regarded them silently for a moment then bowed it's head and pawed the ground once. Aerline got carefully to her feet and approached it cautiously. It lifted its head as she approached, watching her. She stopped a few feet away and lifted both hands out in front of her then stood waiting. The unicorn eyed her, then took several cautious steps toward her. When she didn't move, the Unicorn tossed it's mane, then trotted up to where she stood, and dipped its head, touching her hands with the tip of its horn. A golden light swirled around its horn then filled her hands. She stood there, motionless, the light filling her hands like golden liquid. The unicorn lifted its head after a moment, then turned and fled back into the trees out of sight.

"Quick!" Aerline commanded, not moving. "Someone bring me a full water bag!"
Faran jumped to his feet, grabbed one of the bags, and ran to where she stood.
"Open it please," she requested, still not moving. "Like you were going to fill it."
He did so then looked at her expectantly.
"Put it under my hands so I can pour this into the water," she directed.
He positioned the opening under her hands then held it still as she carefully opened them, allowing the golden light to swirl into the bag. She took the bag from him after her hands were empty and closed the opening back up.
"Keep that separate from the rest of the bags," she instructed. "The water in it will heal anything now. But we can't refill it, so we have to be careful only to use it when we really need to."
Faran nodded and took the bag back to the horses. Jarl walked over to him with a charred stick from the fire in his hands.
"Here," he said, handing Faran the stick. "Mark the bag on both sides. Then we won't get it mixed up." Faran nodded and scribbled dark black dusty lines all over both sides of the bag, then hung it over the saddle horn on Dale's horse.
"There," he declared, satisfied. "That should work."

Aerline walked back over to the fire, a look of amazement on her face and sat back down, shaking her head.
"Dale," she mused after a moment, looking up at him. "I don't know if you are aware what just happened, but unicorns are rarely seen. Usually they only appear if there is a desperate situation. Their horn can heal anything and they've been seen at times on battlefields trotting from body to body, healing those who aren't completely dead. But this one, he gave me his healing power. He came here specifically to do that. He said it would be needed at the end. He gave me all he had." She frowned for a moment in thought then shook her head. "He said the end of all things hangs

by a thread and not to use it until 'He who rips the heaven's apart' has been found in the land which talks to the stars."
Dale winced and reached up to rub his eyes with his right hand, then climbed to his feet.
"Jarl," he said as he walked into the trees.
Jarl frowned slightly then followed him.

Dale walked out of earshot of the others then leaned unhappily against a tree, his arms crossed.
"What'd I do now," Jarl asked but Dale shook his head.
"You didn't do anything," he replied. "But you need to know what's going on." He looked over at his friend and took a deep breath. "I'm stuck here because of a rather nasty space warp," he explained. "I was trying to close it and I lost the fight. Got sucked into it and dropped on this planet. My powers are still blocked because of it and from the resistance I've gotten when I've tried to break free, someone has me blocked on purpose."
"You think someone opened that warp on purpose?" Jarl asked and Dale nodded.
"I think that they not only opened that warp on purpose, but are the reason I can't use my powers. I also think," he continued, looking at Jarl seriously. "That they are the one behind the Gorg. Who ever it is wants me real bad. The first attack there were three of them. The second, there were five. It didn't make any sense to me until that vision the dragon told us about."
"You don't think," Jarl began, his face turning pale.
"I think," Dale replied, interrupting him. "That someone opened that warp to transport an invading army of Gorg here and I got in the way. And I think that if we don't stop them this world will be destroyed. Think about what the dragon said."

Jarl nodded, running back over the dragons words in his mind.
"Falling stars, a swarming army and he recognized that knife from his vision," Dale went on. "And now this. A creature with incredible healing skills comes specifically to give us a powerful

healing mixture, and says it will be needed when 'he who rips the heaven's apart' is found."
Jarl nodded again.
"Yeah," he agreed. "You could be very right. But why didn't Sssversth say anything when he was here the other day?"
"Why should he?" Dale responded. "Dealing with this sort of stuff isn't his job, it's ours. He'll deal with US though if we don't keep the Gorg from taking over this world and I'd prefer not to have to explain our failure."

Jarl nodded in agreement.
"I'd prefer not to have to talk to him again at all," he remarked. "But why didn't you tell the others?"
"I will. But I want your input first. They're not going to understand what we're facing. Not really. You do."
"True," Jarl replied then took a deep breath. "If the Gorg are true to form," he said, thinking out loud, "they're going to wipe out everything in their path as they advance. So they'll move slowly. I wish I knew when they'd landed."
"If they have landed." Dale replied. "They may not have done so yet. It's been just slightly over a month since I failed to close that warp."
"A month," Jarl mused. "How big was the warp?"
"Not terribly large," Dale responded. "Not big enough to fly a ship through by any means."
"So he's sending them through individually?" Jarl blinked. "Do you think he'd have increased it after you fell through?"

"No. It was full size already," Dale shook his head. "And besides, it was in a pretty visible area. Any bigger and Sssversth would have stepped in to close it."
"Ok," Jarl nodded. "He'll have to send them through individually, at the most in small groups. So depending on the size of the army he could be landing them for quite a while yet."

"If they've already started," Dale agreed. "Whatever the case, they'll be landing in a very remote areas so that no one tips his hand before he's ready."
"Then we still have some breathing room," Jarl replied, thinking. "At least a little. Maybe more if they haven't even started landing yet."
"We still don't have any idea who King Yaybar is...or where he is," Dale pointed out. "But I suspect that he'll be someone important in whatever area the Gorg attack first. I need a globe."
"Can't help you there," Jarl replied. "But maybe they'll have some maps at the college when we get there."
"I hope so," Dale agreed. "I'm also hoping we can get a bunch of wizards to help us with this. The magic here is pretty powerful. I had to fight one lousy wizard a few weeks back and I almost drained my blaster before he went down."
"That's impressive," Jarl commented.
"Yeah," Dale nodded. "Especially since I had it on full. And from what I gather from listening to Aerline, he wasn't anyone all that important. He certainly wasn't making his living on magic...he was trying to kidnap Faran for ransom."
"That's frightening," Jarl replied, shivering.
"What is?" Dale asked.
"That he could be that powerful and turn out to be some small potatoes hedge mage around here," Jarl answered.
"Yeah," Dale said. "Which is why I want to get some of them on our side before we have to face the Gorg." He shook his head then stood up away from the tree.
"We'll just have to play it by ear," Jarl commented as they began the walk back to the others.
"Yes I know," Dale agreed reluctantly, "I'm just not thrilled with the prospect."

They walked back out of the trees and rejoined the others who were still sitting around the clear area, talking. Kheri looked up as

they sat down and Dale suddenly realized he'd heard every word he and Jarl had just spoken.
"I didn't know you were listening," Dale thought at him.
"I wasn't trying to," Kheri thought back. "They fell pretty easy when Faran and I fought them though," he pointed out silently. "His sword went right through that armor they were wearing as if it wasn't there. And they strangle easy too." He patted the pocket where his Garrote lay hidden.
Dale smiled slightly, hope suddenly blossoming, then spoke.
"Alright," he explained, for the benefit of Faran and Aerline. "I think I know what is going on now and if I'm right it's not going to be fun."

"What?" Faran asked, watching him.
"From the description of that vision the dragon gave us," he explained. "I think there's an army of Gorg massing somewhere and we are going to have to stop them before they wipe out all life on this world."
Faran turned pale and stared at him, then set his jaw and nodded.
"What's a Gorg?" Aerline asked.
"Think ogre on a bad day," Kheri interrupted. "Only a little smaller...with much better weapons."
"I mentioned them to you before and you saw them when they invaded my camp," Dale explained. "Those are Gorg. A few might not have looked impressive to you but can you conceive of several thousand all charging at you at the same time?"
Aerline blinked and stared at him.
"That's horrible!" she exclaimed.
"Yes," Dale replied. "Their army is usually anywhere from two to ten thousand in number. Sometimes larger."

She stared at him, her mouth open.
"Can you think of any village, town or city that would survive an onslaught like that?" he asked.

"Well," she replied thoughtfully. "The smaller ones might not, but any that had a wizard would have a pretty good chance."
Dale nodded.
"That's one reason we're headed for Villenspell," he explained. "I don't know if we can convince any of the wizards there to assist us but we have to try."
She nodded but looked doubtful.
"Some of the students perhaps," she decided. "But the professors aren't likely to be all that interested."
"We still have to try," Dale replied, then stood up and brushed his pants off. "Let's get going. The afternoon is wearing away quickly."

Chapter Twenty-Four

The company set off several minutes later, following the road as it wound down the other side of the hill and re-entered the woods. It snaked back and forth through the trees and very slowly they became aware that it had leveled out and was climbing again. At last, as evening was drawing near, they left the fringes of the trees and saw before them a long sward of grass with the road running through it. On the other side, in the far distance, the road began it's ascent into the mountains they had been traveling steadily toward. They rode on in silence for several more minutes until they reached a small stream that bubbled merrily across the road and Dale called a halt.
"Alright," he declared, his voice tired. "This is far enough. I don't want to tackle those mountains in the dark. We'll camp here."

They dismounted and led their horses off to the side of the road, setting up camp beside the stream. The forest was several minutes ride behind them but there were a few trees growing nearby and they managed to find enough dead wood under them to get a decent fire going. The crickets filled the air with a symphony chirps as darkness arrived and the air above the grass for as far as they could see came to life with tiny lights flitting erratically around. Faran watched them for several minutes then glanced at Kheri.
"What are those?" he asked, looking back at the lights.
"Fireflies," Kheri replied, looking up from sharpening his dagger. "Hundreds of fireflies."

Faran watched the lights in fascination for a few more seconds then glanced at Kheri.
"What are fireflies?" he asked curiously.
Kheri stared at him for a moment.
"You've never seen a firefly?" He asked in disbelief. Faran shook his head.

"No," he replied innocently. "What are they?"
"Dale?" Kheri asked by way of response. Dale glanced around at the bits of light flickering through the darkness, and grinned, then nodded his head.
"Just don't go very far," he responded.
"We'll stay close," Kheri agreed and got to his feet.
"Come on," he told Faran, pulling on his arm. "Let's take a walk."
Faran got up and followed Kheri down the stream into the darkness, still staring at the lights.
"He's lived a very sheltered life," Dale explained in answer to the question on Aerline's face as they watched the boys walking into the darkness. "Being the son of the Baron is evidently not a ticket to much of anything at all."

Some feet away, hidden in the darkness and silence, several sets of eyes also observed the fireflies. The lights held no interest for them however, it was the horses that drew their attention.
"You think we can take 'em?" a low voice growled a whispered question.
"Yeah," came the answer. "No trouble at all."
"Quiet, both of you," a third voice snarled, it's tone low and full of malice.
"They're not asleep yet."
"I'm tired of waiting," the first voice complained. "Let's take 'em now. There's only three of 'em."
"The other two aren't gone for good you dolt!" the second voice responded and a low
'WHAP!' sounded through the air.
"Shut up!" the third voice demanded. "Or I'll skin you both alive. We wait until they are asleep. Erlan, go get the others and bring them here."

Dale paused but didn't look up as the whap reached his ears. It was the faint, unmistakable sound of something hitting flesh and he closed his eyes, reaching out to the edge of his scan range, searching for the source. Three men, belly down in the grass on the other side of the road, came into view as his mind brushed over them and he paused. As he watched, one of the men rose to his feet and moved quickly back toward the edge of the forest. The other two remained silent, watching the camp across the road from themselves. Ancient reflexes reacted, centuries of training directing his actions, and he keyed the daylight effects sensors on his suit then stood up facing the road, stretching.

Without the cloaking darkness it was easy for him to spot the two men in the grass not far away. He turned nonchalantly and walked over to the horses, then stood stroking his mare on the nose. His body was relaxed, to an outward observer he seemed engrossed in the horse but his mind was busily searching the eves of the forest at the edge of his scan range. As he stood, talking quietly to his horse, several more people emerged from the forest then ran to join the two still laying in the grass.
"Ten," he mused softly. "Wonder what they're up to."

Kheri and Faran had followed the stream for a short ways and were engrossed in sneaking up on the lights flickering in the grass. It took them several minutes but finally Faran let out a cry of delight.
"Hey! I got one!" he exclaimed, closing his hands around a light that hadn't taken to the air in time. He opened his hands carefully and looked down at the small insect that was crawling around in them, its light flashing off and on.
Kheri grinned.
"My aunt used to catch these when I was young," he explained. "She'd put a jar of them in my room at night so I wouldn't be scared of the dark."
"What do you feed them?" Faran wondered aloud, watching the firefly as it climbed out of his hands and flew off.
"I dunno," Kheri answered. "She never told me."

They watched the lights for a few more minutes then suddenly Kheri stiffened and stood still. Faran looked at him curiously but Kheri lifted a hand and motioned him to silence.

Dale waited long enough to be sure that no one else was going to join the ambush, then he turned and walked back to the fire.
"Kheri," he thought, his mental voice urgent. "We have company. Other side of the road. Thirteen of them and if they're friendly then I'm Paw Tucker."
"Got it," Kheri acknowledged, nodding his head slightly. He glanced at Faran.
"You wearing your sword?" he asked and Faran nodded.
"Always," he replied.
"We've got visitors," Kheri explained softly. "Other side of the road. I'm waiting for Dale to tell me what he wants done."

Dale sat down by the fire and picked up a piece of wood then causally began breaking bits off of it. He caught Jarl's eye and nodded imperceptibly. Jarl stood in response without visibly acknowledging him, yawned then scratched the back of his neck.
"I'm think I'm gonna take a walk," he commented to no one in particular. "See what's down that stream. I'll be back in a while."
"Watch that you don't fall in," Aerline admonished him.
He made a face at her, then wandered off down the stream and out of the firelight.
"Aerline," Dale whispered, his voice urgent and barely audible "are there any animals around right now that you can control?"
"Why," she asked, dropping her voice to match his. "What is wrong?"
"Do not look around," he replied quietly, catching her eyes. "There are thirteen uninvited guests on the other side of the road. I assume waiting on us to go to sleep."
"Oh," she breathed. "I'll see what I can find."
"Thanks," he replied, tossing the stick into the fire.

Jarl paused after he was out of the light and flipped a switch on his belt, turning his force field on for the first time since he'd been trapped. It hummed to life, flickered slightly, then stabilized. He tuned the controls, setting it for solid objects, then keyed the sensors in his suit. Instantly the lights came on and he looked back at the road, studying the layout. On the other side of the road he could see a number of crouching bodies. He counted quickly, then nodded. They were all there, providing Dale had counted correctly, and didn't appear to realize they'd been spotted. He flipped the sound dampers on and waded across the stream, no more than a wisp of shadow, moving in an arch that brought him behind them.

"I'm in position," he thought at Dale. "Give the signal."

"Stay there," Dale thought back. "And tell me if any of them move."

"Will do," he responded, waiting.

"Kheri," Dale thought and Kheri responded with a mental nod.

"Yes?" came his reply.

"You and Faran stay out of the light," he instructed. "Move to where you can join rapidly and wait till the fighting starts."

"On our way," Kheri replied and motioned to Faran.

"Come on," he said softly. "We've got to go back to the road."

Faran nodded and followed him as silently as possible.

Aerline was quiet, her eyes closed, whispering soundlessly. Dale watched her for a moment then looked up as an owl soared over head. It was followed by four more then Aerline opened her eyes.

"Best I could do," she told him quietly. "Everything's asleep."

"Stay here," Dale instructed, his voice low. "If the fighting gets too close, have them protect you."

She nodded and picked up a twig then broke bits off of it, dropping them into the fire as if she were bored. Dale readied himself, then stood and strode over to the road.

"What's going on," the first voice growled roughly. "I thought you said they'd be going to sleep?"
"They will you idiot," the third voice snarled. "Now shut up."
"He's coming over here though," the first voice protested and was rewarded by a fist striking him sharply on the top of the head.
"I said shut up!" the other snapped. "Or I'll stick a dagger in you and shut you up permanently."
Dale set his jaw and deliberately walked over to the road then stopped directly in front of where the bandits were hiding. He crossed his arms, looked right at them and shook his head.
"Clumsy," he remarked dryly. "Very. You might as well come out, I've known you were there for twenty minutes."
The night exploded into activity as most of the men jumped rapidly to their feet then charged him.

Jarl pulled several long slender darts out of a pocket and threw them as the men began to move, his aim guided by heat seeking sensors on their shafts. Several of the men fell and lay still, a dart buried in their neck. Kheri whipped out his daggers and sent them flying through the air, accounting for several more and Faran charged, his sword a flashing silver light in the starlit night.

Dale leaped aside as the first man to reach him swung his sword and the stroke whistled harmlessly past. He swept the second man's feet out from under him, then whirled, dodged and threw a punch at the third. The fight swirled around him, and he heard voices in the distance. Reinforcements were headed toward them from the eves of the forest. He ducked under a swing that came out of no where, then sidestepped his attacker and dived out of the way.

Rolling to his feet he glanced around and spotted the leader off to the side, out of the way of the fighting. He moved cat-like behind the man, then grabbed him as he had Kheri, squeezing his throat.

"Call them off!" Dale hissed in his ear as the reinforcements arrived. "Unless you wish to die."
"Stand!" the bandit yelled, and winced as Dale applied pressure to the man's arm, forcing it up higher behind his back. "Now! Drop your weapons and stand back!" he shouted at the top of his voice.
The remaining bandits looked around confused, then did as ordered, raising their hands reluctantly into the air. The night was suddenly lit with blinding flashes of light and seven Gorg materialized in the middle of the road. Dale froze, then let go of the bandit leader, shoving him toward the forest.
"Run!" he commanded sharply as he drew his blaster and took aim at the greater threat.

Three of the Gorg were also armed with blasters and they found themselves separated from their target by a mass of bodies. They fired with deadly accuracy, disintegrating anything in their path as they advanced toward Dale. The other Gorg were armed with long, curved knives and they also advanced, throwing bleeding, mangled bodies out of their way as they did so.

Dale flipped the blaster beam to pinpoint and aimed at one of the knife wielding Gorg then pulled the trigger. It's armor flamed as the blaster's energy hit it, then vanished. An instant later, the Gorg vanished as well. The night was suddenly full of wings as the owls Aerline had called swooped down, their talons ripping into several of the Gorg's faces. Blood gushed from suddenly empty eye sockets and the night was rent with anguished, infuriated screams of agony from the now blinded Gorg. Dale backed slightly, adjusted the blaster's beam and took aim at a second Gorg, then fired again. The Gorg vanished in a flare of incandescent light as the beam hit it, leaving an empty spot in the night.

Kheri ducked, pulled out his remaining dagger, then threw it at a Gorg who was leveling it's blaster at Faran's back. The dagger flashed as it sailed through the moonlight, then buried itself in the Gorg's right temple up to it's hilt, penetrating the monster's brain. The Gorg clawed at the dagger for a moment then toppled over and hit the ground with a resounding thud!

It was over as fast as it had begun and Dale stood, his heart pounding, looking at the carnage. Most of the bandits were dead, and the majority of the attacking Gorg were scattered on top of them, acidic blood eating away at the ground beneath. Kheri was walking among them, methodically recollecting his daggers and slitting open Gorg throats, making sure they would not be rising again. Faran pulled his sword out of the one he'd just finished and set about wiping it off, the look in his eyes hard and dangerous. Dale thumbed the safety on the blaster and reattached it to his belt, then turned and looked around for Jarl.

His partner was standing not far away, one of the Gorg's long knives in his hand, his foot on he back of the bandit leader who was laying on his stomach with his hands behind his head. He glanced up at Dale, an angry scowl on his face.
"Kheri," Dale called and Kheri paused, then looked at him questioningly. "You and Faran strip the bodies, all of them, and let me know when you're finished." Kheri wrinkled his nose in disgust but nodded and turned to the task at hand.

Dale walked over to where Jarl stood then looked down at the man on the ground for a moment.
"Why," he asked, looking back up at Jarl, "are you standing on him?"
"Because," Jarl explained, "I didn't want him to get away."
"The Gorg..." Dale began.
"Were all dead by the time I got ahold of him," Jarl interrupted.
Dale crossed his arms and regarded him silently.
"He tried to rob us, ok?" Jarl explained hotly. "And Gorg or not, I didn't think he should get away with it."

"And why's that?" Dale asked him.
"Because I wouldn't have gotten away with it!" Jarl retorted, then shoved the man back down to the ground as he tried to rise.
Dale snickered.

"Besides," Jarl argued. "How many more does he have hiding back there in the forest to throw against us when we're not looking?"
"I don't know," Dale replied. "You could ask him."
"You ask him," Jarl replied, and shoved the man back down to the ground again.
Dale shrugged then gestured at the pile of bodies.
"At the moment, there's a bit of a mess to clean up," he pointed out.
"So you deal with this guy and I'll go clean," Jarl replied.
Dale nodded then reached down and grabbed the man's arm. Jarl removed his foot and stepped back as Dale hauled his prisoner to his feet.
"Help Kheri and Faran strip the bodies," Dale instructed him. "And vaporize the Gorg. Keep their weapons though. We may need them. We'll deal with the bandits after it's light."
"And what are you going to do?" Jarl asked, slipping the knife into a sheath he'd removed from one of the dead Gorg.
"I'm going to make sure Aerline is ok," Dale replied. "And explain to this guy why he doesn't want to make any of us any angrier."
"Can I have one of the extra blasters?" Jarl asked, his eyes glinting from more than just moonlight.
"Yeah," Dale replied. "There should be three of them laying around on the ground some where. Let me know when you find them."
"Sure," Jarl agreed, attaching the sheath to his belt.
"And," Dale said, stopping him as he started to walk off. "See if anything these guys were wearing will fit you. You stick out like a sore thumb in that jump suit."
"Will do," Jarl replied, then went to help with the bodies.

Dale watched him walk off then shoved his captive slightly.
"Let's go," he commanded. "Walk over to the fire."
The man stumbled forward slightly then started walking silently toward the other side of the road. They made their way around the bodies strewn across the ground to where Aerline was sitting by the fire, an owl perched on her shoulder. Dale stopped him when they reached it then placed a hand on his shoulder and pushed lightly. The bandit sank obediently down to the ground and wrapped his arms tightly around his knees then sat staring into the fire.
"Do I need to warn you about trying to escape?" Dale asked.
The man shook his head silently, still watching the fire.
Aerline reached up and stroked the owl on its head.
"We'll be fine right here," she replied, looking across the fire at their prisoner.
The owl hooted in response and swiveled it's head around to regard Dale with wide, yellow eyes. He looked back at it, then smiled faintly.
"Alright, I'll go dispose of the Gorg," he replied, then glanced down at the prisoner. "I don't suggest you move," he cautioned. "Owls have very sharp talons."
The man glanced up briefly at the owl.
"I ain't moving," he mumbled, and sat motionless, watching the fire.

They worked quickly and within half an hour all the Gorg had been disposed of and all the bandits had been checked for useful items and valuables. The Gorg had been viciously effective with their knives and Faran had to stop after a short time, unable to deal with the savage results of their attack. Kheri lasted longer but he also gave up before the job was done and joined Faran at the stream, trying to control his stomach. Dale and Jarl worked methodically, hardened by long years of dealing with far worse situations. They dragged the Gorg to the side and used the blasters on them, reducing them to their component atoms, then lined the bandits up side by side in preparation for a mass grave.

They were nearly done when Dale stopped and knelt swiftly down beside one of the bodies they hadn't yet moved. He listened for a moment then keyed the sensors in his suit and read over the display.
"Jarl!" he thought sharply, causing his friend to jump. "Get me that bag of healing waters from the unicorn and do it fast!" Jarl dropped what he was doing and sprinted to the horses, returning in very few seconds with the precious bag. Dale had torn the clothing off of the body and lifted it's head up slightly.
"Here," Jarl said, handing him the bag.
Dale shook his head.
"No," he replied. "I can't hold him up and use that at the same time. Pour a small amount into his mouth."

Jarl knelt down as well and very carefully dribbled a thin stream into the slightly open mouth, then poured a bit on each of the wounds. As the water came in contact with the open flesh there was a slight sparkling and the wounds closed rapidly, vanishing completely with in a few seconds. The chest gave a sudden heave, a moan escaped the lips then suddenly the eyes flew open and the nearly dead corpse came violently to back to life. He screamed and thrashed for several seconds, then passed back out.
"He'll survive at least," Dale remarked, standing and lifting the unconscious bandit up in his arms. "Check the rest of them carefully and see if anyone else can be saved. I'll be right back."
Jarl nodded and Dale walked back across the road to the fire then placed the man gently on the ground by his leader.
"He's alive," he explained to the unvoiced question in Aerline's eyes. "We're looking to see who else might have made it.

After making sure that they hadn't overlooked anyone else, Dale set his blaster on a wide spray and turned it on the bodies. They flamed briefly as the energies hit them and were consumed, turning rapidly to ash.

"I thought you wanted to bury them," Jarl commented, watching as Dale disposed of them.

"I changed my mind," Dale replied. "Didn't want some wild animal to come along and dig them up or drag them off before dawn. Besides," he asked as he lowered the blaster. "Do you have anything to dig a hole with?"

Jarl shook his head.

"Hard to bury someone if you can't dig a grave," Dale pointed out as he keyed the blaster off.

"Yeah," Jarl agreed, his voice showing signs of weariness. They carried what was useful of the bandit's attire and possessions back over to their campsite then Dale joined the others by the fire.

The second bandit had awakened and was sitting up trying to figure out what had happened to him. His leader glanced at him as he stirred but said nothing. He looked around and rubbed his head, confusion on his face. Dale's return interrupted his thoughts.

"Good," Dale commented, looking at the second bandit. "You're awake. One of you want to explain to me exactly what you thought you were going to do earlier?"

"You know what we were gonna do," the leader replied, looking up definitely. "You and I ain't fools, so just kill us and get it done."

"I have no intention of causing your death," Dale responded mildly, crossing his arms and regarding both captives with an expressionless face. "Nor am I the reason your men are dead. What exactly were you after?"

The bandit leader looked at him.

"The horses," he replied. "And whatever else we coulda gotten."

"Be glad you didn't succeed," Dale told him. "Being kicked to death by flying horse hooves isn't something I'd want to experience."

The bandit leader glanced over at the horses then shrugged.

"Makes no difference," he shrugged, turning back to Dale. "Dead is dead. And it ain't gonna happen now anyway. So now what?"

"That I am going to leave up to you," Dale replied. "Remember those large, ugly creatures that appeared rather suddenly?"

The man nodded with a shudder.

"There is an army of those," Dale explained, watching the others face. "A large army, as vast as the number of stars in the sky. It's a long way off but it's coming and we are trying to stop it."
The man said nothing, watching him without expression.
"You can have the choice of aiding us," Dale continued. "Or returning to the forest. However if you return to the forest I had better not ever hear of you waylaying travellers again. I will hunt you down no matter where you hide and when I get through with you, you'll wish you had never been born."
The man nodded slightly, waiting for Dale to finish.
"If you aid us there is a good possibility you'll die," he went on, stressing his words to make a point, "but if the army isn't stopped it will destroy everything that lives in this world and you'll die anyway."
"I ain't no fighter," the man replied when he was sure Dale had finished. "I wouldn't do nothing but get in the way."
"Then go back to the forest," Dale told him. "But heed my words because I do not make idle threats."
The man nodded again then started as Jarl squatted down beside him.

"And if you're thinking that maybe Dale doesn't mean it," he warned, his voice low and dark, "Then go back to thieving and see what happens." He placed the point of his knife under the man's chin and forced his head up slightly. "There are far worse things than dying, my friend," he threatened, watching the other sweat. "Far worse." He looked into the bandit's eyes for a moment then pulled the knife away and stood up. The man swallowed and rubbed at the place where the knife point had rested then looked back at Dale.
"Point made and taken," he acknowledged.
"Then leave," Dale commanded, watching him.

The bandit nodded, stood up and walked off without a glance back toward the fire or those around it. The second bandit watched him go then looked over at Dale nervously.
"The same choice is yours," Dale told him. "Aid us or go back to the forest."
"And so is the same warning," Jarl warned.
The man glanced quickly between them, then sprang to his feet and dashed off toward the safety of the forest in the distance.

Jarl watched them go then shrugged.
"They'll be right back to thieving by tomorrow," he remarked, looking sideways at Dale. "You realize that don't you?"
"Maybe," Dale admitted. "Maybe not. I'll deal with that if I have to. Did you find anything you could wear?"
"Yeah," Jarl responded. "Not much though, most of it's too bloody or shredded. I'll be back in a minute." He picked up a bundle of cloth from the ground, stood and walked off out of the firelight.
Aerline watched him go then turned to Dale.
"Why did you let them leave?" she asked.
"What good could they possibly have done us?" Dale responded turning to look at her.
"They might have been useful," she replied.
"For what?" Dale asked. "Cannon fodder? They wouldn't last five seconds against the Gorg army. They didn't even hold up against the seven that showed up here tonight."
"I suppose," she replied. "I just don't like knowing that they're out there where they can attack us again without our knowledge."
"They won't," Kheri interrupted. "Unless they're both dumber than rocks."

Jarl walked back into the firelight a few minutes later, dressed now in a black tunic and pair of pants. He sat down next to the fire and stared into it silently.
"Something wrong?" Faran asked sleepily, watching him.

"Yeah kid," he said, looking over at the boy who was curled up on the ground. "There's several things wrong."
"What's the matter?" Faran asked, propping himself up on one arm.
"Don't worry about it," Jarl replied. "I always get like this when I've had to kill somebody."
Faran looked at him for a moment, then shrugged and lay back down. "Well they started it," he mumbled as he fell asleep.
Aerline glanced over at Faran then shook her head.
"He'll learn", Dale told her. "Remember he's lived all his life behind castle walls. When we found him, he was playing bandit because he was bored. He hasn't seen enough of the world yet, it's still basically a game to him."
"I certainly hope he gets over that attitude quickly," she replied.
She stood and released the owls, then watched them fly off into the night. Throwing her cloak around herself, she lay down on the ground without another word and fell asleep.

"Dale..." Kheri asked after a moment as silence descended on the camp once more, "do you think they'll leave people alone now?"
"Probably for a while," Dale responded, looking over at him. "But not likely forever. They had a horrible scare tonight though, so who knows."
Kheri nodded silently, his face more thoughtful than normal. After a few minutes he looked back over at Dale. "Thank you," he said.
"For?" Dale asked.
"For pulling me out of that kind of life," Kheri explained. "I was headed down that road I think."
Dale nodded, then smiled at him.
"You're welcome," he replied. "Now I suggest we all get some sleep."

Chapter Twenty-Five

The moon rose about an hour later, bathing the landscape in silvery light. The fire had died down to coals and everything was quiet. Faran stirred and woke suddenly, then sat up and looked around. The sound of a twig snapping underfoot nearby echoed through the still night air and he nudged Kheri's foot slightly. Kheri didn't move, though his snoring became slightly louder. Faran wrinkled his nose then quietly picked up his sword, and moved carefully away from what was left of the campfire into the darkness then stood, listening to the night. The moon was full and the land was lit fairly well. He crouched down and silently searched the area around the camp with his eyes, looking for movement. One of the horses snorted suddenly. There was a muffled cry and a thud as something hit the ground. Faran dashed for the horses, then skidded to a stop and stood, shaking his head. Sprawled on the ground near the horses was a young man of about his age. Faran's horse was standing next to him, her ears back, and her front hoof raised.

"Easy," Faran soothed in a low voice. "Easy girl."

The horse snorted, then put her hoof on the ground, eyeing the intruder wickedly. Faran walked over to her and stroked her nose, then looked down at the kid on the ground.

"That was dumb," he stated flatly as the kid struggled to sit up. "What'd you want?"

The boy eyed the horse and stood.

"I want to come with you guys," he explained, straightening his clothes.

"You what?" Faran asked, surprised. "who are you? Where'd you come from? And how do you know anything about us?"

"I'm Galdur," the stranger replied. "My dad's the leader of the bandits and I over- heard what he said when he came back tonight."

Faran looked at him for a moment.

"Does your dad know you're here?" he asked.
Galdur shook his head.
"No," he answered. "He'd a beat me good if he knew."
Faran regarded him for a moment then nodded.
"Come on," he decided and strode back over to where Dale was sleeping.

Dale had awakened when Faran slipped out of camp, and had lain still, listening to the boys talk. He sat up as they finished their conversation and tossed some sticks on the coals, then waited for them to approach the campfire.
"He wants to talk to you," Faran said as they walked up to where Dale was sitting, jerking his thumb at the young man behind him.
Dale looked up at Galdur then motioned at the ground. "Have a seat," he said.
Galdur looked around then sat cross legged on the grass.
"So what do you want to talk to me about?" Dale asked him.
Galdur glanced up at Faran, then looked back at Dale.
"Like I told him," he replied. "I want to come with you guys."
"Maybe we don't want anyone else," Dale tried, watching for a reaction.
"Yeah you do," Galdur replied. "My dad said..."
"Your dad?" Dale asked, interrupting. "Who's your dad?"
"My dad's the leader of the bandits," Galdur explained. "He called all the guys together when he got back tonight and I heard him talking about you and what you told him."

"Go on," Dale prompted, keying his sensors and watching Galdur's vital signs flickering across the heads-up display.
"Well he told everyone else," Galdur explained, "not me cause he thought I was asleep and he never tells me anything anyway, that we had to move tomorrow. He said you had a big army you were gonna go get then come after us with."
Dale said nothing and Galdur went on after a moment.

"Anyway, Sneaker jumped up and said no you didn't, that you were gonna go fight an army and my dad popped him one."
"Popped him one?" Dale asked.
"Yeah," Galdur explained. "Punched him in the face. They got in a fight, like they do every night, and I snuck out."
"And you thought," Dale asked, "that you could just walk up and tell us to take you along?"
"Well..." Galdur shrugged. "I thought I'd try anyway. If you said no I wouldn't be any worse off than I am now."
"Do you have any idea just how powerful the army we're facing is?" Dale asked and
Galdur shook his head.
"No," he replied. "But I'm tired of my Dad hitting me all the time."

"So run away," Faran suggested.
"I can't," Galdur responded. "There's no where to run to. Just woods. 'Sides...I've tried a couple times and he always finds me."
"So does your dad know where you are now?" Faran asked.
Galdur shook his head.
"No, I snuck out," he repeated.
"Not very well," Dale responded, standing. He sighed and turned, looking out into the darkness.
"Come on over here," he called loudly. "You're about as quiet as a flock of geese."
There was motion in the darkness and the bandit leader, accompanied with two very nervous men, stepped into sight.
"That there's my kid," the leader stated, his voice shaking slightly. "You got no right to him."

Dale crossed his arms and regarded the man was some hostility. The others were awake now, watching silently.
"And?" Dale asked when he didn't say anything else.

"And I want you to give him back," the man demanded, his voice betraying how nervous he was.
"I can't give back something I haven't taken," Dale explained.
"You're standing between me and my boy," the leader snarled, clinching his fists.
"He came to me," Dale responded, his voice taking on a warning tone, "and I'm not so sure you deserve to have him back."
The two of them regarded each other for a long moment, then the leader relaxed slightly.

"He's a coward," the man declared, a calculating look flickering across his eyes, "but I tell you what. You want him, you pay me for him and you can have him."
"Pay you for him?" Dale repeated incredulously. "You would sell your own son?"
"You want him," the leader repeated, "you pay for him. He's cost me plenty raising him."
Dale took a deep breath and let it out slowly, forcing himself to control his rising anger.
"How much do you want," Dale asked, his voice suddenly very unfriendly.
"Five Gill," the other shot back.
Dale looked at him for a moment, then reached into his pocket and pulled out five small pieces of paper.
"Take it," he commanded, a steely edge to his voice now, and threw the money on the ground at the man's feet. "If I ever see your face again," he continued angrily as the bandit bent down to pick up the bits, "you won't survive the encounter! Now get out of my sight!"
The man looked quickly at the money, then turned and strode off into the night without another word. His men glanced at each other, then turned and hurried after him.

Dale stood motionlessly, his fists clinched, watching them leave. Faran glanced up at him, then quietly sat down next to Galdur.

"You ok?" he asked and Galdur nodded.
"Yeah," he replied, relaxing slightly. "I think so."
"Dale," Jarl asked from the other side of the campfire. "Shall I?"
Dale took a deep breath, then nodded and unclenched his fists.
"Yes," he replied, glancing back down at Galdur. "Finish it."
Jarl nodded, then keyed the sound dampers on his suit and slipped away like the night breeze.
"He's not gonna kill him," Galdur asked fearfully, looking up at Dale. "Is he?"
Dale shook his head.
"No," he replied. "He's just going to make sure your father won't be bothering us, or anyone else, for a very long time."

Chapter Twenty-Six

Jarl flipped on the daylight effects sensors in his suit then activated a special control on his belt. Everything became bright then vanished as light bent around him, rendering him completely invisible. The air in front of him flickered for a second as his heads-up display sprang to life, painting the world in various shades of red. Jarl paused and adjusted the settings on it, then nodded in satisfaction and spent a few seconds studying the information scrolling across the screen. "Left me a trail a blind man could follow," he muttered with a grin.

He ran quickly across the grass, slowed to a walk at the edge of the trees, then cautiously followed the leader and his men into the forest. He trailed them through the trees for several minutes, keeping well out of the way behind them, finally arriving at a large clearing. Tents were scattered around it, the sounds of snoring rising from them, and a fire was burning in a large stone ring. The leader walked over to a log next to the fire and sat down.
"Heh," he chuckled, glancing over at one of the men that had accompanied him.
"Who'd a thunk that lazy brat was worth so much?"
"Yeah," one of his men replied. "You pulled a good one that time."
"You want we should go get him back now?" the other asked, looking at his leader.

The man shook his head.
"No." he replied. "He's worthless anyway, jest eats and gets in the way. He can stay where he is."
"So what're we gonna do now?" the first man asked.
"I figure," the leader told him, "that we can move a few days ride to the north. Should be alright there. We'll wait a couple weeks though before pulling any more jobs. Give them time enough to get gone."

"Sure boss," the second man replied. "What'cha wantta do with the prisoners?"
"We ain't heard nothing back on the ransom yet?" the leader asked and the second man shook his head.
"Nope. Been a month or more too."
"Kill 'em." the leader decided. "I'm tired of waiting."
"Ok boss," the second man acknowledged, drawing his knife.
"Not now you idiot," the leader growled. "I swear you got brains made of wood. Wait till we leave. You think I want dead bodies hanging around?"
"Oh," the second man replied and put his knife away. "Can I have a little fun tonight at least?"
"Yeah whatever," the leader shrugged and the man chuckled evilly, then walked over to the other side of the camp and stepped into the trees. Jarl frowned, then followed him quickly.

The man walked noisily through the underbrush for several minutes, making his way to a small cave in the side of the hill behind the camp. A set of iron bars had been secured over the mouth of the cave, and behind them Jarl could see several people. The man paused and looked through the bars.
"Hey," he said, "just wanted to let you know, that ransom ain't come yet." He chuckled as the prisoners looked at him. "So the boss," he continued. "He's tired o' waiting. Says to kill you."
"No!" one of the men exclaimed. "Why can't you just let us go?"
"Well," he explained, enjoying their fear. "The boss, he ain't too happy. And if we let you go, then word'd spread. We'd never get no ransoms from no-one else. So you gotta die. But don't worry," he continued with a snicker. "We'll kill you quick like, unless you struggle. Then we might just take our time, make it kinda painful... see how loud you kin scream and all. Maybe break a few bones, cut a few pieces off, 'n let you jest bleed ta death kinda slow like..." his eyes glinted with undisguised malice and he chuckled evilly. "We'll make sure the animals don't get ya afterward though."
He reached into a pocket and pulled out a heavy, iron key.

"Now," he went on, twirling the key around on the end of his finger. "I got me a use for the little lady there. So I'm gonna open this door and if she don't come out, I'll just have to do something nasty. She'll be just as tasty without those feet as with 'em."

Jarl stepped silently up behind him and grabbed his head with both hands, then twisted sharply. There was a popping sound and the man went limp. Jarl dropped the body and turned off the light bending function on his belt, flickering back into view.
"Shhh," he cautioned the terrified prisoners, and bent down to pick up the key from the ground.
"Who are you?" one of the men whispered and Jarl shook his head.
"There's no time for that right now," he replied. "Listen carefully. I'm going to open this door but don't move yet. In a few minutes, the bandit camp is going to become very noisy. When that happens, get out of here and make for the edge of the forest." He gestured back toward the camp. "You'll find a trail on the other side of the camp. Stay away from the light, and follow the trail till you're out of the trees then stay out of sight. I'll join you there as soon as I can." The man nodded, and Jarl turned the key in the lock. There was a muffled click and the door moved slightly.
"Here," he said, handing the key to the man. "Remember, stay out of the light and meet me at the edge of the forest."
"Right," the man replied, then jumped as Jarl vanished from sight again.

"Dale," Jarl thought as he flipped the control back on and vanished. "We're gonna have company."
"Who now?" came the response.
"Six people," Jarl thought as he made his way silently back into the bandit camp.
"Four men and two women. Prisoners they were about to kill."
"Alright," Dale replied. "Anyone hurt?"
"Not currently," Jarl growled. "But someone's about to be."

"Don't kill him," Dale responded.
"Oh I don't plan on it," Jarl replied. "He's just going to wish I had."

He stepped back into the camp and glanced around. Everything was quiet and even the guards appeared to be napping at their posts. He studied the layout for a moment, glanced at the tents, then strode to the fire.
"This would be a lot easier," he thought. "If that blasted spell didn't have my powers blocked."
He reached down and grabbed the end of a stick then pulled it carefully out of the fire.

About half of it's length was flaming and he made his way quickly around to the back of the tents then set the first one on fire. Moving rapidly he caught each tent on fire around the camp's perimeter then tossed the still flaming stick into the leaders tent. The first tent was blazing now and its occupant had awoken. Bedlam ensued a few seconds later as people woke to find themselves in burning tents and scrambled to get out. He pulled the blaster off his belt and adjusted the controls then waited. The leader woke suddenly a few moments later and realized with horror that his bedding was on fire. He grabbed his pants and dashed out of the tent. Jarl aimed then fired and the entire tent vanished behind him in a blaze of light. He changed aim and fired again, vaporizing another tent.
One of the men made a mad dash out of the camp and Jarl grabbed him as he ran past, then tossed him into the air. He screamed as he sailed up several feet then fell, landing on top of another man who was desperately trying to put out the flames on his tent. The camp was in chaos now and Jarl dodged fleeing bandits, then vaporized several more tents.

"Ghosts!" someone shouted, and the cry was instantly taken up by the rest as they fled in all directions into the forest. The leader found himself standing alone in the middle of the devastated camp, watching in disbelief as tent after tent vanished in a flash of light. Jarl stepped up behind him silently, then hit him over the head. He crumpled soundlessly to the ground and lay still.

Jarl picked him up and carried him out of the camp, stripped him naked and dropped him on top of a rather large anthill not far away, then tossed the bandit's clothing up into the branches of a nearby tree. Looking around, he located a fairly sturdy stick and poked it into the ant hill.
"There are several things," he thought as he stirred up the hill with the stick, infuriating the ants within, "that are considerably worse than dying." He left the unconscious bandit leader draped across the hill, covered with swarming, furious ants, and walked back to what was left of the bandit camp.

The few horses that the bandits had were hobbled not far away, and Jarl found them fairly easily. He took note of their position, then spent several minutes tracking down the bandits that had fled. Most had gone deep into the forest but a few were crouched together not far from the camp, whispering. He adjusted the controls on his belt and became partly visible then stepped into their line of sight and vaporized a bush next to them. They looked up startled, then jumped to their feet as one man and dashed off into the trees. He watched them go, then flipped the visibility control off completely and turned back to the camp. It was deserted now, the fire still burning in the middle of it and the bandits possessions scattered around. He checked the prison cave and noted with satisfaction that it was empty, the door standing wide open.
"Good," he thought. "Hopefully they got out safely."

He searched the camp rapidly, then paused.
"Dale," he thought and waited for the response.
"Yes?" came Dale's reply after a moment.
"I'm done here but I hate to leave all this stuff behind," he thought back, "and I can't control all eight horses by myself."

"What do you need?" Dale responded.
"Access to my powers for a few minutes," he explained.
"You don't have access?" Dale asked.
"No," Jarl responded. "That spell keeps me from using them unless given a direct order."
"Ah, I forgot about that," Dale replied. "Do whatever you need to but get back here in the next twenty minutes."
"Thanks," Jarl responded.
He picked up a small bag that was laying on the ground and concentrated briefly, then began shoving things inside it. He worked rapidly and within a few minutes there were only a few old blankets and other useless items left. Walking over to the horses he put the bag over the first one's nose then braced as it sparkled suddenly and was sucked into the opening. He moved on to the next one and shortly had all eight in the bag. Their tack had been piled nearby and it quickly followed the horses into the bag as well.
"Ten minutes," he thought as he pushed the last saddle into the bag. "And it's full. I've got to get back."
He slung the bag over his shoulder, then headed down the trail toward the edge of the forest.

The people he had rescued were not waiting for him at the edge of the forest as he had instructed and he glanced around, then shrugged. The twenty minutes Dale had given him were nearly gone and the spell tugged at him painfully, forcing him to give up the search and run back to their camp. He re-entered its perimeter with five seconds to spare and paused, panting, as the pressure released. He caught his breath then looked around and realized why no one had been waiting for him.

Around the campfire, which was now burning brightly again, sat all six of the bandit's former prisoners. Dale was talking with one of the men and Aerline was busy examining the rest for wounds that needed attention. Jarl took a deep breath and relaxed then

walked over to Dale and handed him the bag without a word. Dale glanced at it, then nodded.
"Thank you," he replied. "What did you do with the bandits?"
"They're scattered," he explained. "Some of them are probably still running."
"And the leader?" Dale asked.
"Sent him to sleep and left him dreaming on an anthill," Jarl replied tersely.

Dale snickered at the mental image Jarl projected and the man he was talking to chuckled.
"Now that I would have loved to have witnessed," the stranger remarked. 'But you were kinder to him that I would have been."
Jarl grinned, then walked over out of the way and sat down. He was exhausted now, but sleep evaded him, so he sat silently, listening to the conversation.
"I wouldn't suggest returning through that forest," Dale was saying. "The bandits are still in there, though from what Jarl says, they're pretty impotent right now."
"I tend to agree," the man replied. "But we really don't have much choice. The other roads will take us almost a years travel before we reach Baron Eleriem. We were to have been there nearly two months ago now as it is."
"It's your choice," Dale responded. "We'll try to make sure you're armed at least, before you leave."
"Thank you," the man replied, smiling. "We do appreciate all your assistance."

"I just want to know why they never paid the ransom," one of the other men whined peevishly.
"The Baron probably never got the ransom note," the first man replied. "Or I'm sure he'd have paid it."
"Well I should certainly hope so," the second man declared with an ingratiating sniff. "He'd better have a good explanation when we get there."

"Now Lord Rheoddry," the first man responded, his voice strained. "I'm sure the Baron will have a very good reason for not sending the ransom."
"Yeah," Faran remarked darkly. "Probably didn't pay it cause you wouldn't sleep with him."
Everyone stopped and stared at Faran who was poking a stick angrily into the fire.
"What did you say??" Lord Rheoddry demanded, his voice stiff and angry.
"You're not a woman," Faran explained, looking at him. "He probably just laughed when he got the note."
Lord Rheoddry pulled himself up arrogantly "Do you know who I am??" he demanded scornfully.
"Yeah," Faran replied nonplused. "Do you know who I am?" He met Lord Rheoddry's eyes with an icy glare. No one moved for more than a minute then the man relaxed.
"Of course not," he exclaimed imperiously. "Why would I even care who you are?! Stupid peasant!"
He got up, tossed his head and flounced from the camp with his nose in the air.

Faran's mouth dropped open as he watched him walk off, then he burst out laughing.
"Dale," he asked, tears streaming down his face. "Was I that bad?"
"Yes," Dale replied. "Just about."
"I take back everything bad I ever said or thought about you," Faran said, shaking his head. "What an idiot!"
Dale grinned.
"You have courage, young man," the man who Dale had been speaking with told him. "But it might not be wise to challenge His Lordship, or insult the Baron as you have."
"Why?" Faran asked. "We're outside the Barony."
"True," he replied. "But you might not be outside it forever and I hear the Baron can be a vengeful man."

Faran shrugged.
"That'd be something new," he commented, poking the stick further into the fire. "My father, bothering to take notice of me for any reason. Hah! That'll be the day."
The man stared at him for a second then looked at Dale.

"His father," Dale explained, "IS the Baron. So I wouldn't worry about his reaction too much if I were you."
"I guess not," the other blinked. "Well that certainly sets things in a different light. Don't take His Lordship too seriously," he told Faran. "He's a bit out of his element right now."
"Don't worry about it," Faran replied, then grinned at Dale. "I was pretty bad myself a few weeks ago."
"I can see there's quite a story here," the man commented then glanced back over to where Lord Rheoddry was standing in the darkness. "But I think I'll pass on hearing it. It takes forever to get him calmed down once he starts acting like this. I'd better go talk to him."
"No," Dale said quietly, arresting the other man's movement. "Leave him alone. If he wants attention, he can come over here where we are."
The man started to protest but caught the look in Dale's eyes and thought better of it.
"Perhaps you're right," he mused, and sat down on the ground. "It might be better at that."
"It's late," Dale stated as he handed the other man one of the blankets Jarl had liberated. "I suggest we all get some sleep. In the morning we'll give you what assistance we can and you can decide which way to travel."

Lord Rheoddry stood, fuming, in the darkness then stared in disbelief as the group around the campfire began bedding down for what was left of the night.

"How dare they!?" he thought, tapping his foot on the ground furiously. "Without my permission! Why I'll have them drawn and quartered!"

No one paid him any attention however and he finally stalked back over to the fire, his face a mask of indignation. Faran looked up as he strode back in and stood.

"Don't," he warned before Lord Rheoddry could speak. "You want to throw a temper tantrum, do it somewhere else." Lord Rheoddry opened his mouth and Faran drew his sword, pointing it at him. "I said don't," he repeated firmly. "I do NOT have to put up with your nonsense and neither does anyone else here."

Lord Rheoddry spluttered indignantly and Faran walked around the fire, still pointing the sword at him. No one moved though all eyes were on the two of them.

"Why you dirty little rodent!" Lord Rheoddry fumed and Faran spun the sword, smacking him with the flat on his unprotected backside. He let out a surprised yelp and backed away.

"You are fortunate not to still be back in the clutches of the bandits," Faran informed him, his eyes smoldering. "You are NOT going to stand there, and insult the hospitality my Lord has shown you! Now shut up and sit down!!"

Lord Rheoddry tripped as he stepped backwards and fell sprawling on the ground. Faran bent forward and touched the sword point to his chest.

"For your information," he said sharply, glaring down at the unfortunate noble on the ground before him. "I am Alain Herauso Feliks the fifth of House Eleriem, son of Baron Eleriem and I out rank you! You are a guest here, and in debt to my Lord for your life. Keep your tongue still unless it is to say thank you or I will remove it, along with your worthless head, with the edge of this blade!"

Lord Rheoddry stared at the sword, looked up at it's wielder and gulped. He nodded quickly, and Faran stepped away from him, but kept the sword at ready.

"I think," Dale said, "that if Lord Rheoddry has no further objections, we should all be getting to sleep."
Lord Rheoddry glanced up at where Faran still stood, watching him, and licked his lips.
"No further objections," he agreed quickly. "None what so ever."
"Good," Dale replied. "Faran get him a blanket and put the fire out."
"Yes sir," Faran replied, and sheathed his sword, then went to do as Dale had directed.

Chapter Twenty-Seven

As the sun peeked over the trees, it found itself shining down on a rather strange sight. Dale had walked some distance from the camp and stood now, holding the bag that Jarl had brought back from the bandit camp. He reached into it then removed his hand and a horse appeared to grow rapidly out of the mouth of the bag until it stood next to him on the grass. Aerline stepped up to the horse and whispered at it for a moment then led it to the side. Dale waited till she was done then repeated the action. In short order they had eight horses standing patiently, their tails flicking away an occasional fly. Dale looked them over and nodded.

"They look healthy," he commented. "Now lets see what their tack looks like."

He reached back into the bag and began pulling the saddles out one at a time. The bridles and saddle blankets were next and with in a few seconds he had a large pile on the ground. He looked them over then nodded.

"All in decent condition," he observed. "We'll give them their pick."

"What about the extra two?" Aerline asked, stroking one of them on the nose.

"We have an extra person now," Dale reminded her. "We'll keep one for a pack horse and Galdur will ride the other."

He reached down and picked up one of the saddle blankets, then flung it over the nearest horse.

"Help me get them saddled," he requested.

They worked quickly and before long had the horses saddled, and ready for riding. Aerline paused then whispered something to them. They snorted, tossed their heads and followed her back over to the campsite.

It took nearly two hours that morning to rouse everyone from sleep and sort out supplies. Lord Rheoddry insisted on taking the shortest route to the Baron's castle so it was decided that they would brave the forest and hope the bandits were too scattered to bother them. Dale provided them with food and weapons out of what Jarl had collected from the bandit's camp the night before, then they mounted and set out for the forest. Faran stood, his hands on his hips, watching them go.

"He'll fit right in," he mused as the riders entered the woods and vanished from sight.

"With what?" Kheri asked, busily packing the saddlebags.

"My fathers court," Faran replied, turning away from the forest. "Unless he's so late that he loses his head for his troubles."

"Would your father really behead someone for being late?" Kheri asked, looking up at him in surprise.

"No," Faran replied. "But the Vice-Chancelor would," he explained, looking at Kheri seriously, "and has. Probably why he's so worried about taking the shortest route."

"Man," Kheri remarked sarcastically, shaking his head. "What a nice guy."

"Not really," Faran agreed. "Not a nice guy at all."

"I wasn't serious," Kheri replied, standing up and brushing his hands off.

"Alright let's GO!" Dale shouted, already sitting impatiently on his horse. The company took several more seconds to hastily finish repacking, then mounted up and set off on the next leg of the journey.

The road wound it's way into the mountains up a fairly gentle slope but before they had been riding for an hour, it had become quite steep and began switching back and forth. Tall pine trees grew thickly on either side and the air was much cooler now. The horses walked slowly, and the creak of the saddles was loud in the still mountain air. Rocks could be seen laying around the sides of the road at times and high over head, the dark specks of circling hawks could just be discerned against the sky. The cry of an eagle drifted to them on a slight breeze as they rounded a curve and they found themselves looking out over a mist enshrouded forest which filled the valley they had left far below. They sat, looking down at it for a few minutes, each wrapped in their own thoughts, then turned and continued on up the road.

As the day was coming to a close, the road topped the first rise and they found themselves looking across a meadow of bright yellow and pink flowers. The road cut straight through them, and then disappeared into a dark opening in the mountain on the other side.

"That is the Wizard's Cut," Aerline explained. "Legend has it that the mage Flavorius got drunk one night and chased what he thought was a maiden through the city streets. When he caught her however, he discovered she was no maiden at all but a rival wizard. They dueled, destroying the town, and were sealed in rock for eternity as punishment by the Wizard's Council. But one day two hundred years later, there was a terrible earthquake that shook the mountain and rained fiery rock down on the valley below. When it was over, there was a piece of the mountain missing. Some say that Flavorius and his rival had spent two hundred years building up power and had destroyed each other along with that section of the mountain in a final fit of passion."

"What nonsense," Faran scoffed and Aerline looked at him.

"It's not nonsense," she insisted. "There have been wizard duels in the past that burned down whole forests or did other terrible things. It's one reason the wizards college was established. To make sure that anyone with that kind of power was not running around loose to destroy the world."

"Regardless of how it got there," Dale remarked. "It appears to be useful now."

"Yes," Aerline agreed, looking back across the meadow. "It would be impossible to get over these mountains without it."

They rode a short way into the meadow and camped beside a small spring that bubbled out of the ground. The sun was well on the way to setting and the light had taken on a reddish hue, setting the clouds above them ablaze. Aerline surprised them with several rabbits and before long the smell of roasting meat drifted through the air. Dale waited until camp was set up and dinner under way then he motioned to Galdur and walked a short way off. Galdur glanced at Faran who shrugged, then got to his feet and went to join him.

Dale stood silently for several minutes, looking over the meadow and considering the road ahead. Galdur walked reluctantly over to him and stood, fidgeting. After a few moments, Dale turned and looked at him.

"What skills do you have?" Dale asked, and Galdur blinked.

"Huh?" he replied. "I thought I'd done something wrong."

"No," Dale shook his head. "Why would you think that?"

Galdur shrugged.

"I dunno," he shrugged. "I guess just cause you wanted to talk private like."

"No," Dale reassured him, "I need to know what you can do."

"Nuttin," Galdur said. "'Cept cook and take care of the horses."

Dale regarded him thoughtfully for a moment.

"Have you ever handled a weapon before?" he asked and Galdur shook his head.

"My dad woulda flayed me alive!" He replied vehemently. "He'd a cut my hands off at the elbows and fed 'em to me!"

"We're getting ready to journey into very dangerous territory," Dale explained. "On the other side of that cut up there, the mountains are wild and there's no telling what we might meet in them. Cooking and taking care of the horses will do you no good if we meet up with a dragon...or worse."

Galdur nodded and glanced past him at the dark line on the mountain.

"So," Dale continued. "We'll have to teach you how to at least defend yourself."

"I'll try," Galdur agreed doubtfully, "but I probably won't be any good."
"What makes you think that?" Dale asked, studying his face.
Galdur shrugged.
"I'm just no good at anything," he replied. "Cept cooking."
"We'll see," Dale told him. "For right now, go keep Faran from burning the rabbits."
"Sure," Galdur responded and ran back over to the campfire.

Dale stood and looked around the meadow, thinking. Jarl and Kheri had walked away from the campfire and were talking. Aerline was happily petting a small skunk that was curled up in her lap. Faran and Galdur were sitting by the fire, turning the rabbits and laughing. He watched them for several minutes, wishing desperately that there were no Gorg in the universe, and no reason to drag them into a battle they might not survive.
"Dale," came Kheri's quiet thought. "What's wrong?"
"Nothing," Dale replied, blocking communication.
Kheri blinked, then looked over at Jarl.
"Don't worry about it," Jarl told him. "He's moody sometimes. He'll get over it before too long. Best to leave him alone though when he's like this. He'll get over it faster."
"You're sure?" Kheri asked and Jarl grinned at him.
"Yes," he replied. "Don't worry about it."

Darkness fell and the meadow came alive with fireflies. Faran watched them flitting, just as fascinated as he had been the night before, then poked Galdur in the ribs.
"Hey!" came Galdur's startled reaction, but Faran was up on his feet and running. Galdur jumped to his feet and gave chase, and tackled Faran several feet from the fire. They went down in a heap, startling a pheasant into the air. She passed over their heads with a loud whirring of wings and disappeared into the darkness.
"What was that?" Faran asked, getting back to his feet.

"Bird of some kind," Galdur replied. "There must be a nest around here."

They hunted carefully through the grass, trying not to step on anything breakable but didn't find any nest.

"It's too dark to see," Galdur decided after a few minutes. "We'll never find it at night."

"I caught a firefly!" Faran exclaimed excitedly, forgetting about the nest. "Look!"

He held his hands out and the firefly climbed up onto his thumb then flew off. Dale watched the boys chasing after the fireflies for a few minutes, then walked back over to the campfire and turned the rabbits.

As the night deepened and the company finished eating, the air became chill, reminding them that the snow wasn't very far above their heads now. They threw more wood on the fire and wrapped up on their blankets then slowly drifted off to sleep. Dale woke up at first light, shivering with the cold.

"Why am I so cold?" he wondered aloud, checking the suits sensors. Everything appeared to be functioning correctly. He kicked the heating elements on slightly and wrapped his blanket around himself tightly, waiting for them to warm up.

Faran rolled over, yawned, and sat up blinking in the early morning light.

"It's cold!" he complained, shivering as he looked around for his blanket. He threw it around his shoulders and huddled under it, shivering and looking miserable.

"Stop whining," Kheri admonished him, sitting up. "If you're cold, get up and go get wood. It'll warm you up."

Faran made a face at him and buried his nose under his blanket.

"Faran," Dale said, prodding him. "Take Kheri and go get wood. We need to get a fire going."

Faran looked up, a sour expression on his face, and stood up sullenly.

"See what you did?" he groused, glaring at Kheri, then dropped his blanket to the ground. "Come on," he demanded and stomped off toward the closest trees.
"Why me?" Kheri griped as he stood. "I wasn't the one complaining."
"I know," Dale replied. "Now go get wood."

Kheri made a face then reluctantly followed Faran to the trees.
"You got me in trouble," he grumbled to Faran as they picked wood up off the ground.
"Sorry," Faran griped. "I wasn't trying to..." He paused, then looked over at Kheri. "Wait a minute," he paused. "You're the one that told me to stop whining, so how'd I get you in trouble?"
Kheri glared at him and Faran dropped the wood then stood up, clinching his fists. Kheri dropped what wood he was holding and took a step toward him then winced suddenly.

"Ummm..." he said, stepping back. "Maybe it's not your fault after all." He picked the wood back up quickly and headed back to the campsite without another word. Faran watched him go in surprise, bent down and picked up the wood he'd dropped and walked slowly back to camp, confused. Kheri was busy building the fire back up when he returned and the others were stirring. He dropped the wood on the ground next to Kheri's pile, then shook Galdur awake.
"Come on," he urged, dragging him to his feet without explanation, then headed back toward the trees. Galdur blinked sleepily and stretched, then followed after him, yawning. Kheri finished with the fire, then refilled the water bags at the spring. By the time he returned, everyone else was awake and breakfast was in progress. He set the water bags down, stood up and looked around.

Dale was standing not far away, watching the boys as they collected wood. Kheri walked up to him and stood silently, waiting.
"Yes?" Dale asked after a moment without turning to face him.

"I'm sorry," he apologized, looking down at his hands.
"Why must you pick fights with Faran?" Dale asked, looking at him. Kheri shook his head.
"I didn't mean to start a fight," he explained. "I just got up in a bad mood I guess."
"Well kindly get out of it then," Dale told him. "We have more than enough enemies without fighting among ourselves as well."
Kheri nodded.
"I'm sorry Dale," he apologized again. "I'll watch myself."
"Thank you," Dale replied, turning back to watch the boys for a moment.

"I need you to work with Galdur," he said after minute or so. "Teach him how to dodge at least. His father never allowed him to do anything but cook and take care of the horses."
Kheri shot Dale an incredulous look then shook his head and started across the meadow.
"What's with all these no-good dads?" he wondered as he walked over to the boys.
Faran looked up as he got near, and motioned excitedly.
"Look what we found!" he exclaimed, then turned his attention back to the ground.
Kheri walked over curiously and looked down.
The boys had moved a log and underneath it was an indentation in the ground. Grass had been placed inside it, creating a nest and six tiny mice peered back up at him sleepily.
"Mice," he stated.
"They're so tiny!" Faran said, kneeling down to look at them closer.
"They're babies," Kheri explained. "You guys should put their house back before they get cold."
"Oh yeah," Faran agreed, grabbing the log. "Come on Galdur, help me."

They dragged the log back over the baby mice and set it back in position then Faran got down on his stomach to make sure that the mother could still get back into the nest when she returned. Kheri grinned, watching him.
"Faran," he said after a moment. "I'm sorry about picking a fight this morning."
"It's ok," Faran replied, standing up and brushing the dirt off of his shirt. He grinned at the log a last time, then picked the wood up that he'd forgotten about in his excitement of finding the mice.
"Come on Galdur," he commanded. "Let's get this wood back to camp."

Kheri watched them walk back to camp and chuckled slightly. "Now that's an unlikely friendship," he thought, thinking about how different the boy's lives had been until recently. He followed them back to camp then caught Faran's eye and motioned him over.
"What's up?" Faran asked as he walked over.
"Galdur," Kheri explained. "Dale wants me to teach him to dodge. Evidently he's never learned how to do anything but cook and take care of horses."
Faran frowned.
"That's not gonna work very well," he replied.
"Especially if we get attacked by Gorg again," Kheri agreed.
"Well I can teach him to use a sword," Faran stated. "We've got lots of extras now."
"Most of 'em are in pretty bad shape," Kheri objected. "But ask Dale. I think it would be a good idea for him to learn to use some weapon at least."
Faran nodded.
"Yeah." he agreed. "I can't believe he was living with a bunch of bandits and never learned."
"Guess you'll have to ask him about that," Kheri replied. "I'll teach him to dodge and throw. You teach him how to use a sword."

"Kheri," Dale called from the other side of the camp, interrupting them. "If you intend to eat before we get back on the road, I suggest you do so now."
Kheri started, then left Faran where he stood and went in rapid search of food.

They were packed and back in the saddle not long afterward, and Faran urged his horse up next to Dale's.
"We found some mice earlier," he said, his eyes shining. "Babies. They were only this big!" he held his thumb and forefinger apart to show Dale the size.
Dale grinned at him and listened as he went on to talk about the fat spider in her web he'd discovered, and the pheasant he and Galdur had startled the previous evening. He grew serious after a few minutes however and glanced back to make sure he couldn't be overheard.

"Would you mind if I taught Galdur how to use a sword?" he asked in a quiet voice.
"You're welcome to try," Dale replied. "I'm not sure whether he'll agree to it or not though."
"Well he has to learn how to use some kind of weapon," Faran argued, glancing back again.
"And why is that?" Dale asked, turning to look at him.
"Because," Faran replied, then frowned and tried to think of a good reason.
"Well?" Dale asked after a few minutes.
"Because he might need to know how," Faran finished then shrugged.
"Not everyone is suited to be a fighter," Dale explained patiently. "He does need to know how to get out of the way. but before we start teaching him how to fight, let's find out a little bit more about him ok?"
"Well, alright," Faran agreed reluctantly. "But what if the Gorg come back?"

"The Gorg," Dale replied, "are after me. At least the ones that have attacked us have been. They'll come for me and kill anything in their way. He'll need to know how to get out of their way and stay out of their way. We can't possibly turn him into a fighter who is skilled enough to take out even one Gorg without several years to train him."

Faran looked doubtful but acquiesced to Dale's assessment.

"We'll see what he says," Dale told him, sensing Faran's frustration. "If he's interested in learning the sword, you can try teaching him."

"Alright," Faran agreed, brightening.

Chapter Twenty-Eight

The Wizard's Cut loomed ahead of them now, dark and threatening, as if no light from the sun could penetrate the space between the high rock walls. A shimmering filled the entrance and nothing could be seen on the other side. The others rode forward unconcerned but Kheri felt the hair rising on the back of his neck and reined his horse in suddenly. Dale jumped as Kheri's sudden panic flooded through his mind and brought his horse to a stand still a few feet in front of the entrance to the cut. The others reined in sharply as well and looked about confused. Dale took a deep breath, forcing down the panic that was still flowing from Kheri, then dismounted and walked up to the entrance.

The shimmering hummed slightly, and he could feel the power behind it. He looked at it curiously, then reached forward. As his hand encountered the field, the sensors in his suit came to light and flashed data across the heads-up display, scrolling faster than he could follow. He waited until the scrolling stopped then pulled his hand back and studied the read-out for a moment, then flipped the display off.
"Well," he declared, turning around to the others. "I know what happened to that mage."
"What mage?" Jarl said.
"The one Aerline told us about yesterday," Dale replied. "Flavorsomething I think was the name?"
Aerline nodded.
"Yes," she replied. "Mage Flavorius. The one that was sealed away in the rock for punishment."
"He's still in there," Dale explained and she stared. "The rock's not gone either."

"Of course it's gone," Aerline protested. "Look, the road goes right through it."

"No it doesn't," Dale replied. "It goes around it. The rock," he paused, trying to figure out how to explain jump-space to someone with no technology. "Look," he explained. "Think about it like this." He pulled a long blade of grass and held it up. "Pretend that you were an ant crawling from the bottom to the top. Now pretend that somehow the grass got bent," he went on, bending a large loop out of the middle of the grass. "When you got to here," he pointed to where the bottom and top of the grass was now touching, "you could step across from the bottom part, to the top part, without ever touching the middle."

"So are you saying that the rock is bent?" Aerline asked, wrinkling her nose and peering at the apparent opening in the mountain.
"Yes," Dale said. "That's exactly what I'm saying. Not bent like this grass, but the space it occupies has been bent out of the way. The reason we can go through here is because there's a magical wedge that's keeping it bent out of the way."
Aerline got down off her horse and walked up to the entrance. She studied it for a moment then turned to Dale.
"What would happen if the wedge vanished?" She asked, casting a critical glance at the rock.
"Then the opening would vanish," Dale explained.
"And anyone inside?" she asked, looking at him.

Dale shook his head.
"No one's ever actually inside," he explained. "Remember that the ant just travels from the bottom part of the grass to the top part without ever going along the part that's in the loop."
"But it seems to take such a long time to travel through," Aerline protested.
"That's because it takes a certain amount of time to fully enter the field that the wedge is producing," Dale explained. "And then the same amount to exit it on the other side. The actual travel from one side to the other is in an instant. So," he continued. "If the wedge vanished while someone was traveling from one side to the

other, they'd find themselves being thrown violently back where they started or violently forward to where they were going."

He turned back and looked at the field again, then looked at Aerline.
"The reason it's still there after all this time is because it's constantly being renewed." he continued. "That mage is still in the rock, and his magic is what's powering the wedge. I don't know why he hasn't stopped it, perhaps he can't."
"So as long as he still lives we'll still have a road here?" Aerline asked.
"Yes," Dale said. "Or until he figures out how to get free."
"Time-stop," Jarl put in and Dale nodded.
"Maybe, but not full stop," he agreed. "Or anything entering the field would stop moving too."
"Yeah, but close," Jarl stated. "Which would also account for how long it takes to get from one side to the other."
"Which means," Dale agreed with a nod. "That the other wizard is still in there too and they're still fighting."

"How is that possible?" Aerline asked looking at the entrance again.
"Because," Dale explained, "Their time is running so slowly, that they are probably still just casting the spell that caused this."
"But that was six thousand years ago!" Aerline protested.
"Yes, and it might take them another six thousand years to finish it," Dale agreed. "Or they might finish it five minutes from now."
"Oh this is terrible," Aerline exclaimed. "I wonder if the wizards at the college know."
"Probably not," Jarl put in. "And I bet they wouldn't believe you if you told them."
"No," Aerline agreed. "They'd never believe me about this."

Dale walked back to Kheri's horse and looked up at him. He was sitting, staring at the entrance, his face pale.

"Kheri." Dale said, reaching up for the horse's reins.
Kheri closed his eyes and shuddered, then looked down at Dale.
"I can't go through there," he whispered. "I just can't."
"Dismount," Dale commanded gently. "Please."
Kheri swung down slowly, and Dale took the reins from him.
"Here," he said, handing the reins up to Jarl.
Jarl took the reins and nodded.
"I'll lead it through," he replied.
"Come on," Dale told Kheri, and led the way back to his horse.
Kheri shivered then followed closely behind him, trying to avoid looking at the entrance of the cut.

Dale swung back up onto the horse, then reached his hand down to Kheri.
"Get up in front of me," he instructed the younger man.
Kheri took a deep breath and fought down rising panic, then mounted and settled into the saddle in front of Dale, closed his eyes and gripped the horse's mane with both hands. Dale waited until Aerline had remounted, then urged his horse forward. They rode up to the entrance single file. As Dale's horse entered the leading edge of the field Kheri suddenly cried out in terror and tried to throw himself out of the saddle. Dale wrapped both arms around him and held him tightly.
"Kheri," he thought. "Talk to me."
"I can't see!" came the panicked response. "I can't feel anything."
"It's ok," Dale thought back at him. "You'll be ok. Just hang on to me and we'll get through this."
"I can't!" came Kheri's hysterical reply. "I don't know where you are!"
"I'm right here," Dale assured him. "You can hear me can't you?"
"Yes," Kheri agreed, his thoughts shaking. "I can hear you."

"Alright," Dale responded. "Now think. You were sitting on the horse in front of me when we entered the field. You're still sitting on the horse. I'm not going to allow anything to happen to you."
"But it's so cold," Kheri thought, his mental voice fading slightly.
"Jarl!" Dale thought quickly.
"Yeah?" came Jarl's rather bored response.
"Keep an eye on my horse," he directed. "I've got a full-blown case of jump-sickness to deal with."
"Kheri not doing well?" Jarl asked.
"No," Dale responded. "He's in total panic."
"Alright," came Jarl's response. "I'll watch the horse."

Dale turned his attention back to Kheri. The younger man was shivering now and pressed back hard against him.
"Kheri," Dale thought, trying to get his attention.
"I'm c-c-cold," came Kheri's reply.
"It's not cold," Dale thought. "It's only cold in your imagination."
"But," Kheri thought back and Dale interrupted him.
"Kheri," Dale thought firmly. "It only feels cold, it only seems dark, because you are afraid. Get ahold of yourself."
Kheri didn't respond but his body relaxed slightly and stopped shivering so hard.
"Talk to me," Dale thought.
"What about?" Kheri's reply was sluggish but not as panicked.
"Tell me about Paw Tucker," Dale answered, searching for something that would capture Kheri's attention for a while.
"Paw Tucker?" came Kheri's response, less sluggish now. "You met him, He's my aunt's neighbor. Remember? We got the horses there?"
"What are his kids names?" Dale asked.
"His kids..." Kheri replied, and relaxed further as his mind became distracted and less fearful. Dale glanced at the readout on his suit

and sighed in relief. Kheri's vital signs were slowly returning to normal.

It took nearly thirty minutes for them to pass through the Wizard's Cut. Dale spent the entire time talking to Kheri and trying to keep him distracted. As the horse took a final step and exited the field, Kheri jumped and let out a cry, then dropped his head in his hands and began sobbing. Dale let the horse walk a few feet out of the way of the others then reined it to a stop and sat still. He said nothing, just continued to hold Kheri and let him cry for several minutes.

Kheri's emotions were in chaos. It took him nearly ten minutes to calm down enough to stop sobbing. He could hear Dale directing the others to continue riding, then he felt the horse begin to move again but he kept his face covered with his hands, afraid to look and see the awful darkness that had tried to destroy him.
"Kheri?" Dale asked quietly several minutes later after the sobbing had finally stopped.
"What?" came Kheri's muffled response.
"Just making sure you were still with me," Dale explained gently.
Kheri relaxed slightly, then took a deep breath and cautiously lowered his hands. The woods they were passing through now looked normal and he wiped the tears from his face.
"Gonna make it?" Dale asked as he felt Kheri stir.
"I think so," Kheri replied then shivered.
"Take it easy," Dale said. "You're not completely recovered yet."
Kheri nodded then closed his eyes and relaxed, listening to the horse plodding along over the stony ground. He sighed slightly and fell asleep, his emotions totally drained.

They rode on for several more hours, past tall stately pines and huge boulders that forced the road to curve around them. Dale waited until it was fairly late in the afternoon, then called a halt next to a

small brook that burbled happily down the mountain. He handed the still unconscious Kheri down to Jarl, then dismounted.
"What's wrong with him?" Faran asked as Jarl laid Kheri down on a blanket out of the way.
"He had a fright back there in the Wizard's Cut," Jarl replied. "And he's gotta sleep it off."
"What scared him?" Faran wondered. "I didn't see anything."
"There wasn't anything," Jarl explained, standing back up. "But some people just get scared. Takes a while to get used to it."
"Is he gonna be ok?" Faran asked, looking down at Kheri, a worried expression on his face.
"Yeah," Jarl responded. "He'll probably sleep for the next two days though."
"Two days!?" Faran exclaimed.
"Yeah." Jarl nodded. "That's about the norm. Some people it's longer. Took me a week the first time I went through before I woke back up."
"You've been through the Wizard's Cut before?" Faran asked and Jarl shook his head.
"No. Just been through what's causing the Wizard's Cut."
Faran looked confused.
"Don't worry about it kid," Jarl told him with a grin and patted Faran on the shoulder then walked off to help with the horses.

They stayed by the stream while Kheri recovered from the exhaustion traveling through the Wizard's Cut had caused in him. Faran and Galdur spent the hours exploring, their friendship rapidly becoming unbreakable. Aerline discovered a fox's den with several pups just old enough to venture outside and spent the time playing with them. Jarl spent most of the time sleeping, grateful for the chance. Dale spent the time worrying alternately about a possible Gorg attack and Kheri. His worries were unfounded however, and about six pm on the second day that they'd been camped by the stream, Kheri finally awoke.

He sat up and rubbed his eyes, then looked around. The memory of the passage through the Wizard's Cut was dulled somewhat and he felt embarrassed to have given in to panic so badly. Dale noticed him stirring and sat down beside the blanket as he woke up.
"Here," he handed Kheri a bowl of stew they'd made earlier in the day. "Eat."
Kheri took the bowl and sniffed at it then was suddenly overwhelmed with hunger. He nearly inhaled it, so rapidly did the contents empty from the bowl. Dale watched him with a slight grin on his face, then took the empty bowl and refilled it.
"Here," he said, handing him the bowl. "Let me know if you want more when that's empty."
Kheri finished off three bowls of stew and part of a fourth before the hunger was abated. He set the bowl down on the ground when he realized he couldn't eat any more, then looked up at Dale who was sitting on a stump nearby, watching him.

"Thank you," he said sheepishly. "I didn't know I could eat that much."
Dale grinned.
"Jump-sickness will do that," he explained.
"Jump-sickness?" Kheri asked, confused.
"Yes," Dale replied. "That's the term for what happened to you when we entered the Wizard's Cut."
Kheri looked at him uncomprehendingly.
"It doesn't have anything to do with jumping up and down Kheri," Jarl commented, from somewhere to his left.
He glanced over at Jarl and frowned.
"I don't get it," he said.
"Don't worry about it," Jarl replied, grinning at him. "That's just what it's called."
Kheri looked back at Dale.
"Why do I feel like I'm missing something?" he asked.
Dale chuckled.
"I'll try to explain," he told him and Kheri nodded.

"Remember that I come from out there," Dale began, pointing up. "In the stars."
"Yes," Kheri replied.
"And remember that I said the stars are actually suns," Dale went on, "just so far away that they look tiny."
Kheri nodded.
"Yes," he repeated.
"Now," Dale explained, "those stars are also very far away from each other. The amount of time it would take you to ride a horse from one to another is incredibly long. Millions and millions of years. However," he went on, trying to find a way to simplify interstellar travel, "that takes far too long. No one would ever get anywhere at that rate. So to make it faster, we use the same sort of thing that causes the Wizards' Cut to work. Only we call it jumping, because it seems like jumping from one star to the other. And we call anything related to it jump- something. The field we went through in the Wizard's Cut is called jump-space because going into it is what allows you to move between two points that are far apart without having to cover the space in between, just like physically jumping will allow you to move between two points that are several feet apart without walking across the ground in between. With me so far?"

Kheri nodded silently and Dale grinned at him then went on.
"What happened to you as a result of going into that field is called jump-sickness. It's a fairly common reaction the first time through and some people never get over it. I'm not sure why the rest of the company wasn't affected. It might have something to do with so much magic in this world."
"So I'm not a coward?" Kheri asked, unspoken worries coloring his voice, and Dale shook his head.
"No," he replied. "Far from it. You actually did very well."
Kheri looked relieved and smiled lopsidedly.

"Thanks," he said. "I don't remember much of what happened, I just felt like I was being swallowed by the darkness."
Dale nodded.
"Your imagination was playing tricks on you," he explained. "There's no darkness in jump-space. There's isn't anything at all but the mind doesn't like that and tries to fill in the nothing with something. The others saw a road running through the mountain because that's what they expected to see. You saw darkness because your fear got the better of you."
"What'd you see?" Kheri asked curiously.
"The same thing I always see," Dale answered. "Grey fog."

Chapter Twenty-Nine

As evening fell, the stars came out overhead and peppered the sky with bits of glittering light. Kheri walked a short ways from camp as soon as it was fully dark and stood, looking up at the stars in silence. Faran found him there sometime later as he was carrying the water bags down to the stream and looked at him curiously.
"Are you ok?" he asked, breaking the silence.
Kheri nodded.
"Yeah," he replied distractedly. "I'm ok."
He glanced over at Faran, then looked back up at the stars.
"You know," he mused, still looking up. "Some day I'm going to go out there."
"Out where?" Faran asked, looking around.
"Out there," Kheri replied, pointing up at the stars. "Where Dale and Jarl come from."
Faran looked up at the stars for a second, looked back at Kheri and shook his head.
"You're crazy," he said.
"I am not," Kheri protested. "I want to see what's out there." Faran looked at him doubtfully and shook his head again, then continued on down to the stream.

With Kheri once more in good health, they resumed their journey to Villenspell the next morning soon after it was light. The road continued it's winding path across the mountain range and after a few hours they found themselves climbing again. The trees became increasingly more scrubby and windblown, the landscape far more barren and rocky. Large boulders lay scattered about and the icy wind whipped past them, stinging any unprotected skin with bits of frozen mist from the snow field that they were approaching. The air became thin and breathing difficult as they neared the lowest edge of the snow field, and Dale called a halt early in the afternoon, unwilling to chance being caught in the snow after dark.

"Not the best spot to camp," he commented, as they dismounted. "But it's the best we've passed for sometime now."

There were mostly rocks and a few scrubby bushes near at hand. No grass grew out of the desolate ground but lichen and other strange plants clung to the sides of the boulders. The company built a small fire in front of a large boulder, then huddled together between it and the rock, wrapped in blankets, as darkness fell. The temperature plummeted and loud noises filled the air as the mountain protested the loss of heat from the sun.
"There are voices in that wind," Galdur whispered suddenly. "Listen. You can hear them."
The others listened for a few moments then Dale shrugged.
"It's just the rocks cooling off."
"No," Galdur argued, shaking his head. "There are voices. I can't understand what they're saying but I can hear them."

Dale regarded him for a moment then glanced at Kheri who shrugged.
"I have no idea," he replied. "I don't hear anything but the wind."
"There may be," Aerline commented, trying to peer out into the darkness. "The mountains are said to be haunted by all manner of strange creatures. Wolves wouldn't range this high but there are Giants, and Ogres and of course Nighthaunts and Wyrdlings. They would be right at home in this place."
Dale glanced at the horses who were standing in a small protected area formed by two boulders then closed his eyes and mentally reached out into the night. He opened his eyes after a second and shook his head.

"I don't like this," he said, glancing around nervously.
"What's wrong?" Jarl asked, instantly on guard.
"I can't scan through these rocks," Dale explained.

Jarl looked at him for a second then keyed his suits daylight effects sensors. Nothing happened. He tried again with the same result then kicked the heating element on briefly. His suit warmed up and the heads-up display obediently told him it's temperature but refused to even register the near-by fire. He killed the display and looked at Dale.
"I don't like this either," he declared. "At all."

"We'll set a guard tonight," Dale decided. "And everyone sleep light. With your weapons at hand in case we need them. Perhaps whatever's out there will ignore us but I'd rather not take the chance."
"We're gonna need more wood," Kheri pointed out unnecessarily.
"It's too cold to go get more wood!" Faran protested, trying to huddle as close to the rock they were sheltering beside as possible.
"We have to have it," Kheri explained. "We'll freeze to death without it. It's cold enough with the fire as it is."
"You're right," Dale agreed. "It's going to be much colder than I expected. Jarl and I will go get the wood. The rest of you stay here." He kicked on the heating element in his suit and set the temperature, then flipped on his belts force-field.
"We'll be back shortly," Jarl said, standing as well.
"Do NOT," Dale admonished firmly, turning to look at the others, "decide to come look for us, no matter what, until the sun is back in the sky. We can survive these temperatures without the benefit of fire. You will not."
The others looked up at them and Kheri nodded.
"We'll stay here," he agreed. "Just don't get lost."
Dale grinned at him then turned and walked over to Jarl. They talked quickly then vanished into the night.

With the fire behind them, the darkness was less complete. Jarl tried the daylight effects function again and shook his head, annoyed.
"I can't get any light," he grumbled.
"Do you get anything at all?" Dale asked, kicking the gain up on his sensors.
"A little. It looks like washed out moonlight," Jarl responded.
"Kick the gain up," Dale suggested as he carefully adjusted the settings.
"I have," Jarl replied. "I set it to max. It didn't help. A pair of night vision goggles would come in real handy right about now."
"Sorry," Dale responded. "Can't help you there."

Jarl pulled the blaster off his belt and checked the gage, then fired a short burst at a nearby rock. The lichen on it caught fire and blazed but the rock showed no effect whatever.
"What are these things made out of?" he asked, walking over to the rock which was now covered with ash where the lichen had been.
"I don't know," Dale replied. "Let's just hope it's as resistant to magic as it is energy weapons."
"This whole world's resistant to everything!" Jarl griped, putting the blaster back on his belt.
"Not entirely," Dale said as he finished adjusting his sensors for maximum effect. "Now, if you are through complaining?"

Jarl glanced at him and nodded.
"I'm through," he replied, annoyance creeping into his voice.
"Then let's get the wood and get back to the others."
"There's not much around here but scrub brush," Jarl pointed out, looking around.
"Then we collect a couple of the larger bushes," Dale said. They stood still, studying the mountainside for several minutes, then Jarl pointed.

“Dale,” he hissed, pointing back down the mountainside. “Look.”

Dale turned and looked down the mountain. There on the slope below, was a long white creature slithering rapidly toward them. Red flames shot off of it’s tail as it whipped it back and forth, splashing against the rocks and setting the bushes on fire that it passed. Dale took a step back, pulled his blaster out and fired. Jarl whipped his own blaster out and joined him. They backed slowly up the mountain, continuing to fire. The night was suddenly rent with an unearthly shriek as the creature collapsed a few feet below them and Dale spun around, looking for other enemies.

“Look!” Jarl exclaimed and Dale glanced back over his shoulder then stared. The creature was now covered with blue glowing lines and as they watched, it broke apart into pieces which vanished in puffs of green and orange light. They looked at each other, then quickly grabbed two of the nearest bushes and headed back to the fire.

“That,” Aerline explained, as she helped break the bushes up into useable lengths, “was a Nighthaunt. They’re living magic, or so the books say. They were used in the first Wizard’s War fifty thousand years ago and when it was over, the surviving wizards lacked the ability to control them. They also lacked the knowledge to destroy them. However they were able to chase them out of the civilized lands into the devastation left by the war. That’s where we are now.”

“Then they don’t hunt for food?” Jarl asked.

“No,” Aerline replied, shaking her head. “They don’t eat. They just hunt to destroy. They’re still operating under the same spells that were cast when they were created.”

“They’re still fighting the same war,” Galdur said, looking over at Aerline. “Aren’t they?”

“Probably,” she replied, snapping another branch off the bush. “They’re not intelligent after all, they’re just tools left over by the wizards that made them.”

"Why was it after us?" Dale asked. "We hardly fit the description of a wizard."

"Who knows," Aerline shrugged. "They don't usually do anything but crawl around and look frightening. I've never crossed these mountains, but there were Nighthaunts not too far from where I grew up. All the kids used to go out at night and ride them. We had contests to see who could stay on them the longest."
"Dale..." Jarl said, his voice thoughtful. "We don't fit the description of the wizards now, but..."
Dale stared at him and the color suddenly drained out of his face as comprehension dawned.
"We might more than fit the description of the wizards fifty thousand years ago," he whispered, and Jarl nodded.
"At least," Dale went on, in a more normal tone of voice, "The wizards they were created to hunt."
"And that would explain why everything is so resistant to our equipment," Jarl replied.
"As well as why two feuding wizards were able to create jump-space on a mountain,"
Dale finished. "Oh my head hurts."
"And it may very well explain," Jarl went on relentlessly, looking at him with hardness in his eyes, "why that warp dropped you here and why there's a Gorg army currently trying to take over this place."
Dale stared back at him silently for a moment then took a deep breath and nodded.

"What are you two talking about?" Aerline interrupted, completely confused.
"How much has this world changed in the last fifty thousand years?" Dale asked, looking at her.
"Why I have no idea," she replied, astounded at the question. "Why?"

"The devastated lands," Dale said. "Why are they on top of the mountains?"
"They weren't always," Aerline explained. "These mountains used to be valleys and plains. But after the war, they were so badly destroyed that all the surviving wizards cast many spells and slowly lifted them up to become what they are today. This allowed the good land that had been covered by the oceans to breath the air and flourish, providing homes for the people and animals not destroyed by the war. Or at least that's what the history books at the college say."
"Terraformers," Jarl thought and Dale nodded.
"Yes," he thought back. "Only done with such a heavy amount of magic, that the world is still reeking of it fifty thousand years later. No wonder everything is so energy resistant."
"But why do the Gorg want this world then," Jarl asked silently and Dale shook his head.
"They don't," he thought back. "They're just a tool. There's someone behind them and I badly want to know who."

They built the fire up to a good blaze and decided on watches, then made an attempt at dozing. Their nerves were on edge however and the night was far from quiet. The wind continued whipping around them, its mournful wailing sounding much more like lost souls seeking release from their torment than air moving past rocks. At times, when the wind died down sufficiently to allow other sounds, they could hear the far off crashing of rocks echoing across the mountainside. Other noises, some distant and some close at hand shattered the night, and sleep became nearly impossible for all except Aerline. She curled up between Jarl and Kheri, then dozed off with a contented smile on her face.

The night trudged on, and Dale's nerves were close to fraying as badly as Kheri's had done in the Wizard's Cut when the first light of morning washed over the sky. He threw more wood on the fire then stood up, and looked around at the landscape which was now

beginning to take on a pale cast as the light broadened. Nothing moved and he sighed in relief, then turned his suits sensors off, praying that they wouldn't have to spend another night on the forbidding heights. The others stirred as he moved, and Kheri sat up, looking quickly around.
"What's wrong?" he asked, his voice betraying his apprehension.
"Nothing," Dale answered tiredly. "Just tired of sitting."

The wood was nearly gone now and they threw what little was left on the fire in preparation for breakfast. The water had frozen in the bags and Kheri got up, picked up a pot then trekked off to the edge of the snowfield. He returned several minutes later with a pot full of snow and set it on the edge of the stone ring they'd built to contain the flames.
"My Aunt," he explained to Faran who was looking at him curiously, "always does this in the winter. The well doesn't freeze but the snow's cleaner."

The snow melted rapidly and Kheri took it off the fire while a few bits of snow still floated in it, took a drink then passed it around. They made short work of breaking camp, saddling the horses in the chill morning air, and then put the fire out. The sun had barely cleared the lowest peak when they were back on the road once more, their thoughts bent on traversing the pass as rapidly as possible and starting the descent before night fell once again.

The road was steep now, and slippery in places where the snow covered it. They were forced to dismount and lead the horses several times, but finally just past noon, they reached the top of the pass. It was a long narrow path running around the side of the shortest peak and they dismounted again, leading their horses well away from the sheer drop to their left. They were almost to the other side of the pass when there was a loud rumbling from above.

"Against the wall!" Dale shouted and pulled his horse to the side then flattened himself against the rock, throwing his arms up over his face. Snow mixed with large chunks of ice and rock came crashing down around them, burying the path several inches deep. One of the rocks hit the path only a few feet from where Galdur stood, spraying him with chunks of rock as it broke apart and a thick chunk of ice glanced off Kheri's arm. The avalanche rumbled on for several long seconds then the rumbling ceased and everything was silent.

Dale cautiously lowered his arms and looked around. The snow had covered the path several inches deep but it hadn't buried it completely. He stepped away from the wall and counted heads quickly, then breathed a sigh of relief. Everyone appeared to have survived in one piece though Galdur's face had been cut by the spraying rock and Kheri was holding his left arm tightly.
"Is everyone alright?" He asked and several heads nodded.
"I'm not," Kheri winced, pain filling his voice. "But I'll make it."
"If you can still walk," Dale said, "we need to get out of this pass as fast as possible before more snow comes down."
"I can walk," Kheri responded through clinched teeth. "I'll be ok."

They carefully led the horses through the snow, staying as close to the wall on their right as possible. It took nearly fifteen, very tense, minutes before they reached the edge of the avalanche's effect and could mount again. The path widened out a few feet further on and within a short time they found themselves on the other side of the pass looking out over a landscape of high mountain peaks and thick green forests. The road wound away down the rocky mountainside as it made for the forest floor several hundred feet below. Dale reined his horse at the first safe stopping point and dismounted.

"We need a break," he decided, his voice betraying the stress his emotions were still under. "We'll go on in an hour or so."
The others dismounted tiredly, grateful to be over the pass and out of the danger of falling snow. The air was still thin and cold as they were still very high on the mountain but the sun had reached zenith and its rays warmed the rocks satisfactorily.

Kheri slipped as he dismounted and fell, landing with a thud on the rocks. He let out a cry of pain and curled up in a ball, holding his left arm tightly.
"Dale," he thought weakly, blinking back tears, "help!"
Dale glanced up then ran back to where Kheri lay on the ground.
"Jarl," he thought sharply. "Get me a blanket!"
He picked Kheri up off of the ground and carried him over to the blanket Jarl had spread out, then put him down gently and helped him sit up. Jarl threw a second blanket around Kheri's shoulders.

"Easy," Jarl cautioned as Kheri winced. "What happened?"
"I slipped," Kheri explained through gritted teeth. "I lost hold of the saddle as I was dismounting."
"Take your shirt off," Dale directed. "I want to see that arm."
Kheri struggled to pull the shirt over his head but was unable to lift his arm high enough to do so.
"I can't," he gasped, clutching his arm again. "It hurts too much."

Galdur had stood silently, watching with concern as Dale tended to Kheri. He could almost feel the pain himself, and when Kheri tried to lift his arm, he winced at the same time. He stood for a moment longer then walked over to where Kheri was sitting.
"Can I see?" he asked. "Please?"
Dale glanced at him.
"There's nothing to see Galdur," Dale replied, brushing him off brusquely.
"No," Galdur argued. "I don't mean like that. Please?"

Dale regarded him for a moment, then stepped back out of the way.

Galdur sat down on the blanket facing Kheri then reached over and took his hand. He closed his eyes and Kheri suddenly relaxed, then blinked and looked at his arm.
"Huh?" he asked.
"Wait," Galdur told him, "I'm not done."
Kheri sat still, a look of confusion on his face. Galdur said nothing else for several moments then released Kheri's hand, opened his eyes, and sat back.
"See if you can use it now," he requested.

Kheri looked at him, then carefully tried to lift the arm over his head. He blinked in surprise, then looked up at Dale. "It doesn't hurt," he remarked incredulously. He pulled his shirt off and looked at the place where the ice had hit him. The arm looked perfectly normal, no sign of even a bruise. "Wow," he exclaimed, looking back over at Galdur. "How did you do that?"
Galdur shrugged.
"It's just something I've always done," he replied. "I just close my eyes and I can see what's hurt and how to fix it."
"Why didn't you tell us?" Dale asked. "Did your father know?"
"No," Galdur shook his head. "I just used it on birds and stuff before. Didn't really know if I could use it on people. But I had to try."
"Thank you," Kheri told him, breaking into a grin. "That really hurt."
"It was broken," Galdur stated. "But it's ok now."
"Yeah," Kheri agreed. "It's better than ok. Thank you."
"You're welcome," Galdur replied, smiling, then stood up.
"Can I have something to eat?" He asked Dale quietly. "I'm kinda hungry now."
"Certainly," Dale agreed. "In fact, I think that's an excellent idea for all of us."

They broke out rations and ate, sitting around the fire. The sun was beginning it's descent into afternoon when they finally remounted and started down the mountain again. The going was slow as the road was steep and rocky, and Dale tried not to give into impatience at the snails pace they were forced to maintain. At last, after nearly a hour of very slow going, the road flattened out and began a series of normal switch backs as it descended into the forest.

Chapter Thirty

Huge boulders were scattered across the mountainside and the road snaked around them. Just as they rounded the second pile of boulders a rock whizzed past in front of Dale's horse and crashed on the road in front of them. Several more came flying out of the trees ahead, narrowly missing the rest of the company. They ducked then flung themselves off the horses and tried to wedge into the spaces between the boulders. One of the horses screamed in anguish as a rock hit it on the head, splattering its brains on the road. It's body fell to the ground, its legs kicking wildly. The rest of the horses reared in panic and took to flight back up the mountain they had just come down.

"I'm going to wring some necks!" Jarl growled, flipping his force shield on.
"I'll help you," Dale agreed, doing the same.
He looked around at the others who were huddled in the back of the small cave like space between the boulders.
"Kheri," he commanded. "You and Faran stay here and stay on guard." Kheri nodded, and drew his dagger. Faran glanced at Dale, his sword already in his hand.
"We'll be fine," he stated, returning his attention to the opening.
Dale nodded, drew his blaster, and ducked outside, running for the cover of the trees nearby. Aerline sank down to the ground and rested against the rock. She closed her eyes and began searching for nearby animals or birds. Several small minds caught her attention and she whispered instructions then continued her searching.

Dale paused as he reached the cover of the trees and crouched down behind a bush. Jarl joined him a second later.
"How many do you think?" he thought and Jarl shook his head.
"From the amount of rocks," he thought back, "I'd say at least three if not four. Either that or someone's got a rapid fire catapult."

They crouched there in the bushes for a few moments longer studying the forest and waiting. No more rocks were forthcoming however and even the wind seemed to be holding it's breath in anticipation.

"I'll go that way," Dale thought, indicating a path away from the road. "You scout along the road."

Jarl nodded, then flipped the controls on his belt and vanished as the light bent around him. He keyed the sound dampers and stood, then waited while his sensors reported back on any life forms. A map flickered to life covered with tiny red dots. Near the center of it, several larger dots blinked slowly. He paused, changed the display to numeric then shook his head.

"Dale..." he thought, still studying the display.

"What?" Dale asked as he stood up and adjusted his force field.

"Either my sensors are really off," Jarl replied. "or we're about to fight several seventeen foot tall guys."

Dale stopped, and kicked his own sensors on, then searched the nearby area for life forms. The display flickered to life and he read it over then sighed, turning it back off.

"Your sensors are fine," he thought back at Jarl. "Let's just hope none of them are wizards."

"You're comforting," Jarl thought back and readied his blaster.

A loud yell rang out suddenly and the forest shook. Several more thunderous exclamations split the air, accompanied by what sounded like a herd of wild elephants stampeding. As they watched, open mouthed, five hill giants burst from the trees not far down the road and dashed off, pursued at top speed by an army of skunks. Dale sat back down on the ground, laughing so hard he couldn't see. Jarl just stared as the giants vanished into the forest, then ran back out again, their heads obscured by angry, screeching birds. They turned at right angles to the road and sprinted off up the mountain, flapping their arms wildly in an attempt to chase the birds away. Jarl stood, his blaster hanging limply by his side, unable to look away, as they disappeared into the distance, with the birds still swarming around them, fiercely intent on drawing blood. As they disappeared from sight, he looked down at his blaster, then back up at the army of skunks that were primly parading back into the forest and shook his head.

"I don't believe I just saw that," he remarked, flipping the safety back on.
"I don't either," Dale agreed, wiping the tears from his face and standing up.
"What I wouldn't give for a recorder right about now," Jarl responded as he re-attached the blaster to his belt.
"NO one would ever believe you didn't stage it," Dale told him as they turned back toward the boulders.
"True," Jarl replied. "But I'd still love to have that for my collection."

The others stepped out onto the road as they approached and Aerline smiled sweetly at Jarl.
"Did you enjoy my skunks?" She asked. He grinned at her and shook his head.
"That was either the most amazing thing I've ever seen," he told her. "Or the silliest. What did you do?"
"Nothing much," she replied with a giggle. "Just asked them if they'd be willing to do me a little favor."
"It appears they were willing," Dale commented, glancing back where the skunks had been. "Remind me not to make you angry when we're near a forest."
Aerline giggled again, then grew serious.
"What about the dead horse?" she asked, looking down at where it's carcass lay in the road.
"We can't do anything for it," Dale told her. "And I'm not going to dig it a grave. We'll just have to do without a pack horse."

They removed what it had been carrying, then Dale turned his blaster on the carcass, incinerating it.
"At least he wont be food," Kheri commented, watching the body turn to ash. "Too bad Galdur couldn't do something."
"I can heal stuff," Galdur replied then shook his head. "But not like that."
"I know," Kheri replied. "Just wish we coulda saved him."
"Be thankful it was only one of the horses," Dale told him, as he set the safety on his blaster and put it back on his belt. "If their aim had been any better, it would have been one of us."
"Unless they meant to kill the horse," Jarl pointed out.
"Why would they want to kill a horse?" Dale asked.
"Could be lots of reasons," Jarl replied, shrugging.
"Well if that was their intent," Dale said dryly, "they succeeded. I hope they enjoy Aerline's pay back for a long time."
"Oh they'll be running for a while yet," Aerline smiled. "I asked the birds to chase them all the way to the Wizard's Cut."
Dale's mouth dropped open and he stared at her then broke out laughing again.
"You certainly can be vindictive when you want to be," he remarked.
"I wanted to be sure they wouldn't come back," she replied with a grin.

"Can you get our horses back?" Faran interrupted. "They took off earlier."
'They'll come back on their own," Jarl said.
"Maybe," Aerline agreed doubtfully. "But there are Wyrdlings in the mountains and they might get eaten." She looked at Faran then shook her head.
"No," she told him. "I'm sorry but they ran too far away. I can only talk to things that are close by."
Dale sighed, then turned to Kheri.
"Would you, Faran and Galdur please go collect fire wood?" he asked. "We'll plan on camping here tonight and hope the horses

come back before morning. There should be good shelter between these boulders."
"Sure," Kheri replied. "Come on guys. Let's see how much we can get." He turned and strode off toward the forest. Faran sheathed his sword, then he and Galdur ran after him and disappeared into the trees.

"How far is Villenspell?" Dale asked, looking at Aerline.
"It's about a weeks ride," she replied. "It'll take much longer on foot."
Dale nodded, then leaned against one of the rocks and rubbed his eyes tiredly.
"Come on," Jarl said softly to Aerline. "Let's take a walk."
She glanced at Dale, then nodded, and accompanied Jarl a short distance away.
"Can you call some rabbits or something?" he asked. "all the food was on the other horses."
"Sure," she replied. "how many?"
"Just enough for tonight," he replied. "I'm going to go try and find water."
"Ok," she agreed. "Just be careful. Those woods are really not very safe."
"I'll keep an eye out," Jarl stated, and flipped on the controls on his belt. His force field flickered back to life and he vanished from sight as the light bent around him once more.

Aerline sat down on the ground and closed her eyes.
"Rabbits," she thought. "Just rabbits." she searched through a number of small minds, and finally located a rabbit.
"Come here bunny," she whispered. "And bring your friends. I need you."
She opened her eyes and waited. Several minutes passed, then there was a stirring in the under brush on the other side of the road. A rabbit hopped out, then sat up in the open, his nose quivering. Deciding that the area was safe, he went back down on all fours

and hopped slowly over to where Aerline was sitting. The bushes stirred again and several more rabbits hopped out, following him. Within a few minutes there were sixteen rabbits clustered around her, all looking up at her with trusting eyes. She reached out and stroked one on the head then glanced at Dale. He was standing by the boulder, watching her silently.

"Jarl asked me to get a few for dinner," she explained. "I didn't expect so many." She looked back at the rabbits and shook her head. "And I can't watch while you kill them either," she finished, getting to her feet.
Dale shook his head.
"I'm not going to kill them," he told her. "Turn them loose. We'll find something else for supper tonight."
Aerline looked at him gratefully, then whispered something to the rabbits. They milled around for a moment, then turned and hopped back into the forest.
"Thank you," she said gratefully. "I don't think I could have eaten them either."
"It's ok," Dale reassured her. "Jarl shouldn't have asked you to do that any way."
"Maybe he'll find a stream," she remarked hopefully. "Fish don't bother me the way rabbits do."
"Perhaps," Dale agreed, then stood up away from the rock and turned his force field on.
"Will you be ok here until the others come back?" he asked, adjusting the sensors in his suit.
"I should be," Aerline replied. "Why? Where are you going?"
"To find the horses," Dale explained. "We have to be able to ride. Walking will take far too long."
"Please be careful," Aerline cautioned, worry creeping into her voice. "There are Nighthaunts on this side of the pass too, and Wyrdlings."
"I'll be careful," he promised. "Trust me. Tell Jarl I said to stay here and guard till I get back."

She nodded and watched silently as he walked off up the mountain in pursuit of the horses.

"Kheri ... Jarl ..." Dale thought as he climbed up the road.
"Yes?" came Kheris mental reply.
"What?" Jarl asked, slightly distracted.
"I'm tracking the horses," Dale explained. "Aerline's back at the boulders alone. Get a fire going if you can please and try to stay out of sight, just in case those giants come back."
"Sure," Kheri agreed.
"I found a stream," Jarl responded, "so I'm headed back now as it is."
"Jarl, you're on guard till I get back," Dale instructed.
"Understood," came Jarl's response.
"And don't ask Aerline to call up rabbits again," Dale thought firmly. "Show her where the stream is and let her get some fish."
"Sorry," Jarl apologized, aware of the irritation in Dale's thoughts. "It won't happen again."

Dale turned his attention to the road he was climbing, and flipped on the infrared sensors in his belt. The horses hadn't left much of a heat signature as they thundered over the ground and no sign of their passing now remained. He flipped the infrared sensors back off and keyed the life signs function in his suit, setting it for maximum range, then stopped climbing. The heads up display darkened and a stylized map of the mountain range almost a mile in diameter flickered into view. It was covered with tiny dots, and Dale searched them over, looking for an indication of the horses. A small cluster of dots not too far away caught his eye and he ordered the display to narrow the search to the vicinity of the cluster. The map flickered and changed, then showed him an area just below the mountain pass.

Six individual dots stood out there, clustered together and not moving.

"Crud," Dale thought. "I hope that's live horses too scared to move and not dying horses or horses stuck in some impossible snow drift." He flipped off the display and pushed himself to a faster pace up the mountain.

The climb was steep and as he neared the top he slowed almost to the same pace that they'd used on the descent. The rocks were treacherous and slippery and he was forced to use the road instead of cutting across the mountainside as he had been lower down. The air was thinner than he was used to as well and breathing became difficult. He stopped finally, gulping for air, and adjusted the controls on his belt to deal with a hostile atmosphere then took a deep breath as the gases inside the force shield became enriched. Glancing down at the charge indicator on the belt he frowned and shook his head.

"Half an hour left," he muttered, starting to climb again. "I hate this. We have got to get down out of these mountains and back to a somewhat normal energy flow. Nothing works right with all this magical interference."

He climbed faster now and reached the area indicated on the display with several minutes left before his belt ran out of power. He held his breath and flipped the field off then slowly let the air out of his lungs. He tried a short breath and was forced to sit down, engulfed in a wave of dizziness as his body rejected the suddenly much thinner air. Dropping his head in his hands, he sat bent over, fighting to keep from passing out. The dizziness passed slowly as he became acclimated once again and he managed to get back up to his feet after several minutes. He stood back up and looked around then keyed the display back on. The dots were close, but slightly higher than where he stood, almost at the entrance of the pass. He turned the display back off and forced himself up the final slope of the mountain.

The horses were standing in a group near the entrance to the pass. They noticed Dale as he got close and watched him advance but did not move beyond the occasional flick of a tail. He climbed up to where they stood and looked around, searching for a reason to their lack of movement. The snow wasn't especially deep here and there were no holes in the ground. He frowned, confused, then took a hold of his horse's reins. The horse twitched her ears, then bumped him with her nose, knocking him back a step. He smiled lopsidedly.

"You big coward," he chastised her. "Why did you have to run all the way up here? Come on now, I need to ride. I can't walk any more."
She swished her tail then obediently followed him back to the road. The other horses, seeing her move, also stirred and walked back to the road behind her. Dale collected the reins of all the other horses, then struggled to mount his mare, barely managing to swing his leg up over the saddle.
"You got taller," he remarked, panting, as he settled into place. "Ok, let's go back down the mountain girl."

The horse seemed to understand his words and set off at a gentle walk back down the road. The others followed along behind, their reins slack in Dales hand. By the time the boulders came in view the afternoon was getting late. The smell of a small cook fire burning beside them drifted through the air and Dale felt an enormous sense of relief sweep over him at the sight of it. He let out a sigh and relaxed, grateful to have made it back down the mountain in one piece.

Chapter Thirty-One

Jarl walked back out of the woods a few minutes after finding the stream and looked around for Aerline. She was sitting just outside the opening in the boulders, looking at something on the ground. There, crawling across the open space, was a long slender snake. It was green, with a bright purple stripe down it's back and it slithered silently over the rocky terrain, then disappeared down a hole.

"He was hunting," she explained, looking up at Jarl. "I don't think he's found anything to eat yet."

"Let's hope he doesn't take a liking to people," Jarl replied, then held his hand out. "Come on," he urged, assisting her to her feet. "I found a stream."

She took his hand briefly and got to her feet, then looked back up the mountain and inconspicuously wiped her hand off on her skirt.

Dale was completely out of sight now and she frowned slightly.

"He'll be ok," Jarl reassured her as he turned, trying to ignore her veiled insult, and glanced where she was looking. "He's pretty smart."

"I know," she replied, "but still...it's about the time of day when the Wyrdlings begin to come out. I hope nothing happens."

"Me too," Jarl muttered looking up the mountain. "Me too."

"Ok," Aerline asked in a more businesslike tone as she tore her eyes away from the mountain that towered above them. "What are we going to put the fish in?"

All of the containers they possessed were on the horses which had run away. The pack horse had carried the extra weapons they'd gotten from the bandits as well as some bags of valuable items that might bring good prices once they reached another town, but nothing useful for carrying fish. Jarl rummaged through it, then

walked over to a bush and cut a long forked branch. Peeling the leaves off of it, he sharpened both ends of the fork with his knife. "We'll just have to spear 'em on this," he stated, handing her the branch. "Best I can do."
Aerline took the branch then nodded reluctantly, and followed him as he led the way back to the stream.

The water was icy, since it was born of the snows near at hand, and it gurgled melodically along in the rocky stream bed as it made it's way down the mountain to the forest floor below. They walked down it together for a ways, looking for fish, but it appeared devoid of life. Aerline stopped after several minutes and sat down on the bank, closed her eyes and began whispering faintly. Jarl stood silently watching her for a few moments, then grew bored and turned his attention to the forest around them.

The sunlight filtering through the trees dappled the leaves on the forest floor with golds and bright greens. A bright red bird swinging on a branch nearby cocked it's head as his gaze fell on it, then it let out a trill and took to the air. The forest felt peaceful and Jarl found himself growing sleepy. He fought the desire to sit down for several minutes then just as he was yielding, happened to glance down at Aerline and realized she had fallen asleep.
"This is not good," he thought to himself and slapped his hand on the emergency life support switch on his belt. His force field snapped on and darkened completely. Powerful energies crackled through the outer layer of the shielding, weaving a protective net around him and a high pitched whine filled the air as his suit reacted, filtering the gases outside the shield. Something smashed into him and he was knocked to the side slightly as his heads-up display flickered to life, awash with red-light from the creature which had just attacked him.

Floating only inches away from Aerline was what looked like a small whirlwind. Intense energies of various wavelengths swirled

through it, brilliant flashes of light shot out of it in all directions and a long, thin, tendril of power snaked from it to Aerline's head. A second tendril suddenly shot out of the whirlwind, cracked against his force-field and rocked him backward, nearly throwing him to the ground.
"Alright," Jarl thought, narrowing his eyes. "You want to play rough? Let's see how you like this."

He drew his blaster, set the beam to needle width, and flipped the safety off. Grasping the blaster with both hands, he braced himself then aimed at the center of the whirlwind and held down the fire button. The beam hit the whirlwind dead center and a small, dark patch appeared on the display as it's energies were neutralized there. The whirlwind reacted violently. shooting out several more tendrils with lighting speed, cracking them across his force-field in rapid succession. The blows buffeted him as they hit, knocking him backwards and his aim slid down toward the ground. He jerked his arms back up, continuing to fire and mentally ordered his suit to anchor him.

The shielding shot down into the ground, cutting into the rock several feet below, and rooting him to the spot. The whirlwind snapped more glowing tendrils of light at him, as the dark patch on it's outer surface continued to grow but the anchor held and he ignored them.
"Come on," he thought urgently, glancing at the rapidly emptying charge indicator on the blaster, "how much more of this can you take?!"

As the remaining blaster charge crept closer and closer to empty, Jarl began to sweat. Massive tentacles of power cracked in rapid fire across his shields now as the whirlwind fought desperately for it's life, draining power from what little energy was left in his belt with each hit. A bright yellow warning flashed across the heads-up display as his shielding rapidly weakened, and Jarl grimaced, then narrowed his eyes.

The dark patch on the whirlwind had spread and it's spinning was becoming erratic. Jarl flipped the controls on the blaster to maximum and emptied the last of the charge into the whirlwind in a final, intense, pulse. The whirlwind shuddered, then suddenly exploded into minute fragments. The fragments flared into brilliant flashes of light, momentarily overloading his sensor display, and were gone.

"Off," Jarl thought at his suit, deactivated his belt's emergency shields and collapsed on the stream bank. Aerline blinked, and looked around.

"Why I think I took a nap," she yawned, then looked over at Jarl. "I don't think there are any fish in this stream," she decided. "I couldn't find any."

He nodded then stood back up.

"Come on," he told her, reattaching the blaster to his belt. "We need to get out of here while we still can."

She stood and looked at him curiously, then shrugged and followed him silently back out of the forest.

When they got back to the boulders, there was a small fire burning and Kheri was busily skinning a pair of wild chickens he had caught.

"Where are the boys?" Jarl asked, his voice extremely tense.

"They're getting more wood," Kheri explained, looking up. "What's wrong with you?"

"I just fought a whirlwind," Jarl replied. "I almost didn't win."

"A whirlwind?" Kheri asked. "Why were you fighting a whirlwind?"

"Because it was trying to kill me," Jarl responded, dropping down beside the fire.

"Go get the boys and everyone stay out of that forest until Dale gets back."

Kheri stood up, worry now lining his face, and ran for the trees on the other side of the road. Aerline walked over and sat down where Kheri had been, then picked up the skinning knife.

"What was that about a whirlwind?" she asked.
"Just what I said," Jarl replied. "Not real large, but pretty powerful. That's why you fell asleep. It was doing something to you and it didn't like my interfering one bit."
Her eyes widened.
"Thank you," she told him, picking up the chicken Kheri had dropped and trying to continue with the skinning. She made a face after a few seconds and set it back on the ground. Jarl grinned slightly and took the skinning knife away from her.
"I'll do it," he offered. "It's not the most pleasant job in the world."
"I'm sorry," she replied. "It's just so ... so ... slimy."
She looked around, disgust flickering across her face.
"What's wrong now?" Jarl asked as he made short work of the chicken.
"My hands are all covered with it," she complained. "And it stinks."
Jarl just shook his head.
"Never take a job as a butcher," he commented, skinning the other chicken then slitting both of them open. Aerline's eyes got suddenly wide and she got up then ran behind the boulders. The unmistakable sound of violent heaving drifted back to Jarl's ears and he sighed.
"I hope Dale found the horses," he thought, "or this trip could become real unpleasant."

He cleaned the entrails out of the chickens, and tossed them off to the side, then speared the them on the forked branch and set them over the fire to roast. Kheri came back out of the forest at that moment, followed closely by the boys, their arms loaded down with wood, a worried expression on his face.

"The woods are too quiet," he told Jarl when they got back to the fire. "Everything just suddenly stopped making noise."
Jarl glanced over at the trees.
"Great," he grumbled. "My blaster's totally discharged and my belt's close to empty. Go get Aerline, she's around behind the boulders, and let's just stay close to the fire. Maybe whatever it is will leave us alone if we don't bother it any further."

Kheri nodded and walked off around behind the boulders. Aerline was leaning heavily on the rock, her eyes closed. He walked over to her and put his hand on her shoulder.
"You ok?" he asked, as she opened her eyes and looked at him.
"Yes," she managed faintly. "But I don't think I'll be eating any of that chicken tonight. Or much of anything for that matter."
He nodded then tugged gently on her arm.
"Come on, we need to go back. There's something brewing in the forest and Jarl wants us all to stay close to the fire."

The feeling of something watchful and angry had begun to affect them all by the time that Kheri and Aerline returned to the fire. Everyone sat silently around the fire, watching the chickens roast and glancing uneasily at the shadows under the trees every few minutes. The feeling continued to grow and suddenly Jarl stood.
"Alright," he commanded, a slight tremor to his voice. "Everyone stay here. I'll be back...I hope."
He took a deep breath, then set off across the road for the trees.

The darkness under the trees had become foreboding and Jarl paused before entering it. The sensation of being watched made him want to turn and look behind himself but he knew that all he would see was empty road. He searched the shadows carefully then activated the sensors on his suit. The heads-up display flickered for a second then died, the power totally exhausted.
"Figures," he thought. "Dale?"
There was no response, just a feeling of intense concentration.

"Great," he thought. "I get to do this alone. Let's hope whatever it is can be reasoned with."

He took a deep breath in an attempt to calm his nerves, stilled his thoughts, then stepped into the trees and cautiously walked a short distance across the grass. Nothing stirred as he passed, but his nervousness grew rapidly and he stopped suddenly not far from the road, afraid to go any farther.

"Alright," he told the empty forest apprehensively, "I'm here. What do you want of me?"

The air in front of him coalesced suddenly into a swirl of rainbow colors and a woman materialized. A soft yellow glow surrounded her and she regarded Jarl silently. He gulped, then quickly dropped down to one knee before her, and bowed his head, staring at the ground.

"Explain your unwarranted attack on my child," she demanded, her voice crystalline in the still forest air.

"He was hurting my friend," Jarl replied, not daring to look up, his voice shaking. "And I thought he was trying to kill her."

"Are you so uncouth that you act first and discover whether your actions are warranted after the destruction?!" she demanded. "What proof do you have that SHE meant any harm?"

Jarl shook his head and desperately fought down the fear that was rising inside him.

"I have no proof," he replied, staring at the grass. "We have been hounded and attacked ceaselessly for days. I feared that this was yet again to be the case."

"You have not been attacked by my children," she stated firmly, her voice slightly calmer. "But I can see you tell me the truth. She was merely curious and meant you no harm."

Jarl nodded silently, his heart pounding.

"Yet...you have hurt my child badly. It will be days before she recovers," the woman continued. "I can NOT allow that to go unpunished."

Jarl flinched and nodded, then looked up.
"Please, M'lady, may I make one request?" he pleaded, his voice trembling.
"What is it?" she asked, looking down at him.
"Would you please wait to pass judgment on me until my Lord returns with our horses?" he begged.
She paused and considered, then nodded.
"I was unaware that you were under task to another," she replied. "Were you acting with his knowledge?"
Jarl thought for a moment then nodded.
"I was following his instructions," he explained, "when I encountered your child. I acted to protect a member of our company and while I did not specifically have his permission to do so, had he been aware of what was happening, he would have given it."
"Then I will wait and speak with him at his return," she decided. "When do you expect him?"
"He went after our horses," Jarl explained. "They ran in terror at the rocks the giants were throwing at us and he is trying to retrieve them."
"You will stay here," she commanded firmly. "And we shall wait for him."
"As you will," Jarl replied, his heart sinking, then sat down on the grass before her to wait.

Dale swung down off his horse beside the boulders and stretched. The exhaustion that had overpowered him in the climb up the mountain had lifted, though he still felt tired. He looked around, wondering where the others were. Kheri noticed his arrival and stepped out from inside the crevasse between the boulders. "I was afraid you wouldn't make it back," he said, his voice tense.
"I was rather afraid of that myself," Dale answered. "Where's everyone else?"

"Faran, Galdur and Aerline are in there," Kheri explained, pointing between the boulders. "Jarl hasn't come back from the forest yet."
Dale paused, the tone of Kheri's voice catching his attention.
"Jarl?" he thought, slightly worried.
"Dale!" came Jarl's immediate reply, relief mixed with fear flooding from him.
"Where are you?" Dale asked silently, instantly on guard.
"I'm...in trouble," Jarl responded. "Aerline and I were looking for fish and I thought we were being attacked. I think I made a very big mistake."

Dale sighed.
"Where are you?" he repeated, wondering just what had happened now.
"On the other side of the road," came the reply. "Not too far into the trees."
"And I suppose you can't leave for some reason?" Dale questioned.
"Ummm..." came Jarl's hesitant response, "No. The person I upset wants to talk to you...rather badly. I'm currently her prisoner."
"Wonderful," Dale grumbled out loud, and handed the reins of his horse to Kheri.
"Would you unsaddle the horses please," he requested. "I have to go try to rescue Jarl from his impetuousness."
Kheri grinned and nodded, then began unsaddling Dale's horse.

Dale walked across the road cautiously, wondering just what was waiting for him under the shadow of the trees. He stepped into the wood and immediately felt a presence watching him. He glanced around, then noticed a glimmer in the near distance. He took a deep breath and forced himself to remain calm, then walked toward it, careful not to appear threatening, his apprehension mounting as he got closer. Jarl was still sitting on the grass and he looked up as Dale stepped into view, then glanced up at the woman who was floating in the air nearby. The glow around her suffused the area with a soft yellow light and Dale stared, then bowed in her direction.

"Well," she commented , crystalline tones drifting through the air as she spoke. "At least one of you appears to have manners."
Dale straightened back up, then glanced at Jarl.
"M'Lady," he replied, looking back at the woman. "I am at your disposal. What has occurred here?"
"Is this your servant?" she asked, and Dale nodded.
"Yes," he replied, "he is. Has he done something wrong?"
"Yes," she said. "Though perhaps it was an honest mistake. He has attacked, and badly injured, one of my children."
Dale blinked and glanced at Jarl again, then looked back up at her.
"I would like to hear what happened," he requested. "If you would allow him to explain?"
She nodded and floated backwards.

Jarl relaxed slightly then looked up at Dale.
"Well?" Dale asked, crossing his arms and looking down at his friend. "Exactly what did you do?"
"Aerline and I were trying to find fish," Jarl explained, picking at the grass as he talked. "We walked down the stream for a ways without finding any and she eventually sat down next it. She went off into that trance of hers and I got bored. I was staring out into the forest, not really thinking about anything, when I suddenly started getting sleepy. I noticed she'd fallen asleep and I panicked. I honestly thought we were under attack by one of those Wyrdlings that she said were likely to show up." He paused, his thoughts caught up in the events of the afternoon once more.
"And?" Dale prompted after a moment.

Jarl blinked, remembered what he was supposed to be doing, and continued talking.

"I flipped on life support," he explained, "just in case there was sleep gas in the air, and this...whirlwind, with long tendrils of light shooting out of it, showed up on the display. It had one of them attached to Aerline's head. It hit me with another of them as soon as my shield came on and just about knocked me over, so I assumed it was attacking her and didn't want me to interfere." He paused for a moment, thinking back to the fight, then went on. "I couldn't see any other reason she would have fallen asleep like that," he explained, frowning slightly, "...or any reason that I should have suddenly gotten drowsy. I assumed that whatever it was doing to her had put her to sleep and I turned my blaster on it. It fought back. It drained my shields Dale," he said, tension written across his face. "I nearly lost. I don't know how much power it was blasting me with but I had use bedrock to anchor. It exploded just as my blaster ran out of charge and as soon as it let go of Aerline, she woke up. We went back to the boulders then, to wait for you, but the forest got far too quiet all of a sudden and I could feel anger directed at me. That's when I realized that I'd probably just made a huge mistake."

"You did," the woman interrupted calmly. "She was not trying to hurt you."
"M'Lady," Dale asked, looking back up at her. "Was your child killed?"
"No," she replied, "but she is hurt. She will recover though it will take time. She is young and was simply curious about creatures she'd never seen before."
"Was Aerline's sleep something she caused?" Dale asked.
"I am unsure of the answer to your question," the woman replied. "A moment and I will inquire."

Dale nodded and the glow around the woman deepened. The forest became absolutely silent and not even the sound of the nearby stream could be heard. Several minutes passed then the glow lessened and she turned back to Dale.

"Apparently so," she remarked. "Though it was not her intention."
"Then Jarl's reaction was some what justified," Dale replied.
The woman considered for a moment then nodded.
"Perhaps." she stated, her voice trailing off. Her eyes glowed briefly as she considered Dale's words. "I will accept that," she decided at last, "however I do not believe it was necessary for him to damage her to the extent he did."
"But she was attacking me!" Jarl exclaimed unhappily, unable to keep silent any longer. "She hit me first and she hit me so hard my shields almost failed with that first blow! I would have been killed instantly had she used even a fraction more power! And she kept hitting me! I have NEVER been blasted that hard before!"

Dale glanced down at him, motioning him to silence, then looked back at the woman.
"Perhaps your child didn't realize," Dale remarked, "just how deadly her curiosity evidently can be to creatures like Jarl and Aerline. He would not have reacted as he did, had he not been in danger, even if the danger was unintentional on the part of your child."
The woman thought for a moment then nodded.
"Perhaps you are right," she mused.

"Also," Dale continued, "even if she did not intend any harm to Aerline, there is no assurance that her magic was not in reality going to do so. As you said, your child is young. Inexperienced. Perhaps it would be best if she learned familiarity with the world around her before you allowed her to explore it alone."
"I shall consider your words," the woman agreed. "Your form is much more fragile than anything my children are used to. Now that the situation is clear to me, I will not require your servant be punished, though I would ask that he act with more discretion in the future, at least as long as you are within my borders."
Dale nodded.

"I will see that he does so," he agreed, glancing back down at Jarl, who was once again watching them silently.
"It would also be wise," the woman stated, looking down into Jarl's eyes, "if he were to learn not to interrupt, and to wait for his Lord to give him permission to speak, when on trial for his actions."
Jarl reddened in embarassment and looked back down at the ground.

Dale smiled faintly and nodded.
"May I ask where your borders extend to?" he asked, changing the subject.
"They encompass the entire forest that lies within this valley," the woman replied. "They end where the trees do up upon the slopes of the surrounding mountains."
"Thank you," Dale told her, "I apologize for Jarl's actions and am grateful you are willing to show mercy to him. We shall try not to disturb you further. I do have one question however, if I may?."
"What might that be?" she asked.
"There were giants hiding in the trees when we first arrived," Dale explained. "They flung stones at us and killed one of our horses. They tried to kill us as well. May I ask why this was?"

"The giants are NOT my children," the woman explained, her eyes flashing angrily. "They are vile creatures that live in the rocky heights and enter the forest only to cause destruction! Why they flung stones at you, I do not know, however I will see to it that nothing of the sort happens again while you are within my borders."
"Thank you," Dale replied. "I'm sorry you were troubled."
"The situation is resolved," she stated. "You have my leave to walk among the trees, only do not hurt any more of my children."
"May I ask," Dale requested, "who your children are so we can avoid doing exactly that?"

"The spirits of the forest," she explained. "the fairys, the sprites, the elves and the will o' wisps. The gnomes and their kin, the brownies and all other magical beings that live in this valley."
"And the animals?" Dale asked.
The woman shook her head.
"No, the animals are not my children," she replied, "however they ARE under my protection. I ask only that you do not harass them or kill them for pleasure. I know men, though it has been many long years since I've seen your kind. And I understand your needs. You may hunt if you wish, but only as much as you truly require. Nothing more."

Dale nodded, then bowed once more.
"You are generous," he told her, "and gracious. You have my gratitude and the thanks of those that travel with me."
He glanced at Jarl.
Jarl looked up, then nodded.
"I'll stay out of trouble," he promised, then looked up at the woman. "May I speak please?"

She considered him for a moment then nodded.
"If your Lord has no objections," she replied.
"He has my permission," Dale told her.
"Very well then," she stated, looking down at Jarl, "you may speak."
"Thank you M'Lady," Jarl responded. "I am truly sorry for the hurt I've caused your child and apologize for my actions. There is one that travels with us and he has skill with healing. Perhaps he can aid her?"
The woman smiled but shook her head.
"She will recover," she replied, "however your apology is accepted and your offer is appreciated."
She lifted her hand in farewell then vanished in a burst of rainbow colored light.
Jarl sighed in relief, then stood, and looked at Dale.

"I really didn't ... " he began.
"I know you didn't," Dale interrupted, dropping a hand on his partner's shoulder, "and things are worked out now, but I think we'd better be extra careful until we reach the other side of the valley."

They left the forest and walked back to where the others were waiting by the boulders. The fire was burning brightly and they could smell food cooking in one of the pots. Aerline looked up as they approached and relief swept over her face.
"I was getting worried," she told them. "It will be dark soon and the Nighthaunts will be out."
"We were discussing things with the Lady of the Forest," Dale explained. "We have safe passage through her realm now, but we have to be very careful not to bother any of her children."
"Or anything else," Jarl put in. "I think if we make her mad again, she won't even ask questions, we'll just find lighting bolts headed our way all of a sudden."
"Oh I doubt that," Dale remarked, looking at him sideways. "She seemed like a fairly civilized person. Better manners than some I could mention."
Jarl made a face at him and picked up the water bags.
"I'm going to go get water," he replied tersely, and stalked off toward the stream.

Chapter Thirty-Two

The shades of evening lengthened and the sky became streaked with reds and golds as the sun bid goodnight to the mountains and dipped out of sight behind them. Jarl returned as the twilight was deepening into night, the full water bags slung over his shoulders and a large catfish speared on a stick. He placed the water bags off to the side then sat down and began cleaning the catfish.
"Where'd you get that?" Faran asked curiously, "and what is it?"
"It's a catfish," Jarl explained. "See the whiskers? They meow too."
"No they don't," Galdur argued. "But they taste pretty good."
Jarl grinned at him and Faran crossed his arms, aware he'd been the brunt of a joke again.
"I hate it when you do that," he complained crossly.
"Do what?" Jarl asked without looking up.
"Make fun of me like that," Faran clarified, glaring at him.
"Don't get your knickers in a twist kid," Jarl chuckled. "I was just funn'n with ya."
Faran stuck his tongue out at the back of Jarl's head and made a face.

Jarl dropped the fish and flipped around, then tackled Faran, pinning him on the ground.
"What was that?" he asked in mock anger.
"Get off me!" Faran yelled, struggling. "You're heavy!"
Jarl just grinned at him.
"Hey Galdur," he called over his shoulder. "Look what I caught."
Faran set his jaw and brought his knee up sharply, catching Jarl off guard. Jarl's eyes widened and he winced then fell to his side and lay there, eyes squeezed tightly shut in pain, curled into a ball.
"Told you to get OFF me," Faran declared triumphantly, getting back to his feet. He brushed the dirt off his pants, and ducked back into the crevasse between the boulders.

Galdur watched Jarl for a moment then walked over and knelt down next to him. He put a hand on Jarl's shoulder and winced, then closed his eyes for a few moments. Jarl gasped as the pain vanished then sighed in relief and sat back up cautiously. Galdur opened his eyes and looked at him, then shook his head disapprovingly. He got up without a word and followed Faran into the crevasse.

"You're just batting a thousand today," Dale's voice commented from somewhere behind Jarl's back. He glanced around and saw Dale leaning against the boulder, his arms crossed, watching him.
"Yeah," he grumbled. "I was just playing with the kid."
"Shoulda worn a cup," Dale commented. "He doesn't fight fair."
"I noticed," Jarl growled, picking the fish back up. He went back to cleaning it, pointedly ignoring anything else Dale had to say.

The night closed down around them and the sound of crickets filled the air. Jarl finished cleaning the fish then set a flat piece of stone over the flames and carefully fried it. Aerline peeked out of the crevasse and sniffed then made a face in disgust.
"You're actually going to eat that?" She asked as she stepped out and squatted down by the fire.
"Was planning on it," Jarl replied. "Or at least part of it. Why?"
"Just smells nasty," she told him, eyeing the fish suspiciously.
"Then don't eat any of it," Jarl replied, his temper wearing thin. She shrugged and got up, then walked over to the horses. He finished frying the fish a few minutes later and looked around.
"Anyone else want any of this?" he asked.
"No," came Faran's response from inside the crevasse.
"I do," Kheri said quietly, sitting down next to him. "If there's enough."
"There's enough," Jarl answered tersely, thinly veiled anger coloring his voice. "Get me a bowl."

Kheri got up silently and went to the saddle bags, returning a minute later with two bowls and spoons. He handed them to Jarl and sat back down. Jarl divided up the fish and handed him back one of the bowls then sat eating silently.
Kheri picked at the fish for a few minutes then looked over at Jarl.
"What's the matter?" he asked.
"Nothing!" Jarl growled sharply. He set his bowl down roughly on the ground then stood up and stalked angrily away from the fire. Kheri watched him go, puzzled, and feeling that somehow Jarl's bad mood was his fault.

Dale was laying on top of the boulders, looking up at the sky and thinking. He waited until Jarl had walked a fair distance from the fire, then slid off the boulders and went after him. The moon had already risen and it washed the landscape with silver light, making the mountainside appear unearthly. Jarl was sitting on a rock now, his shoulders hunched over and his head in his hands. Dale walked silently up beside him, then put a hand on his shoulder.
"Hey," he said, his voice gentle. "Talk to me."
Jarl shook his head.
"There's nothing to talk about," he replied, his voice muffled. "Just in a bad mood's all."
"I can see that," Dale responded, sitting down on the rock next to him. "What's eating at you?"
Jarl dropped his hands and looked up at the stars, then took a deep breath.
"Everything," he replied, knowing that if Dale really wanted to, he could simply read his mind. "I'm still under that stupid spell," he went on, rambling slightly. "I've lost my freedom to you, probably forever. I'm in the wrong for trying to keep myself and Aerline from getting killed today. I've managed to insult one of the major powers in this section of the world just by existing and now it seems I can't even cook a fish right! My blasters worthless, at least till tomorrow night, my suit's out of power and refuses to

recharge, I've blown the shielding circuits on my belt and I don't have the tools to fix them, and everyone's mad at me!"

"Everyone's not mad at you," Dale corrected gently.
"Seems like it," Jarl replied miserably.
"I'm not mad at you," Dale pointed out.
"Yeah, but you should be," Jarl countered.
"Why?" Dale asked and his friend shrugged unhappily, thinking of all the stupid things he'd ever done.
"Jarl," Dale told him gently, "everyone's on edge. This hasn't been the easiest trek for anyone. I'm powerless and it's got me jumpy. I have to bite my tongue several times every day to keep from biting someone's head off just because I'm so tense. I'm terrified of the Gorg showing up again, and I have no idea how I'm going to stop that army but I have to, I don't have any choice. My suit won't recharge either, it's all the magical interference on this mountain and I very nearly didn't make it to the top when I went after the horses."
Jarl turned and looked at him as he talked, but said nothing.

"I don't think you've insulted the Lady we talked to this afternoon," Dale went on. "She seemed very reasonable and understood the situation once she had all the facts. She's just not human and didn't realize how powerful her children are. I'm also not convinced that the thing wasn't actually trying to harm you guys. But that's beside the point. You did nothing wrong and she should have found out all the facts before she got angry in the first place."
Jarl shrugged but continued to listen.
"I can't do anything about that spell right now," Dale continued. "We're going to visit Sourbane as soon as we get to Villenspell. Hopefully he can remove the spell or at least tone it down somewhat and I'll talk to Sssversth about unblocking your powers as soon as he's had time to calm down. I can't release you, you'll cease to exist," he went on, "but just how much have I restricted your freedom?"

Jarl shook his head.
"You haven't," he admitted. "I'm just feeling sorry for myself I guess."

Dale nodded.
"We're all tense," he went on. "Thankfully the Lady of the Forest agreed to protect us till we leave this valley. That means that for tonight at least, and most of tomorrow, we don't have to worry about something leaping out of the landscape and trying to kill us."
"I wonder how she'd do against the Gorg," Jarl said.
"I don't know," Dale replied, "but I have a feeling they wouldn't survive the encounter."
"Maybe we should try to recruit her then," Jarl suggested.
Dale shook his head.
"She's tied to this forest," he explained. "I doubt she'd be very powerful outside it. She might not even be able to leave it if she wanted to. If the army comes through here, she'll put quite a dent in them I'm sure, but otherwise we can't count on her assistance." He stopped and looked around, thinking.

"You know," he speculated thoughtfully after a moment, "there are probably a lot of other powers in this world like her. Tied to some area, unable to leave it, but quiet possibly unassailable while in it. That might make it a lot less likely that the Gorg will succeed in their attack. They might even be having a hard time landing if they're trying to do so where there's enough magic and they're not wanted."

"Yeah," Jarl agreed. "But there's probably just as many who would like to see them destroy all the human population, at least, and might even be willing to help them."
"You're probably right," Dale replied. "I wish I knew more of the history of this place."
"The history?" Jarl asked quizzically and Dale nodded.

"Yeah." he said. "Like that wizards war fifty thousand years ago. Why did it happen? What were they fighting for so intensely that all the land was destroyed? How did it end?"
"Did it end?" Jarl interrupted, looking at him.
Dale caught the look in his eyes and sat up straighter, thinking.
"Yeah," he mused out loud after a few minutes. "Did it end?" He shivered and looked up at the stars. "Maybe it didn't," he spoke quietly, his thoughts spinning, then looked back at Jarl. "The Gorg are being used by someone who wants to wipe out all life here, that much is evident. The vision the dragon told us points to that."

"So maybe the person behind them," Jarl interjected, "has something to do with the original battle?"
"Maybe," Dale agreed. "Maybe a descendant out for revenge."
"Maybe," Jarl said darkly, "one of the original wizards, trying to finish things."
Dale stared at him and turned pale.
"I seriously hope not," he replied.
Jarl shrugged.
"You know what I think?" he mused after a moment.
"What?" Dale asked, watching him.
"I've been pondering over a few things," Jarl explained. "The stories Aerline's told us, the things we've encountered, the fact that magic is so high here that our equipment almost doesn't work." Dale nodded silently.

"And while I was sitting on the grass, waiting for you to get back this afternoon," Jarl went on, "since I had nothing better to do, I was mentally running over some pieces of ancient history from one of the classes at the academy. First year stuff. You remember, they make you learn all about the fleet and it's history?"
"Yes," Dale replied. "I was bored stiff, spent most of my time sleeping. Couldn't tell you what any of it was now if you paid me."

"So did everyone else but I was interested," Jarl grinning. "Always have been interested in history. Been so long though, I don't really remember much of it. But there were some accounts that fascinated me enough to stick with me. There was one that told about a time long ago when planets suddenly started disappearing out of star systems. The fleet got called in to stop it and there was a huge battle. I was fascinated because the battle was between Intergalactic Patrol and a bunch of Wizards. I had never thought wizards really existed before and frankly, till I wound up here, I still didn't think they did. That's why I was thinking about it, because not only are we surrounded by wizards, I was the prisoner of a very unhappy, extremely powerful one, and that brought it back to mind."

Dale nodded silently, waiting for him to go on.
"Anyway," Jarl continued. "The account only said that after the huge battle, in which IGP lost a large number of forces to the wizards, the fighting ended and no more planets were stolen. I assumed that we had won." Dale looked at him, thinking about the ramifications of what Jarl had just told him. "The Nighthaunts," Jarl said pointedly, watching Dale's face. "They never bother the kids that are born here. Aerline told us that. They just crawl around and look frightening. They were created during that war, by the wizards, as a tool to attack the other side. What if IGP WAS the other side?"
Dale nodded slowly
"That would explain," he replied, his voice almost a whisper, "why it attacked us last night. Our shields would have attracted it."
"And why," Jarl went on, "we almost couldn't kill it. It was created to be almost totally resistant to our energy weapons. Maybe even totally, because the blasters we're using aren't IGP issue, they're Gorg!" Dale shivered, but didn't interrupt.

"What if," Jarl mused, thinking out loud, "the battle didn't really end. What if one of the wizards got away somehow."

"But why would he be using an army of Gorg to kill off his own people?" Dale asked. "Wouldn't it make more sense for him to go after fleet headquarters or something?"
"Not," Jarl replied, his voice intense, "if HE was the one stealing planets to start with and what he wanted all along was to be able to steal this one TOO. Maybe he needs the magic that this land reeks of and doesn't want to share it with anyone else. Maybe he doesn't even come from here and these people aren't related to him at all, just innocents he doesn't mind slaughtering. Fifty thousand years...what if it's taken him this long to recover...maybe he's been under a spell all this time and just recently woke up...he might not even realize how long it's been."
Dale paled and stared at him then shook his head.
"Oh I hope you are wrong," Dale told him. "If we're facing an army of Gorg, controlled by a fifty thousand year old Wizard with the ability to make entire planets disappear, who the entire fleet couldn't put down, how are we supposed to have even a slight chance of winning?!"

Jarl shrugged.
"Everyone makes mistakes," he pointed out. "He hasn't won yet, whoever he is. Besides," he added, trying to calm Dale down. "I could be wrong."
"You could be," Dale agreed.
"Well," Jarl decided after a moment, looking back up at the stars. "We'll just have to play it by ear. We can always try a beacon if we need to. This IS, after all, a blue coded planet...as you pointed out several days back."
"Yes," Dale replied. "On the extreme edge of the Galaxy. If anyone heard the beacon, it'd probably be the pirate fleet instead of IGP."
"You're just full of optimism." Jarl chided him gently.
Dale looked at him, then grinned slightly.
"Yeah," he agreed. "I think I need sleep."

Chapter Thirty-Three

The morning came far too early. The sun peeked over the mountains, then shone directly into the crevasse, washing them all with the warm promise of a new day. Kheri opened his eyes and squinted, then looked around. Everyone else was still sound asleep and he toyed with the idea of rejoining them, but responsibility called. He was far too used to Dale wanting to be up and moving at first light, and he lay back down but felt too guilty to stay there. Giving up with a sigh, he reached over and prodded Faran in the back.

"Hey," he said. "Wake up."

"Goway," Faran mumbled, pulling the blankets over his head.

"Get up," he repeated, grabbing the blankets and dragging them off him. "It's morning."

"Why do I have to get up," Faran demanded grouchily. "Dale's not."

"He will be," Kheri pointed out. "You know he doesn't like to waste any time. Get Galdur up and let's get breakfast started."

Faran made a face that would have soured new milk, but sat up, then reached over and shook Galdur.

"Uhnh?" Galdur groaned then opened one eye.

"Get up," Faran commanded grumpily. "We gotta help Kheri make breakfast."

"Breakfast?" Galdur asked, squinting at the sun. "We just ate dinner."

"That was hours ago," Kheri replied, folding his blanket up. "When it was still dark. Now come ON!"

He stood up and stepped over a snoring pile of blankets then walked out into the morning light. Faran, still complaining silently, tossed his blanket aside and stood up as well, then clambered none too gracefully over the snoring obstacles in his way. Galdur yawned and stretched, then carefully made his way out of the crevasse to join them outside.

Jarl woke several minutes later and sat up, then looked around confused. The smell of smoke drifted in through the opening and he blinked in the morning sun, then realized that Dale was still soundly asleep, wrapped in his blanket. He grinned, then left the crevasse. The boys had been busy outside and a decent fire was crackling in the stone ring, a pot of water just beginning to boil at it's edge but they were no where to be seen. He glanced around, wondering where they'd gotten off to, then ducked back inside the crevasse and set about rousting the others from sleep. Aerline woke fairly easily but it took Jarl a full ten minutes to drag Dale out of dreamland and back to reality.
"Come ON Dale," he demanded, getting frustrated as he shook him for the third time, then pulled the blankets off of him. "Get UP!"

Dale grumbled but finally set up at last and squinted at him sleepily.
"I don't remember asking for a wake up call," he muttered.
"You didn't," Jarl replied. "Just returning the favor."
He grinned and Dale grabbed the blanket Jarl was still holding, then jerked sharply. Jarl fell forward slightly, then braced himself and yanked back. Dale looked at him, clinched his teeth and pulled harder. Jarl narrowed his eyes, then heaved, attempting to wrench the blanket from Dale's grasp. Dale released the blanket, then sat there grinning at him as Jarl sprawled backwards on the ground.
"You think so huh?" Jarl asked, his eyes glittering with mischief as he sat back up. "You wait, I'll get even later."
"You'll try, you mean," Dale replied, still grinning.
"Watch your back," Jarl cautioned.
"Watch your own," Dale shot back. "Two can play that game you know."
Jarl grinned at him the tossed the blanket back.
"Come on," he urged, standing. "Everyone else's already up."
He straightened his tunic then stepped back out of the crevasse without further comment, leaving Dale to his own devices.

The boys returned several minutes later, their hands full of red berries from a bush near the stream. Kheri gone back to where he'd found the chickens and had discovered six eggs in a nest hidden under a bush. He walked over to the fire, squatted down then held the egg up and peered at it. Faran watched him for a minute, curious.
"What're you doing that for?" he asked finally as Kheri turned the egg shell around, trying to get the light to shine through it.
"Trying to see if it's got a chicken," he replied, then lowered the egg.
"I need a candle," he complained. "And a dark room. This isn't going to work."
"Maybe Aerline can do something," Faran suggested. "If there's a baby, wouldn't she be able to talk to it?"
"I dunno," Kheri replied. "Maybe. I'll go ask her."
He glanced around, then stood up and carried the eggs over to where Aerline was sitting. He returned a few minutes later and shook his head.
"She said that if there's babies in there, they can't talk yet and she doesn't know," he said, setting the eggs down on the ground.
"So crack 'em open and find out," Faran suggested practically. "If there is, we don't eat it."
"Yeah," Kheri agreed. "But if there is, the baby'll die, dummy. I didn't want that to happen."

"The babies are likely dead already," Dale remarked as he stepped outside. "Unless you got those from some other nest than the one belonging to the chicken you butchered yesterday."
Kheri glanced up at him, a guilty look on his face.
"I didn't know they had eggs," he protested.
Dale nodded.
"Didn't say you did," he replied. "But if the babies spent last night in a cold nest, they probably died. When you kill something Kheri," he explained, sitting down on the ground next to him,

"there will always be something that's hurt by it. You might not ever know about it but you will have caused something else pain. If you catch a fish," he said, ticking creatures off on his fingers as he went on, "kill a chicken, destroy a Gorg, you've killed, not only that creature but millions of others. You've now destroyed any hope of life for what would have been that creature's future descendants and you may also have left orphans behind, who are far too young to live without their parent." Kheri winced at the thought and glanced down at the egg he was still holding. "If it had a mate," Dale continued, catching Kheri's eyes as he looked back up, "that mate may die also as some are so terribly affected by the loss of their partner that they lose their will to live. In some cases you have no choice, but never take life without thought or just cause."

Kheri chewed on his lower lip then looked down at the eggs feeling guilty.
"Now what do I do," he wondered out loud and looked back up at Dale.
"That," Dale told him, "is something you'll have to figure out on your own." He stood up and patted Kheri on his shoulder, then walked off toward the horses.
Kheri watched him go, looked over at Faran and then stared down at the eggs.
"Man," he muttered. "Now I feel terrible."
"Yeah," Faran agreed soberly. "I don't think I'm gonna eat animals any more."

Jarl had been standing silently to the side, listening to Dale. He shook his head, then squatted down beside Kheri.
"Here," he said, holding out his hands. "Let me see them."
Kheri handed him the eggs carefully and Jarl stood, then walked across the road and disappeared into the forest. He carried the eggs back to the spot where they'd spoken with the Lady the day before, then put them gently down on the grass.

"I hate to bother you," he said, looking around. "But my Lord's squire killed a couple chickens yesterday and now he's found that there were eggs. We can't tell if there are chicks in them or if they are still alive. Can you please help us?" There was silence for a few moments then a soft yellow glow spread over the eggs.
"There are no chicks," came the Lady's crystalline voice. "The eggs would not have hatched."
Jarl bowed his head.
"Thank you," he replied, then gathered up the eggs. "He did not mean to cause harm and has, I think, just learned a lesson about life." There was no response. Jarl waited a moment longer, then turned and walked back to camp.

Kheri was still sitting by the fire, stirring the food bubbling in the pan, when Jarl walked up.
"Here," he handed Kheri back the eggs. "There aren't any chicks in them."
"You're sure?" Kheri asked doubtfully, taking the eggs back.
"I'm sure," Jarl replied. "Whether they're still good or not, that I don't know."
"I don't want them now," Kheri said. "I'd feel too guilty to eat them."
"So go dig a hole and bury 'em then," Jarl suggested and sat down next to the fire.

They were slow breaking camp and the sun was well on it's way toward noon by the time they were back on the road. Dale felt reluctant to leave the valley and the promise, however fleeting, it offered of safety for a time. His sleep had been restless, filled with dreams of an insane wizard with unlimited power driving a relentless Gorg army across the universe destroying everything in sight. He sat on his horse now as they began their descent to the valley floor, his mind far away. The horses plodded along, content to amble at a slow pace as their riders didn't seem to mind. The others also felt reluctant to hurry the trip and by the time they reached the valley floor, the sun had passed zenith and was on it's way down toward the mountains.

Jarl had said nothing as they rode, but he was growing concerned. When they halted for the night, they had barely covered five miles and Dale hadn't said a word all day. They dismounted and Dale walked silently over to a log, then sat on it, staring out into the trees. Jarl watched him for a moment, then shook his head.
"Kheri," he asked. "Would you please see to the horses and get camp set up?"
"Sure," Kheri responded. "What's wrong?"
"I need to talk to Dale about something," Jarl replied, and Kheri nodded.

Jarl left him in charge of making camp, then walked over to where Dale was sitting and sat down next to him.
"Alright," he told him. "Your turn. Talk to me."
Dale sighed, then looked at him.
"I can't do this," he told Jarl bluntly. "I just can't do this."
"Do what?" Jarl asked, confused.
"This," Dale answered, gesturing around with his hand. "I don't have the ability to fight off a Gorg army, I sure don't have the ability to fight off a fifty thousand year old wizard. Shoot, I don't even have the ability to break the blocks on my powers and get off this rock. I feel like a mountains been dropped on my shoulders and I don't have the strength to hold it up."
Jarl nodded silently, then put his hand on Dale's shoulder.
"Yeah," he agreed. "I'm scared too. But you're not alone, and this place has some pretty powerful resources. It'll work out."
"But the dragon saw us fail," Dale answered despondently.
"No he didn't," Jarl argued. "He saw two possibilities. How many times have you told me that the future is not absolute? That no matter how many possibilities you can see and plan for, something else is bound to come along? Listen to yourself," he continued. "You're starting to sound like me."

Dale lifted an eyebrow in Jarl's direction.
"You are," he insisted. "You're sitting over here, feeling sorry for yourself and you sound just like I do when I'm coming off a three week drunk. And I'm sitting here sounded way too much like you for my own piece of mind." He glanced back at camp, then wrinkled his nose. "Come to think of it," he commented after a moment, "everyone's acting odd. It's almost like this forest doesn't want us to leave it and it's draining our willpower. Look how far we didn't get today. At that rate it's going to take us a month to get out of this valley."
Dale regarded him silently, Jarl's words finally reaching him through the fog of despair that had settled on his soul during the day. He looked around at the silent trees, then back at Jarl.
"We can't stay here tonight," he decided abruptly, standing up.
"What?" Jarl asked, looking up at him in surprise.
"You're right," he replied. "The forest IS doing something to us. Just like that whirlwind you fought yesterday, only this is more subtle. We have GOT to get out of this valley tonight. Now. If we don't we may never leave it."

Jarl nodded and stood.
"I can't do this alone," he said, placing a hand on Dale's arm. "The others don't respect my authority, they look to you. You'll have to get them moving."
Dale nodded but his heart wasn't in it. Jarl frowned then caught his eyes.
"What would Admiral Balchard say if he saw you like this?" he asked sharply.
Dale looked back at him, then set his jaw.
"He'd be a whole lot less than pleased," he replied and took a deep breath. "Thanks, I needed that reminder." He squared his shoulders, forcing the depression away by strength of will alone, then strode back over to the others.

Everyone was sitting around on the ground, staring off into the trees. The horses stood, still saddled, swishing their tails. Kheri looked up at him as he approached and shook his head.
"I can't get them to do anything," he whined. "They won't listen to me."
"They'll listen to me," Dale responded, his voice hard. "It's this forest. Tie the reins of their horses to yours, mine and Jarl's. We have GOT to leave here...NOW!"
Kheri shrugged, then nodded and set about slowly carrying out Dale's orders. Dale took a deep breath then turned to face the others.
"Up!" he commanded sharply. "Get back on those horses and do it now!"
The others looked up at him then climbed sluggishly to their feet. They wandered slowly over to the horse's and stood, staring at them.
"It's too high," Faran complained. "I can't get up there."
"Yes you can," Jarl argued, then lifted him up onto the horse. "Put your feet in the stirrups."
Faran didn't respond and Jarl shoved his feet roughly into the stirrups then went to Galdur.

Aerline didn't move, just sat on the ground, a dreamy look on her face, whispering silently to herself. Dale shook her, waved his hand in front of her eyes then scowled. He gave up after several seconds, bent down and scooped her up then carried her to her horse and set her down in the saddle.
"Jarl," he ordered, holding Aerline steady on her horse. "Get some rope and lash them into their saddles. I don't want anyone suddenly deciding to dismount or falling off."
Jarl nodded and did so rapidly, completely ignored by the three who now sat on their horses lost in a daze.

"Dale!" Kheri hollered frantically from somewhere behind him. "Help!"

Dale looked around, then ran to where Kheri had fallen into a large clump of what appeared to be ferns. He reached down and grasped Kheri's hand, attempting to pull him to his feet. Kheri grunted then grabbed Dale's forearm in both hands, struggling desperately to rise.
"Jarl!" Dale shouted, adrenaline washing away all traces of the previous depression, "get over here and help me!"
Jarl glanced around then sprinted to where Dale was fighting to pull Kheri free of the ferns.
"Somethings got ahold of him," Dale explained through clinched teeth, "and I can't get him loose. If I pull any harder, I'll pull his arms off. Get down in there and see if you can find out what's got him."

Jarl nodded, then drew his knife and knelt down beside the ferns, then carefully spread the fronds apart, peering down into them.
"Ah," he muttered after a few seconds, "I see the problem."
He stuck his knife into the ferns and sliced quickly then jumped back. Something shrieked and Kheri shot free, knocking Dale to the ground and sprawling on top of him. A stream of purple liquid spewed out into the air from the center of the plant then the fern curled up into a tight ball, wrapping itself with vines as it did so.
"What was that!" Kheri exclaimed as he got to his feet and turned to stare at what was left of the fern.
"Something that wanted to use you for fertilizer," Jarl remarked. "Let's get out of here."
They ran back for the horses and remounted as rapidly as possible.

"Jarl," Dale directed as they settled into their saddles. "Take point and lead Aerline's horse. I'll take Faran and bring up the rear. Kheri, stay in the middle, take Galdur and watch for trouble. Everyone keep a close eye on the person you are leading."
"Got it," Jarl replied, grabbed Aerline's reins, and urged his horse to a walk.

Kheri nodded silently and narrowed his eyes as he glanced around, gripping Galdur's reins tightly. "The sooner we are out of here," he thought, "the better." He looked suspiciously at the shadows under the trees, lengthening now as the sun began to fall behind the mountains. "I hope we can get out of here before it's dark, I'm afraid of what will happen if we don't."

As they rode away from the valley floor a tangible resistance began to oppose them, and the horses became recalcitrant. They fought with them for almost an hour then Dale stopped, dismounted and grabbed his horses reins.
"Get down," he called to Jarl and Kheri. "We're going to have to lead them."
Kheri dismounted and looked around, worry crossing his face.
"This is going to take all night," he muttered, as he untied Faran's horse from his saddle horn.
"It might," Dale agreed as he did the same to Galdur's horse. "Do you have an better suggestion?"
"One that will actually get the horses out of this valley," Jarl put in before Kheri could answer.
Kheri shook his head and pulled on his reins ungently, then nearly dragged his horse back to the road.
"Come on you," he growled. "We're going THIS way!"

They toiled up the road, sweating from the exertion of forcing the unwilling horses to leave the valley floor and begin the climb up the next mountain they had to cross. Night fell and darkness flowed around them like an unseen river, cascading down from the peaks above, threatening to sweep them back down into the valley. The feeling was unnerving and they all found themselves struggling to move forward.
"LET GO!!" Jarl shouted finally. "Just let us leave will you?!"

Laughter filled the air around them and the night was suddenly full of small, twinkling lights. They stopped, their feet rooted to the spot, unable to summon the will to move any further. Dale closed his eyes and mentally reached out for Jarl. Jarl looked around at the lights and something in the back of his mind whispered 'Danger'. He shut his eyes tightly and concentrated on the sounds in the forest around them. Dale's mental touch came an instant later and he reacted swiftly to accept the contact. Together their minds reached for Kheri and found him floating limply in a sea of illusions. They grabbed hold of him and wrenched him out of the mental trap that the fairys were weaving about him, enclosing him within their own sphere of protection. Kheri's eyes snapped open and his will hardened, furious now at the forest and everything in it for what was happening.

Dale caught his attention again, then wove the three of them into one single consciousness with enough willpower to fight off the fairy's spell. They stood silently in the road, the battle raging in sprit and mind, for several very long minutes then suddenly the lights vanished as the fairy's fled and the night was silent. They stumbled forward as something snapped, and the opposing force disappeared, freeing them to continue the climb out of the valley. The piece that had been Dale relaxed and the weaving frayed, breaking the bindings and forcing them back into themselves. Kheri blinked and looked around amazed, then stared at Dale.

Dale took a deep breath and let it out slowly, then opened his eyes.
"Let's get out of here," he commanded, his voice tense. "Before they come back."
The horses were back to normal now, but the other members of the party still stared slack jawed off into space, looking at things no one else could see. They swung themselves back up onto their horses and urged them to the fastest pace possible, intent on rapidly climbing out of the valley.

Chapter Thirty-Four

The moon had risen and the night was growing old when they left the last of the trees behind and began the steep ascent toward the second pass. Aerline yawned and looked around, then let out a shriek.

"Hey!" she protested, struggling with the ropes which bound her tightly to the saddle. "Why am I tied up? Let me go!"

Dale reined his horse to a halt as soon as she spoke, and swung down, then ran up to her.

"I'll explain later," he explained, undoing the ropes rapidly. "But right now, please, just accept we had no choice. We can't stop here."

He handed her the reins to her horse, then quickly remounted his own. Faran stirred as Dale was finishing with Aerline and Galdur followed a few moments later.

"What's going on?" Faran asked, his voice a mixture of fear and anger. "Where are we?"

"Hang loose kid," Jarl told him, uniting him from the saddle as fast as he could. "We'll explain as soon as it's safe to stop and talk."

Galdur didn't say anything, just waited patiently as Kheri freed him, then sat quietly on his horse as they got underway again.

With the entire company awake once more, Dale was tempted to stop for the night but the fear of retaliation from the forest or it's inhabitants was too strong and he forced them to continue climbing for another hour. When the forest at last lay like a silent shadow below them, and the air was so cold that they were all shivering uncontrollably, he stopped his horse and swung down.

"This is far enough," he decided, stamping feeling back into his feet and looking around. "There's less shelter here than I would like but we can't go any farther tonight and it's far enough away from the forest to be safe."

They made camp as rapidly as possible and discovered to their dismay that there was nothing burnable around. No trees grew on these slopes and even the scrub bushes were only visible on the slopes lower down. They broke out the tarps and weighed their corners down with rocks next to a large boulder, then huddled beneath them, wrapped in blankets. The wind howled around their pitiful shelter, ripping the corners out from under their inadequate anchors. They fought with this for several minutes, then gave up on the rocks and resorted to sitting on the corners instead. With the canvass now secured, and the wind at bay, they huddled together for warmth, dozing in fitful spurts.

Night crawled slowly past, filled with unearthly shrieks and the distant sounds of falling rock. Dale drifted in and out of consciousness, too tense to sleep and too tired to stay awake. He thought back over the trip through the forest and kicked himself for not recognizing the trap he'd fallen into. Jarl nudged him in the ribs after a while.

"Stop it," he whispered. "Will you please just let it go and settle down?"

"I can't," Dale whispered back. "I'm too wound up."

"Then go take a walk or something," Jarl muttered, pulling his blanket up around his ears.

Dale frowned in Jarl's general direction, but made a sincere effort to relax and fall asleep.

Icy rain began to fall a short while later and the company awoke suddenly to find themselves awash in near-frozen mud. Dale stood up, cursing, and threw the tarp off himself.

"Alright up!" he demanded. "We'll freeze to death if we stay here."

The company struggled to their feet and fought to remount in the pouring rain. Dale swung up on his horse and keyed the daylight effects sensors in his suit. Nothing happened and he gritted his teeth then forced his horse up the mountain toward the pass. The others followed miserably behind still huddled in somewhat soggy blankets, the only protection they had against the freezing rain.

As they neared the pass, the moon broke out from behind the clouds and the rain slowed to a drizzle then slowly ceased. The ground was icy and treacherous but the horses managed to pick their way over it without too much difficulty. The pass was lower than the first one they had crossed and there was no snow on the ground, but the wind whistled through it, punishing them for daring to brave it's wrath. Several feet inside the pass, they came unexpectedly on a small cave. Dale dismounted without a word and ducked inside briefly.
"It's not very large," he told the others as he re-emerged. "But it's dry. We can get out of the wind at least until the sun comes up." The others slid tiredly off their horses and led them inside the cave mouth, then sank down despondently on the ground, huddling together under the tarp as far from the opening as possible.

The blankets were made of wool and somewhat waterproof but the rain had thoroughly soaked them, and the company was forced make do with only the tarp for protection from the cold. They sat crowded together under it's poor shelter, listening to the wind whipping through the pass just outside. Slowly the chill left them as their bodies warmed the air under the tarp, and sleep prodded at them once again. Exhaustion overtook them at last and they fell into a deep slumber.

Galdur woke sometime later and looked around. Everyone else was still sound asleep and the horses were still standing inside the cave entrance but something seemed wrong. He sat up and sniffed then thought for a moment. The faint smell of smoke was drifting on the air.
"Now how is that possible?" he wondered. "There's nothing up here to burn?"

He got to his feet and went to the cave entrance, then stood shivering in the early morning air and looked out into the pass.

The rain clouds had blown away and there was a bright sun shining down on the lands below his feet. Thick forests covered most of what he could see but behind one of the distant mountains he could see a dark haze. He watched it curiously for a few minutes, then ducked back inside and tried to go back to sleep. The afternoon was getting late when life returned to the party and everyone awoke at last. The air in the cave was now fairly warm but their clothes were still wet and the temperature was unpleasant. They spent a minimal amount of time readying the horses, then remounted and left the cave.

The pass was winding and narrow, with rocks strew haphazardly about. Several times Dale and Jarl were forced to dismount and move several large chunks so that the horses had room to walk between them. The afternoon wore on and as the sun was setting, they exited the pass to stand looking over a deep green sea of trees stretching into thc hazy distance.
"Villenspell," Aerline explained, pointing, "is over there".

On the other side of the valley they could another mountain and just slightly above the trees, near it's peak, was a shining light.
"What's it made of?" Kheri whispered, suddenly awestruck.
"Why?" Aerline asked, looking at him curiously.
"It's so bright," he replied in a more normal tone of voice. "Why's it shinning like that?"
"Oh." She nodded in understanding. "The city is enclosed in a protective warding. You can't see it from inside...it's not solid after all...but it does look pretty from out here, doesn't it?"
"Where's the college?" Faran asked.
"It's in the middle of the city," Aerline explained. "The college was built there long ago when that mountain was a valley filled with a huge lake. It was built on the shore of the lake. But after the

wizards war, it was suddenly on the top of a mountain and very difficult to get to. Students would live at the college then, and they started building places to spend time when they weren't studying. The city slowly grew up around the college and now there are far more people just living in the city than actually attend the college. It's a very large city with almost three million people living in it."

Faran stared at her.

"Three million people!?" he exclaimed. "I didn't know the world had that many people in it!"

She giggled

"It's got lots more than that Faran," she replied. "But most of them don't go to the wizard's college."

She smiled at him and he blushed, then quickly looked somewhere else.

The road down from the pass was less winding and steep than any they'd traversed in the mountains so far and the horses made good time. They entered the trees as night was falling and Dale halted at the first clearing.

"Anyone want to go on?" he asked, looking back at the others.

"No." Jarl replied, grumpily. "I'm tired, I'm wet, I'm cold, I'm hungry and I want OFF this horse!"

"Yeah," Kheri agreed. "I want a fire and dry clothes."

"If everything in the saddlebags didn't get soaked again," Faran groused.

"I'd settle for a dry blanket," Galdur said. "At least it's warmer down here."

"Some of us," Dale replied, looking hard at Kheri and Faran, "could have changed clothes back in the cave."

Kheri's mouth dropped open and he smacked his forehead.

"I'm an idiot," he exclaimed then whirled toward Faran. "And don't you say ANYTHING!"

Faran grinned at him and slid down off his horse.

"Who, me?" he asked innocently. "Why should I tell you what you already know?"
"ooooo!' Kheri fumed and swung down off his horse.
"Stop!" Dale's command cut through the air. "The two of you can roughhouse later. Let's get camp set up, a fire going and food in us first."
Kheri paused, then looked back at Faran.
"You just wait," he warned. "You'll get yours."
"You and what army?" Faran replied, grinning at him.
"I don't need an army," Kheri threatened, taking a step toward him. Dale dropped a hand solidly on his shoulder and he jumped then froze in place.
"I said later," Dale told him firmly.
"Yessir," Kheri replied quickly and got busy unsaddling his horse.

They hung the blankets on bushes near the fire which was crackling happily a few minutes later and those who possessed dry things changed into them. The others dug through the things Jarl had liberated from the bandits and succeeded in finding enough clothing to fit them. Galdur smiled happily as he held up a shirt.
"This was my dads," he grinned. "He won it in a card game. He whipped me good for spilling water on him when he was wearing it one day. Kinda like the fact he doesn't get to have it any more. Mine now."

Aerline pulled out a long, yellow piece of cloth, looked at it then turned and frowned at Dale, her hands on her hips.
"Just how well did you go through this stuff before you made us pack it away?" she asked.
He glanced up at her, confused.
"I glanced through it," he stated. "But I didn't catalog everything. Why?"
"Because," she replied, shaking out the yellow cloth. "There's oilskin in here. Lots of it. Enough to make everyone a cloak. And

there's several fur lined wool capes, some gloves and all sorts of other things that would have been NICE to have the last few nights."

Jarl crossed his arms and looked at Dale. Dale blinked, stared at Aerline, then got up and walked over to where she was standing.
"That's what happens when you get obsessed," Jarl muttered. "You start missing the obvious details."
Dale looked back over at him.
"I'm not obsessed," he argued.
"You are so," Jarl replied irritably. "The only thing you're thinking about is the Gorg. You wouldn't even let the rest of us stop to eat or sleep if you didn't have to!"

Dale started to answer then stopped and regarded Jarl silently. Jarl looked back at him defiantly.
"Admit it," he challenged after a moment. "If you'd been a little less worried about getting back on the road, you'd have known what all we had because you'd have looked at it better when we packed it. But you didn't. You just dumped it all on the ground, ordered everyone to get it packed and paced till we were riding again. And because of that we've nearly frozen to death several times in the last few days. Not to mention spending the last twenty-four hours soaking wet!"
Dale took a deep breath, then let it out and nodded.
"You're right," he admitted, ashamed. "I wasn't thinking and I cost us. I can't keep doing that or we will pay dearly for it. We need to know what supplies we actually have, we need more sleep than we've been getting and we have to eat more than once a day. I'll back off, starting tonight and we'll keep to a more reasonable pace tomorrow."
Jarl nodded.
"Punch me," Dale requested, looking at him, "if I start pushing too hard again."

"Count on it," Jarl replied seriously. "I'll mop the floor up with you if I have to."
Dale grinned weakly.
"I don't think that'll be necessary," he responded.

Aerline had watched the exchange and now looked at Dale with a bit of a smile on her face.
"Would you do us all a favor?" he asked as he turned around.
"Sure," she agreed. "What?"
"Would you go through all the supplies," he asked, "and make a good, clear list of everything we have? And what we need to pick up as soon as possible?"
"I'd be glad to," she told him. "Galdur can help me."
"Thank you," Dale said. "I'm sorry I've put everyone through this."
"Don't worry about it," Aerline replied, patting him on the arm. "We'll survive."
She started pulling things out of the bags and piling them on the ground.
"Come on Galdur," she called over her shoulder. "The others can cook dinner, I need your help over here."

Within an hour, Aerline had sorted out all the extra supplies and equipment that they had. She divided up the clothing according to who each item fit best, striving to make certain that everyone had at least one or two things that were warm and a long piece of oilskin in case of wet weather. Everyone wound up with several sets of clothing as well. Some of the equipment was in poor condition, but still useable and spirits rose as they took stock of what they actually owned. This, combined with the cheery flames of the fire and the badly needed food, lifted their mood back out of the depths to which it had sunk and allowed a feeling of optimism to pervade the camp once more.

Once dinner was over and everything was packed away again, Kheri walked over to where Jarl was sitting on a stump whittling. "You busy?" he asked. Jarl looked up then shook his head.
"No," he replied. "Why?"
"Well," Kheri explained. "It's Galdur. I've tried everything I can think of to teach him how to dodge, Faran's been trying to teach him how to use a sword. I'm starting to think he's incapable of understanding the concept survival."
"I'm pretty sure he understands how to survive," Jarl remarked. "He did grow up with a large group of bandits remember."
"Yes," Kheri agreed. "And he survived by allowing them to beat him up and hiding when he could get away with it. I told him to throw a punch at me so I could demonstrate how to dodge it and he looked like I'd just asked him to murder his best friend. I swear I even saw tears in his eyes."
Jarl blinked.
"O...k...," he remarked. "That's a bit extreme."
"Not only that," Kheri went on. "I've watched how upset he gets when ever anyone raises their voice. It's almost like someone's punched him in the stomach or something."
"I'll talk to him," Jarl told him and stood up, putting the whittling away.

Galdur was sitting by himself under a tree watching as the moon drifted slowly through the sky. A peaceful smile softened his face and he almost seemed to be dreaming. Jarl walked up and looked at him for a moment, then sat down on the ground beside him.
"Isn't it pretty?" Galdur whispered, still watching the moon. "I dream about what it must be like to live there sometimes. I wish I could go see."
"You do?" Jarl asked.
"Sure," Galdur replied. "It must be a beautiful place, all shining and white. I'm sure the people have cities that sparkle and no one ever goes hungry." "Umm, no." Jarl said but Galdur went on as if he hadn't heard. "I think that they must have forests of trees

with sliver leaves and flowers of the purest gold. Streams of crystal clear water and nothing unpleasant ever happens."

"Galdur," Jarl interrupted. "That's a lovely fantasy, but there's no air on the moon. Nothing lives there."
Galdur looked at him and frowned.
"How do you know?" he asked.
"I've been there," Jarl replied. "It's actually a very dreary place, with freezing cold shadows and only slightly warmer areas of stark light where the sun's shining. Nothing grows, there's no water and no air."
"How'd you live then," Galdur asked, unwilling to accept Jarl's description.
"I had something to protect me," Jarl explained simply.
Galdur looked at him for a moment then looked back up at the moon.
"Well," he decided a few seconds later. "Even if it's not true, I like my story better."

Jarl sat silently for a moment, then sighed.
"Dale," he thought, "this is impossible. We're never going to be able to convince Galdur that he needs to learn how to fight, even to just protect himself."
"What makes you say that?" Dale asked.
"He just told me that he thinks the moon is a paradise where no one's ever unhappy," Jarl thought back. "And when I told him what it's really like, he told me he didn't care, he liked his version better."
"And?" Dale asked again.
"He started crying when Kheri asked him to throw a punch so he could show him how to dodge," Jarl said.
"Crying?" Dale replied, slightly incredulous.
"That's what Kheri said," Jarl answered, looking back at Galdur who was still staring at the moon with a happy smile drifting across his face. He waited a moment longer then got up and

walked back to the fire, leaving Galdur to dream about moon-men with gardens full of silver trees.

"They both jumped and turned around then stood, staring guiltily at the man who was leaning against a tree with his arms crossed, watching them."

Chapter Thirty-Five

The sun rose far too early the next morning and Faran woke up with a start as a woodpecker not far above his head decided that it was time for breakfast. He picked up a stick and heaved it at the bird, missing badly. The woodpecker went on serenely drilling holes in the tree bark and Faran growled, then jumped to his feet.
"GET LOST!!" he yelled, heaving another stick at it. The stick hit the tree and bounced off, smacking Kheri in the face as it ricocheted to the ground.
"OW!" Kheri exclaimed, sitting up and rubbing his face. "What was that for?!"
"I wasn't aiming at you," Faran snarled, flinging another stick at the woodpecker who was still drilling holes in the tree. "I was aiming at him!"
The third stick smacked the woodpecker on the tail and it jumped into the air with a squawk then flew off to a different tree.
"And stay gone," Faran grumbled, watching it leave.
"You're worse than the woodpecker," Kheri complained. "At least he didn't hit me as well as wake me up."
"Shut up!" Faran shot back furiously. "I'm not in the mood for it."
He stomped off into the bushes leaving Kheri scowling at where he'd been standing.

Kheri glared after him, threw his blanket off, his temper fraying, and strode off after him. Faran had walked quite a distance from camp by the time Kheri caught up with him and was standing with his arms crossed, glowering at nothing.
"Get back to camp!" Kheri demanded, walking up to where he stood.
"Go away," Faran growled. "Just leave me alone."
"So you can get eaten by a bear or something?" Kheri snapped. "No. Go back to camp!"

He took hold of Faran's arm. Faran jerked away, spun around and punched Kheri in the stomach. The punch landed solidly and Kheri gasped then threw his arm up to block Faran's follow up swing. He caught Faran's wrist, twisted, and flipped him over. Faran hit the ground, then scrambled back up to his feet, his eyes blazing.

"I said leave me alone!" He yelled. "I don't need you to tell me what to do!"
"Then I'll go get Dale and HE can tell you what to do!" Kheri shot back.
They stood glaring at each other for several seconds, then the quiet snap of a twig caught their attention. They both jumped and turned around then stood, staring guiltily at the man who was leaning against a tree with his arms crossed, watching them.
"Finished yet?" Dale asked, uncrossing his arms and standing away from the tree.
"Uh..." Kheri replied, backing up slightly. "Yeah."
Faran bit his lower lip and nodded, watching Dale warily.
"Someone tell me the reason for all the noise." Dale requested, studying them both.

They glanced at each other, then Kheri took a deep breath.
"I yelled at him for waking me up," he explained. "And he left camp. I came after him cause I didn't want him to get lost, or worse, and he wouldn't come back. I kinda forced the issue and we started fighting."
Dale nodded.
"And why were you yelling at him for waking you up?" he asked.
"Well..." Kheri started.
"I hit him with a stick," Faran interrupted. "But I didn't mean to. I was throwing it at the stupid woodpecker!"
"I see." Dale replied, and studied them thoughtfully. "Didn't I warn the two of you what would happen the next time you got into a brawl?"

They nodded nervously and Faran put one hand over his rear.

"Dale," Kheri said with a glance at Faran. "This one's my fault. I could have just let him calm down."
"Yes," Dale agreed. "You could have."
Faran swallowed then shook his head.
"No," he argued. "It's just as much my fault. I threw the first punch."
"And you went much farther from camp that is safe," Dale pointed out.
Faran nodded miserably.
"I know," he replied. "I was mad so I didn't care."
Dale nodded.
"So," he said, regarding the two of them. "What do you think should happen now?"

Kheri winced. He stared at the ground for a moment then looked up into Dale's eyes.
"I'm sorry," he apologized. "I got out of line and I broke the rules. I'll take whatever you decide I deserve."
"Alright," Dale replied, then looked at Faran.
Faran shut his eyes tightly for a second, then looked sideways at Dale.
"I did too," he admitted, taking a deep breath. "I shouldn't have yelled at Kheri, I shouldn't have punched him and I shouldn't have left camp." He winced and chewed on his lower lip. "I just woke up in a real bad mood. I'm sorry. I'll take whatever you give me."
He bit his lip, and waited tensely for Dale to respond.

Dale regarded the two of them silently for a minute.
"We're all exhausted," he decided finally. "I've been driving us too hard and everyone's temper is thin. I'll let you both off this time because I feel that has a lot to do with your behavior this morning. But," he admonished them firmly as they started to relax.

"I expect you both to go out of your way for the rest of the day to get along. With everyone. Understand me?"
They nodded quickly.
"Yes sir," Faran replied. "I promise."
"So do I," Kheri agreed.
"Alright," Dale said. "Then let's get back to camp."

Galdur had breakfast cooking when they returned and the smell of food made Kheri's stomach suddenly growl quite loudly. He blushed as everyone looked at him then shrugged.
"So I'm hungry," he remarked sourly, then caught Dale looking at him and swallowed the rest of his comment.
"If you get me a bowl," Galdur told him, "it's ready to eat."

Dale took his bowl and went to sit under a tree. The sun was warm and the air smelled of oak and pine. Birds called through the forest and a soft breeze blew past, ruffling his hair. Aerline walked over after a few minutes and sat down next to him.
"It's such a nice morning," she smiled. "It's too bad the other forest wasn't this pleasant."
Dale shivered, not liking the reminder.
"I hope we don't encounter any more forests like that one," he muttered, picking at his food. "We almost didn't get out of there."

"The fairies would have let us go eventually," she explained. "They were just playing."
"Eventually?" Dale asked. "How eventually?"
"Oh, two, maybe three hundred years," she replied. "They'd have gotten bored after a while."
Dale looked at her silently.
"Somehow," he said after a moment, "I think that we'd have starved to death long before then."
"Oh no," Aerline told him, shaking her head. "They'd never hurt anyone they decided to play with. We'd have been fine."

"Just prisoners of the Gorg long before then," Dale pointed out. "Along with everyone that they didn't kill off."
"Maybe," she agreed. "But they were still only playing."
"Well the next time someone wants me to be their toy," Dale replied. "I'd appreciate it if they'd ask my permission first."
"That," Aerline told him firmly as she stood, "is something I wouldn't count on. Especially since you have no magic what-so-ever."
She walked back to join the others, leaving Dale to mull over what her words. They broke camp not too long afterward and set out on the road again. Dale held to his promise of the day before and set an easier pace than they were used to. The woods were pleasant and the company found themselves relaxing, a sense of peacefulness from the forest around them filling the air. Just past noon the road ran out of a thicket and they found themselves riding across a wide meadow. In the direct center of the meadow the road forked and ran off in two different directions. They road up to the fork and looked around.

A large sign had been erected on the right hand leg of the fork and the word Villenspell had been carved into it, with an arrow pointing to the right. Dale studied it for a second.
"I wonder where the other leg goes," Jarl mused.
"Out into the unknown," Aerline replied.
"It's awfully well taken care," Jarl argued. "Someone uses it."
"Well of course someone uses it," Aerline stated, looking at him. "What good is a road if you don't use it?"
Jarl just shook his head and refrained from saying anything else.

"It's fairly obvious," Dale remarked, "that the road we want is that one. However," he went on, and turned to look at the others, "I get very nervous when I think about going down it. Anyone else having any problems?"

The others glanced at the road. Faran shrugged and shook his head. Kheri looked at it for a moment then shrugged, "I don't feel anything."
Galdur studied the road for several seconds. "There is something wrong," he agreed at last. "But I can't tell what it is."
"Aerline?" Dale asked.
"None of the animals here are talking to me," she frowned, then shook her head. "Either that, or there aren't any animals anywhere close."

Dale glanced at Jarl who nodded.
"Yeah," he replied. "I get the same reaction. Something bad's waiting down that road if we take it."
"But how are we going to get to Villenspell if we don't use it?" Aerline asked.
"Isn't there another way in?" Dale asked.
"Well yes," she responded. "If you want to go all the way back to the inn, then go all the way around the mountains to get to it. It'll only take about three years that way."
"No thanks," Dale replied.
"Then we take this road," she stated firmly, "or we just don't go." She crossed her arms with finality and looked Dale in the eye.
He sighed and nodded.
"Alright," he decided. "We take this road. However," he looked around at the rest of the company. "Everyone be on your guard. There is an ambush, a trap, or something worse, waiting down this road and I would prefer we saw it before it saw us."
They nodded and he looked directly at Galdur.

"You've refused to learn how to defend yourself," he said, his voice hard. "You are a walking target and a danger to the entire company. You will stay in the middle of the group and if danger threatens you will stay as close to me as you can get. And after we get to Villenspell you will have a choice. You can either get a grip and learn how to defend yourself, or you can take your leave of us

and go elsewhere on your own." Galdur stared at him, shocked. "I will not have someone else killed trying to protect you, when you refuse to protect yourself," Dale went on. "I don't care if you think fighting is wrong, or it scares you or anything else. The wilds are dangerous and nothing that wishes to kill you is going to change it's mind just because you do not wish to fight it. I also don't care if you feel every blow you inflict on something. If you are going to travel with us past Villenspell, you WILL learn how to defend yourself. Do I make myself clear?"
Galdur nodded sullenly.
"Yes," he replied. "I don't want to, but I'll do what you say."
"Good," Dale said, then turned back toward the road. "Jarl, take rear guard. I'll take point this time. Everyone else in pairs between us. And be ready for trouble."

They readied themselves, then slowly made their way down the road. Dale flipped his force field on and was relieved as the shields flickered to life.
"Jarl," he thought. "Try your belt. Mines finally recharged."
Jarl glanced up, then slapped the shield button on his belt.
"Yes!" came his elated response. "I didn't blow the circuits after all!"
"It was the mountain," Dale thought back. "My suits at full power again as well. My blaster is still drained however."
Jarl checked his equipment over and nodded.
"I'm in the same boat," he responded. "But I'll take this over what I've had."
"I as well," Dale replied, then keyed the life signs sensors in his suit. The heads-up display flickered to life and a few large red dots drew his attention. "Up ahead," he thought, directing the thought to both Jarl and Kheri. "Several large creatures, about fifteen or so. Looks like we'll ride fairly close to them"

He keyed the display off and closed his eyes, then relaxed and tried to scan down the road. A wave of nausea swept over him and

he blinked, then shook his head and reined his horse up sharply. The others stopped just as suddenly behind him and looked around in confusion. Dale dropped his head in his hands and fought down the desire to throw up. The feeling persisted for several minutes then slowly faded, leaving him with a blinding headache. Jarl winced, the headache filtering down to him through their link, and rubbed his temples.
"Galdur," he said, his voice tight. "Something's happened to Dale. Can you do anything?"
"Maybe," Galdur replied. "What's wrong with him?"
"I don't know," Jarl shook his head then winced again. "Can you just go see please?"
"Alright," Galdur replied, slightly confused, and urged his horse up even with Dale's.

He reached over and put his hand on Dale's arm, then closed his eyes. The two of them sat immobile for several minutes then Dale suddenly relaxed and slumped slightly forward. Galdur smiled and took his hand away.
"You ok now?" he asked and Dale nodded, sitting back up on his horse.
"Yes," he replied and took a deep breath. "Thank you."
"Sure," Galdur smiled. "What happened?"
"I don't know," Dale answered, shaking his head. "It just hit me out of nowhere."
Galdur nodded, then turned his horse around and rode back to his place in the party.
"What was wrong with him?" Aerline asked as Galdur settled in beside her once more.
"Bad headache," he replied then shrugged. "He's ok now."
Dale flipped his sensors back on and keyed the display.
"I'll make do with this," he thought. "I have no idea what that was but I don't care to experience it twice."

They continued down the road at a walk, and before long had re-entered the trees. The air was cooler than it had been in the meadow but the forest was quiet and the feeling that something was watching them began to grow on the entire party after a short time. Aerline closed her eyes and whispered for a few minutes then gave up.
"I still can't get any of the animals to talk to me," she frowned. "I'm getting worried."
"Maybe you just don't speak their language," Galdur suggested.
She smiled gently at him.
"Maybe but I don't think that's the problem," she replied. "I think something else is wrong."

The road ran quite straight for a fair distance then turned a corner around a large tree. As they rounded the corner there was a loud growl and a huge white wolf sprang out of the underbrush and stood bristling in the road in front of them. Dale reined his horse to a sudden stop and sat looking at the wolf.

It stood fully six feet high from the ground to it's shoulders and stared back at him with ice blue eyes. Its growl deepened, warning him away, and it took a step forward toward them.
"Now what?" Dale wondered. "What is it with the forests of this planet?"
"Dale!" Faran shouted. "There are more of them! Behind us!"
"I'm on it," Jarl shouted back, swinging down from his horse. "Faran, back me up!"
Faran swung down from his horse and ran back to stand beside Jarl, his sword at ready. Dale sat unmoving, staring at the wolf in front of them. Kheri quietly slipped off his horse and faded into the trees. The wolf growled again and readied itself to spring then collapsed on the road. Dale blinked.
"What..?" he asked, looking around. Kheri walked out of the trees and went to retrieve something from the wolf's neck.

"Good shot," Dale told him, grinning, as he swung down from his horse.
"Thanks," Kheri replied, and disappeared into the trees again.

"Aerline," Dale instructed as he stepped onto the road. "Talk to the horses please. Keep them from panicking."
"I was already doing so," she replied and he nodded.
He bent over the wolf and listened to it for a moment, then stood back up.
"Something's weird with this wolf," he remarked, turning to Aerline. "It's not breathing."
"Did Kheri kill it with that dart?" she asked, astonished.
"Shouldn't have," he said. "It didn't kill you, just put you to sleep."
"How odd," she replied, then paused. "Maybe not so odd after all," she mused thoughtfully. "These woods ARE Villenspell property and the wolves could be part of the protective spells guarding the college."

Dale glanced at her then looked back at the wolf. "We're an awfully long way from the college," he replied doubtfully.
"True," Aerline agreed. "But we passed the perimeter of the wards just before you got so ill back there. Didn't you feel it?"
Dale stared at her for a second.
"So that's what happened!" he exclaimed. "It thought I was attacking."
"What did?" she asked curiously.
"I tried to scan down the road, see what was waiting for us," Dale explained, "and as soon as I touched it, I felt horrible. I couldn't see, I was dizzy, I almost couldn't keep from throwing up and then I got a blinding headache."

Aerline nodded.
"Yes," she agreed. "That sounds about right. That's the first defense. Woven by Magister Rommalt himself. It's very annoying."

"Annoying isn't the word I'd use for that," Dale grumbled, then glanced back at the wolf on the ground. "So you really think these are part of the defense?"

"Yes," Aerline replied. "And I suggest you don't kill it."

"Why not?" Dale asked, looking up at her.

"Because if you do," she explained, "the spell will react with something more powerful. As long as the wolves aren't vanquished, the spell won't think we're too much of a danger. If you kill everything it sends at you, eventually you wind up with something you can't beat."

"How does anyone get to the college then?" Dale demanded, frustrated with this turn of events.

"Students don't come in this way," Aerline explained. "The other leg back there really does lead off into the unknown. People travel it sometimes but not often. Anyone from the civilized lands that want to journey to the college will take the other road. Only troublemakers and things best not mentioned come in this way."

"That's comforting to know," Dale replied with a sigh. "Alright we won't kill the wolves but that's not going to keep them from trying to kill us very long.

"Just put them to sleep," Aerline suggested. "Like you did that one."

"Kheri," Dale called and Kheri stepped back out of the trees.

"How many uses does that dart have left?"

"Five for today," he replied. "Why?"

"We can't kill these wolves," Dale explained. "They're not actually alive and Aerline thinks that they're part of the college's protective wards. If we destroy them, something nastier will come along and we'll be in trouble."

"We're already in trouble," Kheri remarked, glancing back. "The rest are just about on top of Jarl and Faran."

"Maybe you can leave just one," Aerline suggested. "If they don't all die, maybe that'll be enough to stop the spell from making anything else."
"And if that isn't the case?" Dale asked.
"Then we ride really fast and try to get to Villenspell before whatever it is gets to us." Aerline replied. "But do you have any other choice?"
"Not really," Dale acknowledged, drawing his sword. "Not that I see at least."

He and Kheri ran back to the position that Jarl and Faran were holding in the road behind them.
"Good news and bad news," Dale said as he ran up.
"What's that?" Jarl asked, watching the wolves as they advanced.
"Well," Dale explained. "Those aren't real wolves. They're part of the spell protecting the college. They'll probably die pretty easy."
"So what's the bad news," Jarl asked.
"If we kill them, the spell will send something worse after us. And if we kill that, it'll send something even worse," Dale explained. "Until we can't fight what it sends and we get killed."
Jarl turned and looked at him.
"You are kidding me," he stated. "Correct?"
"Nope," Dale shook his head, dropping into a ready stance. "Wish I was. Aerline thinks that if we don't kill all of them, the spell might not activate and send anything new."
"Great," Jarl growled. "So we leave one alive then try to out run it?"
"No," Dale replied. "We leave one unconscious on the road up front and kill these, THEN try to get to the college as fast as we can."

The wolves continued their slow advance, then stopped several feet away from them and stood growling. Dale watched them for a few minutes then frowned.

"What now?" he wondered, and turned around to check on the lead wolf in the front. It was still laying on the ground unmoving where it had fallen. He turned back and looked at the wolves that had been advancing from the rear.
"Alright," he said out loud. "Either attack us or go away."
The wolves ignored him and simply stood there growling. He relaxed, sheathed his sword, then strode over to the closest one. Nothing happened and he stopped in front of it then reached out and touched it. The wolf didn't move or change the pitch of it's growl. Dale thought for a second then grinned.
"They're stuck," he said, looking at Jarl.
"They're what?" Jarl asked looking over at Dale then glancing back at the wolves.
"They're stuck," he repeated. "They're stuck in a for loop."
Jarl frowned, then put his knife away and walked over to one of the wolves. It too didn't move or even acknowledge his presence.
"Well what do you know," he grinned, examining the wolf. "They're zombied."

"What," Kheri asked, "is a for loop?"
"Umm..." Dale replied, searching for an explanation Kheri would comprehend. "It's a piece of a spell. It tells something that the spell has made how to know when it should do something or not."
Kheri lifted an eyebrow at him.
"The explanation didn't," he remarked. "What is going on?"
"These guys are supposed to attack invaders," Dale explained. "The wolves back here from behind and that one up there from the front. That's the leader," he said, pointing at the wolf in the road ahead of them, "and these'll react based on what it does. It's supposed to either kill the invaders or be killed. It's not supposed to just stop moving and lay down in the road."

Jarl turned and glanced down the road, then grinned.
"The parent process went to sleep." he commented.

"The wolf did," Kheri replied. "If that's what you mean. I stuck it with a sleep dart."
"Yeah," Jarl agreed, "the wolf. The main wolf. It went to sleep and the rest of these are waiting for it to tell them what to do."
"It won't stay asleep forever," Kheri pointed out but Jarl shook his head.
"Yes it will," he argued. "Unless the spell's been designed to wake it up at some point and that's pretty unlikely. I doubt the prog... err, wizard gave any thought to his deamon being put to sleep, just killed."
"It won't wake up on it's own?" Kheri asked.
"Not likely," Dale replied. "It'll probably lay there forever now unless something resets the spell."

"Meanwhile," Jarl interjected, glancing back at the motionless, growling wolves and grinning, "the spell can't make anything new, because these all still exist. But it can't remove them because it wasn't designed to deal with this."
"Right," Dale agreed. "At least as long as we stay here. What will happen if we try to ride past the wolf in the road up there, I'm not real sure."
"Pretty lousy AI's," Jarl commented, poking the wolf with his knife point.
"Lazy programmer and lack of beta testing," Dale snickered.
"So what do we do now?" Jarl asked.
"We'll go back to the horses and lead them carefully around the wolf," Dale decided. "Since the spell seems to be designed to react based on what's happening, we'll make absolutely certain we do not get off the road. No telling what spells might activate if the invaders are sneaking through the trees."
Jarl nodded and they walked back to the horses.
"We'll have to lead the horses carefully around the lead wolf," Dale told Aerline and Galdur, then quickly explained what had happened. Aerline giggled as he finished the explanation and

nodded her head, then gathered her reins tightly in her hand and stood waiting.

Dale walked back to his horse and paused. waiting until everyone had dismounted and were ready.
"We go single file," he instructed them. "This is critical so pay attention please. Do NOT allow yourself, or your horse, to step on the wolf and do NOT allow yourself or your horse to step off the road. If you do we may have even worse problems to deal with."
He waited until they had all acknowledged him then turned and carefully led his horse around the wolf and down the road a short way. The others followed slowly, sticking to the middle of the road after they passed the wolf and in a few minutes the party was clear of the ambush. Dale looked around, then keyed his sensors back on.

The heads-up display flickered to life and tiny red dots covered it but nothing large appeared to be nearby. He studied it for a few minutes, then satisfied he hadn't missed anything, set it to alert him if anything larger came into range and remounted.

The forest thickened as they rode forward and the sound of birds could be heard now. Normal noises that had been missing began to occur and the feeling of watchfulness fell away behind them. Dale grinned and relaxed slightly.
"The whole spell seems to be stuck on the road behind us," he thought.
"Let's hope it stays that way," Jarl responded silently.
"Dale, when did you become a wizard?" came Kheris mental question.
"I'm not," Dale replied. "What made you think I was?"
"The way you and Jarl were talking about why the wolves weren't attacking," he explained. "That was pretty deep stuff. I didn't understand most of it."
Dale grinned again.

"Someday," he promised, "once I'm no longer stranded here, I'll see that you get an explanation Kheri. Right now you'd just get more confused at anything I could say."
"Ok," came Kheri's response. "I'll hold you to that."

They picked up the pace now that the danger appeared to be behind them and proceeded at a gallop down the road. No one had any desire to find out what spells activated at night in the forest or suggested stopping as the afternoon wore on and evening began to fall. A sense of urgency had begun to grow on the company now and they concentrated on the road ahead, trying to reach the mountain before dark.

Just as twilight was beginning, they came to another sign beside the road. A face wearing a terrifying expression had been carved in it and the words 'Beware Of Ogre' were written in flowing script beneath the face. Dale glanced at it as he thundered past, and began the climb up the side of the mountain at last. The others followed as rapidly as possible, striving to ascend above the tree line before it became fully dark.

So rapidly were they moving that the rock which should have hit the road just in front of them missed totally and landed a few feet behind Jarl. They glanced around, but didn't slow the pace, leaving a very frustrated Ogre jumping up and down on a boulder behind them.
"I don't think he appreciates being ignored," Faran remarked, glancing back.
"Too bad," Kheri responded. "He'll get over it."

Darkness settled down around them as they left the last of the trees behind and the road steepened as it climbed toward the city shining high above them in the darkness. The stars glittered over head and the temperature began to fall as the mountain lost the warmth of the sun. They paused briefly to break out warmer clothing, then continued climbing, the sight of the city glimmering high above drawing them on like moths to a flame.

Continued in Book Two, Villenspell - City of Wizards